MORE PRAISE FOR RAGE FACTOR

"A definite page-turner
—*Rendezvous*

"Lives up to the promise of [Rogers's] excellent debut . . .
Will have readers begging for more."
—*Romantic Times*

"A gripping, tightly woven tale of suspense."
—*Old Book Barn Gazette*

"What author Rogers does best is deliver taut, frightening
action scenes that have you on the edge of your seat."
—*The Mystery Reader*

"Rogers knows how to build suspense."
—*San Antonio Express-News*

RAVES FOR BITCH FACTOR

"The best new heroine to come along in years!"
—*Library Journal*

"Funny, clever, and entertaining."
—*The Washington Times*

"One of the year's most stellar debuts."
—*Romantic Times*

"Riveting . . . Dixie is . . . full of sass and surprises."
—*Woman's Own*

"And while Dixie walks the walk and talks the talk . . . she
remains appealing and sympathetic. The novel's climax is
likely to leave readers chilled long after they close the book."
—*The Plain Dealer*, Cleveland

BANTAM BOOKS BY CHRIS ROGERS

Rage Factor

Bitch Factor

RAGE FACTOR

CHRIS ROGERS

BANTAM BOOKS

New York • Toronto • London • Sydney • Auckland

This edition contains the complete text
of the original hardcover edition
NOT ONE WORD HAS BEEN OMITTED.

RAGE FACTOR

A Bantam Book

PUBLISHING HISTORY
Bantam hardcover edition published February 1999
Bantam mass market edition / January 2000

Library of Congress Catalog Card Number: 98-8835.

ISBN 0-553-58070-1

Published simultaneously in the United States and Canada

Bantam Books are published by Bantam Books, a division of Random House, Inc. Its trademark, consisting of the words "Bantam Books" and the portrayal of a rooster, is Registered
in U.S. Patent and Trademark Office and in other countries. Marca Registrada. Bantam
Books, 1540 Broadway, New York, New York 10036.

PRINTED IN THE UNITED STATES OF AMERICA

OPM   10   9   8   7   6   5   4   3   2   1

This book is dedicated to the memory of
Stan Houston, a fine writer who made me laugh,
and to all the fans who loved *Bitch Factor*.

ACKNOWLEDGMENTS

Any mistakes in this book are entirely my own. The best of it I owe to some exceptional people:

The entire staff of Internal Audit and everyone at Bank United, especially Lisa and (our friend) Candace.

John W. Moore II, Certified Protection Professional.

Robin McKenzie, Larry Schkade, and all the talented folks at Ideas.

Jennifer Robinson, Peter Miller, and all the staff at PMA Literary & Film Management, Inc.

Kate, Amanda, Susan, Jessica; and everyone whose fingers touched it at Bantam Books, with a special thanks to Jamie S. Warren Youll, for a bitchin image.

My family and friends, for their inspiration and encouragement.

Jo Bremer, for her friendship and experience.

Adelaide and Janet; Amelia, Laurel, Linda, Mary, and Steve for their unflagging support; with special thanks to Margaret Anderson, Kay Finch, Ann Jennings, Glenn Gotschall, Amy Sharp, and Leann Sweeney, for pulling double duty, and to Ron Scott, who warned me this one wouldn't be easy.

Rage Factor

Prologue

February 14

Cold.

Bone-piercing cold needled Sissy's muscles.

A vile stench invaded her nose. The back of her head throbbed, each pulsating beat ringing like steel on an anvil. Her mind, muggy with something deeper than sleep, faltered at the rustling near her face.

Somewhere, a motor whined.

Were her eyes open? Darkness wrapped her so completely she couldn't be sure. She tightened them, opened—

Ohh! One eye stayed shut, hurt when she tried to force it. The other opened only halfway. She reached to touch her face—

Pain ripped through her arm into her chest. She couldn't breathe—

Ah . . . there, subsiding now. She swallowed carefully, barely moving, didn't want the pain again . . . then sipped a shallow, tentative breath—

And gasped! Pain knifed through her lungs.

Sweat dampened her upper lip. Clammy. She shuddered.

Sissy's cheek rested on her knees, knees drawn tight against her chest. Trapped.

He must have locked her in the metal storage room again, among the dusty boxes of keepsakes and lumpy plastic bags of old clothes. The plastic felt chill and smooth against her fingers.

Dear Lord, what was that stench? Like something rotten, decaying, making her want to vomit. A rat must have crawled into the storage room and died—

The rustling—? There could be more rats! Oohhhh, God. Her stomach knotted in dry heaves. How could she hurt so much and still be alive?

She recalled the blows now, her husband's merciless fist pounding her, his snakeskin boot with its nickel-plated toe swinging again and again, aiming for her stomach—striking whatever got in its way.

It was her own fault. She had forgotten to take out the garbage, so busy making supper. Lean pork chops, browned just right. Stewed apples, julienne carrots, fresh bread. It was Valentine's Day, and Sissy wanted everything perfect. He looked so handsome—he always looked handsome, but tonight he wore a brown tweed jacket and a yellow shirt that made his blond hair brighten like spun gold. Sissy wore one of her college skirts, the waist taken in. She looked all right.

He liked her cooking. Everything would have been fine, *just fine,* if only she had remembered the garbage. It was her own fault he had complained all through the meal, not even noticing his food.

"What the hell's wrong with you, you can't remember one simple thing? Now I'll have to haul the freakin bags to a Dumpster somewhere." Their town house had room for only two cans in the redwood caddy beside the garage. He hated seeing the cans overflow, bags stacked alongside.

"Maybe I could take them—"

"Oh, wouldn't that look great, my wife hauling trash all

hours of the night? You'd have to walk. You don't even have a goddamn driver's license."

When her renewal notice came, he'd said they didn't need two drivers in the family. Where the hell did she ever go without him? he'd said.

"I'll have to clean the car after stinking up the trunk with those goddamn bags. You like that, don't you, me doing grub work? Don't know why I ever married such a worthless dumb shit."

He was drunk, had come home already half-drunk after stopping with his friends from work. He mixed a Stoli martini before supper, then another to bring to the table, and another. He ranted on throughout the meal, saying the hateful things he always said, only this time his black rage came on faster than usual.

"I'm not one of those pissy-faced candyasses you went to law school with. My daddy practically owns this goddamn town and you better not forget it."

Law school. Sometimes Sissy wondered where she would be if she'd stuck it out, gotten her law degree —

"You better learn to bygod do your part. It's not like I ask a hell of a lot, is it? Keep the freakin house clean, cook a decent meal. Spread your goddamn legs a few times a week. AND TAKE OUT THE GODDAMN GARBAGE."

His huge fist had struck fast, closing that eye. Then he reached for the tennis racket he kept in the hall closet, clamped in its thick wood frame, handy for Saturday morning matches.

Sissy saw the rage like sparks of blood in his brown eyes. She turned to run. "Help me, Jesus," she whispered.

He hit her spine, knocked her into a chair, and she stumbled. Once she was down, he kept hitting her, his rage darker than ever before, and didn't stop even when he heard her collarbone crack. A satisfied gleam had leapt into his eyes as he raised the racket one more time.

Sissy shuddered, trying to remember what happened

later, him carrying her to the storage room and dumping her. But nothing came. She must have passed out.

Dear Lord, she hurt everywhere, pain like a hundred ice picks jabbing her. And she was so cramped, couldn't even raise her head off her knees.

A truck rumbled nearby—loud, as if right outside the garage—and there was that whine again. Familiar.

Risking the pain she knew would come, Sissy reached out to explore the limits of her confinement. . . . Plastic.

All around, plastic. A long rip—

Jesus help her! He'd stuffed her in a plastic bag. And dear God, she knew that whine, knew it.

Knew it.

The Dumpster truck.

A thin mewling leaked from Sissy's lips. She wasn't in the closet at all, but in a plastic garbage bag inside a Dumpster.

Saliva snaked from her lip down her bare leg and she felt ashamed of her terror. Her mind begged to close down, to reject what she knew was happening. She tried to pray.

Did he think he'd killed her?

No.

No! He was just teaching her a lesson, that's all. A lesson. That's all there was to it. When the truck whined on by, he would come back to get her, tell her to clean herself up, make him some breakfast. Not to even think about seeing a doctor. There would be fresh flowers in the crystal vase. He always gave her flowers after one of their . . . spats.

All right.

All right, as God was her savior, she would learn something valuable from this. She would learn to make lists every day of what needed to be done so that never again, *ever*, would she forget anything important.

Holding very still, Sissy whispered the Lord's prayer as she listened to the truck rumble closer.

Metal clanged.

The Dumpster shifted. The steel jaws had clamped on to it.

Pain exploded in Sissy's shoulder as the truck jostled her skyward and fed her into its gaping maw. She tumbled with a crush of garbage, fear shattering her prayer, her screams swallowed in the motor's whine.

Chapter One

January 14, ten years later

The Parrot Lounge, like a pulse point in a sleeping giant, nestles in a low corner of a three-star vintage hotel in downtown Houston. The hotel's ads, aimed at attracting traveling businesswomen, do their job well. Any happy hour, Monday through Friday, at least a dozen solitary women enjoy a predinner cocktail at the Parrot, while listening to the tinkling chords of sexy piano music and wishing for a more exciting evening than they'll find on cable TV.

Dixie Flannigan, feeling conspicuous in her jeans and sweatshirt, fingercombed her short brown hair and scanned the sleekly professional clientele as she sauntered to a rear table. The skip she'd spent the afternoon locating sat at the piano bar. His Armani suit brushed the silk skirt of a trim brunette, who smiled up at him, all lips and eyelashes. As Dixie ordered a club soda with a twist, the brunette laughed vivaciously, apparently at some witticism the skip had whispered in her ear.

Lawrence Riley Coombs, Dixie recalled from his file sheet, was known to be a charmer. Tall, rich, handsome, and politically connected, Coombs personified the exact opposite of men she usually hauled back to justice. Treat him gently, the bondsman had told her.

When the waiter, sweeping a disdainful glance over Dixie's attire, minced away to fetch her drink, she rang up the bonding office number on her cell phone.

"I have a fix on Coombs. You want to notify HPD, or should I?"

"We'll do it." The crisp female voice belonged to an undergraduate enrolled in the Criminal Justice program. The girl nurtured visions of single-handedly curtailing world crime and worked the bonding office night desk to pay her tuition.

"If you get a unit dispatched right away," Dixie suggested, "maybe I'll arrive home tonight before my friend feeds my dinner to the dog."

"I'll get right on it. Uh . . . you don't want to bring Coombs in yourself?"

Not if I can avoid it. He stood six-one, 190 pounds, according to his arrest sheet—and Dixie could see plenty of muscle filling out his fancy suit.

"I think your boss wants this one handled by Houston's finest," she hedged, watching Coombs lean close to the brunette, his hand resting on her thigh. The woman glanced at another woman beside her and appeared to be blushing.

Everybody had been shocked, the bondsman claimed, when Coombs missed his trial date that morning. His family was old money and, while Coombs was a laze-about, dividing his time among gambling, small game hunting, and women, he'd never been in any real trouble with the law before. Dixie, a former Assistant District Attorney, had followed the case closely in the newspapers. Lawrence Coombs was accused of having raped Regan Salles, a thirty-five-year-old hairdresser at one of the city's upscale salons. Date rape, the newspapers called it. But Dixie knew the ADA on the

case and had seen photographs of Salles after it happened—
two ribs broken, bruises blackening her entire pelvic region—
damage that wouldn't show in ordinary street clothes. Dixie
wondered if the vivacious brunette at the piano bar was practiced in self-defense.

Assured that the bonding agent would "get somebody
out there pronto," Dixie thumbed the phone's DISCON-
NECT button and relaxed for the wait. Her part of the job was
finished.

She watched Coombs speak to the piano player, slip a few
folded bills into the musician's tip jar, and return his attention to the blushing brunette. When the music instantly
segued into the opening chords of "Some Enchanted Evening," Coombs took the woman's hand and led her to a
postage-stamp dance floor near Dixie's table. Whatever else
the man was, he was drop-dead handsome and silver-spoon
elegant.

In a resonant baritone, Coombs began to sing, intimately,
as if the words were meant only for the woman in his arms,
yet loud enough for others to hear.

"Some enchanted evening . . ."

Conversation quieted. The man was worth a listen. His
voice was full, warm, and smooth. He moved with a sexy,
graceful ease, holding the woman as if she were fine crystal.

Was she special? Dixie wondered. Or had Regan Salles
also received such ardent attention from Coombs before
their "date" turned ugly?

When a club soda appeared at Dixie's elbow, she paid
rather than run a tab. The minute Coombs was in custody,
she intended to split. For the first time ever—and Dixie was
fast approaching forty—she was in a relationship that mattered to her. She didn't want to screw it up. Yet five nights
this week, work had kept her out late, and her excuses were
beginning to sound lame even to her own ears.

She watched the handsome couple whirl about the floor,
totally into themselves, as if everyone else in the room had
ceased to exist. When they brushed past, Coombs still croon-

ing softly, Dixie read raw desire in the woman's flushed face. The skip certainly had a knack for cozying up fast.

Two other couples had joined Coombs and his partner on the dance floor, but everyone else in the room was either alone, as Dixie was, or with a group. Did all these women have as tough a time as she did making a relationship work?

Dixie jabbed her swizzle stick at the lemon twist in her glass. Why did life have to be so damn complicated? She wanted closeness. Companionship. At the same time she wanted freedom and solitude. How could she expect a man to understand such a dilemma when she didn't understand it herself?

As her eyes slid past the bar, they locked on someone she knew, someone she did *not* want to talk with tonight.

Too late. Casey James, stringer for the sort of tabloids that feature alien sightings and virgin births, was already off her bar stool and beelining for Dixie's table.

"Counselor! I *knew* that was you sitting there!" Casey waved a fat cigar in one hand, a drink in the other, as she pushed toward Dixie between tables, a camera swinging from one shoulder. "I haven't seen you since our interview after that murder case you cracked!"

She stopped short of the table, slapped the cigar hand over her mouth, and looked hastily from side to side.

"Oh, Judas Priest, are you on a case now?"

Dixie had already darted a glance at Coombs. He seemed absorbed in stroking the brunette's silken hip and serenading her ear. Whether or not he'd heard, the worst was done. No point now in being rude.

"Hello, Casey. What brings you to the Parrot?"

Casey set her drink on Dixie's table and dropped her squatty body into an empty chair.

"Oh, honey, it's absolutely the *best* place for picking up stories. Buy a woman a drink, she'll tell the wickedest tales you ever heard—truth! Clients stealing from other clients, secretaries setting their bosses up for divorce or blackmail, or both, couriers delivering anonymous packages containing live snakes, spiders. Every one of those stories I learned from buying a woman a drink." She paused to draw on the cigar, piggish black eyes ogling Dixie. "May I buy *you* a drink, honey?"

Dixie couldn't help grinning at Casey's gall.

But when she looked back at the dance floor, and the piano bar beyond it, Coombs and the brunette were nowhere in sight.

Chapter Two

Casey James was a problem. If she discovered Dixie had followed a skip to the Parrot Lounge and the skip had just bolted, she'd stick to Dixie like Krazy Glue.

"Actually, Casey," Dixie offered, waving the waiter over, "I do have a story you might like." Standing, she swallowed the last of her club soda and hitched at her jeans. "How about ordering another round while I recycle this one? Then we'll talk."

Casey's greedy eyes widened a fraction. "Sex or violence?"

Already moving toward the door, Dixie shrugged. "Both."

Pacing her stride to appear unrushed, she stepped through the doorway and scanned the hall for Coombs. No luck. Except for the Parrot Lounge, only empty meeting rooms occupied this floor. No service personnel in sight. To the right, Dixie could see the elevator niche. To the left, an EXIT sign pointed to an enclosed stairwell that no doubt led to a parking area. The stairwell reentries were probably kept locked.

Hearing a hum that could be the elevator ascending, she jogged to the right. The hotel's main dining room on the twenty-seventh floor offered some of the best food in the city. If the brunette was registered here, she and Coombs might be planning to catch dinner while he romanced her into inviting him back to her suite.

Dusky blue carpet muffled Dixie's footsteps as she sprinted down the hall, hoping the elevator was the old-fashioned kind with lighted numbers to show where it stopped. She came abreast of the second meeting room, and the door opened.

A hand snapped around her wrist, yanked her into the room.

"Looking for me, darlin'?"

Coombs' blue eyes stared down at her.

Uh-oh.

"Don't flatter yourself, jerk." Dixie twisted away, but his hand on her wrist was like a steel band. When she tried to knee him, he spun her around and enveloped her with his body, his arms pinning hers like baling straps.

"Heard somebody was asking about me this afternoon," he drawled softly. "Guess that must be you."

He smelled of Aramis, one of Dixie's favorite men's colognes. Until now.

She brought her boot heel down hard on his Italian loafers. He flinched, but his grip remained as tight as ever, and suddenly she could feel his wet breath in her ear. A shiver went through her. She wondered briefly about the brunette, figured it'd been her in the elevator.

"The judge missed you this morning, Coombs."

He chuckled low, his mouth still at her ear. "The judge will get over it. Had to visit my sick mother."

"Sure you did." Expecting merely to finger Coombs for the HPD, Dixie had entered the hotel unarmed, except for the Kubaton, a six-inch hard-plastic rod, always on her key ring. If she could reach it . . .

"You have the tightest, roundest little ass under those jeans. Don't you darlin'? Tight, round . . . hot."

His hand snaked between her legs.

Dixie used the motion against him, tucking quickly to flip him over her shoulders onto his back. He knew the right moves and rolled as he landed, one arm reaching out to grab her ankle. He jerked her off balance.

She hit solid on her rump, jarring her spine all the way up. Pain laced through her teeth and skull.

Then he was on top of her, pinning her arms beneath her, slamming his fist into her right breast. Dixie's breath flew out of her as pain rushed in. She arched, trying to force him off, trying to free her hands, but his weight was like lead.

"Look at me, darlin'," Coombs whispered. "Look at me." He grabbed a handful of her hair and yanked. "Let me see the pain shining in those sweet brown eyes."

His other hand worked at the front of her jeans.

Dixie twisted sideways and shouldered him into a chair. The chair fell, bounced off Coombs, and landed like an iron fist on the side of Dixie's face.

Her vision wobbled. She tasted blood, felt it dribble from her mouth. She tried again to twist beneath him, but he was too strong, too heavy.

"Since you were so hot to find me, pretty lady, I'm going to give you a treat. I'm going to bury my cock right up to your belly." He licked the blood off her mouth.

Dixie clamped her teeth on his lower lip and bit down, jerking her head side to side like a pit bull.

Coombs grunted, loosening his hold on her hair.

She slammed a knee into his groin, but the angle was all wrong. Blood flowed from his torn lip into her mouth. She could feel her teeth click together in the thin skin beneath his lip, and the thought that she might bite it off sickened her.

Finally freeing one of her hands, she gouged at his eye. Her thumb had barely connected when a hammer blow of his fist hit her face. Pain lashed through her cheekbone, splintering into bright red shards of light inside her head.

But she refused to let go of his lip. His whiskey breath filled her nostrils.

How can this be happening in a busy hotel? she wondered lamely. *Can't anyone hear?*

But it'd been only a minute, maybe two, since he surprised her in the hall. And how much noise had they actually made?

Her ears rang. She'd go for Coombs' eye again, but she wasn't sure where her hand was or how to make it work.

She felt his thumbs on her jaw, prying her mouth open. With one abrupt thrust, she heaved him off, releasing his lip. She scrambled away, spitting blood.

"Casey!" she yelled—knowing the Parrot Lounge was too far away. Her vision had cleared, but her head felt ready to explode. Spotting the fallen chair, she grabbed it and swung upward, striking Coombs' hip. He barely noticed.

"So you like it rough, do you, babe? Let's see just *how* rough." He scooped up a chair by its legs.

Dixie backed away, her chest screaking pain where Coombs had pounded it. She could hold her own against a lot of men, but at five-two, 120 pounds, she was no match for this man. He hadn't built those muscles at a piano bar.

"Casey!" Dixie yelled again. "*Casey!*"

Coombs swung the chair. Dixie dodged, but the metal frame cracked against her foot and ankle. As the blow sent her sprawling, she heard herself scream. Fury burst inside her like a Fourth of July rocket.

Hobbling to her feet, she dove at Coombs, shoving him into the wall, and this time her knee connected with his testicles. When he doubled over, Dixie butted the top of her head into his face. Blood spattered her shoulders. She kneed him again, fury driving her leg like a piston.

The door crashed open.

"There she is!"

Through her rage, Dixie saw Casey James rush through

the doorway, blue uniforms crowding behind. For a furious instant, Dixie was only mildly grateful. Another minute alone with Coombs and she'd have stomped his bastard balls into a bloody pulp, nullifying any future rape plans.

"Are you all right, honey?" Casey's camera flashed in Dixie's face. "Truth, woman! When you promise a story, you deliver in spades!"

Chapter Three

"Aunt Dix, when you get your cast, I'm the first to sign it. Okay?" Ryan, Dixie's twelve-year-old nephew, watched intently as a doctor probed her ankle.

She lay on a narrow emergency-room bed, stoic face firmly in place. Her family had gotten wind somehow of her scuffle with Coombs and had rushed to the hospital, insisting on crowding into the tiny treatment cubicle. Ryan's slender neck stretched forward, taking in the doctor's every move.

Dixie's bouts with danger fascinated the boy when he heard about them thirdhand, but actually seeing his aunt injured had stiffened him up like boiled starch. Dixie wished he'd relax and not worry about her. Hooking a finger in the back pocket of his jeans, she tugged him toward her, wincing at the pain that laced every muscle in her body.

"Sorry, kid, you'll have to sign my Ace bandage." Her jaw didn't want to work right on its hinge, slurring her words a bit. "No cast. The ankle's only bruised. Right, Doc?"

"Mmmmmm . . . possibly."

"Just wrap it up and let me go home." She hated such fuss over a simple injury that never would've happened if she hadn't been such a dumbass, letting Coombs spot her. Now she'd have to endure another round of family lectures on choosing a less dangerous profession.

But she felt a pang of selfishness, seeing the pallor of her sister's face as Amy fluffed up the bed pillows like giant marsh-mallows. When a hospital aide approached, Amy snatched a blanket from the young man's arms.

"There you are! You people keep this room way too chilly."

"Thank you," Dixie mumbled to the aide.

Amy never meant to be rude, but on mother-hen duty she developed tunnel vision. Blond bob frazzled above a woolly lavender sweater, she had rushed in worried and clucking, demanding the blanket as soon as she saw Dixie's skimpy paper coverlet.

"I don't understand a hospital that insists on stripping you down to nothing," she said, "then freezes you blue." Now she snapped the blanket in the air, spread it, and patted it into place. "Ryan, don't get in the doctor's way. He needs that light you're blocking."

"I'm not in his way, Mom. Just watching. You're going to need X rays, Aunt Dix."

"X rays!" Amy tucked the soft washed cotton around Dixie's neck. "That's a good idea. Don't you think so, Doctor?"

Tiny silver bells on Amy's charm bracelet tinkled in Dixie's ear. Amy had worn silver bells on the day they met, Dixie recalled, the day Amy's parents, Barney and Kathleen Flannigan, brought Dixie home from the halfway house, ink barely dry on the adoption papers. The bells had dangled from Amy's ears that day, glinting in the sunlight, framing a broad welcoming smile. Nearly three years older than Dixie, Amy had been the best big sister any girl could want. Sometimes, though, her patting and tucking got tedious. Dixie pulled the blanket away from her chin.

"Yep." The doctor straightened and scribbled on Dixie's chart. "We'll take a few pictures, see what's going on in there. Are you planning to be a doctor, young man?"

"No, sir. An airplane pilot. But I might need to set a broken bone, in case of a plane crash."

"Ry-an!" Amy's bells tinkled nervously as she waved aside her son's comment. "Parker said the plane is perfectly safe."

Parker Dann, bold as a pirate and solid as steel—the man who made Dixie's toes curl every time he smiled—stood a few feet from the bed, talking to Amy's husband, Carson Royal. Parker had promised to take the whole family flying next weekend. Amy still had the flutters about going up.

"Isn't it safe, Parker?" she insisted.

"Safer than the Parrot Lounge, anyway." Parker's dark brows hooded fierce blue eyes as he studied Dixie, thick mustache tracing a narrow smile.

His gaze hadn't left Dixie's face since he stormed into the emergency room like a knight on a white charger. A girlish part of her—a part Dixie scarcely knew existed—felt as maidenly as Guinevere. Nevertheless, she'd turned her stoic face on him, declaring she was fine.

"Aunt Dix can still go flying on Sunday, can't she?" Ryan looked worriedly at the doctor. "And teach our self-defense class?"

The doctor, pushing the cubicle curtain aside to wave in a nurse with a wheelchair, cocked an eyebrow at Ryan.

"Why don't we wait until after the X rays to talk about what your aunt can do?"

He winked and walked out whistling. Dixie wasn't sure whether a whistling doctor was a good thing.

A buzz of activity had greeted her when she arrived at the hospital shortly after Coombs. Apparently, Casey James had spread the word that Dixie was responsible for the damage to Coombs' face. His nose and lip had swelled, turning his handsome features grotesque. Seeing the teeth marks, the doctor had immediately ordered blood tests. Until that moment, Dixie hadn't considered the possibility of AIDS. Another dumbass move, biting him.

The nurse positioned the wheelchair close to the bed. "Can you sit up, Ms. Flannigan?"

"Sure." Dixie's entire left side objected screamingly, but for Ryan's sake she bit back the cowardly moan that threatened to spill out.

With the nurse's help, Dixie eased off the bed and into the wheelchair. A tone chimed outside the cubicle. The nurse frowned toward the sound, glanced back at Dixie, then turned to leave.

"We're a bit shorthanded," she explained, "but I'll send someone to take you upstairs."

Parker grasped the wheelchair handles. "I'll take her. Where do we go?"

The nurse paused, as if considering. The chime sounded again.

"Radiology. Second floor. Just follow the signs." She dashed away.

As Parker wheeled the chair around and aimed it toward the cubicle opening, her brother-in-law stepped forward to hold the curtain.

"This is precisely why I'm saying she ought to think about missing persons," Carl told Parker, making himself skinny for the wheelchair to pass. "Friend of mine says *everybody's* looking for somebody these days. Missing mothers, fathers, kids."

Parker didn't answer, but in the silence Dixie could sense his agreement. The only time he turned bearish and surly was when Dixie's job got her into a scrap, which in the past weeks—and she'd barely known Parker three weeks—had happened more frequently than she cared to think about.

"I like Carl's idea," Amy said. She'd whipped the blanket off the bed, and now she settled it on Dixie's lap, tucking it around her legs. "All those missing kids, somebody needs to find them, Dixie, and you're good at that. She found you quick enough, didn't she, Parker?"

"Like I had a red beacon blinking on my tail."

Dixie looked up to find him smiling. He hadn't thought it humorous at the time, though, her bringing him back from North Dakota after he'd skipped out on his trial. Parker's case had made Dixie reevaluate her conviction that innocent suspects don't run.

"Problem is," her brother-in-law persisted, "police departments don't have enough manpower to look for missing persons. Opens up a whole new industry—runaways, divorced parents stealing their own kids. What I'm saying, Parker, there's a need out there that's not being filled. Your sales ability, Dixie's street sense, the pair of you could rake in a bundle."

"Keep talking, Carl," Parker told him. "Sooner or later some of it's going to land between her stubborn ears." He pointed the chair toward an elevator bank and kept moving.

"Guess this was another of your quick, safe, simple jobs," he muttered to Dixie. "Did you see the size of that bruise on your face?"

"I've been needing a new hairstyle anyway." She drew a strand of her short hair over the bruise, then continued, speaking gingerly around the pain in her jaw. "Maybe I'll get one that swings over my cheek, all sultry like that actress from the thirties. What was her name?"

Parker jabbed the elevator button. Behind them, Ryan was bumming vending-machine change from his parents. Maybe that meant they wouldn't all follow her upstairs.

"Tallulah Bankhead. And stop changing the subject. Carl has a point this time. If this missing persons investigator needs a partner—"

"*I* don't need a partner to find lost kids or lost parents."

The elevator doors opened. Parker pushed the chair into the empty car and punched a button for the second floor. Dixie could feel his frustration pulsing behind her as he stood waiting for the doors to close. When the car began to move, he leaned over, captured her hands for a gentle squeeze, and kissed the top of her head. Then he held on, as if drawing her energy inside him. His breath escaped into her hair. The warm scent of him enveloped her.

"Dixie, do what you have to do. But don't expect me not to worry about you."

She turned her face up to meet his lips. Instantly, all the pain and frustration of the past few hours began to dissipate, like ashes on a lake. Much too soon, the elevator bumped to a halt and the doors slid open. A white-coated technician stood in the hall.

"Ms. Desiree Flannigan?"

"It's *Dixie* Flannigan." Her blood mother, an incurable romantic, had christened her Desiree Alexandra, which Dixie promptly shed at the age of twelve, except on legal papers.

"The doctor wants pictures of your foot. My, that *is* swollen, isn't it?"

Twenty minutes later, after being x-rayed, turned, x-rayed some more—feeling a whole lot like a piece of microwaved beef—Dixie eased into the wheelchair again, and Parker maneuvered her back down to the ER. Ryan bounded up beside her.

"Is it broken?"

"Don't know yet." Dixie hooked an arm around his scrawny neck and pulled him down to eye level. "What's with all the enthusiasm? Are you trying to get a school paper out of this?"

He grinned sheepishly, wriggling in her grasp as they continued down the corridor. Her escapades had gained Ryan at least one A in creativity and a lot of attention from his classmates. She planted a loud kiss on his cheek, then whispered in his ear, "You can *claim* it's broken, if you want."

She dropped several more wet kisses on him while he squirmed, finally freeing himself.

"That reporter lady said the man you beat up is in jail." He scrubbed a hand over his damp cheek.

"Let's hope he stays there."

"What'd he do?"

They'd reached the treatment cubicle, where Carl and Amy loitered outside the curtain, along with a new visitor, Brenda Benson, prosecutor on the Coombs case.

Small but sturdy, Brenda was striking without being pretty, with amber eyes, a strong jaw, and magnificent yellow-gold hair that made you think of sunny beaches, even on the stormiest winter day. In grade school, Dixie recalled, her hair had invoked taunts—"Hey, Straw Head," "Hey, Mellow Yellow," or even "Hey, Pee Brain." But the jibes bounced off Brenda like water off a hot griddle, and now, at nearly forty, her yellow hair looked as lustrous as ever, despite the unforgiving hospital lights.

As Parker coasted the wheelchair to a stop, Brenda raked back a long strand that had escaped its clip. Dixie wondered if her friend had torn herself away from a prosecutor's crushing workload just to check on a sprained foot. Probably. Compassionate, aggressively single, stubborn as a dripping faucet, Brenda had once snipped off her own beautiful locks to support a classmate who was humiliated for having a case of head lice. Afterward, without the golden mane waving above her coarse features, Brenda was frequently mistaken for a boy. Any other girl would've been insulted. Brenda had seen both humor and opportunity in the situation, encouraging the misconception anytime being a boy offered advantage.

Tonight her amber eyes shone with the same intensity as when she and Dixie, as ten-year-olds, had shared their darkest secrets. She wore a smart camel suit, somewhat wilted, simple alligator pumps, and an expression of intense worry.

To ease her friend's concern, Dixie flashed a grin.

"Hey, Mellow Yellow. Next time a worm wriggles off your line, I want a bigger net to catch him with."

Brenda's weary smile barely lifted the corners of her thin lips.

"From what I hear, you gaffed the sonofa—" She cut her eyes toward Ryan, and the smile brightened a watt or two. "To answer your question," she told Ryan, "Lawrence Coombs committed as many rotten, dirty deeds as any video-game monster. Your aunt zapped the sucker, thus doing the women of Houston a supreme justice."

"Really?" Ryan beamed at Dixie.

"Glad I could help." She managed another grin, ignoring the ache in her jaw.

Amy plucked at Ryan's shirt, straightening the collar. Then taking a firm hold on the boy's shoulder, and another on Carl's arm, she shot a meaningful glance at Parker.

"Come on, fellows. Let's give these two lawyers a chance to talk in peace." She herded the three males down the hall toward the vending machines.

Brenda's amber gaze followed them out of earshot, then swung back to Dixie.

"For months I've been trying to get enough evidence to convict Coombs. He's injured other women before Regan Salles, but they're all too scared to sign a complaint."

"Can't say I blame them." Dixie recalled Coombs' height-ened pleasure as he watched each vicious blow register on her face.

"With both you and Regan testifying, I think I can get a conviction."

"You *think*? Surely his failure to appear at trial will sour his case." Testifying in court was Dixie's least favorite part of skip tracing.

Brenda's mouth twisted bitterly. "It seems Coombs left an emergency message for his attorney early this morning, claiming he had to see his mother at a nursing home in Galveston. Marianne Coombs is a stroke patient, and Coombs *did* show up there, but so far no one's saying what the emergency was. His attorney didn't receive the message until after court convened." She peeled the wrapper from a chunk of nicotine gum, popped the gum into her mouth, then rolled the wrapper into a tight ball. "Considering Coombs' fine family history in political circles, the judge will jump hoops to be lenient."

"Visits his sick mother in the morning, then trolls the Parrot Lounge that night?" Dixie shook her head at the double standard. "Don't worry so much, Brenda. You're good. You'll nail him."

"With your help, I'll have a better chance."

Dixie sighed. She and Brenda shared a lot of history. At twelve, when Dixie moved away with adoptive parents, the girls remained pen pals. Years later, they reunited at law school, only to drift apart again after graduation, losing track completely until the day four years ago when Brenda applied for a job as Assistant DA. And once again, Dixie had moved on. After ten years of frustration with Texas' swinging-door justice, and reaping a bumper crop of stomach ulcers to show for it, Dixie had drifted into the fringes of the judicial system—bounty hunter, bodyguard, occasionally a finder of lost persons. Have Mustang, will travel. Ulcer-free and pig-simple.

But Brenda worked harder than anyone in the department, making a personal commitment to every assault case against women or children that crossed her desk. Now, in the familiar lines of her face and the exhausted slope of her shoulders, Dixie could see the ravages of too much work and worry.

But she still didn't relish taking the witness stand.

"A bounty hunter who gets popped a few times by a skip won't gain many points with a jury," she grumbled.

"The officer said Coombs jumped you. Tried to rape you. You have a bruised jaw, Dixie, and a broken ankle—"

"Sprained." Dixie shifted in the wheelchair to relieve a twinge in her battered ribs. "Listen, Bren, what I'd like most is to never set eyes on Lawrence Coombs again. But if you need me, I'll be there. You know that." What else could she say?

Abruptly, the ADA bent awkwardly over Dixie's chair to throw both arms around her. Shalimar—a scent Brenda had always loved and wore too heavily—took Dixie's breath away.

"I knew I could count on you. But I needed to hear you

say it." Brenda's voice broke. She cleared her throat and straightened self-consciously, releasing Dixie's shoulders. Then she grabbed her friend's hand and held on. "This case—" She swallowed. "We *can't lose* this one."

Her hand felt cold in Dixie's.

"After you *win* it, Bren, take a vacation. A *long* vacation. You deserve a break from all the misery you take on." An orderly appeared with Dixie's X rays. Hearing the Happy Whistler, she looked around to see the doctor headed their way, as well. She turned back to Brenda. "Try the West Indies. I hear St. Martin is virtually crime free."

Brenda nodded and released her hand. "I'll think about it. Meanwhile, I hope you don't expect that sprained foot to get you out of racquetball next week."

"Not sprained," the doctor said cheerfully, snapping Dixie's X rays onto a light box. "Fractured. Looks like your nephew gets to sign a cast after all."

Chapter Four

Two hours and twenty miles later, Dixie struggled with a temporary splint as she attempted to climb out of Parker's Cadillac—her own Mustang still parked in the hotel garage. "The cast will come later," the doctor had told her. "After the swelling subsides."

She'd barely pushed open the car door when Mean Ugly Dog, her half Doberman, nosed under her arm. Mud usually waited in the kitchen, all grins and wags when she opened the door. He must have sensed something wrong tonight. Sometimes the ugly mutt astonished her with his perceptiveness.

He sniffed out the bulky foreign substance on her left foot, a high thin whine drifting softly on his breath. Then, planting two heavy front paws on her lap, he gave her face a thorough tongue bath—Mud's version of reassurance.

"It's okay, boy." Dixie nudged him gently aside to reach her crutches in the backseat.

"Hang on," Parker said sharply. "I'll come around and help you."

On the long, quiet ride from the hospital, Parker's few words had been brusque. Grouchy. Whatever he was chewing on, Dixie wished he'd spit it out.

"I'll be okay. The sooner I start using these sticks, the sooner I'll quit feeling clumsy."

"You'll have plenty of time to practice."

Four to six weeks, according to the doctor. "Lucky girl," he'd announced, teeth gleaming in his wide smile. "It's the foot that's fractured, not the ankle." Ten years younger than her and calling her "girl"? She'd felt like tweaking the twerp's nose.

It was after the doctor's pronouncement that Parker turned quiet. But Dixie's questions had elicited only terse replies, capped by, "I'm not angry, Dixie."

The foot wasn't her first broken bone, probably wouldn't be the last, but it was her first time on crutches. Already she hated the handicap. How the hell did you climb out of a car and manage the damn sticks at the same time?

A brisk January wind whistled around the car as she leveraged herself off the seat. Mud sniffed the rubber-tipped crutch, then sat back on his haunches to observe. Sliding her injured left foot awkwardly, trying not to bump it, Dixie hopped back to clear the car's threshold—and a stab of pain in her battered ribs caused her to drop a crutch, nearly doubling her over. She swallowed back a yelp. If Parker knew about the bruised chest, he'd get even surlier.

After retrieving the crutch, she turned to find him and Mud standing side by side, two anxious faces in the yellow porch light. The sight made her smile.

"It's *okay*, guys. Bones heal. I'll be fine in no time."

"Until the next job," Parker said. "The next cut, scrape, broken bone, gunshot wound—"

"I've never been shot." She maneuvered the crutches under her arms and took her first step toward the house.

She'd never realized 120 pounds of human flesh could be so heavy.

But she could do this. She could.

Parker slammed the car door and walked behind as she approached the porch, Mud sniffing worriedly at her splint. She hadn't a clue how to get up the steps.

"Why don't you put your car in the garage?" she suggested. Carl had offered to drive her Mustang home from the hotel, but it wouldn't arrive until tomorrow.

"The car's fine."

"Didn't you just wash it? The wind smells like rain."

"Dixie, if you fall, you'll break another bone."

"I'm not going to fall." *I hope.*

Mud tramped up the stairs ahead of her, as if to show the way. Then he turned and studied her misshapen foot again.

Approaching the first step, Dixie hesitated.

"Go ahead and unlock the door while I figure out how to do this." Did she put the crutches on the step and swing up? Or try to lever herself up, pulling the sticks behind her? Maybe she should just sit down and scoot up backward on her butt.

"Crutches are useless going up stairs," Parker said. "You have to hold the rail and hop."

"Hey, that's right. You've used these things before." As a kid, after a tractor accident. She grinned at him, hoping for a smile back. No dice. "So what do I do with them while I hop?"

"Both in your left hand, hold the rail with your right. Or just *hand me* the friggin crutches."

"Parker, I'd rather practice the whole thing while you're here to coach me."

He nodded grudgingly.

Balanced on her good foot, the unwieldy splint crooked behind, she transferred both sticks to one hand and grabbed the stair rail. It was awkward, but she managed to mount the three steps to the porch, then reposition the crutches and clump to the door.

Inside, she suddenly noticed how much furniture Kathleen had squeezed into the cozy living room. When her adoptive parents died within two years of each other, Dixie had inherited the house along with the family pecan farm. Amy, less nostalgic and more practical than Dixie, received the summer home in Maine. Dixie adored the old Texas farmhouse, loved every dusty collectible inside it, but at the moment it looked as inviting as an obstacle course for combat training. On a side table, one of Kathleen's miniature needlepoint maxims framed in ornate silver had never seemed more appropriate: A *Worm Is the Only Creature that Can't Fall Down.*

Parker moved ahead, clearing a path, while Dixie eased tentatively forward.

"Ow!" She'd misjudged the jutting edge of a table and cracked her splint against it. Hurt like a sonofabitch.

Mud sniffed at the table, her foot, the crutch stem, and managed to stay precisely in her path as she continued toward the kitchen.

"What do you want for dinner?"

"Anything." What she wanted most was to sit down, but her stomach felt as hollow as a gourd. "Something simple. Is there pizza in the freezer?" She usually kept an emergency supply of frozen pizzas and Jimmy Dean sausage biscuits.

"You don't think a broken foot's enough to keep you awake tonight, you want indigestion, too?" Parker's tone was as harsh as his words.

Dixie knew he was merely frustrated with not being able to take away her pain or clobber Lawrence Coombs for causing it, but apparently Mud wasn't as certain. He nosed protectively between them, teeth sharp and gleaming, his sleek back as high as Dixie's waist.

Parker scowled at the dog.

"Ease up, Mud. I didn't break her damn foot." When Mud stood his ground, Parker sighed. "I'll make an omelet."

Parker's omelets were like golden slices of heaven.

"Sounds terrific." Dixie's mouth watered at the mere mention of it.

She scratched Mud's ears and hobbled to the breakfast
nook, a padded booth Barney had built the year after Dixie
became part of the family. She still preferred eating most
meals there, instead of the long dining table with its eight
side chairs. But managing her splinted left foot while sliding
onto the blue leather seat she usually chose proved
daunting, especially when she was hungry, tired, and irri-
table. She switched to the opposite side, Amy's side in the
old days, Parker's in the past few weeks.

Grateful to be off the crutches, she stroked Mud's neck as
she watched Parker move with lazy efficiency between the
refrigerator and stove. Maybe cooking would warm up his
chilly attitude. A big man, with powerful, densely muscled
shoulders, he should look klutzy in Kathleen's gingham-
curtained kitchen. But he chopped, sliced, and sautéed as
gracefully as a master chef—which continuously amazed
Dixie, since she could scarcely scramble eggs without turning them rubbery. His face and arms had bronzed up on his
new boat-selling job at Clear Lake. A fresh haircut had
squared off the dark fringe around his collar, leaving the
wavy locks thick on the top and sides, as unruly as a small
boy's except when freshly combed. As she watched him
work, a tender passion curled up to nestle around Dixie's
heart.

Three weeks ago, Parker Dann had been a name in a file,
a mug shot, a bounty job she'd tried to turn down because it
interfered with her Christmas holidays. Most of the days
since then had been spent with the two of them under the
same roof, six days with Parker as her prisoner while she investigated a vehicular manslaughter charge against him.
Only after proving his innocence had she allowed herself to
respond to the emotions he stirred.

Now, his former neighborhood no longer appealing and
his new house under construction eighty miles away on
Galveston Island, he usually stayed at her place. They were
exploring the boundaries of a relationship. Like chunky fruit
Jell-O, it didn't fit smoothly into a mold. For Dixie's part, she

already knew she wanted him in her life until long after his dark hair turned white and his rakishly handsome face leathered with time lines. But neither of them had a good history for long-lasting male-female relationships. Parker Dann was a drifter; any day he might drift right out of her life. She was afraid to care *too* much.

The tempting aroma of onions, mushrooms, and sausage wafted from the stove. Moments later, Parker set a warm plate in front of her, omelet perfectly browned, folded, and accompanied by a slice of melon, another plate for himself, and a tall glass of milk for each of them. She didn't have to look to know Mud would be scarfing up similar fare.

"Milk?" she asked. They usually had wine with dinner.

"Drink it. It'll help that bone to mend." He sat across from her and tucked into his meal without meeting her gaze. Grouchy.

"Parker, if I agree to discuss the missing kids thing with Carl, will you stop with the silent treatment?"

"What silent treatment?"

"Okay. Maybe 'silence' is not precisely descriptive. How about, 'silence salted with terse orders'?"

His blue eyes tilted up at her from under his dark, shaggy eyebrows.

"I just don't see where Carl's idea is so wrong. How can chasing bail jumpers be more rewarding than finding missing kids?"

"I never said it was more rewarding."

"Is it the challenge? A 'liberated female' thing? Why do you insist on putting yourself in the middle of dangerous situations?"

"Finding Coombs wasn't supposed to be dangerous," she pointed out.

"You knew he was charged with rape and battery."

"The job went sour. You think a parent who's stolen a child isn't dangerous? Picture a mama lion."

He looked away from her. "Eat your omelet before it gets cold."

Dixie didn't want to argue with him. Nor did she want to go to bed with the anger simmering between them. She forked up a bite, but continued to watch him discreetly from beneath her lashes. His broad shoulders were rigid with tension, his jaw rock hard, barely moving as he chewed. Parker's concern for her was comforting at times, but she couldn't respond to his fears by taking a desk job somewhere. And she simply didn't know the answers to his questions. She'd never consciously decided to become a bounty hunter. It was a thing that needed doing, so she did it. After ending her career as a prosecutor, she hadn't really planned the rest of her life. She was making it up day by day, taking on whatever seemed to need doing. Which today had included finding an accused rapist who hadn't appeared for trial. And dammit, despite the broken foot and painful bruises, this was a day she felt good about her job. Lawrence Riley Coombs was one devil she wanted to see burn.

Parker speared a mushroom as if to kill it.

"I just feel so friggin impotent, not being there, like there must be something I could've done. Almost wish Coombs wasn't locked up, so I could go beat the shit out of him."

"Thanks for feeling that way." Dixie meant it. The male gallantry thing might be chauvinistic, but she appreciated his wanting to protect her.

Parker shoved his plate away. "It isn't easy loving you, Dixie. Knowing any day I might get a call that you're seriously injured or . . . worse."

Loving her? That's a word they hadn't used before.

"How would you feel if it was the other way around?" he demanded. "If I was the one in danger of coming home in a box?"

Dixie had dated a cop once. The worry and uncertainty had made her as mean as a homeless wasp at times, and she hadn't cared half as much about the cop as she did about the man sitting across from her. She reached for Parker's hand and linked a finger around his broader one.

"Do you have any idea how good you made me feel, showing up at the ER?"

His gaze caught hers, and his mouth softened at the corners.

"Embarrassing, wasn't it, all of us crowded around while a doctor poked at you?"

"I wasn't talking about Amy, Carl, and Ryan. I'm used to their mother-hen act. But Coombs . . . well, his kind of attack makes a woman feel . . . dirty. When I looked up and saw your big, beautiful, worried face, everything that happened in that hotel meeting room vanished like a bad dream."

With his free hand, he nudged a strand of hair away from her cheek. "A bad dream that left an imprint," he reminded her.

"It'll heal."

He nodded. "This time."

"Believe me, tonight was not typical. These past *weeks* haven't been typical."

"No?" He touched her neck where a knife wound had scarcely healed. Then he turned her hand over and rubbed the back of her knuckles with his thumb. "Figured you'd be pissed when I showed up at the hospital. But I had to come. Make sure you were all right."

"I was more all right after you got there." She retrieved her hand and returned part of her attention to her food. "You know, if Lawrence Coombs isn't convicted, he'll go right on doing to other women what he did to Regan Salles. What he tried to do to me."

"Which means you'll testify against him?"

"How would you feel about that?"

"Your having to say in front of a courtroom what he tried to do? Hellfire, Dixie, the sonofabitch belongs in prison. Putting him down for the count is the *only* way to make up for those bruises and that broken foot. I want to be right there in court to hear you crucify him."

Dixie didn't think Coombs' attack on her would crucify him, since he hadn't been successful in raping her. A jury might reason that any woman figuring she had balls enough to be a bounty hunter should expect a few bruises. Juries were unpredictable. But she was glad Parker felt the same way she did about testifying. Men could also be unpredictable.

When she'd put away the last of her omelet and half a package of cookies to make the milk drinkable, she battled the crutches to lend a hand with the dishes.

"Give it up," Parker told her. "You're not helping."

"Thanks." Dixie hung up her dish towel and gimped to the living room to read the newspaper.

Later, wind whistling around the windows, they flicked on the bedroom television and prepared to snuggle together in her big four-poster bed. Kathleen's patchwork quilt would keep them warm enough. In the past couple weeks, the ten o'clock news followed by *The Tonight Show* had become Dixie's favorite time of day. The snuggling invariably turned serious about halfway through Leno's monologue.

Dixie knew that wouldn't happen tonight, when the only square inch of her that didn't hurt was her navel. Her hands had gone numb from using the crutches, and her armpits ached as much as her bruised ribs from carrying her weight. But she still craved the comfort of curling up in bed with Parker.

While he was in the bathroom, she clumped to the dresser and peeled off her sweatshirt. The left side of her chest had turned an ugly purple. Quickly, before Parker could see it, she slipped on a fresh oversized T-shirt. Tomorrow she'd have to learn how to shower without getting the cast wet. Fiberglass would be lighter, and waterproof, the doc had told her. But he was out of it.

During the first commercial, Parker turned off the sound.

"Will you really talk to Carl about his investigator friend who wants a partner?"

"I'll *talk*. That doesn't mean I'll take the offer."

"What if I was part of it? Like Carl said, doing what I do best."

Dixie hated that idea. She wanted two working partners less than she wanted one.

"There's not a whole lot of selling to be done in investigation. Think about it. Would you knock on someone's door and say, 'Hey, lady, for twenty thousand bucks, we'll locate that teenager you misplaced last week'? Customers generally come by referral."

Parker nodded, absently smoothing the faded quilt over Dixie's thigh. "How would you feel about spending some time in Galveston—while your foot heals? There's a summer house for rent right next door to mine."

They could watch the new construction go up. Whoopee. But she wouldn't be doing much anyway. And Mud loved the beach.

"Sure," she said.

"I may be busy part of the time, with the yacht business gearing up."

"January is boating season?" Dixie shivered and snuggled closer.

"People start dreaming about warm weather. A lot of money can be made on other people's dreams."

The commercials had ended. He thumbed up the volume, but when the next break came, Dixie took the remote and hit the MUTE button.

"Do you think I do what I do for the money?" she asked.

"I suppose you make a decent living off the pecan farm."

"Yes, I do."

"So you don't really need to work . . . at anything."

"Not for the money. There are other rewards to be had from working." He should know. He'd socked away enough to retire for life.

He caught a strand of her dark hair and wrapped it around a finger.

"I'm a salesman, Dixie. For me, every angle involves money. Besides"—he tugged at the strand of hair—"you *do* take a bounty."

"Of course I do, it's business. But—" She sighed. "But money alone wouldn't make me take a job I didn't believe in."

Smoothing her hair aside, he nuzzled her ear. His lips felt soft, his breath warm. His tongue tickled.

"You don't believe in finding lost kids?"

"Some of those kids don't want to be found—and for good reason. Some will be found with needle tracks up their arms and fried brains. Others will never be found—alive. It's a heartbreaking business."

His eyes narrowed and his expressive mouth turned down at the corners. "I hadn't thought about it like that."

She tossed the remote on the nightstand and snuggled gingerly under the covers, wanting to wrap her good right leg over his, but the splint was like a stone wall between them, and every movement sent a fresh shiver of hurt in one direction or another.

"Nevertheless," she murmured sleepily, "I'll talk to Carl's friend."

He kissed her forehead, then her cheek, then slid down beside her to capture her lips.

Outside, the wind whistled fiercely under the eaves, while inside, Kathleen's quilt cocooned them and the flickering TV screen bathed them in colored light.

Six weeks, the doctor had said. *Not if she could help it.*

Chapter Five

Monday, February 10

Dixie's pager shuddered silently against her hip. She checked the number, then tossed away the remainder of her sandwich. Julie Colby, the victim-witness coordinator, liaison to Brenda's staff, had promised to beep her as soon as the jury reached a verdict. Seeing the familiar number, Dixie paid her lunch tab and clumped hurriedly along a tunnel with lime-green walls. She could get around now without the crutches, but she carried one along when she knew she'd be swinging the four-pound cast for a while. Squeezing into a crowded elevator, she rose to the fifth floor and eased open the door of Judge Engleton's court. From the low collective babble, she knew the jury was still out.

The courtroom was packed. Dixie slid into a back row, shed her jacket, and plucked a speck of gray lint off her tan sweatshirt. The drive from Galveston had been frustratingly bumper-to-bumper, due to construction on the Interstate. She'd rushed through several errands before Julie paged her, and now she wondered if her deodorant was still on the job. Sniffing, she wrinkled her nose.

"Could be worse," offered the man sitting next to her. White-haired and small-boned, he looked like everybody's favorite uncle. His blue eyes glinted. "Better a little honest sweat than that godawful flowery smell women spray all over themselves."

Dixie had to agree. "Morning elevators are the worst. Hair spray, talcum powder, cologne, and *men's* aftershave lotion."

He poked her with a bony elbow, glanced around, and lowered his voice suggestively. "A spot of perfume behind a woman's ears, now, that ain't so bad, but there's one place a woman oughta smell like a woman—"

"Hey! Stow that thought, goat-twerp!" She scooted away, ignoring his lecherous wink. Just her luck to sit beside a dirty old man. Now a jungle of Rastafarian braids blocked her view. But leaning sideways, she found a wide enough opening between the braids and a tall, baby-patting mother to get a clear view of Lawrence Riley Coombs.

The defendant looked as dashing as ever, sitting there in his conservative gray suit, hundred-dollar tie, and those trust-me blue eyes. Dixie had to commend counsel's shrewdness in assigning one of their female junior partners to the case, as if to say, "This attractive young woman would never defend a man guilty of rape."

But it would take more than smart lawyers to set Lawrence Coombs free. It would take a jury of blind, deaf monkeys.

"He'll walk." Belle Richards slid her classy rump onto a vacated spot on the bench. "Trust me."

Dixie recognized her Bill Blass suit from a *Fortune* magazine article touting Belle as Texas' "hottest female defense lawyer."

"Not a chance he'll walk. Unless every woman on the jury is a Stepford Wife."

"Worth a wager?"

Dixie hesitated. "A week at your Caribbean condo." She hesitated again. "Against what?"

"Against a favor."

The artful gleam in Belle's eye made Dixie instantly wary. "What sort of favor?"

"I need someone to play bodyguard to the teenage daughter of one of the firm's best clients."

Dixie was itching to work again. Four sedentary weeks watching Parker's house go up were enough already. But the teen years often turned adorable kids into sullen, smart-mouthed terrors, hanging out on street corners, selling drugs in school yards. She hoped Ryan would escape the adolescent process and go straight from fantastic twelve-year-old to sensible adult.

"Bodyguard or bratsitter?"

"Our client received threats," Belle said, "against her own life *and* the girl's. The client was worried enough to take her daughter out of a pricey school—she's some kind of whiz kid—and bring her along."

"Along from where?"

"L.A. To work in Houston for four days." Belle snapped her purse open and paused to check her lipstick in a palm-size mirror. "This is a VIP account, Flannigan. I need someone on the case I can trust." She dropped a set of keys into Dixie's lap. "In addition to your usual outrageous fee, you get to chauffeur the girl around town in the company Porsche." Belle knew how to sweeten a deal to make it damn near irresistible. "Targa 911," she coaxed. "Gas included."

"Four days. How long do I have to think about this?"

"The wager or the job? I need someone to pick up the girl tomorrow morning."

Dixie grinned. "Then you'd better lay out a backup plan. My week in Martinique is cinched. Hearing the jury's verdict is only a formality."

"You wouldn't think so if you'd heard the victim testify—"

Belle clamped her mouth shut, then, "Oh, shit! I forgot you'd had a run-in with Coombs yourself."

"Got a nice souvenir from the occasion." Dixie tapped the crutch propped beside her. As a witness herself, she hadn't been allowed in the courtroom during the trial, but she'd followed it in the news and had occasional conversations with Brenda Benson.

Belle looked down at Dixie's cast. "You know, Coombs' father made sizable donations to a number of political campaigns, including those of some prominent judges. And his playboy son has sense enough to keep the money flowing."

"Sounds like the kind of back-scratching crap that made me get out of this business three years ago."

Dixie slid her gaze across the courtroom to Regan Salles, the victim who'd had enough guts to accuse Coombs: full-breasted, full-hipped, with china-doll skin, platinum curls, and a pouty attitude that attracted men like kids to a cookie jar. Regan had demonstrated strength and composure the first time Dixie saw her in the courtroom. Now she looked angry and spiteful; not the best persona for influencing a jury. Julie Colby, the tall, phlegmatic witness coordinator clasping Regan's hand in support, was speaking as if to calm her, but the rape victim appeared locked in her own anger.

"I saw Regan's photographs after Coombs worked her over," Dixie said. "That was enough to convince me of what's true. It'll convince a jury."

"Truth and testimony are two entirely different concepts, Flannigan. How did you manage to miss that in law school?"

"I caught it. I didn't want to believe it."

"Trust me, in rape cases, Engleton is a man's judge."

"The jury still decides the verdict—"

"Based on evidence presented and *allowed*. Which in Engleton's court can get skewed."

Dixie was the first to admit that the Texas legal system rarely measured up to the wide-eyed ideals she'd harbored as a junior prosecutor. And Belle was right about Engleton. Unfortunately, he wasn't—in her opinion—the only judge who allowed bias to taint the ideal of due process.

She scanned past Regan to a third woman—Clarissa Thomas, slender and stylish, with a thin pinched face, pale hair, pale eyes, pale expensive designer clothes, and a strident determination to right wrongs. Clarissa had stumbled upon the rape scene in a suburban park after leaving her stalled car on the roadside. In search of a phone to call her husband, she arrived in time to see Coombs slink off through the trees. Later, she'd picked him from a lineup without hesitation. But now she seemed to cower from Coombs' mocking stare. That cowering could translate as uncertainty.

Yet, surely a jury could see through Coombs' slick posturing. According to Brenda, the man was suspected of raping and beating at least five women in two years. His victims described him as charming, generous, and thoughtful—until sometime around the third date. Dixie had seen that charm at the Parrot Lounge. She'd seen his other side, too.

Women admitted being willing to have sex with Coombs, but apparently he wasn't interested in willing sexual partners. His game was to win a woman's confidence, then come on rough, using his fists. Sometimes he used a knife.

A jury was not privy to unsubstantiated reports, though, and the other victims were too terrified of Coombs, or too ashamed and frightened of cross-examination, to go to court with what they'd suffered. Dixie couldn't actually blame them. A good defense lawyer could twist a rape victim's words until she sounded like a whore.

Brenda Benson had won tougher trials. She knew how to elicit strong testimony, and her final arguments never failed to touch a jury where it mattered. Brenda could convince a stone to roll over. Yet, lately, some of her big cases had gone south.

"How was the prosecution's cross?" Dixie asked Belle.

"Benson was good. She was damn good." Belle shook her head. "But that slimy bastard turned on his thousand-watt smile and dampened the crotch of every female on the jury."

It figured. "What about the men? Sometimes they're more astute than we give them credit for. They'll see right through Coombs."

Belle shrugged. "Trust me, all the men would kill to have Coombs' style and money and good looks. Secretly, they admire the bastard." Belle's gaze shifted to a middle-aged couple sitting across the aisle. She lowered her voice. "Did you know about the girl who's been catatonic since Coombs 'allegedly' finished with her? That's her parents."

The couple appeared to be in their fifties, the man sad-eyed and shrunken, the woman dark and intense. She kept twisting the strap of her alligator handbag so hard Dixie expected to hear it snap. If a look of hatred could kill, Coombs would never hear the jury's verdict.

"Brenda's counting on this conviction," Dixie said.

"I hope she gets it." Belle plucked at a racquetball glove peeking out of Dixie's pocket. "Tell me you aren't nuts enough to attempt a game with a broken foot."

"A game, a workout, and a rip-roaring celebration, if the jury brings in the right verdict. The foot is healed." Well, practically. "Why don't you join us?"

"I have to meet a client. Flannigan, call me when you're finished at the gym. By nine o'clock at the latest. If you don't take this job, I have to find someone to pick up the girl by seven A.M. tomorrow."

Dixie nodded vaguely. She hated bodyguard jobs almost as much as she hated sitting on her butt watching paint dry.

"But about that cast," Belle said, as if reconsidering, "when does it come off?"

"Tomorrow." Actually, tomorrow was pushing it, but Dixie had badgered the doctor into using ultrasound to hasten the healing process. She was optimistic. She turned her gaze on Lawrence Coombs.

"What do you think makes a man take pleasure from inflicting pain on women?" she asked Belle.

"Who knows? Early abandonment by his mother? Punishment or humiliation suffered as a child?"

"Or maybe a chunk of his neurological cells mutated while the bastard was still in the womb."

"You're a cynic, Flannigan."

"Some of us have to be."

Such unanswerable questions were part of the reason Dixie no longer sat in the prosecutor's chair. She believed in justice, not law. She believed the negative emotions that triggered crimes were common to all humans—greed, lust, frustration, anger, fear—and that criminals could be lumped into three classes. Third-class criminals were ordinary people pushed too far. They genuinely regretted their mistakes; given a second chance, they could usually reestablish themselves as worthwhile citizens. Second-class criminals were low-life scum indoctrinated early with the wrong values; occasionally, second-class criminals were "rehabilitated" by the system. But there was one sort of monster that no amount of punishment or counseling would change. Lawrence Riley Coombs was such a monster. A verdict of "not guilty" today would be tantamount to issuing Coombs a license to assault and rape.

A hush swept through the courtroom as the door opened to the judge's chambers.

"All rise," droned the bailiff.

Judge Engleton took his seat behind the bench. As the jury filed into the room, Dixie tried to read their faces. Drawing only blanks, she turned her attention to the prosecutor's table. Brenda Benson scuffed her chair around for a better view of the jury.

"Brenda's aged since this trial started," Dixie whispered. Her friend's lithe body looked ten pounds thinner under a smart gray suit. If Coombs walked, she knew, Brenda would take it as a personal failure.

Stepping forward in the jury box, the forewoman handed a folded sheet of paper to the bailiff, who gave it to the judge. The judge donned a pair of reading glasses, unfolded the page, looked at it without a flicker of change in his solemn demeanor, then passed it to the court clerk. The clerk faced the defendant and cleared his throat.

"On the charge of assault, we find the defendant, Lawrence Riley Coombs, not guilty. On the charge of rape, we find the defendant not guilty."

On the wave of silence that filled the courtroom, someone moaned.

"They did it," Belle said softly. "They let the bastard off."

Reporters rushed to capture the defendant's reaction. Defense counsel looked as stunned as the prosecutors.

Seeing Brenda's stricken expression, Dixie knew what her friend was feeling—like being kicked in the stomach. Disbelief—*she hadn't heard right, the jury had made a mistake, the judge would grant a mistrial.* Then guilt—*how could I let this happen? What did I do wrong?*

Murmuring a hasty departure to Belle, Dixie waded into the throng, swinging her crutch past Regan Salles and Clarissa Thomas—huddled together with the witness coordinator, faces pasty with shock, no doubt worrying about reprisal from Coombs. He wasn't the type to let bygones be.

Dixie placed a steadying hand on Brenda's arm. "You'll get another crack at him."

"How many more women will he assault before one is brave enough to turn him in?" Blinking rapidly, as if fighting an emotional torrent, the prosecutor fished a piece of nicotine chewing gum from her pocket and fumbled the wrapper off. Her words came slow, fierce, and deliberate. "Regan Salles was beaten so badly she'll never have children. She almost died, Dixie. The next woman very likely *will* die. Look what he did to you. Of all the reptiles I've watched slither out of this courthouse and back into society, Lawrence Coombs really scares me."

Dixie searched her soul for a crumb of reassurance; Brenda's assessment was exactly right. Future victims would see Coombs' acquittal as proof that their own testimony would go unheard. He could stack up conquests like firewood.

A reporter approached, but Brenda's angry stare turned him away. She slapped a stack of files into her briefcase. "I blew it. I totally blew it."

"You did everything you could. Sometimes the system works, sometimes it doesn't."

"The system *never* works against men like Coombs. He's too high profile, too glibly credible. If we rolled a woman into the courtroom on her deathbed, defense counsel would claim she inflicted her own injuries and blamed Coombs out of spite. And the jury would buy every lying word of it."

Rage smoldered in Brenda's eyes. Dixie knew that rage. She'd felt it too many times herself.

"Hey, girl, it's over," she cautioned softly. "You have to let it go." But she owed Brenda more than useless platitudes. During the dead weeks that followed Dixie's resignation from the DA's office, all that kept her from becoming an embittered bar hag was Brenda's unflagging willingness to alternately hold Dixie's hand and kick her butt. Dixie owed her friend the same support. "Get your gear. Let's work off some of that frustra—"

Someone pushed between them. Dixie looked up to find Coombs' tailored shoulders in her face.

Ignoring her, he leaned forward to whisper in Brenda's ear.

Brenda's face blanched white.

Then Coombs was gone, striding toward the door in a swarm of reporters.

Dixie took Brenda's elbow. "What did he say?"

Mouth slack, eyes wide, the prosecutor glared at the back of Coombs' head. Then she twisted out of Dixie's grasp and snatched up her briefcase.

"Brenda, what did he say?"

"He said, 'Foreplay's over, darlin'. Brace yourself for the main event.' "

Chapter Six

Not guilty? A scream rose in Sissy's throat as she watched the clutch of reporters follow Lawrence Coombs toward the exit.

Jesus help her. How could anyone sit here listening to the evidence day after day, then look that judge in the eye and issue a verdict of not guilty? She longed to slam the jurors one by one against the wall and scream the question at them. Not *guilty?*

A courtroom groupie squeezed past, reeking of old clothes and cheap perfume. Sissy breathed through her mouth, fighting queasiness. How many bottles of cheap perfume had she sprinkled around her apartment trying to purge the Dumpster smells of cat litter and fetid garbage from her nostrils? How many boxes of discarded old clothes had she cleaned and mended to support herself after those months in the hospital?

Lately she had begun to relive the hell of those hours after waking in the Dumpster. In the deadest part of a night, she would jerk erect in bed, soaked in perspiration, the truck's whine in her ears, shame and confusion roiling in her brain. Then, gasping with pain, she'd relive the horror of falling and watching the compactor inch toward her, the fear of being buried alive by the next load of garbage, the agony of climbing broken and bleeding out of the truck.

Hiding in a clump of bushes at the roadside, she'd been afraid to stop a passing motorist, afraid of being taken to a hospital, where she would have to answer questions. Bleeding and humiliated, she dragged herself to a YWCA, and from there had ended up in a women's protection center, where she found help.

A new name. A new life.

A vow to never, ever be frightened again.

And a new goal: to show other victims the way out.

That terrifying time was long past—and so much good had happened since then. But in her nightmares Sissy still felt the blows from her husband's huge fist, saw his silver-toed boot swinging toward her.

During the Coombs trial, she had felt herself filling up again with hate and frustration, and she had fought it. But now, as Lawrence Coombs paused in the doorway to tip a sarcastic salute to the courtroom, Sissy felt a rage that threatened to send her wailing through the crowd to gouge out his eyeballs, to rip out his tongue, to stomp his slimy guts into the green asphalt tile of the courtroom floor. The rage was like a beast, clawing, snapping, eating at her. She had to get out of here. NOW. Before she burst into a thousand bloody fragments.

But she had to do it slowly, calmly.

Be still, Sissy.

Do not make a scene, Sissy.

You must not go back to the hospital.

Someone was asking her a question. She had to answer sensibly, but what? What was the question again?

Chapter Seven

Dixie looped the racquet over her gloved hand and leaned against the wall to wait for Brenda. Her cast felt downright silly with her gym shorts. Outside the glass barrier, two jocks in muscle shirts stole glances at her, making her feel even clumsier. But she intended to get a good workout today if it hair-lipped the devil. After the weeks of inactivity, she felt as if a swarm of bees had been trapped inside her.

From somewhere down the hall came the rah-rah music of an exercise class. This new club, all sparkle and glass, attracted too many dilettantes and spandexed weight-watchers. But the Downtown Y was overcrowded, and with Dixie's uncertain schedule, lead time for reserving a racquetball court had become prohibitive. The new club was only a short drive from the courthouse. And the locker rooms smelled better.

She saw Brenda making her way down the hall, racquet and goggles in hand, hair pulled back in a braid. Brenda Benson had never been pretty. Perhaps a plastic surgeon could've refined her square features; then with her muscular body and magnificent hair she'd be a knockout. But Brenda was more interested in improving the world than improving her looks.

Noting the deep worry lines etching the prosecutor's forehead, Dixie wondered if Lawrence Coombs' parting comment was getting to her. Surely Brenda had been threatened before—hell, who on the DA's staff hadn't? Dixie recalled one red-letter day when she'd personally received three hate notes.

"Let's play." Brenda swung through the door, adjusting her goggles.

Dixie bounced the racquetball.

"You wouldn't rather talk first?" There'd been no chance after the trial to discuss Coombs' cryptic remark.

Brenda's grim smile spread the web of fine lines that encircled her strong mouth. She swiped her palms on the seat of her gym shorts.

"What's to talk about? Are you trying to wangle a handicap for a little foot fracture?"

Dixie bounced the ball again. Perhaps the activity would be better than talking; better, certainly, for dealing with her own frustrations. She hated seeing the bad guys win.

"Can't fault me for trying to get an edge." She bounced the ball once more, then served.

It lobbed off the back wall and fell nicely within Brenda's reach. Brenda whacked the hell out of it, sending it crashing from the wall to hit the front glass on the fly, then almost to the back again before touching down. Lunging, Dixie smacked the ball half as hard as Brenda had, coming down on the bad foot and stumbling.

"I suppose that was Coombs' face you just splattered all over Houston," Dixie taunted.

"You bet it was!"

Dixie hoped the bitterness in Brenda's voice was tempered with humor. As long as the prosecutor could smile as she vented her anger, it wouldn't gnaw at her. Only a fool ignored a threat, yet you couldn't let fear erode your confidence.

"What do you suppose Coombs meant?" Dixie landed on her good knee to save a grounder and winced as floor grit scraped off a layer of skin.

"You know damn well what Coombs meant. He's coming after me." Brenda missed a high ball, plucked it out of the air on the third bounce, and served without losing a beat.

The ball stayed in a slow, easy play for over a minute until Dixie flubbed another grounder, landing on the same knee. Cursing the fancy gym that offered seventeen kinds of fresh-squeezed juice, but couldn't keep the floors swept, she searched until she found a small black pebble, scooped it up, and tossed it into a corner.

Brenda served—*whawp!*

"You've had threats before," Dixie said. "How many bogey-men actually materialized on your doorstep?" *Whawp!*

"Coombs means it."

"You think he's stupid enough to risk jail again?"

"I don't think he's stupid at all." *Whawp!* "But *he* believes he's untouchable."

For several minutes Dixie concentrated on playing. Her foot ached like a bad tooth. To reduce running, she stopped going for wide shots. Soon she was hitting only the balls that lobbed within arm's reach. But the movement felt great.

She knew Brenda was right about Coombs. An egomaniac, he would believe he could wreak vengeance on the ADA without getting caught. When they stopped for a breather, Dixie regarded the woman who'd just creamed her at racquetball.

"Think you need a bodyguard?"

Brenda pulled off her goggles and wiped a towel across her face. "What I'm thinking is maybe I don't want this job anymore."

"Aw, don't say that, Bren. You're too damn good at it. And you're needed. You've locked up so many fist-crazy bastards

I'm surprised the Women's Help Center hasn't given you a medal. Hell, you're the DA's Golden Girl."

The media nickname, coined for Brenda's stunning hair as well as her occasionally brilliant courtroom procedure, failed to draw a smile.

"*You* quit," Brenda said. "And you seem to be doing all right."

Dixie bounced the racquetball so hard it jarred her wrist when she caught it.

"Yeah, I'm doing all right." She didn't regret for an instant her decision to leave the DA's staff, but sometimes she felt like a lily-livered deserter. She'd been good at her job, damn near as good as Brenda. If all the good guys laid down their swords, wouldn't the bad guys finally take over?

Brenda was studying her. "You set your own hours, right? Work at your own pace? You're making more money now."

"A lot more money." *A hell of a lot more money.*

"And you finally have time for a love life."

Dixie felt a sappy grin spread across her face. "Yep, I finally have a love life."

"Aren't you satisfied with what you're doing?"

"I'm satisfied, Brenda, but I don't envision myself a bounty hunter forever. And I'm not contributing much to the greater good."

"Yes, you are! In your own way, you contribute a hell of a lot. We can't convict the bail jumpers who skip off to Mexico only to resurface later doing the same dirty deeds. Working outside the system, you're more effective, in some ways, than any cop."

"What are you leading up to?"

Brenda looped the damp towel around her neck. "Do you think I could do what you're doing? Bounty hunting?"

Dixie could tell the prosecutor was serious, and she didn't want to answer without giving the question some thought. Bouncing the racquetball, she listened to the hollow *thunk, thunk, thunk* echo in the small room.

"You have the guts, Bren," she said finally. "You have the

stamina. And in defense class I've seen you practice hand-to-hand against some tough competition." She looked Brenda square in the eye. "But could you kill a person, if that was your only reasonable choice?"

"You've never killed anyone."

"Not yet. And I hope I never do. But every day of my life I face the possibility."

"I could shoot a dirtball like Coombs, easy."

"Even if you didn't know whether the dirtball was guilty? Remember, I rarely know as much about a skip as I knew about Coombs."

"If they skip, chances are they're guilty."

"I used to think so." Until Parker. "A skip tracer brings them back to trial, and lets a jury decide on their guilt or innocence."

A scowl hardened Brenda's mouth. "I'm not sure I could do that."

"Brenda, it's only in old westerns that bounty hunters get to be judge, jury, and executioner." Dixie wanted to say more, but all that came to mind were the same lame remarks some of her friends had spouted when she stopped practicing law.

They played two more games, Brenda winning all three. Playing with an injured foot had been dumb, but the vigorous exercise had banished the trapped bees. Dixie felt exhilirated. As they prepared to leave, she limped to the corner and retrieved the black pebble she'd tossed there.

"Wait up," she said. "I want to share something—guess you could say it's what keeps me chipping away from the sidelines."

Brenda eyed her warily, but ambled over to where Dixie knelt on the floor, drawing a big imaginary circle with her finger.

"Throw a rock in a lake," Dixie said, cradling the pebble in her palm, then tossing it to the center of the circle. "You'll see ripples. Small, insignificant ripples. Scarcely noticeable." She drew a second circle, smaller than her hand.

"Toss that same rock in a puddle, and the ripples become great outward waves that turn everything to mud. Like that pebble, one evil man among the righteous is insignificant, a single dark shadow on a sunlit pool."

"Careful, preacher." Brenda popped a chunk of nicotine gum in her mouth. "You're sloshing pond water over your chic new footgear."

Dixie's occasional metaphorical lectures, a persuasion technique learned from her Irish adoptive father, were an old joke between them from law school. Tedious or not, Dixie believed some things needed to be said.

"Darkness," she persisted, "is as much a part of nature's scheme as you or me, or this rock. It's not our job to eliminate all the shadows in the world, but to remain part of the light, part of the balance. Without us, the pool shrinks. The light dims. The ripples of darkness spread wider."

Brenda sighed, long, heavy, and defeated. "I get your belabored point. But I'm not sure our society has enough candlepower these days to brighten a broom closet."

Dixie scooped up the pebble and balanced it between her thumb and forefinger.

"Benson, you're one of the brightest spots in the whole system. Next to you, Lawrence Riley Coombs is like a single dust mote in a ray of sunshine." She flipped the pebble off her thumbnail, caught it in the palm of her hand. "Insignificant."

The prosecutor frowned at the shiny black rock. After a moment, Dixie closed her fingers over it and shoved it into her pocket.

They spent the next twenty minutes working out with free weights. Brenda seemed hell-bent on pressing as many pounds as the buff young men in the room. Only when she and Dixie were both thoroughly spent did they head for the showers.

Dixie needed to get home. Parker would be pissed if she was late for dinner again, and she had to call Belle Richards for specifics on where to pick up the client's kid tomorrow morning. But Brenda's mood worried her.

She fished some coins out of her pocket—a phone call would ease Parker's mind.

"Looks like the beer's on me tonight," she told Brenda. "Might be your last big chance to tie one on at my expense."

"Think I can't beat you when your foot's healed?"

"I think there's a Mexican beer at the Suds Club with my name on it, and I could use the company for an hour or so."

Brenda looked at her, not buying it. "I've lost cases before, Dixie. I'm not going to do anything crazy tonight."

Dixie gave her a thin smile. "Crazy is in the eye of the beholder, old friend."

The ADA stalled a second longer, then shrugged. "I suppose the Suds Club will be bubbling with gossip about my failing record of late. Might as well give them an honest target to aim at."

Chapter Eight

The mixture of odors at the Suds Club was like no other bar in town. The small brewery and pub sat alongside a laundromat, taking advantage of a captive clientele waiting for their clothes to dry. Like other lawyers, Dixie had started hanging out there not because she liked doing laundry but because the owner was a friend, another former prosecutor whose golden dreams of making a difference had tarnished. He and four other attorneys—who happened to also be musicians—had formed a band, calling themselves "The Convictions," that played the club on weekends. Damned good vintage rock and roll. Tonight, a neon Wurlitzer provided music at a volume allowing easy conversation.

But Brenda wasn't doing much talking. They'd taken their usual booth in the smoking section. Although Brenda was trying to shuck the habit, and Dixie's one childhood attempt had made her sick enough to swear off for life, their corner niche was tradition.

Simulated padded leather walls and plush wine-red carpet muffled the hum of a hundred conversations. Neon beer signs provided the dim lighting. Brenda stared at a Corona bottle on the bar in front of her, alternately drinking from it, sucking on a lime wedge balanced on its rim, and scraping at the bottle's label.

Dixie's efforts to lift the prosecutor's spirits had struck out. Time for some ass-kicking.

"How many open cases are stacked on your desk right now?" she asked.

"Fifteen. Maybe twenty."

"How many more assault charges you figure were filed today?"

"What's this, Monday? Forty or so, mostly family violence. It'll be over a hundred before midnight." Brenda's fingernail scraped a long tear through the Corona label.

"And how many of those will land on your desk?"

"What's your point, Dixie? We both know there's no shortage of work to be done."

"Precisely. Yet here you sit moaning in your Corona after losing a single case."

Lifting her chin, Brenda swept a somber gaze around the crowded room. Dixie recognized many of the men and women from courtrooms and plea-bargaining tables.

The prosecutor's gaze rested for a beat on a lone man at the bar, fortyish, attractive, and nearly bald. When he raised his glass, Brenda nodded curtly, an odd wistfulness softening her coarse features. An instant later the effect was gone, and Brenda's gaze hurried past.

"Look at them." she said. "How many men do you think will go home later and beat up their wives? Or discipline their children? Or pick up a prostitute and knock her around awhile before kicking her out of the car? Or stop at the liquor store going home, decide hell, why not have some fun with the owner's granddaughter—"

"If you're talking about the Ramirez case—"

"The two SOBs who raped that child are going to walk."

"Maybe not. Mr. Ramirez gave a good description before he died."

"Not good enough. And the girl's too terrified to ID them. The dickhead cop who was first at the scene made sure of it."

Dixie sighed. "Is that the game we're playing now? Male bashing?"

"You think I'm wrong?"

"I think your viewpoint is skewed. As my sainted adoptive mother would say, 'Even men and barbed wire have their good points.'"

Brenda grimaced and took another swallow of her beer.

"There *are* plenty of good men in the world," Dixie persisted. "Only, you won't find them in the case folders stacked on your desk—"

"Hell, Dixie, it's not just men. I had a woman in my office last week left her month-old baby in a shopping mall storage room while she went to work. Said she didn't have money for a sitter. Two months ago we found a seven-year-old girl chained in a bathroom. Dirty, starved, scared. Sores all over. Never been to school a day—could barely talk. Three other kids in the family, all going to school, playing with friends. Father and mother both had good jobs. A normal American household. Except nobody in the neighborhood, *nobody*, knew about that fourth kid, chained in a bathroom, fed table scraps, treated worse than you'd treat a dog. An entire *family*, Dixie, in collusion against one poor child." Brenda pushed her beer aside. "How does such a thing happen?"

Dixie had seen worse during her ten years as a prosecutor, before she quit trying to understand.

"You need some balance to your perspective," she replied. "Get away for a few weeks. Spend a month in the sunshine. Find a brown-skinned island gigolo and get gloriously laid."

"Ha!" Brenda's sudden smile flickered to the balding man at the bar. Her spontaneous hoot turned to a chuckle, then to roaring laughter.

Dixie couldn't help grinning. Brenda had an infectious laugh, deep-throated and tobacco gruff.

But Dixie's comment hadn't been funny enough to elicit the convulsive gales that followed. Brenda pounded the table, tears streaming down her cheeks. People turned to stare, sparking more laughter. Hysterical laughter. Brenda's hair pulled out of its braid. Her skin flushed. With the Beach Boys singing "I Get Around" on the Wurlitzer, Dixie glared at the gawkers until they turned hastily back to their drinks.

Finally, Brenda mopped her face with a wad of napkins, and her laughter subsided.

"Maybe you're right," she gasped. "Maybe the world is sane and it's only my viewpoint that's skewed."

"That's not exactly what I said," Dixie argued.

Brenda popped the lime wedge into her mouth and sucked, then took a long pull on the Corona. Finally, she seemed composed.

"Cases pile up faster than we can clear them," she grumbled. "No matter how many hours I grind away, the stack never gets smaller. The world isn't going to change. As you say, I may as well put blinders on and save my own sanity."

A waitress plucked their empty beer bottles off the table. Brenda twirled her finger to signal another round. Glancing at her watch, Dixie was about to protest when a voice carried from across the room.

"There she is! I knew that was her laugh." Clarissa Thomas, the pale, determined witness from the Coombs trial, started weaving her way through the crowd, accompanied by Regan Salles and Julie Colby, the witness coordinator who'd comforted Regan in the courtroom.

"A hairdresser, a DA liaison, and a socialite housewife," Dixie mused. "What's that old saying? 'Adversity breeds strange bedfellows'?"

Brenda peered at Dixie curiously. "I don't find it so surprising they'd strike up a friendship. When men are the enemy, women have to stick together."

"A man is the enemy," Dixie amended. "Lawrence Coombs

is only one man." She refused to lump all the males in the world into one big bad villain, and she had no desire to get into a pity party with these women over the verdict. Besides, it was time to call Belle Richards about the bodyguard job. Parker would be grumpy, hearing she was working again, but a deal was a deal. She'd lost the bet, including the coveted vacation at Belle's Caribbean condo, which after the past weeks didn't sound half as inviting as it usually did. She needed the job just to be busy at something useful.

"Same time next Monday?" she asked Brenda, dropping bills on the table for the beer tab. "I reserved a court."

Brenda's amber eyes showed a trace of sparkle. "By then, I'll be over my anger, knee-deep in another case, your foot will be stronger, and you'll beat my socks off."

"Yep. That's what I'm counting on. I can carry my weight in class this week, too." She and Brenda taught a self-defense class together, women on Saturdays, Ryan's private school on Thursdays. In the past month, Dixie's foot fracture had kept her from participating.

As she stood to leave, the three women approached. Something in their attitude made Dixie linger. She was sure they hadn't been in the bar when she and Brenda entered.

"You said we'd put him away," Clarissa challenged.

She and Regan were both drinking wine, Julie a draft beer.

"In prison for a very long time." Regan's voice carried a hint of panic. "A very long time, you said. But he walked right out of that court, free to come after us—"

"Just as you told us the restraining order would keep him in line while he was out on bail," Clarissa spat. "It didn't!"

"Sit down," Dixie said firmly, offering her own chair and pulling up another one for Regan. They didn't appear drunk, merely angry.

Clarissa glared at her, but sat. Regan plopped down beside her. Looking uncomfortable, Julie set her beer mug on the table, tapped a thin cigarette from a package of ultralight Capri, and took a seat slightly behind the pair. Apparently, the task of calming the two witnesses after the jury's verdict had not gone well.

"My husband practically lost his job," Clarissa said, "coming home all hours to check on me. Worried out of his mind. He *begged* me to go to my mother's in Boston—"

"Not a bad idea," Brenda told her, maintaining the calm but forceful voice Dixie'd heard her use with distraught victims in the courtroom. "Maybe you *should* go away for a while. Regan, maybe you should, too."

Regan blanched. "You really think—you think Lawrence will come after us?"

"Frankly, I think he'll be . . . looking for fresh game," Brenda hedged. "But I can have patrol cars watching him—"

"That's what you said before!" Clarissa snapped.

And before, when Coombs was charged with a crime, HPD had cause to watch him, Dixie added mentally. He was a free man now.

Clarissa slapped her glass down on the table, spilling a few drops.

"Hey, ladies!" Julie placed her hands on Clarissa's shoulders and began kneading the rigid muscles. "Let's all take a deep breath and start over."

Brenda shot her assistant a look of gratitude.

But Clarissa shrugged off Julie's hand. "You saw his smug smile when that jury gave the verdict." Her face had flushed almost to the color of her wine. "How could they do that? Those women jurors—"

"Maybe he got close to one of them," Julie murmured. "You said he could be enchanting, Regan."

"Like a snake charmer, sweetie. Charm a cobra right out of its basket."

Brenda shook her head emphatically. "There was no indication of jury tampering." Her voice remained even and firm. "Now, listen, we all need to calm down and put this behind us. A bar is no place to discuss it—I know a coffee shop down the street that makes the most decadent desserts you ever put in your mouth. We'll talk about getting you both some protection—until we're certain Coombs has lost interest."

"My husband says we should buy a gun," Clarissa announced, glaring from Brenda to Julie.

"Maybe he's *right*. Maybe we should all carry guns." Regan's voice rose to a screech. "It's legal now, isn't it?"

Brenda shook her head and began herding them toward the door. "Let's talk first." Glancing back at Dixie, she paused, allowing Julie to continue ushering the women ahead of her. "Want to join us?"

"Thanks, but I really need to call Belle, and Parker's probably got supper waiting."

Brenda smiled. "Dixie, I think you scooped up the last good catch in Houston."

Probably, though she wasn't sure Parker could be caught. "Or maybe there's one more terrific guy out there, just waiting for you to poke your head up long enough to notice." Dixie allowed her gaze to flicker toward the balding man at the bar.

But Brenda didn't follow the lead.

"Unfortunately," she muttered, "the only men I meet these days have numbers stenciled under their photographs."

As Brenda turned to go, Dixie realized she was holding the black pebble instead of her car keys. Rolling it between her thumb and forefinger, she watched her friend buck up in the aftermath of failure, frazzled yellow hair swinging above strong, determined shoulders.

Chapter Nine

Lawrence Riley Coombs slipped his hand under the woman's elbow and steered her toward the car, shielding her from the rain with an oversized umbrella. Fat raindrops plopped onto the taut fabric. The night was warm for early February, but a cold front was due to blow in and push the thunderclouds across the state line to Louisiana.

"Watch the puddle, darlin'. Don't get mud on those beautiful toes." *She did have nice feet, set off by strappy high-heeled sandals. Nice legs, too.*

She giggled softly. "I couldn't believe my eyes when I saw you sitting there at the bar all by your lonesome. You're even more handsome in person than you were on TV today."

"Dottie, you say the nicest things, and my bruised ego soaks up every word." They'd reached the Chevy. He handed her the umbrella. The rain had almost stopped. "Give me your keys and I'll get that door for you."

"I never believed for a minute all those hateful things the

newspapers said about you, Larry. Those two women must have been crazy. Why, anyone could just look at you and know you wouldn't hurt a fly."

"It's *Lawrence*, darlin', and I don't want you thinking too harshly of those ladies. You've heard about unrequited love." He opened the car door and brushed off the seat. "I should've been more sensitive, should've let them down easier."

"Now don't you go blaming yourself! You've been through too much misery already, with that awful trial. You need someone to make you forget all that."

Reclaiming the umbrella, he draped a casual arm around her shoulders.

"Dottie, you could make a man forget just about anything." He tweaked her chin playfully, then handed her into the car. "If you really mean what you say . . ."

"Of course I mean it! Why, one weekend at my house on Padre Island, you'll be a brand-new man."

"Sounds mighty temptin', darlin'." He stroked the back of her neck, feeling the fragile bones beneath his palm. Right now he had other plans, plans for a certain golden-haired Assistant District Attorney who didn't know when to back off. "I hope you'll give me a rain check."

"You'll call me, won't you? Tomorrow?" She handed him a folded square of pink paper that smelled of honeysuckle.

"Tomorrow, and that's a promise." He slid the paper into his pocket. But Dottie was entirely too eager. The woman needed a cooling-off period. "I may not be able to get away this week. You know how it is, work piled up on my desk during the trial."

"Surely the work will keep another day or two."

"It'd keep, but I'd be distracted, pretty lady, and I want to give you *all* the attention you deserve." He brushed a light kiss on her yielding lips.

"Mmmmmm . . ." She clutched his lapel, deepening the kiss.

Randy bitch. He loosened her fingers.

"I'll call you tomorrow, darlin'. We'll have dinner next week."

He kissed her fingertips, shut the door firmly, and winked at her through the rain-streaked window. *Easy screw. He'd bet six-to-one she was ready to come in her seat.*

Sliding behind the wheel of his Jaguar, he watched the Chevy's taillights disappear down the street. He'd wait until late tomorrow to phone her. Maybe even wait until next week. She'd be pissed, but flowers would perk her right up. Women were so predictable.

He found the bottle he had tucked between the seats, Johnnie Walker Black, a man's drink. A silky fire, like burying himself in a fiery pussy. He'd bet that ADA's pussy was plenty fiery.

Turning the Jaguar toward Bellaire, he drove to the red brick bungalow with its single gaslight, the swinging nameplate announcing the Benson residence, home of ADA Brenda Benson and her young sister, Gail. Pretty brown-eyed Gail, almost as sweet as her amber-eyed sis. Maybe he should do them both, let Brenda watch while he did the sister.

He coasted to a stop as he neared the driveway. Listening to the rain pelt the Jaguar's metal roof, he took another nip from the bottle.

Lights were on in the front of the house. No car in the driveway, but with a two-car garage, that didn't mean anything. On Monday nights Brenda spent an hour or two at the health club, then stopped at a local newsstand to buy a *Houston Business Journal* before joining her sister at home.

He tilted his watch toward the light. By this time the pair would be tucked up dry and cozy, reading the business news, maybe sipping a cup of hot chocolate. It would be so easy to knock on the door right now, muscle his way in, and do the both of them.

His dick hardened, thinking about it. He shifted on the seat, dropping a hand to his crotch, and eased his pants seam over enough to relieve the tightness. The rain had picked up again, pounding the hell out of the Jaguar's roof. He liked the sound. Rain always made him horny.

Chapter Ten

The dark house gave Dixie a start. The kitchen windows should be lighted, at least, Parker creating something scrumptious at the stove. He'd told her once that he never spent more than three years in any town. Before they met, before he moved in "temporarily" with Dixie, he'd already lived in Houston nearly three years. Every day she half expected to find a note saying he'd moved on. Was this the night he chose to drift away?

When they parted that morning in Galveston, she was certain they'd agreed to sleep at her place tonight. The rented summer cabin was only theirs for a month, and the month was up. Parker's own house on the island wouldn't be finished for several more days.

She didn't look forward to telling him about Belle's bodyguard job. But as Barney'd often said, "If you have to swallow a bullfrog, it's a good idea not to look at it too long." She wanted to get the telling part over with. The work she did was part of her life, part of who she was, what she believed in.

While Mud had been in doggie paradise these past weeks—
running on the beach, chasing waves, worrying sand crabs
out of their holes—and Parker had driven off to sell boats
every day, Dixie'd been bored witless. Even chauffeuring a
teenager around town was beginning to sound exciting.

Driving toward the garage, she looked for smoke wisping
skyward from the chimney. Parker liked sitting by the fire
after dinner. Maybe he'd eaten early, as he sometimes did
when she worked late. But tonight there was no smoke in the
night sky.

She parked her taxicab in the old barn that now served as
a four-car garage, housing a variety of vehicles she used from
time to time. The taxicab made a fine surveillance car, and
was the only one of her recycled vehicles that boasted an automatic transmission. Until her clutch foot was operational
again, the van, tow truck, and Mustang, a retired DPS unit,
were about as useful as a trunk of Confederate money.

At the kitchen door, the *tick-tick-tick* of Mud's toenails
said at least someone was eagerly awaiting her arrival.

"Hey, boy." She patted his great ugly face. "Bet you
thought we forgot you." She stooped to Mud's height, using
the crutch for support. Mud nosed her ear, his warm breath a
small measure of comfort.

Parker was merely working late, she reasoned. Maybe
he'd hit some heavy traffic in the fifty-mile drive from Clear
Lake, where he sold boats. Or maybe he'd stopped off at one
of the gourmet supermarkets he enjoyed shopping at in
Houston. Or maybe he'd driven back to Galveston to check
progress again on his new place.

Dixie switched on the kitchen light and opened the refrigerator. Habit. They'd cleaned it out before leaving for
Galveston, and she wasn't really hungry. The freezer held
leftover spaghetti sauce. Sausage biscuits. The last piece of
fudge pecan pie. She put the pie on the counter, Mud
padding alongside. When he scooted his empty water dish,
Dixie filled it, then noticed the telephone message light
blinking.

Snatching up the receiver, she dialed the message center. The first two calls were solicitations, the third was from Parker.

"You turned the cell phone off again," he said. Outside the window, Dixie saw a pair of headlights swing into the driveway. They paused at the gate. Mud's ears twitched forward. *"If I could've reached you, wherever you are,"* Parker's message continued, *"you'd already know I'll be late tonight. Tell you why when I get there."*

The headlights bounced through the gate. Dixie could hear the faint rumble of Parker's Cadillac. She skinned off her jacket, and hobbled to the kitchen closet to hang it up. By the time his heavy, reassuring footsteps sounded in the utility room, she felt as antsy as Mud, and wondered if her ears were twitched forward, too.

The door opened. Parker's wide grin beneath the dark mustache settled Dixie's fluttering stomach right down.

"You're home! Great!" He scooped her off the floor in a one-armed bear hug, his other arm filled with grocery bags. "How was the game?"

"I lost, and it felt wonderful." Dixie pulled him tight. Holding him felt so damn good, she prolonged it, nuzzling her face into his cool neck.

"Hey, lady," he said softly. "For a greeting like this I'll come home late more often." His lips covered hers in a lingering kiss that quickened Dixie's blood.

Mud nosed insistently between them. Parker ignored him for a moment, then slowly released her. Dixie could have stood there for hours.

"I suspect Mud's enthusiasm is for the steak he smells in this bag." Parker scratched Mud's ears as he set the packages on the counter. "You, however, must have learned to sniff out champagne." He crooked his elbow around her neck, gently forcing her to look up at him. "What gives?"

"Champagne? What are we celebrating?"

"What gives?" He stroked her cheek with his thumb.

"Can't I just be glad you're home? I missed you."

He held her for another moment, testing the truth of it in her eyes, it seemed.

"Missed me after, what, fourteen hours? I like that." Dropping a kiss on her forehead, he let her go and started unloading the grocery bags. "I called your cell number."

"I know. I was in court for the jury verdict. Can't let the phone ring in there, and it won't fit in my gym shorts."

"Heard Coombs got off." He cocked a finger pistol, aimed it out the window, and made a popping noise with his mouth. "Maybe now *I'll* get a shot at the bastard."

Parker was joking, of course. At least she hoped he was. He unwrapped the champagne bottle and, beaming at her, displayed the label with a flourish.

"Whoa!" Dixie didn't buy the good stuff often, but she knew what it cost. "You made a sale today?"

"Not just *a* sale, sweetheart." He emptied the grocery bags: fresh asparagus, cucumbers, lettuce, red bell peppers, and three huge ribeye steaks. "A big sale. A *very* big sale."

"So tell me."

"Welllll." Rinsing the vegetables under cold, slowly running water, he wiggled his eyebrows. "Notice how I draw out the suspense?"

Dixie menaced the butcher knife at him. "A dangerous habit, Dann. Tell me!"

"Okay, okay!" He encircled her and captured the knife, then began slicing a pepper into skinny strips. "Remember last week I told you about a guy I met having lunch at the Clear Lake Hilton? Berinson. Always wanted a fishing boat, but his wife refused to be a weekend widow, and she likes to entertain a lot. Now they're retired."

Dixie rubbed a wooden salad bowl with olive oil and crushed garlic. She wasn't much of a cook, but doing the easy tasks made her feel less like a door prop when Parker was performing his kitchen magic. He finished the pepper and started slicing a cucumber.

"The Berinsons came into the shop today. I took them out on a boat—actually I showed them three. The first was a weekend fishing craft, perfect for the bay area. He loved it, she hated it. I think he'd've bought it anyway, but next week they'd be divorced. Don't need that on my conscience."

He tossed the vegetables into the salad bowl and unwrapped the steaks. Mud paddled closer and rested his muzzle on the ceramic tile counter, his eager nose practically touching the meat. Dixie nudged him aside. She tied the asparagus bundle with string, stood it up in a microwave jar, added water and a dash of salt. She looked up to find Parker watching her.

"Did I ever tell you you're a beautiful woman?" He continued before she could answer. "When you're sixty-five, Dixie, you'll still be beautiful, but *that* woman . . ." He nodded at Mud. "Even Mean Ugly Dog is better-looking."

Mud sat back on his haunches, still watching the steaks.

"Yet, you can tell Berinson loves his wife. So when she starts eyeing at a forty-foot party boat, which any real man could never take his fishing buddies on, he makes like it's okay."

Dixie thought about the dirty old man in the courtroom today, and Lawrence Coombs, and was glad Parker was telling her this story. Sometimes a person's outlook could be distorted by the people she dealt with.

"From the way they're talking," Parker said, "I catch on that the Berinsons aren't too worried where their next meal will come from, so I take them out to where we keep the big mothers, eighty feet and better, the size yacht you can pile in twenty people and travel around the world."

"Do people do that? Just take off and live on a boat for months?" Sounded like fun.

"Some, not many. Mostly they putt-putt out into the Gulf, party all night, maybe fish the next day, then putt-putt back. If you like the water, and you have the money, why not?"

Why not, indeed? Dixie'd never learned the art of leisure. Parker was a master at it. He was a master at a lot of things, like stretching out a story until you wanted to strangle him. By the time he finished describing the boat, the steaks were cooked. By the time he related the couple's oohs and aahs, and explained the negotiations, they'd finished the champagne, the meal, and half a bottle of Bordeaux.

"Nearly time for the news," Parker said. "Why don't you take the coffee into the living room. I'll make a fire." He grinned. "After dessert, I'll tell you the good part."

This time even waving her steak knife at him didn't hurry the words along, so she nuked the leftover slice of fudge pecan pie and placed it on a tray with the coffee, a small bottle of Kahlua, and two forks. Maybe the alcohol, the food, and his good fortune would mellow him out enough that he'd shrug off her new job as no big deal.

"How'd your friend take the verdict on Coombs?" he asked when they'd settled in front of an old movie that preceded the ten o'clock news.

"Brenda? Not well, I'm afraid. But she's tough. Hey, maybe we could invite her to Galveston some weekend, when the house is finished. She needs a distraction."

"Sure, why not?" He cut a piece of the warmed pie with his fork. "Maybe she needs a boat."

"Yeah, well, speaking of boats, what—"

He slid the bite of pie into her mouth. "Curious, are we, George?"

She could only nod. Parker's fudge pecan pie was the most sinfully scrumptious dessert she'd ever tasted. That's why there was only one slice left.

"What have you got to trade?" he asked.

Dixie sipped her coffee. "A back rub?"

"Okay. What else?"

"*What else?* Stop stalling. Tell me."

"You're even more beautiful when you're nosey. Did I ever tell you that?"

"And you're more insufferable than a squeaky wheel." But charmingly insufferable. "Ever heard of being killed in the heat of passion?"

"Heat of passion? Grrrrr, I like the sound of it." He urged her down on the couch, covering her with his huge body, and nibbled her neck. One hand slid under her sweatshirt to cup her breast. "Lady, there's a bump on your chest. I think I need to examine it."

"Mmmmmm." The wine and liqueur had made her feel deliciously relaxed. "Maybe you should."

As his lips nibbled closer to her mouth, and his fingers found their way under her bra, one heavy leg pressed between her thighs. They'd learned weeks ago how to maneuver around the cast. Dixie heard a champagne glass tip over, but the sound seemed to come from very far away.

She awoke shivering an hour later. The fire had died down. Slivers of colored light from the television danced over their bare skin. Parker lay beneath her now on the narrow couch. They'd fallen asleep with her head on his chest, the rest of her spread over and tucked around him like an afghan. She loved the soft rumble of his breathing, the scent of his skin.

But her butt felt like a block of ice, and her body was setting up like concrete. She shifted to unwrap herself.

His arm tightened around her; he opened his eyes.

"Have your way with me, then steal off into the night? Madam, I feel so *used*."

She kissed his chin. "*Useful* is the word. You have proved yourself so outstandingly useful that I've decided not to kill you for dragging out that boat story."

She tried to push herself up, her muscles protesting, but he held her tighter.

"Want to hear the end of it?" he teased.

"Now? Right now I want to jump into a hot shower and a warm robe while you stoke up the fire." She levered herself against his chest, but it was useless. Like pushing against rock.

"Tomorrow, you and I are invited to attend a ribbon-cutting party," he said, "on Mr. and Mrs. Berinson's new yacht. Champagne christening, then sail away for dinner and dancing."

Uh-oh. Tomorrow, she had a brat to sit.

"Just us and them?" Dixie wasn't keen on fancy dinner parties, but the old couple sounded nice. How would they feel about a teenager?

"Twenty or thirty couples. The guest list reads like a roster of retired money magnates—which means yours truly will be racking up a few more sales before summer."

Forty people? All dressed to impress, bubbling with witty good manners and expecting her to make conversation? She could hold her own in a crowd of lawyers, all talking the same language, but—

"Our very first party together." Parker looked as excited as a puppy. Of course he'd be excited, he loved being with people, even in boisterous crowds. He expected her to be at least as enthusiastic.

"What time would I have to be there?" Dixie's hours on the bodyguard job started before dawn and ended well after dark. "I—have this kid I'm taking care of tomorrow."

Parker's arms loosened, and she was able to push herself off him, off the couch. He looked vaguely astonished.

"A kid?"

"Teenager. It's a job for Belle."

His bushy brown eyebrows kicked up suspiciously. "Belle Richards is a criminal defense attorney. Any job you do for her involves criminals."

He would know. Belle was *his* attorney. She'd hired Dixie to find Parker Dann when he skipped out on his trial and took off for Canada.

"This girl isn't a criminal."

"Then she's the daughter of a criminal, or she's running from a criminal. Since when did you take on baby-sitting jobs?"

"Since Belle asked me this afternoon."

"Can't you get out of it?"

"I—don't see how." Dixie scooped up her clothes and headed for the shower.

As the hot water sluiced over her skin, the cast protected by a plastic bag, Dixie counted all the reasons she should go to that party. Number one, Parker wanted her to go. That's what building a relationship was all about, wasn't it—doing things for each other, even things you didn't want to do? Number two, this party was important to him, important to his future. As long as he was doing well at his job, selling boats and enjoying it, he wouldn't drift away to another job, another city. Number three, if Dixie couldn't bring herself to be a part of that life, somebody else would. Parker Dann was attractive, loving, supportive—like Brenda said, he might be the last good catch in Houston.

Then Dixie counted all the reasons she *couldn't* go to the party. Number one, she had a job of her own to do. She could still weasel out of it, get someone else to take it on, but she'd promised. Number two, she was a coward. She was nowhere near as socially adept as Parker. She always felt awkward making small talk. Number three, what would she wear? She'd never been on a yacht in her life. A speedboat, fishing boat, sure, but never a yacht. What did people wear to parties on yachts? *Dance* parties. Number four, she was a spineless, gutless, yellow-bellied, lily-livered coward.

But what about Parker? Did she expect him to sit at home every night, cooking dinner, watching the ten o'clock news? Parker Dann was flamboyant, fun-loving, gregarious—he would hate the sort of life she led. Probably the only reason he hadn't taken off before now was—what? The sex was good? Yeah, the sex was great. Learning the new sales job, that probably took a lot of his attention. And Mud, he liked Mud a lot.

Dixie wrapped her hair in a towel, pulled on her terry-cloth robe, and looked at herself in the mirror. Glamour puss. Tomorrow night Parker would be wining and dining with twenty fancy-assed women.

He'd said he loved her. Sort of. No, he'd said she wasn't easy to love. Well, *he* was, dammit, and it was infuriating, him being so lovable. Maybe there was something wrong with her, but she didn't want a love relationship that required her to change. Well, maybe a *little* change.

She dried her hair, fluffed it, and put on some lipstick. Then she scrubbed off the lipstick. She was going to bed, for Pete's sake.

In the kitchen, Parker had finished the supper dishes, and was rattling pans back into their cupboards. He hung the dish towel on a hook and turned to face her.

"Dixie, this thing tomorrow night . . . it's important that I go."

"I know. I want you to go. I—wish I could go with you." She *did* wish she could go. Even a yellow-bellied, lily-livered coward could make nice with strangers for a few hours.

"There must be someone you could get—"

"There's no one. And it's a kid, a sixteen-year-old kid."

"Dixie, you're not the only reputable bodyguard in Houston. Who would do it if you were sick? Or out of town?"

"I'm not sick or out of town."

"You don't want to go, do you?"

She sighed. "I can't go—unless the kid can go with us. And I'm not sure how her mother will feel about that."

He studied her solemnly for a long moment, then turned and walked into the bathroom.

When Dixie heard the shower going, she clumped over to the telephone. Stared at it awhile. Mud sat on his rump and stared with her. In her mind's eye, Dixie saw one of Kathleen's needlepoint maxims. Though she couldn't recall precisely where in the house it could be found, she could see clearly the brown and green cross-stitching: A *Loose Horse Always Seeks New Pastures*.

She could pick up the receiver, call Belle, and weasel out of the job, at least for tomorrow. But what about the next job that came along inconveniently?

Instead, she opened her locked gun cabinet, hidden behind a sliding bookshelf, and lifted out a battered metal case. The foam insert was shaped to fit a twelve-gauge, pump-action shotgun, a .45 semiautomatic, and a holstered .38 revolver—Smith & Wesson Chief's Special Airweight—the model Dixie preferred when forced to carry a gun concealed. She checked all three weapons, then put the case on the dining table. Stacked ammunition alongside it. Now that she'd taken the job, jeopardizing a perfectly terrific relationship for it, she'd better damn well keep the kid safe.

Chapter Eleven

Lawrence Coombs stowed the Johnnie Walker under the seat and started the Jaguar.

"No, Marianne," he whispered gruffly, "we won't do sexy little Brenda Benson just yet. Let her think about it awhile." Let her worry about what he'd said as he left the courtroom today, wonder if he'd go through with it, and when. He wanted to scare the bitch so bad those amber eyes would roll right back in her head when he slipped the meat to her.

Doing the kid sister while Brenda watched would be a bonus, though, a new experience, something he wanted to think about. Get it just right. Maybe wait until they took one of their long Sunday drives after church, catch them on a country picnic when they'd least expect it. Afterward, leave them tied naked from a tree limb, tied face-to-face, so Brenda would see the pain and shame in her dear sister's eyes.

Before the fun could start, though, he had to figure an angle to keep the bitch quiet later.

A station wagon passed by. He waited until its taillights disappeared around the next corner before easing the
Jaguar away from Brenda's house and starting home, windshield wipers swishing time to a Clint Black tape wailing
from his stereo. At that hour, the drive to his town house
took only minutes. Clint had barely finished two songs when
Lawrence entered the circular driveway to his garage.

He was glad he'd sold the big house with its enormous
yard always needing upkeep. Who the hell needed a yard
when you had all of Memorial Park less than a block away?
Jogging trails, tennis courts, and no gardening bills.

His floodlight was out again. He'd have to fix that. Dark as
hell back here when that light was out.

Garage opener not working, either. Maybe the electricity
was on the blink. Neighbor's lights were on, though. Hadn't
missed paying his bill, had he? Hated doing shit like that,
handled most of it by bank draft at the first of the month.
Probably something screwed up in the Light Company's
computer.

Leaving the motor running, headlights focused on the
garage door, he stepped out of the car, snapping the big umbrella over his head. Water swirled around his shoes as it ran
down the concrete drive. Four-hundred-dollar shoes, goddamn water better not seep in. Any deeper, it'd be over the
tops, up to his ankles. Texas dew, they called it. *Shit!*

Picking his way carefully, he headed for the single bright
path lit by the headlights. Above the drumming of the rain, a
sound like someone coughing cut through the darkness.

He paused, listening.

"Who's there?"

Probably a dog. The woman next door had three dachshunds, creepy, big-eyed, wimpy dogs, never barked. He
thought she'd carved out their voice boxes until one day he
heard one of them growl at a bird. Not loud, just a rumbling
deep in its throat.

He moved toward the light again. That's probably what
he'd heard, one of those wimpy dogs—

Shit! What the—

His feet whipped out from under him. He grabbed hold of the Jaguar's side mirror to keep from sliding facedown in the water—

"Uh!" Something—felt like a goddamn baseball bat—struck his head and this time he did fall. Water splashed over his mouth and nose. A figure standing over him grabbed his arms as he tried to push himself upright. *Goddammit!* Was he going to drown right here in three inches of water?

There, sitting up now, that was better. Hands behind his back, though—

"Wait a goddamn minute!" Something rough like burlap slid over his head, smelling of sawdust. "What the goddamn hell's going on— *Uhh!*"

He was jerked to his feet, wrists yanked high behind his back, wrenching his arm and shoulder muscles as the cord tying his hands was looped around his neck, forcing him to keep his wrists high or strangle. Incredibly, he heard the *whir* of the garage door sliding open. It was working now?

Someone pushed him—stumbling—down the driveway. He bumped against the Jaguar, felt it move. Must be two of them, then, one driving it. Couple of do-gooders, riled up by the trial verdict, planning to teach him a lesson. Well, he'd been taught by meaner fists than theirs. They better hope he didn't get loose.

He heard a car door open, and he was shoved inside. Not the Jaguar, a backseat. Down on the floorboard, knees bent under him. The burlap bag scraped his face where it slid on the floor, and his head hurt where they'd hit him, the dizziness a red haze behind his eyes. A warm droplet trickled a path down his collarbone. Water? Or blood? His head hurt like hell, like it might be cut.

Someone pushed in behind him. He heard the door slam, then a pair of feet planted themselves in the middle of his back, pinning him down. The front car door opened and slammed shut, and then they were moving.

"Couple of goddamn vigilantes, is that it?" he said thickly, raising his mouth off the floor. "Getting even for *Regan*? Let me tell you something, she liked it. She liked every goddamn min—umph!"

One foot had moved from his back to mash his face to the floor again. His nose and mouth inside the bag ground into the carpet. He couldn't breathe. He humped and struggled, trying to squirm onto his side, but the relentless feet kept him pinned. Finally, he stopped struggling and lay still. After a minute or so, the pressure eased off and he could turn his face enough to breathe.

The car stopped. He heard the doors open and close: one, two, three—no that was the trunk—

And then he was yanked out of the car by his belt, shins knocked against the door frame. The rain was only a light mist now as they forced him to walk, hands jacked agonizingly toward his shoulder blades.

His foot struck what felt like a curb and he stumbled, but they yanked him up again, shoving him forward. Wet scrub brush grabbed at his shirt and pants. They walked on and on, his shoes *thuck-thucking* on the soggy ground. Traffic sounds grew muffled, distant.

They were taking him into the park—

"Uhh!" His middle struck something solid.

"*Sorry, Larry.*" A coarse whisper, close to his ear, deep and seductive through the burlap bag. "*That's a park bench. You know about park benches, don't you, Larry?*" A hand struck his back, knocking him forward.

He had done Regan Salles on a park bench, pale, goosefleshed skin inviting against the dark wood. Not at Memorial Park, though, not that close to home ground. Left her tied there when he was finished.

"Regan, is that you, darlin'? If you wanted more, why didn't you tell me?"

The rope jerked tight, yanking his head back, cord biting into his throat, cutting off his air.

"This isn't Regan, Larry. But I'm a friend of women like Regan everywhere. Women who trusted you, might even have loved you, given a chance."

She—it was a she wasn't it?—let the cord go abruptly.

It wasn't Regan Salles. Nothing sexy about Regan's voice, even her whisper would sound whiny. At the end she'd begged him, in that nasal whine, not to hurt her anymore.

Something hard and metallic pushed behind his collar at the back of his neck, scraping the skin. "Ow!" He snapped his head forward; the cord yanked tight across his throat.

"Got to get these clothes off you, Larry. Can't have any fun with all these clothes in the way. You remember that part, don't you?"

He felt his collar being half cut, half ripped. They should use a box razor, he thought uselessly as he gasped for air, a box razor sliced clean and fast. The cord slacked momentarily, and he sucked in a greedy breath through the dusty burlap.

Hands worked at the front of him, loosening his belt, jerking his pants down, while the whisperer cut away his coat and shirt, all the time murmuring in his ear.

"How does it feel, Larry? How does it feel to have your decency stripped away, to stand naked to the world?"

"Don't you know, darlin'?" He tried to keep the fear out of his voice. "If I haven't done you yet, I apologize for the oversight. I'll make it up to you, first chance I get."

"I don't think you'll be playing your clever games anymore, Larry."

He was naked now, except for his shoes and socks, testicles small as acorns in the cold, damp air. He always left a woman's shoes and stockings on, too. If she wore panty hose, he ripped out the crotch and buttocks, cut away the panties. The meager cover on a woman's legs and feet made her feel even more exposed in the places that mattered.

He shuddered at the thought of being found like this tomorrow morning. That's what they meant to do, knock him around, then leave him tied, naked and humiliated. But he was not some stupid broad. He'd find a way to get loose. He wrenched away, trying to free himself from his captor's grasp.

The baseball bat hit him across the shoulder, *hard*. A moan escaped his lips.

The whisperer jerked the cord, forcing his head back, mouth so close to his ear he could feel warm breath through the burlap. She would have to be tall, wouldn't she, to be right at his ear like that? He was nearly six-two.

"That was a dumb move, Larry. Do you feel this?" Her hand under his scrotum, knife blade pricking the skin.

"Yes—" he managed.

"My partner is going to tie your feet now, and I don't want you moving a muscle. Understand?"

"Yes." He hated the sound of his own voice, thin and reedy.

His foot was tugged sideways, almost throwing him to the ground. A scratchy rope wrapped around his ankle, tightened, cutting off circulation. When that foot was secured to the bench leg, the bat struck his other anklebone, knocking his legs apart. Tears of pain sprang to his eyes—and for the first time he wondered if they meant to kill him—but he refused to give his tormentors the satisfaction of another moan.

As they tied his other foot, he felt damp wood brush his penis. He humped away from the contact; must be facing the back of the bench.

"Now, Larry, we're going to untie your hands. Remember, don't move a muscle." The knife bit into his scrotum.

"Okay! All right, take it easy. I won't move."

Feeling his hands released, his throat mercifully free, he considered a quick jab with his elbow, fast and hard in the gut, then grab the knife—

But one upward thrust from that blade would castrate him.

They shoved him forward, over the bench, yanking his arms wide, the injured shoulder screaming with pain. His exposed privates pressed against the wet bench slats as someone retied his hands, one to each corner.

This was how they planned to leave him, spread-eagled

over a goddamn park bench. He pictured himself being found, maybe by his neighbor walking her wimpy dachshunds. His cheeks burned with humiliation.

He tugged against his bonds. They *couldn't* leave him like this! Not right here in his own neighborhood.

A hand slapped the side of his head, sending a bolt of pain through his ear. The whisperer, in front of him now, grabbed his head with both hands and put her face close to his. He could smell her breath through the burlap, the sweet, yeasty odor of beer.

"That's more like it, Larry. Show a little spirit here. Give me a reason to hurt you."

He wrenched his head away, jerking on both wrist bonds. They held tight, the rough twine cutting into his skin, but he scarcely felt it, so hot was his anger. When he got free, this cunt would wish she'd never laid eyes on Lawrence Riley Coombs.

Her fists clubbed both sides of his head.

He butted forward, hoping to connect with her face, bloody her goddamn nose, but his forehead barely brushed her.

"That's good, Larry. Give us a fight. Let my friend see you're not a wuss."

She clubbed him again. His ears rang and a grayness expanded inside his head, like dirty wet cotton. He sagged across the bench, the top of his head grazing the seat, the back slats cutting his gut in half.

Through the grayness, he heard them whispering and didn't give a damn what they said. Suddenly the whole world seemed distant, a cruel echo of life outside this bubble of pain and rage. Whatever punishment they had in store for him, he'd have to endure it. Fighting only made it worse. If he ignored them, maybe they'd get bored and not kill him, leave him alone.

The whisperer cupped his chin, lifted it.

"Don't fade out on us, Larry. It's not as much fun when you won't play. You remember that, don't you?" She fingered the longish hair in his armpit, twisting a strand round and round.

"*Remember how much you enjoy a woman who puts up a fight?*"

She yanked the strand of hair, ripping it out by the roots.

"GODDAMMIT!" He bucked, straining against the ropes. "You better hope I never find you, cunt, because I'll tear the goddamn hair out of your head AND THEN I'll tear the hair out of your goddamn TWAT!"

"*Oh, that's good, Larry. Now you're playing the game like a real man.*" The throaty voice low and seductive, so close he could feel her breath warming the burlap. "*You are a real man, aren't you, Larry? You wouldn't be a little swishy, would you? My friend thinks you're more than a little swishy.*"

"Your friend is full of shit," he mumbled.

The bat struck him across the ass with savage intensity, driving his privates into the wooden bench slats. The jolt shuddered through him with sickening impact.

"*Oh, Larry. I'm afraid my friend is getting bored with the foreplay and ready to move on to the main event. Do you understand what I'm saying, Larry?*"

He couldn't reply. Even if he could get his breath, he was terrified of the answer, had never been so terrified in his life. Inside the burlap bag, he felt incredibly alone.

"*You do understand, don't you, Larry?*" The whisper no longer sounded seductive.

His mind wanted to fold in on itself. His bladder felt heavy, the muscles holding it wanted to let go.

"*Remember the woman you raped with a Coke bottle, Larry?*"

It was so dark inside the bag that he could almost imagine the world outside had disappeared. The fibrous cloth scratched his skin. His breath filled the enclosure, and he smelled the Scotch whiskey he'd drunk in the car.

"*For you, Larry, we have something better than a Coke bottle.*"

In the distance, he heard voices, a couple arguing. The voices drew nearer, until he could almost make out the words.

What would happen if he cried out? Would they hear him

over their own heated conversation? Would they come running? Would they try to help? Or would they pretend they heard nothing, refuse to get involved? This wasn't New York City, for God's sake. Houston still had its share of Good Samaritans.

Part of him wanted to scream for help, but another part saw his helplessness, his nakedness, and was too ashamed.

The whisperer seized his chin and slipped her other hand under the burlap, fingers cool against his neck. She stuffed something into his mouth that smelled of oil and tasted gritty, like a dirty shop rag.

"Just a precaution, Larry. We don't want anyone to horn in on our game, do we?"

Something heavy and cold as steel pressed between the cheeks of his ass. He flinched. But incredibly, he was hard; it quivered against the wooden bench.

"Easy, Larry. The more you fight, the more fun it'll be for us. Isn't that what you tell your victims?"

Strong fingers gripped his shoulder as the person labored behind him, trying to press the heavy object into an opening too narrow and tight. The oily rag sickened him, and he was lost in fear, fear like a hungry rat gnawing at the base of his brain. But fear wasn't all; humiliation burned inside him like a yellow bug light.

The heavy object thrust his cheeks apart. A horrible, tearing pain ripped upward, a pain like nothing he'd ever felt, a pain like no other in the world.

He stared into the blackness of the burlap bag and heard the distant sound of traffic, heard the voices of the arguing couple drifting farther away, and the rat in his head gnawed faster.

"Well, well. What have we here?" Cool fingers encircled his engorged penis. *"Are you going to come for us, Larry?"*

This can't be happening, this can't possibly be happening.

The steel thrust harder. For one agonized second the pain was so bad he was sure the shaft would come bursting through his belly.

Then he exploded in a torrent and sagged against the bench. Laughter crowded his ears as the intrusive object pulled out of him and he heard it fall to the ground. He felt wetness all over and knew that only part of it was blood; another part was surely semen.

Inside the burlap bag, in the darkness, he saw the faces of those who would discover him. He saw contempt and disgust. And he heard their voices. *Look at him. He liked it, didn't he? Why would he have jism all over if he didn't like it?*

He wanted to weep, but there were no tears inside him, only humiliation and a crushing sense of worthlessness. He tugged uselessly against his bonds and listened for his captors, heard nothing, knew they'd gone. A cool breeze ruffled the hairs on his exposed skin, dried the fluids that had run down his legs. If he could pray, he'd pray for rain to wash away his shame. But the cold front had blown in. The rain had finally stopped.

Chapter Twelve

Tuesday, February 11

Dixie entered the elegant Four Seasons Hotel at six fifty-five A.M. When she'd called Belle Richards the night before to accept the job and get the principal's background and itinerary—with the intention of scoping out the destinations in advance—Belle was rushing out the door. Dixie managed to get the name of the kid she was hired to protect, Sarina Page, and not much else.

Standing now in front of the VIP suite, Dixie raised her hand to knock. She'd barely touched the door when it opened an inch.

Snapping alert, she leaned her crutch against the wall and loosened her jacket around the Smith & Wesson holstered beneath her arm. From somewhere inside the suite, a TV commercial battled the drone of a hair dryer.

Dixie placed her knuckles firmly against the door. Tapped. The door opened another inch.

"Hello!" she called.

She heard a third sound—*someone weeping?* But the hair dryer drone blasted over it.

The TV commercial segued to cartoon music.

Between the door and the jamb, a sliver of an opening offered a skinny view of the far right corner of the living room. Dixie eased the door wider. A floor-length mirror reflected the sofa—and someone lying on it. *Crying.* Drunk, maybe. Or hurt.

Sliding the gun from its holster, Dixie eased into the room. Back to the wall, she scanned as she moved, the .38 locked with her probing gaze. A woman lay facedown on the sofa, wearing a robe, long, glossy hair draped across her face. A red scarf trailed from her neck.

Swinging her cast around a wet spot on the floor, Dixie crossed the room in three strides. Still scanning for movement, she placed one hand on the silky kimono, near the shoulder.

"Lady—?"

The body was cold . . . and . . . *rock hard.*

She nudged the blond hair back. A *goddamn dummy!* Then who was crying?

The mirror flickered with movement—the door inching open!

Dropping to one knee, Dixie aimed. As the door swung wide, a mass fell from above it and thumped to the floor.

But no one was there.

She swiveled: aimed at the mirror.

Something wrong with that mirror. It looked . . . wavy . . . as if floating.

"Come out of there!" Dixie cocked the revolver. The click was barely audible over the hair dryer drone. "Now!"

"Okay! Okay, okay, okay." The mirror rolled up like a window shade, revealing a metal stand, a bedroom doorway, and a scrawny teenage girl. "That cannon looks totally *un*friendly. Would you mind pointing it somewhere else?"

Dixie steadied the gun. "Who are you?"

"I'm *her* . . . me! . . . I'm Sarina Page! Stop pointing that thing at me." She fingered a black object in her hand, and the crying stopped. Then she turned her back on Dixie, folded the metal frame, and shoved it into the bedroom.

A trick mirror. A goddamn crying dummy. Where did she get all this stuff? What the hell was going on? Dixie holstered the .38. If anyone but Belle Richards had hired her, she'd walk out right now.

"What's with the practical joke?"

Sarina pointed a remote control at the door. It slammed shut against the stuff that had fallen—which now looked like a trapper's net.

"How did you miss the liquid soap on the floor?" the girl countered.

Dixie glanced at the wet spot she'd avoided.

"You were supposed to slip on the soap, knock the door open on your way down, and release the trap." The girl stomped across the room and kicked the mass of netting aside, allowing the door to close. "The net would've held you long enough for me to grab your gun."

Dixie wished she could wrap her hands around Belle Richards' throat right now.

The girl's thin face was flushed with irritation—or embarrassment—at the failure of her elaborate hoax. Shaggy, collar-length hair framed quick gray eyes, a narrow nose, and an ample mouth. No acne, of course. Rich kids never suffered crooked teeth, pigeon toes, or acne. Above faded black jeans that hugged her thin legs like chimney soot floated an oversized dust-colored shirt. A whiz kid, Belle had called her. Couldn't tell by looking.

"Why would you do that?" Dixie demanded. "*What* is going on?"

"I was proving a point." The girl hopped on a chair and yanked down a wire apparatus that had held the net above the door. "I may be only sixteen—practically seventeen—but I can take care of myself. I *don't* need a bodyguard." She hopped down.

Standing nearly a head taller than Dixie's five feet two inches, she slid an appraising gaze over Dixie, as if buying a used car. "I especially don't need a bodyguard who's not even as big as I am."

A *VIP client,* Belle had said. Suppressing the urge to flip the kid over her lap and spank her, Dixie cocked an eye at the failed contraption. A *crying dummy to lure her into the room, soap to trip her, a net to capture her—all to prove she doesn't need a bodyguard?* "Fortunately, someone who cares about you feels differently."

"My mother." Sarina spotted the cast on Dixie's left foot. "*What* is *that?*"

Dixie shrugged. "Leftover from a previous case. Had to do some serious butt-kicking."

"Cool." A trace of a smile threatened to break through. "Outstandingly cool."

As Sarina tossed the dummy and other items into the bedroom, Dixie sized up the posh suite. Every table held a fat vase of pink flowers—roses, carnations, other varieties Dixie couldn't name. Pink hearts nestled in some of the arrangements. A TV flickered inside a discreetly camouflaged entertainment console, Bugs Bunny chattering over the hair dryer drone still issuing from the bedroom. Abruptly, the hair dryer stopped.

"Was that the whatchamacallit, Sarina?" A woman's voice.

"Bodyguard, Mother. All hundred butt-kicking pounds of her."

"Hundred and twenty pounds," Dixie muttered.

"Tell her I'll be right out." The hair dryer whirred back to life.

"Maybe she thinks you're deaf." Sarina pointed to one ear. "But hey—I, on the other hand, am certain you have exceptional hearing, superb eyesight, and the speed of a hummingbird." Her scathing gaze swept over Dixie again. "Otherwise, I don't have a prayer in hell of escaping the bad guys."

Terrific. A whiz-kid, prank-playing smartass. Dixie glared at the telephone, beginning to understand why Belle had been too rushed to give any details. One phone call would get her out of this mistake.

"How many bad guys you figure we'll have to fight off?"

The girl rubbed at a red spot on her thumb.

"If you listen to my mother, every serial killer in the western hemisphere." She scooped up a high-tech toy of some sort, a foot-high mass of metal and plastic. When she moved a lever protruding from the top, appendages that appeared to be legs and arms moved in synch.

"And do you?" Dixie asked.

The girl raised an eyebrow.

"Listen to your mother?"

The hair dryer stopped again. "Sarina, does the bodyguard know you have a seven-thirty dentist's appointment?"

Dentist? Dixie looked at her watch.

"She knows now, Mother."

The hair dryer droned on.

"It's seven o'clock," Dixie said. Driving anywhere in Houston at this time of day took at least half an hour, especially with a new crop of rain clouds rolling in. February in Houston was crazy-weather time. Scrape ice off your windshield in the morning, wear short sleeves that afternoon. Rain was an everyday threat. "Do you know where the dentist's office is?"

"Not a clue."

On the television, familiar theme music announced a cable rerun of *Guerilla Gold,* an old series about three young women who started their own investigations firm after being ousted from a chauvinistic police academy. When the sultry lead appeared on screen, Sarina strolled nearer the set.

Dixie wondered what had sparked the girl's interest. The show had been off the air for at least ten years. By today's cop show standards, it was as tame as Goldilocks and the Three Bears.

But in the opening scene, the star, Joanna Francis, wore

tight black jeans and a loose-fitting gray shirt similar to Sarina's, collar flipped up around a swirl of auburn hair. Sarina flipped up her own shirt collar. She squared her shoulders like the woman on the screen. Then, suddenly aware she was being watched, the kid cut her eyes at Dixie. With an embarrassed grin, she tweaked the collar again. "So . . . is this totally *un*chic?"

In the oversized shirt, she brought to mind a lanky Oliver Twist. Or a shaggy stray puppy: lost, underfed, but cute.

"You look great," Dixie said, meaning it. "Chic is overrated." Smelling coffee, she spied a service cart laid with fresh fruit, a basket of assorted sweet rolls, and a half-eaten peanut butter sandwich.

"Help yourself." Sarina grabbed the sandwich and flopped on the couch.

Eyeing the chocolate croissants, Dixie merely poured herself a cup of coffee. Black. "What can you tell me about this bad-guy situation?"

Sarina had turned up the TV volume a notch, to conquer the hair dryer noise.

"On the flight from L.A., another card showed up," she said distractedly, eyes glued to the television. "It's on the desk over there. Weirded Mother out big time."

Dixie carried her coffee to the desk and set it on a notepad supplied by the hotel. A square envelope addressed in blocky red letters lay beside a commercial valentine. Dixie lifted the card by its edges, careful not to smudge any fingerprints. Inside, following a short love poem, was a personal message printed in the same square letters: YOU CAN'T RUN AWAY. WE WILL FINALLY MEET IN HOUSTON.

"What do you mean, this *showed up*?" Dixie said.

"Mother found it in her tote bag about twenty minutes before we landed."

Meaning the stalker was either on the plane, in the airport, or had dropped the card in her mother's bag somewhere on the way.

"Did you take a cab to the airport?"

"No. Marty drove us."

Marty? Mercifully, the hair dryer whirred to silence. Now the television seemed to be blasting.

"Turn the TV down," Dixie said. "So we can talk."

"What's to talk about? This nutcase sends notes. That's all I know."

"Sarina, turn down the television."

"I guess good hearing is not one of your qualifications after all." Tossing Dixie a drop-dead look, the girl lowered the volume. On the screen, the star and her two partners were karate-clobbering a gang of nasty-looking men in leather jackets.

"How long have these notes been arriving?" Dixie asked.

"A month or so, I guess."

"Sarina!" The voice from the bedroom. "Are you still here? You'll miss your appointment."

"We need specifics, Mother. Like *who* and *where*."

"Oh, for heaven's sake, it's right there in my address thingy." The speaker appeared in the bedroom doorway. "Good God. *You're* Dixie Flannigan? From Belle's description, I expected an Amazon at the very least. How can you be a bodyguard?"

Dixie looked at the woman, and then at the TV screen, just as Sarina switched channels. *Oh, shit.* Sarina Page was the daughter of TV princess Joanna Francis, the beautiful star of *Guerilla Gold* and at least one other long-running series. Sarina's father would be actor John Page, Joanna Francis' former husband, also a veteran TV star. The only thing in Dixie's book worse than a mouthy teenager was a mouthy teenage celebrity brat.

Joanna Francis was in town to shoot a cable movie. Dixie had read that somewhere. Maybe she'd have caught on quicker, she consoled herself, if Sarina's last name had been Francis.

Unlike the understated young star of *Guerilla Gold*, the veteran actress wore a bright yellow designer suit, an animal print blouse, and tiger-striped fuck-me shoes. Pure Hollywood.

"I can have Belle Richards send someone else," Dixie offered. "If you're worried I can't handle it."

"No." Joanna turned to a mirror near the sofa and scrutinized her famous face. "Belle said you're the best."

"Then, you want to tell me about these notes you've been getting?"

In the mirror, the star's luminous complexion lightened a shade. "They're all like that one. Greeting cards. Christmas first, then New Year's. After that, friendship cards—"

"Where are the others?"

"With my attorney in Los Angeles. Belle didn't fill you in on all this?"

"She hasn't had time. Did you alert the LAPD?"

The actress tossed back her auburn hair with a head movement Dixie recognized from every role she'd ever played.

"My attorney advised against it. He said the police can't keep a secret. They might leak something to the press. And after the incident last year, *any* suggestion that I might not be able to finish the film could jeopardize my contract with the production company."

Dixie recalled the "incident." Joanna had passed out during a press conference, was rushed to a hospital emergency room and treated for drug overdose. Reporters said she was drunk during the interview. It later turned out she'd had an allergic reaction to an antibiotic, but the tabloids preferred their own version of the story.

"Ms. Francis, how do you expect to catch this creep without the police?"

"I don't care if he's caught. I just want him stopped."

The only way to stop him, of course, was to catch him, but Dixie didn't want to argue the point. Her job was clear and simple: keep Sarina Page unharmed until she boarded a plane back to Los Angeles.

"Did all these cards appear out of nowhere, like this one?"

"The first two came in the mail." The star ran her tongue across her perfect lips, as if they'd gone dry. "The others showed up at the studio. In my dressing room. On my lunch tray. Under my car's windshield thingies."

"Were all the messages this subtle? This one sounds more like a smitten fan than a killer."

"One of them claimed we were meant for each other. It said I should stop dating. Save my *purity*."

"Did you stop dating?"

The woman looked down at her daughter sprawled on the sofa.

"I don't like anyone telling me how to live. Marty said my attorney's security people would take care of it. Then another message came, threatening Sarina. I haven't dated since. When I need an escort, Marty Ahrens, my agent—who's sixty-seven and happily married—takes me. But mostly Sarina and I go as a 'couple.' " She mussed her daughter's hair, then smoothed it.

Sarina flinched. "Mother drags me to these boring awards banquets." She switched the TV channel to the morning news. "Pretends I'm along for *her* protection."

Dixie glanced at the desk clock and decided to squeeze more of the details from Belle, who would no doubt be miraculously available now that Dixie knew the worst. She could phone while the dentist performed atrocities on the kid.

"I'll need the address for Sarina's appointment," she said. "We can talk more later."

Joanna's spike heels tapped softly across the carpet to the desk. As she dug through a snakeskin handbag and withdrew her address book, Dixie wandered toward the television, now practically silent. Apparently Sarina wasn't enthralled with local news.

The girl slipped off the couch, opened a closet, and removed a huge black denim bag, along with a gray poncho.

"Sarina, you're not wearing those clothes." Joanna jotted an address on the hotel notepad.

Sarina fingered the shirt collar. "I like these clothes."

On the television, a reporter was broadcasting live from a crime scene that looked like Memorial Park. Too many cops to be a simple mugging. Dixie glanced around for the remote control.

"That *color*, Sarina. It's so drab. Can't you wear something perkier? And your hair—!"

"My hair's fine." A catch in the kid's voice made Dixie look up. Shoulders rigid, mouth tight, Sarina stood facing away from her mother. Moisture glinted in her eyes. "This color is *me*. Decidedly *un*perky."

Joanna opened a bottle of nail polish. "Sarina, you're not leaving until you put on something less depressing."

"I like depressing." The girl stamped across the carpet, jerked open the bedroom door, and closed it behind her, muttering something that sounded like "Codswallop!"

Dixie found the TV remote and punched up the volume.

"*—Lawrence Coombs, acquitted yesterday of sexual assault, was discovered early this morning in Memorial Park by a woman walking her dachshunds. Coombs had been sexually assaulted and beaten. Doctors say he is conscious and in fair condition.*"

Sonofabitch! Dixie barely suppressed a Texas cheer—and instantly felt mortified at her elation. Vigilante justice was not a good thing. Still, if more rapists had to endure the sort of pain they dealt out—

Then she recalled the two women arguing at the Suds Club. Could there be a connection? Regan had been scared, Clarissa plenty angry. And at least one of the pair had a strong, protective man who might believe the jury let the rapist off way too easy.

The newscaster cut to a rerun of Lawrence Coombs strolling from the courtroom yesterday. Recalling what he'd said to Brenda, Dixie couldn't muster any sympathy for him.

The bedroom door flew open. Sarina flounced out.

"We'll be late," she told Dixie. "No time to say hello/good-bye. We're late, we're late, we're late."

The girl had slicked down her hair with gel until it snugged wetly around her head and had pulled a red sequin beret over it. A bright purple boa, draped over the gray poncho, hung to her knees. Multicolored bracelets laced up both arms. She strode to the front door, swung it wide, tossed her head with that same theatrical movement her mother used, and swept into the hall.

She slid a glance back at Dixie. "I can do *perky*."

Joanna, studying her own fingernails, hadn't noticed.

Chapter Thirteen

The whole idea of a sports car with automatic transmission seemed ludicrous, but Dixie was glad for it, since her clutch foot was still not completely dependable. She liked the feel of the Porsche, the leather seats and snazzy curved dash — like sitting in the cockpit of the single-engine airplane Parker had taken her family flying in. With her clumsy cast, Dixie managed to weasel out of the flight without coming off a wimp in front of Ryan. She'd sat in a plane's cockpit before, though. As a kid, she'd dreamed of being another Amelia Earhart — free, adventurous, daring. That was before she learned how much she hated flying.

She did like driving, though, and the Porsche Targa was a honey. Sliding into the early morning traffic from the hotel parking lot, she eyed Sarina.

Slouched low in the passenger seat, the girl screwed an intricate bit of plastic to her odd high-tech toy. The thing looked like a *Star Wars* alien, all teeth and scales. The sequin beret and feather boa lay at the kid's feet, along with her denim bag. A scowl hardened her mouth.

"Toothache can be miserable," Dixie said.

"I don't have a toothache."

"You're going to the dentist?"

The girl squinted at her. "Totally *un*necessary. My mother thinks if I miss my six-month cleaning by even a week, all my teeth will rot and fall out. Our regular guy referred us to someone here."

Dixie supposed stars were allowed to be eccentric. Or maybe mom just wanted the kid to stay busy. As Dixie left the hotel room, Joanna had handed her a long list of local attractions to visit during the week—Museum of Fine Arts, Johnson Space Center, IMAX—and seemed to expect the list to be punched like a dance card.

Sarina fished a square of thin, rubbery material out of her bag and began molding it to the creature.

"What's that you're working on? Some kind of model?"

"Fire Dweller. An original, one-of-a-kind rod puppet." She turned it so Dixie could see. "*My* design."

Rotating a lever, she caused the creature's head to swivel, following Dixie's movements.

Impressive. The thing was incredibly detailed. She could almost imagine it shuddering to life and charging across the car to bite off her nose.

"My nephew would love that."

"You think this is some kind of toy?" Sarina flicked the lever again and the creature's eyes sparked briefly as if lighted from inside. "It's for miniature work. On *professional* film." Insulted, she turned her shoulder to Dixie, shutting off conversation.

Fine. As Dixie maneuvered the Porsche toward the address Joanna had given her, she used her cell phone to call a friend at HPD's Sex Crimes and ask about Lawrence Coombs.

A gray late-model Camry had slipped in behind the Porsche when they left the hotel. Dixie noticed it still back there, not quite close enough to see a license number. She watched for it to follow them onto the freeway, but in the heavy traffic every third car seemed to be a gray Camry. Popular model. There were two in the medical tower parking lot when she pulled in.

In the dentist's waiting room, she found a guest telephone positioned so she could watch for Sarina to emerge from the hygienist's cubicle and at the same time keep an eye on the parking lot. The phone weighed about two ounces; it kept trying to creep over the edge of the glass table as Dixie talked to Belle. But the call was free.

"My contact at the Sex Crimes unit said Coombs was worked over pretty good," Dixie said. "Won't talk about what happened. Just stares out the window, eyes as empty as Saturday night beer bottles."

"That man deserved whatever he got," Belle said evenly.

"You won't hear any argument from me." Dixie hesitated. "Have you talked to Brenda?"

"It's only eight A.M. — I've barely had my morning coffee."

"Coombs' acquittal hit her hard, harder than any case she's lost in a while."

Belle was silent a moment, then, "Benson has better sense than to be part of a revenge mob, if that's what you're thinking."

That was the idea Dixie'd been resisting. "But she might know who did it."

Any involvement could put a rude end to Brenda's career. More important, it signaled a need for professional counseling. For ten years Dixie had walked in the same shoes her friend wore now. She knew the frustration of watching one scuzzball after another thumb his nose at justice, knew how it could eat at you. You felt responsible, even though the verdict was out of your hands. You felt embarrassed that a system you worked so hard to uphold had failed. You felt a burning rage against the judge and jury, and a raging need to see justice done, even if it meant putting your own gun to the scuzzball's head and blasting him into the ozone. If Dixie hadn't walked away from the job when she did, hadn't bottled up the bitterness and pushed it into a cold, dark chamber of her heart, she might herself have wreaked vengeance on Lawrence Coombs.

Maybe she'd given Brenda the wrong advice last night. Perhaps she should've recognized the level of her friend's frustration, encouraged her to quit the system while she could still face herself in the mirror.

Changing the subject, Dixie asked Belle, "Can you get copies of those mash notes Joanna Francis received in L.A.?"

"Already done—but I have an investigator on that part, Flannigan. Your job is to keep Sarina safe."

"What's the harm in my taking a look? Find the stalker—everybody's safe."

"Okay. I'll leave the copies at the front desk."

"Is Joanna's L.A. lawyer doing anything at all to identify this guy?"

"Surveillance. They had someone watching both Joanna and Sarina."

"Did you read the other notes?"

"Briefly. Why?"

"Did any of them mention a face-to-face meeting?"

"They all hint at it, saying things about destiny, divine union, that sort of thing. This last one is the most specific."

Dixie wondered if Joanna's change in location had fueled the stalker's passion or merely offered a favorable time to arrange a meeting.

"While I'm chauffeuring Sarina to dental appointments, who's guarding her mother?"

"Joanna refuses to have a personal bodyguard. Her only concern is her daughter's safety. Until Sarina was threatened, only Joanna and her agent knew about the notes."

"I don't feel good about this. You know how much I hate personal protection of high-profile targets." No matter how vigilantly you guarded a person, a determined assassin would eventually find a moment of opportunity. And nine times out of ten the principal made the job tougher by refusing to take simple precautions.

"You're the best insurance that girl could have for the money, Flannigan."

"*For the money?*"

"You know what I mean. Joanna's budget doesn't approach the national security allotment for protecting the president. I hired the best person for the job."

"Save the faint praise, Ric. Just get me everything the L.A. attorney has compiled on this bozo writing the love notes. At least I only have to brat-sit for four days." The sooner Joanna Francis and her weird daughter flew back to Glitter City, the better Dixie would like it. The longer the job, the greater the chance of something going wrong.

"Ummm, about those four days . . ." Belle left the sentence hanging.

"What about them?"

"Dixie, I've got another call—"

"What about them?"

"Last night's rain flooded the area where part of the shoot was to take place. They're filming other scenes while searching for a new location, but this could add a couple of days to the original time frame."

"A couple of *days*? That would cut into the weekend." But Belle had already hung up. "Coward," Dixie muttered to the dead phone.

She cradled it just as Sarina emerged from the treatment room showing off her puppet to the hygienist. Sarina moved a lever, and the creature reached out one rubbery hand to stroke the woman's arm. She laughed, obviously impressed.

In the parking lot the two gray Camrys had multiplied to three, none of them occupied. Circling the block twice, Dixie assured herself no one was following, and minutes later the red Porsche was back on the expressway headed to Belle's office in the Transco Tower. After she picked up the file of threatening notes, Dixie intended to drop by the DA's office for a heart-to-heart with Brenda, maybe take the prosecutor to lunch. Eventually, Joanna's cultural attractions list would have to be tackled, and sometime during the day, Dixie hoped to squeeze in a visit to the foot doc, talk him into removing the cast.

"Where's Greenspoint?" Sarina asked.

"About fifteen minutes north of downtown. Why?"

"My next appointment is near Greenspoint."

"Not another dentist?" The kid's teeth sparkled; her gums looked pink and healthy.

"No, not a dentist." She clicked on the radio and began punching buttons.

Dixie grimaced. Getting information from this imp was harder than milking a porcupine.

Finding a rap station, Sarina adjusted the bass and began drumming the dash.

"When do you have to be at this unspecified place near Greenspoint?" Dixie asked her.

"Eleven-thirty."

Terrific. Time enough to stop at Belle's office for the file, but not enough time to lunch with Brenda.

The rap song ended, and Sarina punched another button.

"—*Lawrence Coombs is under police protection pending investigation of the eye-for-an-eye beating*—"

Dixie caught Sarina's hand. "Wait, I want to hear this."

"—*as yet Coombs has not given police a description of the assailants dubbed by one officer as 'Avenging Angels.' Meanwhile, a verdict is expected later today in the Carrera versus Carrera civil case.*"

"This is one wild and crazy town," Sarina said. "Avenging Angels?"

"You don't have violence in L.A.?"

"Violence, sure, but—"

"Isn't Hollywood where Charlie Manson, the bogeyman of the century, ran amuck? And what about the Saldana thing? Or the Menendez murders?"

"Yeah, it's creepville, all right. Mother fired our gardener last year because he was 'acting strange.' " Sarina made a leering, grotesque face framed by twisted, menacing hands. Then she changed the radio station to drum along with another song that defied rhythm.

Dixie parked in the Galleria Mall garage, across the street from the Transco Tower. A gray Camry passed and continued to another level. Dixie jotted down the license number, but she'd already decided she was being paranoid. With so many freeways crisscrossing Houston, tailing somebody was difficult enough when you knew the routes. An L.A. stalker would've gone nuts trying to stay on the Porsche's tail this morning.

She checked the dash clock. With luck, she could be in and out of Belle's office in ten minutes, take another ten to drop by Brenda's for a brief chat, and still make Sarina's eleven-thirty appointment.

"I'll stay in the car." Sarina reached for the cell phone. "I need to make a call."

"You can make it from inside. Come on."

"You'll only be in there a couple minutes, right? I'll keep the doors locked." She punched numbers on the dial pad.

"Sarina. Put it down and come on."

"What can happen in broad daylight in a locked car?"

"I'm not interested in finding out."

The girl stared, as if Dixie had sprouted a second head.

"You're kidding about this, aren't you, Flannigan? You're not really telling me we're going to be joined at the hip until Friday!"

"Ms. Flannigan. And no, Sarina, I'm not kidding. For the next four days I'll stick to you like toilet paper to a fresh cut. My job is to keep you out of trouble until you fly back to L.A., where another chump can take over, maybe let you sit alone in a car in a public parking garage. Until that happens, you and I, as you say, are joined at the hip."

"But—"

"Sarina!"

"Hey, all right, Ms. Flannigan. Don't weird out."

She slapped the phone down and climbed out of the car.

They took the skywalk across the street, rode an elevator to the twenty-third floor, scooped up the file, and were back in the Porsche without incident in nine minutes, Dixie feeling slightly abashed about their dispute. Yet she had to make the kid understand up front that even the smallest breach of security was unacceptable. Otherwise, the girl would make life hell during the coming days. Protecting a cooperative principal was tough enough; guarding a target who didn't want to be guarded was a nightmare.

But Dixie didn't like the heavy silence that hung between them.

"You can call me Dixie," she said, steering the Targa toward downtown.

"Is that a Southern thing?" Sarina drawled. "Ah mean, is Dixie like a nickname or the appellation on yore burth certificate?"

Dixie ignored the kid's sarcasm—she couldn't help being a Hollywood brat. But few people knew Dixie's real name. When the Flannigans adopted her, they'd insisted she keep her given name out of respect for her birth mother. Later, changing it hadn't seemed important enough to bother with the paperwork. After all, her full moniker appeared only on her driver's license and other legal documents.

"My birth certificate says I'm Desiree Alexandra." She tossed the kid a shamefaced grin. Maybe sharing what was essentially a minor embarrassment would loosen up communications. "Could you look at this mug and say Desiree Alexandra without cracking up?"

"Well—" Still the sarcastic drawl. "It *is* sweet enough to make mah teeth ache."

"I think my mother pictured me in pink organza on the sweeping lawn of a Southern mansion, mint julep in one hand, ruffled parasol in the other, and a dozen suitors at my feet."

"You mean, she didn't expect you to grow up to be a bodyguard?"

"Even *I* didn't expect me to grow up to be a bodyguard."

Not to mention a bounty hunter. "I wanted to be Chief Justice of the Supreme Court."

"So what happened?" Sarina had dropped the sarcasm, but was fiddling with her rod puppet, apparently losing interest.

Dixie shrugged. "Life happened."

Surprised to find a parking meter within a block of the courthouse, she whipped in, telling Sarina to stay put until she circled to the passenger side of the car. Security inside a deserted parking garage hadn't bothered her nearly as much as out here in the open where an assailant could be anyone who passed. Gray cars in every direction. She hadn't spotted a Camry, but the street was teeming with traffic, as were the cross streets. Who could tell?

Sarina waited without comment while Dixie scanned the area, then she motioned the girl out. As they walked, Dixie instinctively took the side nearest the street.

Inside the courthouse, she surrendered the .38. Even with a carry permit, the law forbids weapons in courtrooms, except on cops. The guard also took the Kubaton from her key chain. It might be only a six-inch cylinder of hard plastic, but in the right hands it was lethal.

As they waited their turn at the receptionist's desk in the busy sixth-floor office suite, District Attorney Sonny Grossman sidled out of his cave.

"What brings you in from the farm, Dix?" He shook hands, giving hers a discreet squeeze.

She and Sonny had engaged in a brief, unspectacular romance after she quit the system, him teasing her constantly about going soft. He'd been supportive when she took up skip tracing, but there remained a mild sexual tension between them.

"I have some questions for Brenda. She around?"

"On the phone a minute ago." Grossman glanced at Sarina. Dixie introduced them without giving the girl's pedigree. "I can flag Brenda down, if it's important."

"No, I'll wait a few minutes. She seemed upset after Coombs' acquittal. How's she doing now?"

"Treated the whole department to breakfast this morning." He nodded toward an orange juice carton and an open box of pastries. "I'd say she's taking it fine. Besides, Coombs didn't exactly escape justice, did he?"

"Any idea who worked him over?"

"If I did, I'd send a thank-you note." He looked at Sarina. "You didn't hear me say that, miss."

"Hear you say what, sir?" Sarina mugged a look of doltish innocence and wandered over to forage for pastries in a blue and white package mottled with grease spots.

"Astute kid," Grossman commented. "Cute, too. Where'd you find her?"

Dixie mentally debated how much she could say without infringing on her client's privilege. News of Joanna Francis arriving in town had already made the papers, and Belle hadn't mentioned that Sarina's presence was a secret. Anyway, it wouldn't hurt to have Grossman alerted, in case the greeting card stalker tried anything more serious than an occasional love note. She briefed Grossman quickly. Then he spotted someone he needed to talk to and was gone. Dixie poured a cup of coffee from a stale-smelling pot. Pondering whether she really wanted to drink it, she saw Brenda approaching, her smile as radiant as her hair.

"Hey, sport. Are you recovered from our game?" The prosecutor looked fresh and vibrant in a brown tweed jacket and tan skirt. No telltale circles under her eyes.

"As a matter of fact, I'm ready for the rematch. How about right now?"

Brenda laughed. "I can appreciate that you might want to get even, but next week will have to do."

She didn't look like a woman riddled with remorse, Dixie noted. She motioned her friend away from the receptionist's eager ears.

"So, what happened last night?"

"What do you mean, what happened?"

"Regan and Clarissa. I left you cooling an argument."

"Oh, that. We had a long talk, a couple of beers, and a few laughs." Brenda shrugged, still smiling.

"How many are a couple?"

"Not enough to need a designated driver. What are you getting at?"

"The Coombs beating. Those two women were upset enough before they started drinking. You don't think . . . *maybe* . . . they decided to teach him a lesson?"

Brenda's smile faded only slightly. "I'm smart enough not to wonder."

"Brenda, wrong is wrong—"

"Listen, kiddo, I have work to do. Catch you later." She turned abruptly and headed back down the hall, a spring in her walk that had definitely been absent the evening before.

"Thursday," Dixie called. "Defense class. It's your turn to be the poor dumb bastard attacker."

Brenda looked back long enough to flash her radiant smile and a quick thumbs-up, then continued down the hall.

Chapter Fourteen

The road to Sarina's eleven-thirty appointment degenerated from pavement to gravel to graded dirt, the Porsche picking up road grime with every mile. Dixie watched for the gray Camry, but if it followed, the driver had to be damned good. Finally, at a pocket of undeveloped land a good five miles east of Greenspoint Mall, the address Sarina had supplied materialized.

"This is it?" Dixie asked. The building looked deserted.

Two-story, windowless aluminum, it jutted among co-lossal pines that shrouded the late-morning sun. The ground had turned marshy from last night's rain, which threatened to start again as she and Sarina picked their way along a broken concrete path. Sarina hurried ahead.

"Are you sure this is the right address?" Dixie called after her. A sign to the right of the metal door said STONED TOAD PRODUCTIONS.

"It's the right place. I'm expected." Sarina pushed the doorbell. Inside the building a buzzer brayed.

"Why would your mother send you way to heck and gone out here?" A car passed on the road. Dixie looked uneasily through the trees.

"She didn't send me."

"What do you mean?" This mysterious appointment wasn't on Joanna's list, but then neither was the dentist.

"Mother doesn't know. If she hadn't hired you to *protect* me, I'd have taken a taxi."

"A taxi would've dumped you at the last turn. If those rain clouds open up, we'll be hubcap-deep in mud." Dixie counted to ten, reminding herself this wasn't really the kid's fault; all teenagers were handicapped with pubescent brain damage. "Sarina, tell me what's going on here."

The girl scuffed her feet on the gravel-studded concrete, her gaze riveted to the silent building.

"You can't tell my mother!"

"You know I won't promise that."

"She'll weird out, and this is really no big deal."

"If it's no big deal, why all the mystery? What *is* this place?"

Sarina pushed the bell again, as if hoping someone would rush out to rescue her.

"*Sarina.*"

"A cinefex studio. Alroy Duncan"—she said the name reverently—"creator of only the *best* innovations since Spielberg—well, small-time stuff, but *good*—sort of invited me to visit his studio."

"*Sort of* invited you?"

"I met him when he came to the premier of *Devil's Walk.* Soon as I heard we were coming to Houston, I called, and Duncan said sure, come on by."

"Cinefex? As in special effects? *Close Encounters? E.T.? Titanic?*" Dixie had heard that film production companies were sprouting in Texas faster than bluebonnets, but this was the first she'd heard of a "cinefex" house in Houston.

"The only way to learn effects, see, is by doing it, inventing as you go, or finding someone who'll take you on as an apprentice."

"You're saying that in all of southern California there's no college course for special effects?"

"Ancient theory—*nothing* hands-on. Nothing that keeps up with technology."

"I take it your mother doesn't approve of your career choice."

Sarina rolled her eyes theatrically. "Totally *un*thrilled would be an understatement. She wants me to learn something *sensible*, become a computer scientist or a bone doctor, or like my aunt, God forbid, a *lawyer*."

Dixie winced: during her own college years, law was considered a worthy profession.

"All mothers want something better for their kids than they had themselves," she reasoned, not sure it was true, and certainly not speaking from experience. Her own mother had scarcely acknowledged having a child. "What does your dad say?" John Page would know the industry as well as anyone.

Sarina whirled from the door, sprinted to the corner, and scanned the side of the building.

"He says the only way to work in film today," she called over her shoulder, "is by landing a job the industry can't get along without." She marched past Dixie to scan the other side of the building. "Writer, director—someone who won't be history"—Sarina turned back and raised both hands to finger-quote—" 'after the bloom of youth is off her cheeks.' "

Dixie recalled seeing part of a new TV series with John Page playing second banana to a virile young hunk. She'd wondered at the time how the veteran actor felt relinquishing his leading-man position. Having started out doing stunts, he might sympathize with his daughter's career choice. Only it wasn't John Page who'd hired Dixie.

"What, specifically, do you plan to accomplish here?"

Sarina thumbed the doorbell. "Find out more about the

industry? Get a dialogue going with a genius on his way to glorification? Learn some shortcuts?"

Hands shoved sullenly into her poncho's deep pockets, the girl stared at the closed door. Dixie could feel her frustration.

"Look," Sarina continued, "I may be only sixteen—practically seventeen—but I know what I'm good at and what I'm not good at. When Mother comes at me with this doctor, lawyer noise, asking why I don't choose a *sensible* profession, I want to say that as far as I'm concerned, I was DNA'd for film when she popped me out of the womb. I might *fake it* by learning to mouth words like a lawyer, but I will never have it *here*." She thumped her chest.

Dixie studied the kid's intense gray eyes. There was quite a lot she apparently wanted to tell her mother but didn't. Or couldn't. The girl reminded Dixie of herself at sixteen-going-on-thirty-five. Dixie hadn't been a whiz kid from a fancy school, but she'd spouted off just as volubly, just as emphatically, about law and justice, good and evil. Although her rose-colored glasses had long since scummed over, she still considered the laws that govern a nation important. Surely they were more important than strobes, explosions, and fake blood.

"Sarina, your mother has walked the walk. She knows how hard it is to make a name in Hollywood. I'm sure she only wants you to have the best future she can provide."

"But she *ignores* what *I* want. She has some crazy notion I'll ruin my life by following in her and Dad's footsteps. What makes her think I won't ruin my life anyway? Would she have stopped auditioning if her parents told her, 'Don't become an actress, Joanna, you'll ruin your life'? *Codswallop!*"

"Maybe she—"

"You know how old Spielberg was when he snagged his big break? My age. He knew what he wanted and went for it—big time. I'm going to grab for what I want."

Before Dixie could reply, the metal door swung open. A

hulk of a man stood in the doorway, bits of modeling clay adhering to his full blond beard, hand extended in welcome, a good-natured twinkle in his sea-green eyes.

"So, you want to come in or what?" He shook hands without bothering to exchange names, his broad paw cool and dry. "You can't read signs?"

"Uh—" Sarina said.

"Little sign under the doorbell? Says 'Ring and Enter'?"

"Sorry—"

"There I was, making a face mold, you leaning on the bell, what am I supposed to do? Mess up an hour's work? Couldn't move until it set up, right?"

"Guess we didn't notice the sign," Sarina said.

"Come on back, but see the cables all over? Watch your step with that crutch, don't give me grief with the insurance company."

Dixie weighed the car keys in her hand and looked back at the Targa. They'd already made the long drive; what could it hurt to let Sarina schmooze with the great Alroy Duncan? Meanwhile, personal security jobs generally included a lot of time spent waiting, so she'd brought the stalker's messages from the car. She could hole up in a corner and examine the notes.

The walls of the huge room they entered stretched to a twenty-foot ceiling, with no permanent dividers other than a small cubicle that Dixie took to be the bathroom. A sharp chemical odor stung her nostrils. Duncan—at least she supposed this was the wizard himself—led the way, zigzagging around folding screens and makeshift curtains that sectioned off odd-shaped areas. Masks and body parts hung from exposed beams. In various dark corners stood hulking monsters, including the skeleton of a tyrannosaur, bony jaws near the ceiling. Past a miniature city strung along one wall, they reached a relatively clear work area. On a table a white model of Duncan's face stared with empty eye sockets.

"I don't have the mixture perfected yet, but look at this."

He grasped an edge of the mask and stretched it. "Practically tear-proof, see?"

"*Un*credible." Sarina bent close. "Good definition. What are you using, alginate?" She sniffed the rubbery material.

"Better than alginate—although it didn't give me quite the high I got with older products." He grinned.

"There's no drip," Sarina noted, examining the mask.

"Right! Come look at—" Duncan stopped to stare at Dixie as if seeing her for the first time. "Who's she?"

"Uh—a friend with wheels," Sarina said quickly. "She's cool. Really."

"You sure she's not a spy? Here to steal my secrets?"

The twinkle had never left Duncan's green eyes, and Dixie wasn't sure if he was serious or just putting them on.

"I won't even look," she promised.

"Hey, if Sarina Page says you're cool, you're cool, right? Come on back."

Duncan stepped behind a curtain. He must have flipped a switch, because Dixie heard a hollow hum as flashes of projected light hit the wall. But then the doorbell buzzed, reverberating in the steel rafters, and the projector clicked off again. Duncan stuck his head around the curtain.

"That'll be the wardrobe tech from your mother's set, here to pick up a headpiece. You folks can take care of yourselves for a minute, right?" He hefted a hat-size cardboard box.

Dixie watched him saunter toward the door. His casual reference to Sarina's mother bothered her.

"Did he know you were Joanna Francis' daughter when he agreed to meet with you?"

"Sure. Totally *un*smart to have righteous connections if you don't use them."

"I thought your mother was shooting a western. Why would she need a headpiece?"

"SF western. Mother's character is a xenomorph, traveling through time and space, transforming to fit in." Sarina pushed the curtain aside and peered into the area where

Duncan had been working. "Come on back, you've got to see this."

Instead, Dixie watched the door open at the other end of the building. The woman who entered wore the standard "techie" gear Dixie'd seen at theaters—black jeans, black T-shirt, black jacket—over her squatty body. When she scanned the room, her piggish gaze landing on Dixie, she grinned broadly and waved.

"Dixie!" Casey James called, pushing her way past Duncan. "I knew you'd lead me to something juicy. Here I was, all set to spend the week trailing Joanna Francis around her set, maybe catch some smoochie-smoochie behind the scenes. First, I camp at the hotel, to find out who Joanna spent the night with, and who do I see driving up at crack of dawn? *Now why,* I say to myself, *is Dixie Flannigan, bounty hunter, visiting Joanna Francis?"*

As Casey crossed the long room, treading with care around the clutter, Alroy Duncan followed behind, looking perplexed. Dixie's mind worked frantically. Belle had made it clear that Joanna wanted nothing about the stalker leaked to the press.

"Then you come out with the daughter." A camera had appeared magically in Casey's hand. "I'm thinking, *drug problem? Kleptomania? What's this kid into?* And since Joanna's film will be shooting all week, I can catch her any-time. But Dixie and the kid? Got to be a story there. Truth! So we arrive at *this* obscure point of interest." The reporter waved a hand at their surroundings. "What's the deal?"

"Casey, I'm glad you stopped by." Dixie hoped her smile didn't look as wooden as it felt. "I want you to meet my cousin, Sarina Page. Sarina, Casey James, freelance reporter. And this is Alroy Duncan."

Sarina cast a cool gaze at Dixie, then slid it over to the reporter. Duncan plucked at his beard, as if his mind was already back on his work.

"Cousin?" Casey looked skeptical.

"Distant," Dixie added. "You know I'm adopted. But Sarina and I have always hit it off, and guess what she wants to be, Casey. A *lawyer*. Joanna asked me to show her around, fill her in on what a lawyer's life is really about."

Casey's shrewd eyes worked over Dixie's face as if trying to read something between the lines. Then she darted a piercing look at Sarina.

"Cousin," she repeated. "What brings you two 'cousins' to a"—she looked at Duncan—"horror lab?"

"Just an errand." Dixie nodded toward the box Duncan held tucked under one arm.

"Ms. Francis' headpiece," he explained, finding a stray bit of clay in his beard and tugging futilely at it. The alginate had evidently dried.

"Mr. Duncan was about to show us his work," Dixie told Casey. "While it's everyday stuff for Sarina, I've never been in a cinefex studio before. Fascinating place. Maybe you could use it in a story. Come see—"

"You're putting me on, honey."

Dixie shrugged. "Sorry. Guess it wouldn't make very good copy. The monsters are all fake."

"Kid," Casey said to Sarina, "you want to know about lawyers, let *me* show you what's what. I follow enough of them around to know the hairy details Dixie won't tell you." She headed toward the door. "Crap! Half the morning wasted."

Dixie strolled alongside her. "Thought I'd take Sarina to visit a few of the more prominent law offices around town. Maybe spend some time at the courthouse. Give her a chance to see both sides. What do you think?"

"I think the girl's nuts."

Watching from the doorway as Casey climbed into a gray Toyota Camry, Dixie hoped she'd deflected the reporter's curiosity. Casey James could be as tough to brush off as cat hair. But at least Dixie knew who'd been tailing them. And now, with only Alroy Duncan to worry about, Stoned Toad Productions might be the safest distraction Sarina could've chosen.

"I made my first film when I was fourteen," Sarina was saying as Dixie joined them. The girl stood before a miniature castle, examining tiny windows and balconies. "Not much to brag about, totally *un*original, but hey—it was hands-on effects work."

"I hear you. My first film doesn't tip a glass to what I do now." Duncan flipped a switch. The castle windows lit up. "But I still get a grin when I watch it. Come see the shadow puppets we created."

"We?" Sarina hunched alongside him.

"When business revs up, I use students from the local schools."

Dixie'd seen enough, and she had a feeling Sarina's fifteen minutes would stretch like cheap panty hose. Removing a stack of magazines from a canvas chair, she settled down with the file of faxed greeting cards and a small notebook.

The first card, postmarked in Los Angeles on December 22, bore a standard Christmas greeting, *Wishing you good cheer at this special time of year*. Beneath it, a blocky printed note said, GOD BLESS YOU, JOANNA. THE MESSAGE IN YOUR NEW MOVIE HAS GIVEN ME REASON TO LIVE.

Dixie didn't see anything particularly threatening in the words, though the phrase "given me reason to live" seemed to indicate the writer was in an emotional state. She wondered what had prompted Joanna to keep the card and its envelope.

The second card, postmarked January 2, bore the stalker's note, THIS IS OUR YEAR TO JOIN IN DIVINE UNITY, JOANNA.

Definitely more personal. The card was illustrated with a simple, stylized drawing of Father Time, similar to the first one. They appeared to be about the same size. Dixie wished she had originals instead of facsimiles. The logo on the back would identify the publisher. If they were purchased from a single location, the stalker could be one of the store's regular patrons; the owner might remember him.

A stretch, she acknowledged, and if the publisher was one

of the big houses, she hadn't a prayer of getting a lead. But these card designs hadn't the slickness she associated with Hallmark or Shoebox. Cases often turned on odd bits of information. She jotted *identify pub. & purch. point* in her notebook.

The third card was received on January 14, according to a penciled notation in a corner of the envelope. No postmark. The sun motif on the front looked to be the same style as the others. The commercial message read, *Get Well Soon.* The penned addition thundered, YOU MUST OVERCOME YOUR ILLNESS, JOANNA! YOUR ILLNESS IS MEN!

The line "overcome your illness" sounded vaguely familiar. Hadn't there been a pop psychology book, *Overcoming Your Illness Through Positive Mental Attitude*?

Four days later the star received a second get-well card. On the blank area inside, the stalker had printed and underscored, NO MORE MEN, JOANNA! IF YOU HAVEN'T THE STRENGTH TO PRESERVE YOUR PURITY, I MUST HELP YOU. YOUR DAUGHTER WILL SACRIFICE FOR YOUR SINS.

Preserve your purity? Somebody had been watching too many bad movies. Dixie couldn't imagine anyone taking this stuff seriously. According to one of Dixie's FBI contacts at Quantico, every celebrity attracted stalkers. The issue they all talked about at parties was, "How many stalkers do *you* have this week?"

But a mother would think twice before dismissing that last line. The words "sacrifice" and "sins" smacked of religious fanaticism. Dixie knew from her prosecuting experience that a religious fanatic was the worst sort of crazy, often driven by voices and portents. Logic was useless against such delusion.

Still, the stalker's messages were laughable for the most part. What had raised Joanna's hackles enough to hang on to those first three? Dixie jotted *why keep early cards*???

The final greeting bore only the single word *Congratulations!* with no illustration. Inside was printed, I KNEW YOU COULD DO IT, JOANNA. NOW WE CAN BE UNITED. This one, dated February 2, sounded as if the stalker approved of Joanna's actions for the two weeks preceding her trip to Houston.

As Sarina's voice drifted near, Dixie glanced at her watch, then added to the file the valentine Joanna had received on her flight from L.A. The card was half an inch larger than the facsimiles and looked more expensive. Dixie wrote in her notebook *why change card style?*

"Being an effects artist isn't a game with me," Sarina was saying.

She and Alroy Duncan stood near one of the computer stations. He was checking out the kid's rod puppet.

"Effects *artist*—I'm glad you put it like that," he said. "I won't take on a dilettante, thinks she's Ms. Somebody Special. I won't have you screwing up one of my jobs just to show off."

"I won't screw it up," Sarina vowed. "I'll pound away for sixteen hours straight—laser shootouts, nickel-a-frame blood-and-gore slasher films, pornographic cartoons, anything. When I'm done, it'll be exactly the way you want it."

The pair shook hands. Dixie had a sinking feeling something had just transpired that she didn't officially want to know about.

Chapter Fifteen

"You're putting me in a rotten position," Dixie shouted, to be heard above the clang, screech, and *vroom* of afternoon traffic. They were parked once again in the garage across from the Transco Tower. She scooped up the file folder that held the stalker's messages. She wanted Belle to find out if Joanna's L.A. attorney had traced the five greeting cards to their point of purchase.

Sarina slammed the passenger door and slouched ahead toward the skywalk. Dixie couldn't help liking the kid, with her damn-it-all determination to follow a dream, but in good conscience she couldn't keep quiet about the deal Sarina had made with Alroy Duncan.

She caught the girl's poncho, drawing the lanky teenager into protection range.

"Now that you've seen Duncan's studio, don't you think it makes more sense to find a school that teaches—"

"There *is* no school. What you saw was it. That's what it looks like."

"But wouldn't it be smarter to get a well-rounded education first? Something—"

"It would be totally *un*smart to pass up a chance with Duncan. Do you know how long I'd have to kiss up to get as good an offer in L.A.?"

"What about something to fall back on in case your movie career takes a dip?"

"Are you kidding? Film is forever! People *need* movies to lift them from the sludge of everyday life."

"That's a worthy outlook, Sarina, but . . ." Dixie shrugged, remembering the bug-eyed, eight-legged, reptilian-faced creature hovering just inside Duncan's door. "Can you really take rubber masks and two-headed lizards seriously?"

"You think a film has to be *serious* to be worthwhile? What about *Star Wars*? You think Lucas didn't create value with that film—beyond the obvious box office megabucks? You think it won't be remembered?"

Dixie had seen *Star Wars* nine times, had rented the video only last week to watch with Ryan. She liked movies that left her smiling.

"Sarina, your mother has a right to know."

"She thinks I'll grow out of it."

At sixteen, it's possible to outgrow anything, Dixie wanted to tell her, including the burning enthusiasm of youth. But at any age it was heartbreaking for someone to squelch your dreams.

"Are you sure your mother understands how strongly you feel about this?"

Sarina opened the glass door that led to the skywalk and waited for Dixie to crutch her way in.

"She doesn't want to understand."

"Maybe we could talk to your father, have him reason with her. You did say he supports your working in film, as long as you don't take up acting."

Sarina moped along, hands shoved deep in her pockets. "If I'd taken a cab this morning, my mother wouldn't find out I'd talked to Duncan until my birthday."

"Don't you think that's being a bit hard on your mother?"

"If she would only *listen* to me." Sarina spread her hands to show the futility of being sixteen and knowing life was already slipping away. "Dixie, you mentioned *E.T.* — only the most often watched movie in the world. Movies like *E.T.* have real heroes kids can relate to. A story line that communicates values kids of all ages can latch on to and believe in. I want to be part of a team that creates such an impact."

Impact? She certainly knew how to hammer a point home. "Did you take debate in high school?"

Sarina grinned. "Made an A plus."

Dixie admired the girl's passion; wished, in fact, she could feel such passion again in practicing law. But Sarina might be selling her mother short, expecting Joanna to automatically veto an apprenticeship. Maybe if Sarina stayed closer to home. . . . "L.A. *must* have better facilities than Houston for studying special effects."

"L.A. doesn't have Alroy Duncan."

A defeated sigh hissed between Dixie's teeth. Her arguments were no match for Sarina's bullheadedness.

"Have you checked out the Houston universities, or are you pinning all your hopes on the mighty Duncan to make you the next Spielberg?"

"There're some good arts programs here. I can get accepted at one of them. And hey, I don't expect to be another Spielberg or another Lucas or another Doug Trumbull, but that's okay. I'll settle for being me, because I'm *good*."

Not to mention humble. "Your little spectacle this morning fell flat," she muttered, recalling the dummy in the hotel room.

Sarina blushed. "An actor would've followed cues."

"And a stalker would've had you cold." Dixie hated being in the middle of a family disagreement. But if the kid was willing to take regular college courses while she trained in special effects, where was the loss? Dixie realized then that she *wanted* the kid to get a shot at her aspiration. Maybe Belle could reason with Joanna.

She'd scarcely ushered Sarina into Belle's reception area when the attorney stormed out of her office.

"Flannigan, where the hell have you been? I've been dialing your mobile phone until my fingers are raw. I left messages on your answering machine, even called Clear Lake to see if Parker had heard from you. I was about to start calling the hospitals."

"Hospitals?" After leaving Stoned Toad Productions, she and Sarina had stopped for a burger. She'd taken the cell phone along, but maybe it wasn't working again. "It's only two-thirty. Sarina's mother won't finish shooting until six. Why all the worry?"

Belle stamped back toward her office, motioning them to follow. "Joanna received another card, found it between the pages of her script—and she swears that script hasn't been out of her reach since she left the hotel. The stalker must be somebody close. Anyway, Joanna called the dentist's office, found out what time you left there, and expected to catch you back at the hotel. I told her you stopped here after the dentist, but—why the hell didn't you let me know where you were?"

"Did you see the string of local attractions we're supposed to take in?" Dixie waved Joanna's list. "I didn't realize we were on a tight leash."

Belle glared at Dixie. Then her anger seemed to cool.

"I told Joanna not to worry as long as Sarina was with you, but she's pretty frantic." She looked at the girl and nodded toward the law library and conference room. "Why don't you telephone your mother and ease her mind?"

"Sure." Sarina crossed to the door and stopped. "Don't heap all the flak on Dixie, Ms. Richards. I asked her to show me around." The door clicked shut behind her.

"What did this latest note say?" Dixie asked.

Belle tossed a plastic Ziploc bag across the desk.

"It's pretty much like the others."

Dixie extracted the card by one corner. No postmark on the envelope. The commercial message said, *To my special*

Valentine . . . may you open your heart today and receive love in. The stalker's note in blocky red letters read: I DREAM OF OUR FUTURE TOGETHER, JOANNA. SOON OUR DREAM WILL BE REALITY.

Dixie slid the card back into the plastic bag. When she closed it, a puff of air whooshed out along with a familiar odor she couldn't quite place.

"Notice anything different about this one?" she asked.

"Different how?" Belle glanced at the plastic-encased valentine. "You mean the writing? The language?"

Dixie spread the facsimiles on Belle's desk, then lined up the two valentine cards in their plastic bags. "Look at the dates. Only one of the seven cards, the fifth one, mentions Sarina. The first five cards arrived about ten days apart, the closest being four days. These last two"—she tapped the valentines—"arrived two days in a row. They both hint of an imminent meeting."

"You think the stalker's closing in."

"Maybe. Valentine's Day is Friday. Maybe the stalker discovered Joanna was leaving town, took vacation time to follow her, and purchased the valentines en route. The creep seems to have more freedom now to play hokey games."

Belle glared. "You don't sound as if you're taking this case seriously."

"Did you read these? This guy's a joke."

"What? You think a sicko will only spout obscenities and satanic verse? We can't ignore—"

"I'm not ignoring anything. Only I'm wondering if Joanna hangs on to every piece of fan mail she receives. These early notes don't threaten anyone. Why save them?"

Belle flipped through the first three cards. "I see what you mean. Nevertheless—"

"Nevertheless, we run down all leads." The most recent card was the largest. Dixie explained about the codes on the back. "Both valentines are from a major publisher, but what about the others? Has anyone tried to locate the point of purchase?"

"I can find out."

"The first five cards have a simplistic design and a West Coast style. If we're lucky, the stalker bought them at a local art mart, a specialty boutique. Then picked up a valentine from a rack at the L.A. airport, the other valentine from somewhere here in town. What about fingerprints? Handwriting and ink analysis? Have these been to a lab?"

Belle folded her arms and crossed to the window, patent leather heels *thupping* the carpet. A thick gray veil shrouded the view of Houston's downtown skyscrapers. The attorney stared out at it, anxiety molded into her rigid back muscles.

"What I'd like to do is turn this whole damn case over to the HPD. But Joanna wants it totally hush-hush. No lab."

"I know a damn good private—"

"Even in a private lab, leaks happen. I have to respect the client's request for confidentiality."

"You're her legal adviser, dammit. Advise her. She might listen if she knows it's the only way to protect Sarina."

"Give the woman some credit, Flannigan. Joanna may act like the typical gotrocks airhead, but she's smart enough to know that every major police force in the country is understaffed and underpaid, that the last place to look for protection is the local cop shop." Belle picked up the latest card and studied it. "Joanna's had a bad year. On every show, accidents happened—lost scripts, busted water pipes, a fire in her dressing room. Accidents, but it doesn't take much to be dubbed a jinx."

"Okay," Dixie relented. "Hush-hush. And . . . maybe Sarina and I should drive over to the film location. Let Mom wrap a wing around her chick, reassure herself the kid's okay." Dixie didn't like hanging out in a crowd, though, where an assailant could pop up anywhere. "Afterward, we'll split for someplace safe." She gathered up the file contents.

"Belle . . . Joanna's hotel room was filled with flowers this morning. Any chance some of them came from the stalker?"

"Possible. But when Joanna travels, Marty sends armloads of flowers."

"Marty? Her agent?"

"To impress visitors, he says. Especially media. I can find out easily enough." She skewered Dixie with a look. "You *will* let me know where you go?"

"Yes. But I'd like to avoid these public places Joanna wants to send us to. One of Parker's clients is hosting a private yacht party in Galveston this evening. It's low risk. Invitation only."

The attorney eyed Dixie searchingly. "How does Parker feel about your working this job?"

"He didn't say much, beyond promising to take Mud to the beach."

Belle grimaced. "Anyone who can make friends with that ugly dog must be a master harmonizer."

"Meaning I'm the one causing all the problems?"

"I didn't say—"

"Actually, it does seem like everything I do lately stacks another brick in the wall between us."

"He worries about you, Flannigan. You're in a dangerous business."

"It's what I do. I've been independent too long to start playing Jane to his Tarzan." She looked out at the skyline, toward Clear Lake. "Anyway, that's not the real problem. We're just so different."

"Opposites attract."

"Right. God must have been laughing when he set up that dichotomy."

Dixie slid all the greeting cards and facsimiles back in the file folder. She had her own sources for checking fingerprints and handwriting, sources that could be counted on for secrecy. She intended to use them.

Chapter Sixteen

Codswallop!

Sarina plunked down the phone and unzipped her tote bag on the conference table. As she extracted a gray spiral notebook, she studied the room. Totally *un*thrilling. Brown dead-cow chairs. Books everywhere.

She opened her notebook to the first clean page, more than halfway back, then rummaged through her bag for a pen. Fire Dweller blocked everything, so she lifted him out and carefully placed him on the table. Granite table. Must weigh as much as a TransAm. Hernia time, bringing it up to the forty-seventh floor.

Finding the pen, she snatched up the notebook and flopped on the floor. Would *not* sit on dead cow.

Dear Dad, she wrote. *She's done it again. Trashed my life. Rips on me every minute and*

She reread what she'd written, set the notebook aside, jumped up, and strode to the window. Yards below, and some distance away, a news helicopter circled to land on a nearby building. Sarina leaned across the humongous table, grabbed her tote, and rummaged until she found her Datman. She queued up sound number 142 and punched the ON button. Instantly, the room filled with the *whoop-whoop* of a helicopter's blades. She lowered the volume, so it wouldn't carry past the heavy wooden library door, then feathered the sound to sync with the helicopter circling below.

A digitized simulation would've taken the bird down slower, less wobble, maybe circle once for form and drama. Sarina became one with the sound, lessening the volume as the copter descended, cutting it completely the instant after the wheels hit the helipad. Perfect!

She dropped the Datman back in her tote and sat down again with the notebook. She scratched through "trashed" and wrote "devastated." Dad would never see it, but she respected his opinion, and he disliked colloquialisms. She scratched through "rips on" and wrote "criticizes."

I know you want me to be patient, but life won't let me. The best part of my art is happening now, right now, and if I can't find a place to express it I know I'll fly apart like an exploded squib.

Sarina slapped the notebook down on the carpet and squinted at the puppet on the table. Fire Dweller was as good as any rod puppet ever built. Smooth action. Micro movement. She had to make Dad understand.

Seventeen is six months—almost seven months—away. What if I lose the touch? What if my talent dries up like an open jar of alginate?

Dropping her pen beside the notebook, she jumped up and circled the table to inspect the bookshelves. Law books. Somewhere in those books there had to be a law against a parent trashing—devastating—her daughter's future.

Chapter Seventeen

Joanna's director was loud, fat, and had an ego problem. Dixie guessed he was pushing fifty. If he lived to be fifty-one, if he didn't croak from emphysema or a heart attack, and if no one murdered him, he should consider himself on overtime. The scene had gone through twelve takes since Dixie's arrival. Each time the director yelled CUT, his hypertension intensified, the blood vessels in his throat and temples throbbed like convulsive snakes.

Production was ALREADY behind schedule, the fat man explained, and NO, Ms. Francis could NOT spare a moment to talk to MS. Flannigan. And if MS. Flannigan didn't make herself scarce immediately, he would be elated to have her bothersome self escorted off the set. Dixie might've reminded him that the "set" was actually a public street, which the city had temporarily cordoned off for the production company's use, and as a tax-paying citizen, she could launch a protest the likes of which he'd never seen. Instead, she

decided to "make nice," a strategy her Irish adoptive mother
had promised would reap greater rewards than otherwise.

Besides, it wasn't the rude director pushing Dixie's trouble alert button. It was the equipment poised to crash down
from a building, or trip someone, or short out and fry anybody standing in a rain puddle. It was the unfamiliar crew. It
was the teeming crowd—some of the watchers permanently
fixed at the perimeter, others stopping and moving on, the
mass pulsing like a giant amoeba.

So while she and Sarina waited for Joanna to get a break,
Dixie studied faces as if through a camera lens. She wanted a
mental snapshot of every crew member and onlooker: one of
them was quite likely Joanna's stalker. She dug out the notebook from her jeans pocket and jotted ideas as they occurred
to her. The first note read, *Find out if fat direc. wanted
Joanna on film.* He certainly seemed to be unnecessarily
rough on his star actress.

On their way downtown, Dixie had stopped to photocopy
the stalker's messages and to ship a set by overnight mail to
Les Crews, her FBI contact at Quantico. A profiler, trained
by the agent credited with inventing the field of medical
criminology, Les had developed almost as many credits as
the guru himself. If anyone could suggest a "type" to watch
for, it was Crews.

Joanna, dressed in a skimpy frock, stood beyond the barri-
cades, hugging herself against a harsh wind and silver
drizzle. A ragged awning snapped and bellied over her head.
A lighting crew fussed with fill lights. Several yards farther
along the sidewalk, a Hollywood killer in a western-tailored
suit and lizardskin boots smoked a cigarette.

The crowd pressed close behind the barrier. The atmosphere buzzed with expectancy, everyone waiting for the director to yell ACTION. Spectators wanted to hear the *zing!* of
bogus bullets, the screams of the killer's prey. Dixie just
wanted to be elsewhere.

Sarina's habit of darting off to chat with friends increased

Dixie's uneasiness. The teenager knew everybody in the film crew and slipped among them like a shadow in her gray attire. Workers from surrounding buildings, suburbanites who'd read about the shoot and driven in to rub elbows with celebrities, students, novices scooped up as extras—all had their eyes fixed on Joanna Francis. Dixie hoped a break would come soon when Sarina could check in with Mom. The less time spent among film people and their unpredictable fans, the better.

Then a face popped into Dixie's view that made her heart leap: Parker. He must've talked to Belle.

He squeezed through the throng and joined her at the perimeter rope.

"Thought you'd be on your way to the boat," Dixie said. "I'm glad you stopped by."

"I didn't like the way we left things."

"Neither did I."

"Guess working for a famous film star is more exciting, anyway, than a boat ride," he said flatly, watching Joanna huddle beneath an awning.

"I'm not here for excitement. I'm here because someone threatened a client and her daughter."

"Sorry. I didn't come to argue." He kissed her forehead, squeezed her shoulder, and let his hand linger there. "Don't suppose you found someone to take over for a while this evening?"

Dixie regarded him in his spiffy navy blue blazer and camel slacks, a tan raincoat draped casually over his shoulders. He looked terrific.

But she had committed to staying at Sarina's side, warding off potential danger, until the girl was tucked safely in bed, where hotel security took over.

"What if she went along?" Dixie suggested.

He glanced at Sarina, a few feet away, talking with a techie. "Is that the girl?"

"Looks like a lost puppy, doesn't she?"

"You have a reputation for picking up strays." He smiled and wiggled his eyebrows. "Lucky for me."

Dixie knew he was considering all the possible ramifications of taking Sarina to the ribbon cutting. The weight of his hand felt good. In companionable silence, they watched the action unfold as the film resumed shooting.

"I don't understand why anyone would choose to be a screen actor," Dixie whispered.

"Money? Fame?"

"Fame only lasts until a new face comes along, and there isn't enough money on this continent to make me put up with what she's endured the past half hour. Look at that dress she's wearing. How she keeps from turning as blue as the silk is a mystery." The temperature was falling rapidly. The wind gusted the misting rain under even the largest umbrella. From a trailer labeled WARDROBE, a red-haired techie hurried across the lot with a slicker to wrap around the star's shoulders.

"Actually, the weather is the reason I was able to stop by," Parker said. "These clouds are supposed to blow north. Hasn't rained a drop in the bay, but the new owner postponed his maiden voyage for an hour to be certain." He stroked a raindrop off her nose. "I think bringing Sarina, daughter of the famous Joanna Francis, will make us the talk of the party. Unless you want to keep her anonymous."

Dixie thought about it. "Anonymous would be good." Provided Joanna approved of this off-the-list excursion.

He handed Dixie a square envelope.

"Here's the slip location. The party starts around six, goes on until midnight. I offered to help with any last-minute errands, but you can show up anytime. There'll be a skiff to ferry latecomers to the yacht."

Taking a small shopping bag from under his raincoat, he thrust it into Dixie's hand, kissed her briefly on the mouth, and was gone. Inside the bag she found a red rose and a new pair of deck shoes in her size. Her sappy grin reappeared, until she realized she'd be clumping around the boat on a cast. Unless she got the doctor to take it off.

And what the devil would she wear? If everyone dressed as snazzy as Parker, her jeans and sweatshirt would embarrass him. Now she almost wished she'd said no.

But when she told Sarina about the party, the girl was surprisingly enthusiastic.

"The cast and crew hang out and go to dinner together after a wrap. I hate that. Mother attracts only the *ungifted* people. A Texas yacht party sounds like having some fun for a change."

When the director finally decided to take a break, Sarina shouted, "Mother! Over here!"

Joanna stamped toward them on heels every bit as high and skinny as the ones she'd worn that morning.

"I can't believe you have the nerve to show up here," she raged at Dixie, her anger hot enough to turn the drizzle to steam. "I instructed Belle Richards to fire you. You are stupid and irresponsible, taking my daughter out of town without checking in. There are telephones—"

"Mother, it wasn't Dixie's fault. Didn't you get my message?"

"Young lady, I'll deal with you later. At least I can understand *your* taking off to that NASA thingy without checking in, but *she's* old enough to know better. And I'm surprised I have to remind you we are not on vacation here. This is a working trip for me. How do you expect me to work if I'm worried sick about you?"

NASA? Dixie looked at Sarina. Somebody had been ad-libbing.

"It was on the list, Mother. If all I can look forward to this week is being imprisoned at the hotel and you ripping on me, I'd rather stay with Dad."

Joanna's beautiful eyes widened as if she'd been slapped. Then her lips mashed together in a hard, straight line.

"Of course you're not a prisoner, Sarina." She glared at Dixie. "That's why I hired someone to keep you . . . company."

"Then let Dixie do her job. And stop worrying."

Dixie hadn't missed the girl's quick, furtive glance to see if her bodyguard would rat on her. Apparently, the conniving twerp had invented a NASA tour to cover her visit with Alroy Duncan. Dixie knew she should tell Joanna the truth . . . but, what the hell, she sympathized with Sarina's determination to apprentice with one of her idols, and Joanna's hostility hadn't won any points. On the other hand, she couldn't let the kid off too easy.

"Why don't you tell your mother what you saw on the NASA tour, Sarina?"

"Ummm, well, I thought I'd tell her later."

"At least tell her the part you liked best."

"Okay, sure, soon as we get to the hotel. Hey—" She pointed desperately toward a row of trailers lined up along the street. "Mother, isn't that the woman we met on the cruise last fall?"

"Tori Pond? Yes, she showed up needing a job, and wardrobe had an opening." Joanna's eyes flashed one last angry spark at Dixie, then she tossed back her damp auburn hair with that famous shrug and began scanning the street. "Actually, Sarina, I *am* expecting someone. You remember Alan Kemp, don't you?"

"Alan from Brussels?" Sarina's diversion had worked perfectly.

Joanna smiled as if her anger of mere moments ago had never existed. "Oh, there he is—*Alan*!" She waved at a silver-haired man standing in a puddle of light, wearing a dark trench coat and black leather gloves. "Over here!"

Alan waggled a knobby cane in response. Then, staving off the rain with a huge umbrella and leaning on the cane, he threaded his way past the production crew busily repositioning cameras and lights. Joanna hooked an outstretched hand around his bicep and pulled him under the awning.

"Ten years since I've seen this gorgeous man. He drops by the set today for lunch as if it's an everyday event."

"Young lady," Kemp told Sarina, "you were scarcely as

tall as my walking stick when I last saw you. You've turned out quite as pretty as your mother." Up close, he appeared to be in his early forties, distinguished mane prematurely silver, voice smooth and rounded. No accent. Stage actor, Dixie figured. If not, he ought to be, with that voice.

"Alan's a syndicated reporter," Sarina told Dixie. "We've been E-mail buddies since I got my first computer." Then, turning back to Kemp, "Mother didn't tell me you'd be in town."

"She didn't know. I only arrived in the States yesterday, on business. When I read in the newspaper last night that Joanna would be shooting a film here, I couldn't let the opportunity pass without seeing the both of you. I hoped we'd all dine together this evening. . . ." He raised an eyebrow quizzically at Dixie.

"Oh!" Joanna exclaimed. "This is Dixie Flannigan, a . . . friend of . . . a friend. She's . . . showing Sarina around while I work. This is Alan Kemp, my cousin."

His grip was firm in the leather glove, and he held Dixie's hand a fraction longer than customary, soft, curious eyes gazing into hers.

"When I was a lad," Kemp said, "my guides were unfailingly quite old and crotchety."

He didn't buy the "friend of a friend" story, Dixie was certain, but he was too excruciatingly polite to question it aloud. She slid her hand free of his glove.

"A decent guide would suggest a drier place for you folks to chat. There's a good restaurant up the street. I can find a taxi—"

"No, Tori's expecting me." Joanna flapped a hand at the young woman watching from the wardrobe trailer. "After this last scene, we'll all go someplace exciting—"

"Mother, Dixie invited me to a party. On a yacht."

"A yacht?" Joanna was intrigued.

Hearing the *whir* of a camera's motor drive, Dixie glanced around to see Casey James sitting in her Camry, head thrust through the car's open window, Nikon busily clicking off frames. The reporter flashed her bold grin, then continued shooting just in time to catch Joanna linking an arm with Alan Kemp. The star's dazzling smile wasn't at all cousin-like. When Casey beckoned insistently, Dixie cast a wary eye at Sarina, decided she was safe under Mom's wing for the moment, and excused herself, to amble over.

"What's up?" Casey's tone held an unmistakable note of accusation. "Thought we were buddies, and now you're letting Kemp scoop me?"

"You know him?"

"You're kidding me, right? Osgood, Kuralt, Harvey, Kemp — don't tell me you've never heard his show, 'Starstruck.' "

Dixie vaguely recalled the name. Basically a radio gossip show about the world's rich and eccentric. But she'd never seen Kemp's face. He was strictly radio.

"How did you recognize him?"

"Eight or nine years ago, before I decided to destroy my reputation as a journalist and go for the dough, Alan Kemp and I covered the same Hollywood beat. I was hard news, he was flash. Truth, honey, Kemp had that sexy silver hair way back then." A wistful expression slid over the reporter's chubby features.

Dixie glanced back at Kemp, whose posture suggested more than a cousinly interest in Joanna Francis, and wondered if Casey had nurtured a crush on the man all these years.

"Kemp is Joanna's cousin," Dixie said softly.

"You, Kemp — that woman has cousins like a dog has fleas."

"He seemed surprised to find Joanna filming here."

"Don't bet on it. That man can tell you what color panties Demi Moore is wearing on any given day. You think he doesn't keep up with who's shooting where with whom? Take off your blinders, honey. Their meeting is no accident."

As Dixie strolled back to the trio under the awning, she heard Casey's motor drive whir into action. Joanna couldn't have missed it. Apparently, the TV queen didn't mind having the press around as long as they were catching her looking beautiful between scenes. At Dixie's approach, she tossed her auburn hair and smiled up at her cousin.

"Alan," she cooed, "wouldn't a yacht party be the perfect escape from this miserable day?" Her eyes rounded at Dixie. "You don't mind, do you, if we tag along?"

Chapter Eighteen

"No problem." Parker sounded pleased when Dixie called to beg two more invitations for Joanna and her cousin. His clients promised not to broadcast to their other guests that the star would be there, but Dixie had little faith they'd keep the secret.

She felt the risk factor escalating. Nevertheless, a private boat in the bay with a few dozen people aboard was still better than a crowded public restaurant with no control at all.

When Joanna insisted Sarina needed appropriate clothes for the occasion and pressed a credit card into her daughter's hand, Dixie started to protest. Busy department stores presented the same risk as busy restaurants. Then she recalled a quiet boutique that Belle claimed was Houston's best-kept secret. Located in River Oaks, an upscale area near downtown, the store was small, exclusive, and anyone entering would be highly visible. Besides, Dixie also needed some party duds. She hoped to find the perfect yacht bash attire to make Parker's eyes light up when he saw her.

While Sarina scuffed along, halfheartedly rummaging the clothing racks for something her mother would approve of, Dixie found a few items for herself. She scrutinized a short red wool blazer with creamy white pants and matching blouse. She couldn't recall ever owning a red blazer. Brown, yes, and bright blue, exactly the color blue Joanna had been wearing with her spike heels, running from a make-believe killer.

"Was it my imagination," Dixie asked Sarina, "or was that director coming down harder than necessary on your mother today?"

"Old Bubble Butt Barton? He has the hots for her, but she told him to lose a hundred pounds, she wasn't into dating hippos."

"So he gets even by making her shoot a scene over and over in freezing rain? Why does she put up with that?"

"He's an unwiped ass, but a talented unwiped ass."

"Sarina!"

"Uh-oh. Now you're the language police as well as the fashion warden."

Dixie made a mental note to have Belle find out if any other actresses had received threats while working on one of Barton's films.

"Does your mother receive a lot of fan mail?"

"Tons."

"And she keeps it all?"

"No way." Sarina zeroed in on a black dress barely long enough to cover her crotch.

Dixie took it out of her hands and found a longer version in kelly green. "What does she do with it?"

"Her mail? Marty's secretary sends every fan a signed glossy and a letter mentioning Mother's latest film."

"What about the anonymous letters?"

"Oh. Mother keeps those, if they're obviously from men."

"She gets love notes from women?"

"Duh!" Sarina gave her a look. "This *is* the nineties."

Of course it is. "Why does she keep anonymous notes from men?"

"She thinks Dad sends them." When Dixie continued staring, she added, "Mother thinks Dad's still in love with her."

"Is he?"

Sarina shoved the green dress savagely back on the rack. "You think he'd tell me? I don't even know why they divorced in the first place."

"How long have they been divorced?"

"*Officially*, eight months."

Dixie wondered what "officially" meant, but after those three bitter words, Sarina's face had closed down. Dixie decided to drop it for now. She could always find out more from Belle about John Page.

"How would this look for a yacht party?" she asked Sarina, modeling the red blazer and cream slacks in front of a mirror.

"What's wrong with your jeans and sweatshirt? Isn't that your, you know, uniform?"

Probably seemed that way. After she stopped having to dress for court, Dixie saw no reason to wear clothes that required panty hose, dry cleaning, and dignified posture.

"A bodyguard needs to blend. In jeans, I'd stand out like spinach on a smile."

"Oh." Sarina scowled at the racks of clothing. "Well, none of this stuff works for me. I'm fine in what I have on."

Not according to her mother. "I *like* what you have on," Dixie said, truthfully. She thought the kid looked like any teenager. Rebellious. "Only, why should I be the only one who has to gussy up for this event?"

"You're the blending bodyguard."

"The bodyguard who *didn't squeal to Mom* about your deal with Alroy Duncan. *Yet.*"

"Sounds like blackmail."

"Let's call it insurance." Dixie slid into the red blazer, smoothed it over her hips, and decided it fit okay. Her cast, which the doctor had adamantly refused to remove, even when Dixie threatened to take a hacksaw to it herself, didn't look quite as obtrusive with the white, full-legged pants over it. She tossed Sarina a similar jacket in pearl gray. "Cooperate on the small stuff, kid, and maybe I won't rat on you about Duncan. At least until the week's out. What's more important to you, a fashion statement or your future as a special-effects wizard?"

"Okay, okay! I get it." Sarina tried on the gray jacket and two others, and in minutes had an outfit even her mother should approve of.

But Dixie wasn't as sure about her own clothes.

"What do you think?" She turned in front of the mirror. The pants fit snugly around her hips, then fell in a soft line to a half inch off the floor, covering the plaster almost completely. The blouse had long sleeves and a low V-shaped neck. The tailored blazer curved just right over her bust, nipped in at the waist, and sported brass buttons, epaulets, and a fancy gold crest on the left breast pocket.

"You'll blend," Sarina said. "Once you put on makeup."

Dixie studied her appearance and had to agree. The dressy outfit made her face look unfinished. She hated worrying with colored creams and powders, had barely accomplished Lipstick 101, but the sales attendant assured her they could do a complete makeover with time to spare.

Half an hour later, Dixie peered in the mirror at a stranger.

"Perfect," Sarina said. "You look totally *un*exceptional. Not at all like a bodyguard. Ordinary."

Ordinary? After spending a wad on clothes and all that time getting painted and fluffed, Dixie had hoped at the very least for smashing.

Chapter Nineteen

The Berinson yacht would've been hard to miss, since it was the biggest boat in the harbor. White with black trim, it sparkled like a diamond, lights glittering, music pulsing. The party was well under way when Dixie and Sarina shuttled out. They could hear a live band playing country rock.

Sarina laughed. "Seafaring shitkickers. Is that not un*credibly* cool?"

She'd directed her question to the young man driving the shuttle, yelling to be heard over the music and the roar of the outboard motor. The man had a lean, tan face, strong hands, and a yearning in his eyes that said he'd just found the uncredibly coolest thing on the water and it wasn't a boat.

"If you think the music's hicksville, wait'll you see the food," he teased, grinning back at her. "Barbecued hog jowls, mustard greens, corn fritters . . ."

Sarina moved closer to him, said something Dixie didn't hear, and by that time the skiff had arrived at the ship. Waiting for Sarina to board ahead of her, Dixie appraised the girl's new appearance. In a charcoal gray blazer with gray and black striped pants and a black turtleneck sweater, she looked more mature than her sixteen years. Along with the clothing, she'd magically donned an air of sophistication. She was acting, Dixie realized, playing the "dazzling young sophisticate." Her Hollywood upbringing had kicked in. No wonder the shuttle driver was salivating.

Dixie only wished her own movements could be as graceful. Even in her new duds, she felt awkward. Sarina had talked her into carrying a brass-headed cane they'd found in the accessories department.

"You'll look eccentric rather than crippled," she'd said.

Dixie hadn't felt *crippled*. But recalling Alan Kemp's elegance as he waved his cane, she'd decided to buy one.

Spotting Parker at the ship's bow, she stood admiring him a moment. He looked as glamorous as a riverboat gambler.

"That's your guy?" Sarina asked.

"Yeah, sort of."

"Then who's the blonde cutting in on your time?"

Dixie hadn't noticed who Parker was talking to. Now she saw the woman—tall and fortyish, with the sort of healthy good looks Dixie associated with orange juice and aerobics. Parker appeared to be explaining the boat's layout.

"Probably a client." Dixie looked away, not wanting anyone else to catch her staring.

When a couple approached—the woman horse-faced and thin as a needle, the man stooped, bald, and beaming as if he'd won the lottery—Dixie guessed they were the Berinsons even before they introduced themselves. Holding hands the entire time, they gushed over Sarina, saying how glad they were that she and her mother had decided to come. Joanna was still coming, wasn't she?

"I'm sure she is," Dixie said.

"Mother never misses a good party." Sarina-the-young-sophisticate showed she could make a hit with all ages.

The Berinsons beamed at her, pointed out the bar and food, then moved on to their other guests. Dixie steered Sarina toward the bar, positioning herself where she could see Parker and the "client" he was with. She should go out there, introduce herself to the woman. Walk up casually, laughing, as if she hadn't been watching them together. Wrap a possessive arm around Parker. She could introduce Sarina. She should do almost anything other than stand here. But a bit of Barney's sage advice popped into her mind: *If you can't run with the big dogs, stay on the porch.* In a courtroom, or on the highway tracking down skips, she could run with the biggest. Here she felt small.

She ordered two club sodas with a twist.

"Soda?" Sarina scoffed. "Totally *un*original. I'll have San Pellegrino."

"No alcohol," Dixie said.

"Sparkling water," the bartender translated.

Dixie turned away from the man's smarmy smile. Since when had water become so damned complicated?

"Make it two." She didn't really like club soda anyway. She wondered if the new yacht owners were going to sail around the world in this luxurious tub, and when Joanna and Alan would finally show up, and who the hell was the blonde Parker was talking to, and why the hell had she agreed to come here in the first place?

"Tell me about Alan Kemp." She ushered Sarina toward a window where they could look out at the shoreline. "Your mother said she hasn't seen him in years. How did he know where to find you?" Through a forward porthole, she could see Parker and the blonde. He was laughing, not a pretentious, polite laugh, but the real thing. They looked good together, both tall, attractive, totally at ease.

"No big mystery," Sarina said. "*Billboard* would've carried the film's location. Cast, crew, all that."

"Has he ever visited any other film she was on?"

"Not that I remember." Sarina stared into her glass, worrying the swizzle stick back and forth. "You don't think it was Alan who sent Mother those notes, do you?"

"Maybe, maybe not." With all his charm, good looks, and

sex appeal, something about the man didn't ring true. "His arriving on precisely the same day as you and your mother bears noticing, that's all."

"But Mother and Alan haven't seen each other in years. And Alan was in Brussels when those cards were sent."

"You know that for certain, do you?"

"His E-mail—"

"Can be sent from anywhere. He *said* he arrived in the States yesterday, but if he's the stalker, isn't that what he'd want us to believe?"

The girl shrugged. "I suppose."

"How often do they keep in touch?"

"They talk on the phone once or twice a year. He always sends gifts at birthdays and Christmas."

"On the flight from Los Angeles, do you remember seeing anyone who might have been Kemp in disguise? Different hair, eyeglasses, maybe padded clothing—?"

"I don't remember anyone like that." Sarina set her drink down and frowned at the carpet. "They're not *close* cousins, I mean by blood. Before Mother married Dad, I think she and Alan had a . . . a thing going." She looked worried.

Dixie patted the girl's arm reassuringly.

"Listen, kid, it's my job to be suspicious. Most of the time my suspicions are unfounded, which is exactly how I like it." Parker and the blonde had disappeared around the deck. Dixie inched along the rail, bringing them back in view. "Now, tell me about Tori Pond."

"The wardrobe tech?"

"You said she showed up at the studio where Joanna was working after they met on a cruise." At the ship's rail, the woman took Parker's arm and pointed toward something on shore.

"Tori hung out with us the whole trip," Sarina said.

"Could she be jealous of your mother? A wanna-be actress, maybe?" Dixie couldn't get past the notion that the stalker's messages were too hokey to be real. Like a bad TV movie. Belle had made a good point—criminals were more likely to be crude than clever. But the notes Joanna received were neither.

"Dixie, Mother's had fans before who got totally intense. I don't see why she's making such a fuss this time."

"Has any fan ever threatened you before?"

"I don't think so."

"That's why your mother's treating this one differently."

The girl puffed out her cheeks and picked up her glass to worry the swizzle stick some more.

"Did you and Joanna continue the friendship with Tori Pond after she joined the studio's staff?"

"Tori doesn't come to our house, if that's what you mean. It'd be okay with me. She does incredible things with costumes and makeup. But a wardrobe tech is not exactly the crowd my mother hangs with."

"There was a tall, red-haired kid who followed your mother around on the set, handing her things—"

"Hap Eggert." Sarina grinned. "Hap's cool. His mother costarred on some of the *Guerilla Gold* segments. Hap's been in the business forever, works lighting, sometimes camera crew, whatever."

A waiter stopped beside Parker with a tray of drinks. He took one for himself and handed one to his "client." When they touched glasses before drinking, Dixie's throat tightened.

"Were Pond and Eggert"—Dixie hesitated—"and the director—on the same flight from L.A. as you and your mother?"

"Sure, but . . . Dixie, we're all like *family*, even the techs. You're not going to hassle them, are you?"

"As I said, it's my job to be suspicious."

"Is that why you're spying on your boyfriend instead of walking right up and telling that blonde to get lost?"

"I'm not spying." Dixie felt her face flush. "Not exactly. I mean, they're only talking. Parker's a salesman, he talks to people. It's business."

"Dixie, maybe *he* thinks it's business, but *she* is Glenn Close in *Fatal Attraction*."

The woman did look awfully intense as she leaned toward Parker in a dress much too revealing for the weather.

"Dixie, go get your man!" Sarina swiveled her gaze toward the loading ramp and smiled wickedly. "And I'm going to get mine."

Her mother and Alan Kemp had arrived, and the young man from the shuttle had boarded with them. Dixie watched Sarina-the-sophisticate slink in their direction. When Dixie looked back, Parker spotted her. He waved. The blonde glanced at Dixie, but suddenly seemed to have other interests. As Parker strolled across the deck, he looked so good, Dixie couldn't blame the woman for wanting to scoop him up.

Sauntering up beside her, he leaned close and whispered, "You look nice. Really nice. Thanks for coming."

Nice? That was a long way from smashing.

"Thanks for inviting me." She wished they were at home, curled up with Mud and Jay Leno.

"Did you meet our hosts?" Parker gently plucked a piece of lint off her new jacket.

"Yes. I'm glad you sold them this boat. They seem to be enjoying it. They seem to enjoy each other."

He nodded. "Like high school sweethearts. Hard to believe they've been married over forty years."

Dixie watched the couple conversing with their celebrity guest. Other guests crowded round. Sarina and the young shuttle driver stood together at the rail, well away from the others, and close enough to be in Dixie's protective reach in a few strides. Couples, couples, couples, everywhere she looked.

"I expected everyone here to be elderly," Dixie told Parker. "But most seem to be . . . our age . . . or even younger."

"The Berinsons' children, their friends. Come on. We should mingle."

Mingling was exactly what Dixie loathed about parties. Mingling meant making intelligent conversation with people she didn't know and had nothing in common with. What should she say, "Did you notice those thugs on TV last night? I caught up with those old boys down in Monterey, after they skipped bail. And how was your week?"

But Parker was a consummate "mingler," and in minutes they were talking to a man who raised emus. Dixie kept an eye on Sarina. At the same time, she tried to keep track of Alan Kemp, another good mingler. Wherever he was, whoever he talked to, his eyes never seemed to leave Joanna. Exactly what business had brought him to Houston? Dixie wondered.

The emu man was funny. As he told a long, convoluted tale about his emu farm, Dixie found herself relaxing. After the story reached its punch line, Parker looked at their empty glasses.

"What are you drinking?"

The man said Scotch, Dixie said soda, unable to remember the name of the sparkling water, and Parker wandered off for refills. Shortly, a waiter appeared with their drinks.

Surprised, Dixie looked around for Parker. She spotted him at the bar, talking to the blonde.

Chapter Twenty

Following a taxi with Joanna and Alan Kemp back to the Four Seasons Hotel, Dixie decided this was one day she was glad to see end. She couldn't recall one thing that had gone right. To top off the uncomfortable evening, a black spot had appeared out of nowhere and landed on the crotch of her new white pants. The club soda–removal trick someone suggested only made it worse. Everybody she talked to the rest of the night seemed to adopt a frozen-faced stare to avoid looking at the stain. And Parker spent most of the evening talking with his blond "client."

To be fair, Dixie hadn't been the ideal date, unable to dance, unwilling to be far from Sarina. How could she blame Parker for being less than attentive? But dammit, he'd wanted her there, hadn't he? The strain between them had not lessened. Would he be at home when she got there? Maybe by the time she saw Sarina safely into the hotel suite, and investigated something that had been nagging her since seeing that latest valentine, she'd have figured out what to say when she finally faced him.

Sarina hopped out of the Porsche. "See you tomorrow."

"Wait! I'm going up with you."

"It's okay. I'll ride up with Mother and Alan."

"I need to check out the suite."

"Okay. We won't go inside until you get there."

"Sarina, I'll only be a minute here. Wait up."

"C'mon, what can happen between here and the hotel room? Are you planning to hold my hand in the shower, too?"

Using her new cane for support, Dixie eased out of the Targa. Her foot ached from standing on it all evening. She accepted a valet ticket and steered the teenager toward the entrance.

"Sarina, you can do this my way or you can break in a new bodyguard."

"*Un*believable! You're making a big deal over a two-minute elevator ride. What about Mother? If Alan's the stalker, isn't she in danger, too?"

Joanna and Alan Kemp were disappearing behind the elevator's gold-tone doors.

"I wasn't hired to protect your mother."

The girl blinked at Dixie, then her eyes narrowed with understanding.

Dixie glanced at her watch. Parker should be home by now, settled down with Mud in front of the fireplace.

"You're saying you'd let my mother walk into danger, while you're protecting *me*?"

"The only way this kind of job can be done is to set priorities. Your safety is my priority. You're the one the stalker threatens." Dixie chose her next words carefully. "If you and Joanna were both in a killer's gun sight, I would save you. Then I'd help Joanna if I could."

Sarina scuffed her shoe over a matted spot on the carpet, mouth thinned into a stubborn line. Then she crossed her arms and stared at the elevator doors until they opened. The day hadn't been bad enough, now Dixie had the kid mad at her, which meant tomorrow would begin on a sour note.

Upstairs, Joanna had kicked off her shoes and was on the phone ordering room service, while Alan sat on the sofa, reading aloud from the menu. The scent of too many flowers thickened the air. Dixie spotted a fresh arrangement on the bar separating the sunken sitting room from a tiny dining area beyond it. She sauntered over and angled a glance at the attached card. *Knock 'em dead, Joanna.* No signature. Another bouquet from her agent?

Snatching up the television remote, Sarina perched on a sofa arm and punched the POWER button, then looked over Alan's shoulder.

"Pizza," she said. "Huge, with everything except anchovies. How about you, Dixie?"

No sulk in her voice. Had she already decided not to be mad?

"Nothing for me, thanks." Dixie felt a peculiar relief. She had enough to deal with tonight. "I just came up to use your telephone—when your mother's finished." She'd purposely left her cell phone in the Porsche's trunk. "Meanwhile, I guess the bathroom is through there?"

She strolled offhandedly toward the bedrooms.

"Yeah." Sarina rolled her eyes behind Kemp's back. "There's another phone, too, if you want privacy."

"Thanks." Dixie shut the bedroom door behind her and quickly searched the closets and under beds. In different circumstances, she would've swept the entire suite before Sarina and her mother set foot in it. But Belle had warned that the film star was as stubborn as a fed mule about maintaining a low profile, and Joanna had indicated as much when she introduced Dixie to her cousin Kemp. Searching the hotel suite had to be totally, as Sarina would say, *un*obvious.

Dixie also wanted to satisfy a hunch. A hunch she hoped wouldn't pan out.

The enormous bathroom had twin sinks, a shower, a

whirlpool bathtub, a separate area for the toilet and bidet, and locking doors that opened into the bedrooms. It didn't take long to see that everything was fine. Fine, that is, unless they'd brought the stalker home with them.

The door popped open just as Dixie rose from looking under the bed. Sarina poked her head in.

"Mother's off the phone."

"Okay. I won't be long."

Lifting the extension, Dixie dialed Belle's unlisted number. She loved interrupting the lawyer's evenings. When Belle answered, Dixie quietly filled her in on Kemp's opportune visit, suggested a background search, then rattled off the other questions on her list.

"I don't feel good about your leaving them alone while Kemp's in the hotel suite," Belle said when she'd finished. "Maybe you should spend the night."

"That wasn't part of our deal." Besides, even though she was suspicious of Kemp's motives, Dixie's hunch might eliminate him as the stalker. "You said Joanna wanted me to disappear when Sarina was with her."

"I didn't know she might invite the viper back to her own nest."

"Kemp's probably exactly what he claims to be—a reporter who happened into town, saw his cousin was filming here, and dropped by to say howdy. Doesn't make sense that he'd stalk Joanna after not seeing her for ten years. Checking him out is just part of doing the job right."

A resigned sigh issued from the phone. "I alerted hotel security. I suppose that's the best we can do."

"No. If you're really worried, you can hire round-the-clock surveillance, not only for Sarina but for Joanna."

Belle's silence stretched until Dixie wondered if she'd disconnected. "Trust me, Flannigan, Joanna won't budge on this subject."

As Dixie cradled the phone, she scanned the bedroom. Judging by the bug-faced space monster residing on the dresser, this was Sarina's room.

Beyond the door, a Lexus commercial changed abruptly
to a sitcom. The kid would be busy for a while, manipulating
the TV control. Dixie slid open dresser drawers and riffled
stacks of cotton underwear, black and gray T-shirts, and
jeans. Then she opened the closet to search through jackets
and shoes. Inside the pocket of a black designer bathrobe
with "SP" embroidered in gold, she found what she'd prayed
wouldn't be there: a white paper sack with a brand-new
valentine inside, along with a cash register receipt and a red
felt-tip pen—as red as the spot on Sarina's thumb that
morning.

According to the receipt, the pen and three cards had
been purchased at a gift shop in the Los Angeles airport. A
tan smear on the side of the bag caught Dixie's eye. She
sniffed it. Peanut butter, the same odor that had puffed out
of the Ziploc bag that held the second valentine at Belle's
office.

Sarina was Joanna's stalker.

Chapter Twenty-one

Arriving home to see the familiar wisp of chimney smoke in the night sky. Dixie'd felt a rush of relief that quickened her spirits like sunshine after a long rainstorm. She found Parker stoking a blaze of pecan shells in the fireplace. And now she was curled in her favorite club chair in the living room, a woolly afghan over her lap, her hands wrapped around a warm mug. Parker had made hot buttered rum.

Mud, having lapped up his own small measure of the savory drink, lay with his muzzle across Dixie's good foot. He snapped to attention when Parker tossed him a homemade cookie.

"I don't understand why the kid would want to terrorize her own mother," Parker said.

Dixie had related what she'd found in Sarina's bathrobe pocket.

"I stood in that closet doorway at least two minutes, staring at the valentine and the red pen and the peanut butter smear, and asking myself that exact question. Sarina obviously sent the cards. But why?"

Dixie didn't want to talk about the blonde at the party, or the fact that Parker had barely said a dozen words to Dixie the entire two hours she was on the boat. But she *did* want to talk. She wanted them to get past the disagreement about her job. Maybe keeping him involved, letting him know what she was doing, would dispel some of his anxiety.

"The thing is," Dixie explained, "if Sarina sent the cards, then she was never in danger. Joanna had no reason to hire a bodyguard, no reason to worry about her daughter — except whether the kid's psychotic. But why would Sarina play such a mean prank on her mother?"

"To get attention?" Parker stood by the fireplace, one foot on the raised hearth, firelight flickering across his handsome features, turning his naturally tanned skin to burnished gold.

They were being unusually formal with each other, Dixie realized, as if a third person were in the room, a stranger. She wanted to break the tension, make Parker laugh — or even yell at her — but she continued talking, talking, talking, about everything except what needed to be discussed. Relationships were such a damned struggle.

"Joanna does seem wrapped up in her own world. Everything she says to Sarina is some sort of complaint or criticism." She remembered how upset Sarina had been when Dixie asked about the divorce. "Maybe Sarina thinks her bizarre prank might bring her parents back together. She wouldn't be the first kid with such hopes."

"Inventing a stalker is no typical adolescent prank."

"Sarina's not a typical adolescent."

"You're making excuses for the girl, Dixie."

Yes, she was. Picturing Sarina calmly composing the stalker's threatening messages, disguising her handwriting with the blocky red letters, and placing the cards where her mother would find them, Dixie wanted to jerk the girl up by her ears and shake till her brains rattled. But she could also picture the kid growing up with Joanna's Hollywood craziness and self-involvement. By contrast, Sarina seemed practical, highly intelligent—a kid any mother should be thrilled to have around, to enjoy being with and getting to know. Sarina—she realized—was a kick.

"She pulled a stupid stunt," Dixie said. "Naturally, I'm surprised, and yeah, I was pissed when I found that card in her robe. But I'm also relieved." The most frightening aspect of a bodyguard job was knowing you might not be adequate to the task, knowing that one slipup could give a killer an opening. "At least I don't have to worry about her ending up on a mortician's slab."

"More likely, on a shrink's couch."

Parker flicked on the television, but left the sound low. A cop show was finishing up, preceding the news. He crossed the room to refill Dixie's mug, then set the carafe on a table and perched on the arm of her chair.

He ran a hand over Mud's back.

"If there's no stalker, then you don't have a job any longer."

"I don't suppose that'll break your heart."

"Not at all." He continued stroking Mud's back, not looking at Dixie. "You didn't have much fun tonight, did you?"

"I'm not much of a party animal." She didn't mind admitting her shortcomings, but admission generally led to some attempt at conquering them. She couldn't see herself ever becoming a social butterfly. "Does *that* break your heart?"

He scratched between Mud's ears. "People prefer buying from someone they know. Circulating at social occasions is better than waiting for boat lovers to get a buying urge and drop by a showroom." He stopped stroking the dog and turned a steady blue gaze at her. "I made good contacts tonight, Dixie. We'll be invited to other parties. I'd like to think you want to be with me."

"I suppose you need a sociable female on your arm while you're circulating." Dixie studied the liquid in her mug. She didn't like the catty sound in her voice, but dammit, the image of Parker laughing on the forward deck with the blonde wouldn't go away.

"No, Dixie, I don't *need* a woman on my arm. But good hosts generally prefer to balance the male-female columns on their guest lists."

Meaning if she wasn't there, another woman would be. God, she hated this conversation.

"So I go along, wearing my rubber smile and making like a proper guest while you ignore me, spend the whole time charming the pants off your 'contacts.' " *Shit!* She'd said it, despite her resolve not to play the jealous lover.

Parker leaned away slightly to stare at her. When Dixie allowed her gaze to meet his, she saw an amused twinkle in his devilish eyes.

"Is that a green glow radiating from your beautiful face?"

Beautiful? Not very damn likely. Just the Parker Dann charm turned on high. Did he say the same words to every female he met? Did he have pet phrases, guaranteed get-laid flattery he portioned out like fish bait?

On the television, a car careered around a corner, a police unit in close pursuit, bullets flying. Dixie would rather be dodging bullets, chasing one of the ten most wanted, than sitting here, taking part in this conversation. Why did male-female situations have to get so damn sticky?

"Parker, I suppose I'm too down-home simple to enjoy the glitzy world you circulate in. And you don't like my world much, do you?"

He rose and stared at the fire. Mud lifted his muzzle off her foot to pant at her, and then at Parker.

"So where does that leave us?" she added miserably, because she knew it had to be said.

"Where do you want it to leave us?"

How did she answer that? She wanted a perfect world,

where she could do her job without being hassled, without worrying that Parker was worrying about her. She wanted to arrive home without that churning in her stomach, searching for signs that he hadn't taken off for more exciting places. She wanted freedom to live her own life, dammit, but assurance that he'd always be a part of that life. How did she put that into words without sounding arrogant?

As silence closed in on them, the room took on the feeling of a funeral parlor. Mud put his paws in Dixie's lap and his muzzle near her face, as if trying to decide whether she needed a good tongue bath. When the news came on, Parker turned up the volume and Dixie welcomed the distraction. Then a familiar face flashed on the screen.

"Lawyers for Lawrence Coombs filed suit against the city today for wrongful arrest and endangerment. Coombs was assaulted last night following his acquittal of a rape charge. A spokesman for the District Attorney's office responded to a citywide outcry supporting Coombs' attackers."

The newscast switched to a location scene in the DA's public relations office. *"There is no place in our society for vigilante justice. This office will assist the police department in pursuing Lawrence Coombs' attackers with the same diligence we allot any criminal investigation."*

"They should've killed the bastard!" Dixie blurted, reliving the rage she'd felt during her last few moments with Coombs, before the cops burst into the room.

Parker's eyebrows dipped low, shading a penetrating gaze. "You sound like you mean that."

"Part of me does. The part that would've shot him had I been armed that day."

Parker nodded solemnly. "Me, too. Will the police really pursue his attackers as they claim?"

"They'll go through the motions. Coombs' lawsuit will galvanize the mayor's office to bring pressure on the DA."

" 'Which is the justice, which is the thief?' Shakespeare asked. I'm wondering if justice has progressed in three centuries."

Parker's own brush with the legal system had given him reason to doubt its merit.

"The system may be fallible," Dixie said. "Sometimes prosecutors and judges and juries make mistakes. But what would replace it?"

The newscaster segued to another story, with a name Dixie recognized.

"A judge ruled today that Patricia Carrera will be reunited with her eight-year-old son, Paulie. The boy's grandparents, Mr. and Mrs. Joseph Carrera, filed for custody after police dropped abuse charges against the mother due to insufficient evidence."

Brenda had worked for weeks trying to build a case against Patricia Carrera, who was accused by a school counselor of battering her son, after the boy came to school repeatedly with cuts and bruises. A team from Domestic Violence had investigated, and no one doubted the woman was guilty of abusing Paulie, but they could never put together enough evidence. And Paulie hadn't held up well to questioning. When forced to drop the criminal case, Brenda had counted on the grandparents' civil suit to protect the boy from future danger. Now the civil process had failed, too.

"So, what are you going to do about the kid?" Parker asked softly.

About Paulie? No, he meant Sarina. Sometimes Dixie was damn glad not to be a mother. It couldn't be easy, or more people would get it right. Parker's cool gaze probed for an answer.

"I want to give Sarina a chance to explain. But from where I sit, there's only one conclusion to draw. And since I wasn't hired to untangle family problems, I'm dumping the whole mess back in Belle's lap."

Dixie stared into the fire, unwilling to search Parker's expression for approval. Her decision had nothing to do with their own problems, it was the only thing that made sense. Dixie worked for Belle Richards, not for the film star or the star's daughter. How much to tell Joanna, and what to do next, would be Belle's decision.

Dixie only wished she could hand off her relationship problems as easily.

Chapter Twenty-two

Sissy sprang from her chair to snap off the six o'clock news. How could the court send that child back to his mother, knowing the unspeakable cruelties he'd suffered at the woman's hand? How could a judge say there wasn't enough evidence against Patricia Carrera? The boy's *testimony* was all the evidence anyone needed.

Hot chocolate splashed from Sissy's cup, scalding her fingers. The pain ignited her anger, and she hurled the cup at the nearest wall. Hearing the satisfying crash, she lifted her chin and watched the chocolate mess slide to the floor.

She looked at her hand and saw it curl into a fist.

The power of the court was the highest power before God. Yet how many times must that power wither in the hands of ineffective judges and weak juries?

Couldn't they see that a small boy would never accuse his own mother of such horrible, torturous acts if they weren't real? Didn't they realize the child would return to more of the same unspeakable treatment?

She kicked a stray porcelain shard against the baseboard and strode to the kitchen for a wet sponge.

Children were God's gift to nurture and protect, totally trusting, totally dependent. A parent who abused that trust, damaged a child, had to be stopped.

Sissy wiped the sponge over the spattered wall, turned the sponge over, and wiped again. The wall would stain. She dropped the pieces of broken cup into a trash bag and carried it to the kitchen. Stuffed it deep into the can.

Then she picked up the phone and punched in a number. Listening to the ring, she watched her fingers open and close, open and close into an ever-tightening fist.

When man's law became so impotent that women and children were no longer safe in their own homes, it was time for a higher, if cruder, form of justice.

Chapter Twenty-three

Patricia Carrera backed slowly through the throng of pro-testers gathered outside her home. *Stupid people.* They could protest until their bleeding hearts shriveled, and it would make no difference. *She* had *won!* Her son was coming home, where he belonged.

Steve's parents has better not give her any trouble tonight. If they did, she would call the cops and demand they force the Carreras to release Paulie. Considering everything the cops and the District Attorney had done to hurt her, it was high time they helped her out.

Patricia turned south, then west into the Carreras' ritzy neighborhood. How many times a week had she made this trip when Steve was alive? Three times? Four? Seemed they were always at his parents' house for some trumped-up oc-casion. After Steve's death, the Carreras had wanted Paulie to stay over more and more often, poking at her with ac-cusing eyes and vicious comments until finally they tried to take Paulie away altogether. But Patricia poked right back, busting their traitorous little scheme. Paulie was *her* son. He *belonged* with her.

Straight ahead, a detour blocked the road to the Carreras' house. ROADWORK, the sign said. Interesting. The streets along here all ended in culs-de-sac. How many of them handled enough traffic to create potholes?

Now what was this, *another* roadblock? Without lights or reflectors, or even a sign directing traffic to an alternate route. *Wait*, the road was only partially blocked, as if someone had dragged the orange-and-white sawhorse into the street as a prank. Probably a kid. Kids had entirely too much freedom these days for causing mischief, too much time on their hands.

Patricia couldn't see any potholes. No open construction. Certainly no good reason to turn back. She was only a few blocks from the Carreras' house, and this was obviously not a legitimate detour. If she shoved the sawhorse back a few feet, she could drive through. Leaving the engine running, she hopped out.

A movement in the hedges startled her. *Probably a cat.* Disgusting, the way people let cats run wild, even in a nice neighborhood like this one.

"Owh!" Something struck the back of her knees, knocking her forward. Her chest hit the sawhorse and she grabbed it for support.

"What—?!" Something was being forced over her head. A plastic bag? "*Stop that!*" She couldn't breathe inside a plastic bag! She fell to her knees as she tried to pull it off—

Her hands were yanked behind her and fastened.

"*Get this off—owh!*" A slap.

"You keep that hole shut." A whisper. "Or I'll stuff a rag in it."

Now Patricia was being dragged, her breath sucking the plastic around her face. She would smother, *she would die!*

She kicked backward at the person forcing her arms up high, *hurting* her—

She was shoved onto a car seat—pushed to the floorboard. She shook her head to dislodge the plastic bag. Her breath had drawn it so tight against her mouth and nose that she knew she would pass out.

"Be still," the voice said.

"I . . . can't . . . breathe," she managed.

"Get that bag off her face," someone said. "I told you to use the burlap." A woman's voice?

The bag was loosened but not removed. Patricia gulped air, tilting her head so the plastic wouldn't cling to her face. By rolling her shoulders forward and tucking her head down, she created an air pocket. After a few gasps, her breathing returned to normal.

Who were these people? Where were they taking her?

The car had picked up speed as if on a freeway; now it slowed again. Stopped. She heard the car doors open. Someone grabbed her wrists by the tape—that's what it was, tape, they'd taped her wrists together—and pulled her backward from the car.

"Who are you?"

A smack across the mouth, catching her lip on the sharp edge of a tooth. She tasted blood. The plastic sucked against her face again—and she panicked—but when she tilted her head and blew a stream of air, the bag fell away. She could breathe, shallowly.

A door scraped open. Pushed, she stumbled into a building that sounded large and empty. Garage? Warehouse? An acrid chemical odor hung in the air. Steps echoed hollowly. Another door opened, and she was shoved into a smaller room. Much smaller. Patricia felt herself being crowded forward, nose pressed into a corner like a bad child's.

A light clicked on overhead. She couldn't see through the plastic bag, it was dark and opaque, but she could see light hitting the floor beneath her. Then the bag ripped away and she stared at two dirty gray walls cornering in front of her. A light hung from the ceiling behind her, a single bulb on a long cord. Shadows shifted on the wall as the bulb swung back and forth. Concrete under her feet, filthy, spattered with something that looked like russet paint.

"Who are you?" she demanded, turning to see and receiving a slap on the back of the head.

"Who are you?"

"Who are you?"

"Who are you?"

Three mimicking voices, close to her ears; at least she thought there were three. At least two. She could feel their breath.

Something spidery brushed her face—she shrank from the touch. Then someone leaned close.

"We are God's fist of justice," the voice whispered. "Your transport to hell."

She felt a small, quick pain above her wrist, then the tape ripped off and her hands were free. She hesitated before drawing them in front to massage the wrists, saw a spot of blood where something sharp had nicked her when they cut the tape. Patricia hated blood.

"Oh, look. She's got an ouchy." Someone clubbed her hard on the back, knocking her forward. "You know about ouchies, don't you, Trisha? You gave Paulie a plague of ouchies."

She had never given Paulie anything he didn't deserve, no matter what these bleeding hearts thought. Their own children were probably spoiled, ungrateful whelps who would grow up to be drunken bums and criminals.

A hand clutched her arm, jerked her around. When she saw the face, Patricia almost cried out. The mask was flesh-colored, a woman's face molded of thin, translucent plastic, the expression horribly vacant. The hair was bright red Raggedy Ann yarn. A print housedress covered a bosom and hips that were obviously padded. A parody, Patricia wondered dizzily, of her own hennaed hair, her own ample figure?

Another "woman" stood nearby. Frizzy yellow hair framed a cartoon face, long Betty Boop eyelashes painted on plastic eyelids. Both "women" wore thin rubber gloves and black rubber boots.

"Look at that dirt on your dress, Trisha," Betty Boop mocked. "Only stupid, clumsy little girls get their dresses dirty. Stupid, clumsy girls."

She—it was a she, wasn't it?—grasped Patricia's hand.

"Trisha needs a reminder not to dirty her nice dress," whispered Raggedy Ann, her voice low and sultry.

She slapped Patricia's palm with a metal egg turner, exactly like the one in Patricia's own kitchen. The holes in the metal stung like ant bites. *It hurt!*

Patricia clinched her hand and spit at the redhead. Spittle oozed down the plastic cheek. Through the translucent face, she could see the "woman's" features twist into a cruel smile.

"That was naughty." The sultry whisper slid over Patricia like syrup. "We all know what happens to naughty little girls, don't we?"

Who *were* these people? And just where did they get off treating her like this?

Betty Boop tried to pry Patricia's hand open, while the redhead gripped her other wrist.

"You don't really want it across the back of your hand, do you, sweetie?" Betty Boop screeched in the reedy falsetto. "It would hurt more, much much more." Her strong fingers ground Patricia's knuckles together until the fingers curled back in pain. Then the egg turner slapped down, stinging.

Tears sprang to Patricia's eyes. She blinked them away. She must keep her wits about her, figure out what was happening, how to get out of here.

"You've been a very naughty girl today, haven't you, Trisha?" Raggedy Ann crooned.

Patricia clamped her lips together. The blonde tightened her grip on Patricia's wrist. The egg turner swooped down again.

"Damn you!" Her palm was on fire.

"Have you been a naughty girl today, Trisha?"

"No!"

The egg turner smacked her palm, sending slivers of pain into her arm. Despite her resolve, tears slid from her eyes.

"Stop this!" she demanded. "This is crazy!"

"You shouldn't lie to us, sweetie," Betty Boop screeched. "Patricia was naughty today, weren't you? Naughty, naughty."

"NO!" She flinched even before the metal stung her skin. "Goddamn you! Stop this!"

"Then tell us the truth, dear," Raggedy Ann whispered softly, sincerely, in her syrupy voice. "You were naughty today."

"N—all right, all right, YES!"

But the egg turner slapped down harder than ever. She screamed a string of curses, tears streaming down her face, calling them every filthy name she could think of.

"My goodness, would you listen to that mouth." The blonde shook her head. "My mother would wash out my mouth with soap if I talked like that. And Mommy always knew best. Always." Reaching into a deep pocket in her print dress, she extracted a small vegetable brush.

"I'll find some soap," the redhead said, and crossed the tiny room to disappear through a door.

Patricia twisted out of the blonde's grip and sprang for the door they had entered. Yanked it open. Dashed through. This room was dark, except for a red EXIT sign at the far end. Footsteps pounded after her, but she didn't look back. Heedless of the cardboard boxes and steel drums that crowded her passage, she ran full out toward the sign . . . and made it.

She prayed the door would not be locked.

Her hands, slick with sweat, slid uselessly around the doorknob. It refused to turn. Panting, hearing the footsteps clamoring closer, Patricia stopped fumbling and breathed deeply to calm her panic. She wiped her hands down the sides of her dress. Lifting the hem of her skirt, she wiped the doorknob. The footsteps were close behind her, and she had no idea what to do when she got outside, except run.

But the knob had to turn. It *had* to.

Wrapping it with her skirt, she turned the knob easily. But when she pushed, the door refused to open.

She shoved harder. Just as she felt hands grab her sleeve, the door gave. She pushed on through, slamming the door shut behind her. Maybe she could block it with—

"Sur-*prise!*"

A flashlight blinded her and Raggedy Ann's horrible painted smile pushed close. Beyond it loomed another mask, this one framed with black hair, blunt-cut and tangled.

"NO!" Patricia lunged past them, but one grabbed her collar, the other her arms, pinning them helplessly behind her again.

"Don't run, Trisha. Only bad little girls run away before the party's over."

Patricia fought, twisting, kicking, to free herself, screaming desperately into the night. But she knew with a chilling certainty there was no one to hear her screams. She was alone with these crazies, and she didn't believe they had gone to so much trouble just to poke fun at her and slap her hands.

They dragged her back inside the building. A silken cloth—a scarf?—encircled her neck, choking off her screams.

"No one can hear you, dear," Raggedy Ann crooned. "But that screeching gives me a headache." She tightened the scarf with a vicious twist.

Patricia choked and coughed.

"You see, dear, there's no one around for miles. When that five o'clock whistle blows, the workers in the area clear out fast." Tugging the scarf, the redhead forced her to walk. The brunette led the way, shining the flashlight ahead of them. "Anyway, this old plant hasn't been used for years."

Where were they taking her? This wasn't the direction she had escaped from.

"The rendering company moved, but they can't tear the building down because of the asbestos, so it sits here empty, except for the drums of old grease and fat and God knows what else they left behind. We found one whole storeroom full of bones, boiled clean, but smelly."

Something squeaked and scurried amongst the litter. The flashlight swung in that direction, freezing tiny pairs of eyes in its beam. Their own footsteps halted, and the silence stretched.

"Just rats," the brunette said finally. "For a moment I thought we might get a glimpse of something more interesting."

They pushed forward.

"Don't let her scare you, dear," Raggedy Ann murmured. "Rumor has it that the company used to buy more than just bones and grease for rendering, that they actually slaughtered animals here. Workers claim the ghosts of dead horses haunt this building, but I don't believe in ghosts. Do you believe in ghosts, Trisha?"

What nonsense. Of course, she didn't believe in ghosts.

The redhead twisted the scarf. Patricia choked and stumbled.

"You must learn to answer quickly, dear." She eased the pressure. "Don't worry, though, we aren't going to kill you. We only want you to sign some documents. Then you'll be free."

"What documents?" Patricia squeaked the words out. It had never occurred to her that these lunatics might intend to kill her. She didn't want to die.

"Papers to put right the wrong you've done. You do believe in atoning for your sins, don't you, dear?"

The syrupy voice, so self-assured and mocking, made Patricia want to slap the redhead until her ears rang. Impossible now, but if they just let her go for one moment—

"Trisha, you do believe in atonement, don't you?"

"What sins?"

The scarf twisted tighter. Patricia gasped.

"The answer, Trisha, is YES or NO. Do you believe in atonement?"

"Yes, but—" The words were so distorted by her burning

throat they were barely recognizable. Then the scarf loosened, and she sucked a raw breath.

"I knew your answer would be yes, dear."

The brunette, juggling the flashlight, turned a key in a padlock and opened a heavy door. The room beyond was totally dark. The stench pouring through the opening made Patricia gag. Raggedy Ann pushed her forward.

"NO." Patricia veered sideways, wedging herself in the doorway. "I won't go in there."

"You *won't?*" the redhead said, the word thick with sarcasm. "My friends and I think you *will*, Trisha. Between the three of us, we can easily force you to go in." She twisted the scarf brutally. "Did little Paulie ever say no, Trisha? Did he ever beg you not to lock him in the dark for hours?"

Please Mommy don't make me please Mommy please. Paulie's whine grated in her memory. But kids had to learn their lessons.

"Maybe she'd rather sign the papers out here," Betty Boop screeched, appearing out of nowhere. The flashlight illuminated her plastic face, carving her eyes into hollow sockets.

"Would you like that, Trisha, dear? Would you like to sign the papers out here?"

"Let me see them," Patricia rasped, stalling. She had no intention of signing anything for these loons.

Raggedy Ann released the knot binding her hands, and the brunette shoved three pages at her, all very legal and important-looking. The first page was a letter to Steve's parents.

> YOU CAN KEEP PAULIE. NOW THAT I'VE WON THE
> BATTLE, I'M LEAVING TOWN. YOU WON'T SEE OR
> HEAR FROM ME AGAIN. PATRICIA

The second was a letter to her lawyer.

> FOR REASONS I'D RATHER NOT DISCLOSE, I MUST
> LEAVE TOWN IMMEDIATELY AND SHALL NOT
> RETURN. I HAVE ATTACHED A POWER OF ATTORNEY

AUTHORIZING YOU TO SELL MY HOUSE, FURNISH-
INGS, AND CAR, AND ASSIGN THE PROCEEDS TO MY
PERSONAL BANK ACCOUNT. PATRICIA CARRERA

The third page was a power of attorney, ready for Patricia's signature.

Already notarized.

"I'm not signing any of these." She thrust them away from her. The nerve of them, thinking they could force her to give up Paulie and leave town.

Betty Boop laughed. "Oh, yes you will, sweetie. You'll sign them." A loud, raucous cackle. "The only question is when? *When?*"

Before Patricia could brace herself again, the redhead shoved her into the darkness. Here the floors were wet and slick. Patricia fell against a wall slimy with dampness. The stink choked her. She retched as bile rose in her throat. Clutching her stomach, she vomited.

"Sonofabitch!" the brunette said in her deep whisper. "I think she got that mess on my shoes."

Patricia's hands were caught behind her and taped while she continued to retch helplessly.

"Here, snap this on," the redhead said.

The scarf was whipped from around Patricia's neck, and a wide strap that felt like leather took its place. Patricia heard the clink of chain as the strap tightened, snug but not choking.

And then she was alone in the room, dry heaving now, with nothing left in her stomach to throw up. She spit, trying to clear the foul taste from her mouth.

"You can't leave me in here!"

She charged toward the open door but was stopped short. Her head yanked back brutally. The collar around her neck was chained to the wall.

"Whew!" Betty Boop stood in the doorway. "Sweetie, I don't know what died in that room before we got here, but your tossing your cookies didn't help. Didn't help at all."

"Let me *out* of here! You can't chain me here like an animal!"

"All you have to do," the brunette whispered, "is sign those papers, and we'll have you on first-class passage to anywhere you want to go outside the state."

"NO!" The word erupted like an explosion. They could not do this to her. She was not a child. "NO! NO! NO!"

"YES! YES! YES!" the echoing voices mocked her.

It was not the mockery, though, but the note of insanity in the voices that raised the hair on the back of Patricia's neck.

"We'll be back, dear," Raggedy Ann crooned. "After you have ample time to consider our offer. While you're thinking, Trisha, think about Paulie spending all those hours alone in the dark, locked in that horrible little cabinet."

The door clicked shut. Patricia heard the rattle of the hasp, the snap of the padlock.

She trembled as their footsteps faded into the distance.

"Please Mommy please," she said quietly.

Chapter Twenty-four

Wednesday, February 12

On the drive to the Richards, Blackmon & Drake office next morning, Sarina attempted to explain her reason for terrorizing her mother, but Dixie refused to listen. She wanted to hear the story for the first time with Belle in the room. Otherwise, she might strangle the kid. Maybe between Dixie and Belle, they could sort out truth from fiction.

"This better be important," Belle said when they arrived. "There's a judge who'll want to gavel my head if I'm late. I have ten minutes."

"It's important." Dixie dropped the valentine, red pen, and white paper bag on the desk pad, then slid a hip onto a corner of the mahogany desk. "Sit down," she told Sarina. "And talk."

The teenager perched on the edge of Belle's white leather guest chair, looking as miserable as a wet cat.

"I can't see why everyone's making such a big deal out of this—"

"Out of what?" Belle said, but Dixie motioned her to let the kid talk.

"Okay, I'm right in the middle of a kick-ass project, a ten-minute Frankenstein spoof—I'm not expecting an Oscar for it, but, hey—nine zillion hours and we're down to the last hundred frames before edit. Only Mother gets weirded by this anonymous fan and drags me to Houston."

She sprang from the chair.

" 'I *can't leave,*' I tell her. Does she listen? Does my mother ever listen? Her head is soundproof. To top it, I can't even tell her *why* I can't go. She goes bonkers when I mention a career in f/x. Arguing with her is like trying to blow out a lightbulb. So I'm stuck."

Crossing her arms tight across her chest, Sarina strode behind the chair and paced.

"Make the best of it, I decide. I swing a meeting with Alroy Duncan, only to make it work I need my mother distracted. We're at the airport, I see the valentines and remember she gets distracted every time one of those cards shows up."

She turned to Belle and dramatically threw her arms wide.

"Only the whole thing backfired. You hired Sherlock here, and now you're going to tell Mother what a jerk I am. When Dad hears about it, even *he* won't back me up on taking an apprenticeship."

During Sarina's explanation, Belle had dropped quietly into her chair. "You mean this whole stalker thing was a . . . a . . . *hoax,* so you could sneak around town—"

"I wasn't sneaking around, I was—"

"Sit down," Dixie said. "And go back to the beginning. Tell us about the cards you sent while you and Joanna were still in L.A."

"What cards?"

"The cards that frightened your mother enough to stop dating," Belle said. "Frightened her enough to want you watched every minute you weren't in school."

"I don't know any more about that than you do."

"You didn't send them?" Dixie persisted.

"No. I . . . NO! I'm not the creep who's coming on to her. I just picked up on his idea and used it."

Belle glanced at her watch and punched a button on the desk phone.

"Ms. Grimm, page Blackmon at the courthouse, will you? Tell him to take over. I'll be there as soon as I get free." She looked at Sarina. "Stalking is a felony offense, which means you could have more crap coming down on your head than either of your parents can shovel off. If you're telling the truth about not sending the cards in L.A., then *maybe* I can keep this from turning into a worse mess than it already is. Sarina, give me a reason to believe you."

Head down, the girl tapped rapidly at the sides of her jeans, thinking about it.

"I can't prove I didn't send the other cards. But I didn't."

Belle heaved an exasperated sigh and buzzed the receptionist again.

"Ms. Grimm, would you bring two cups of coffee and—" She looked the question at Sarina. "Juice? Coffee?"

"Just water."

Belle relayed the order, then released the intercom.

"Sarina, you know where our law library is located." She pointed to a door. "I'd like you to sit in there for a few minutes while Dixie and I talk."

The girl slouched out of the office.

"I hope there's no back door to that room," Dixie said.

"There is, but I keep it locked." When the receptionist arrived with the drinks, Belle sent her into the library with Sarina's water, then opened a drawer and extracted a packet of sweetener. "What made you suspicious of her?"

"Mostly a hunch." And peanut butter.

"You think she's telling the truth about not sending the L.A. cards?"

"I don't know. I want to believe her. But she grew up in a world where the line between reality and make-believe is damned hard to see."

"If she's telling the truth, then we still have a stalker out there."

"No reason to think the stalker's in Houston."

"And no guarantee he isn't."

Dixie wouldn't argue, since the odds could go either way. "What did you find out about Alan Kemp?"

Belle retrieved a fax from her in-box and read from it. "Alan and Joanna are distant blood cousins. Their great-great-grandmothers were sisters, and the family evidently stayed pretty tight. Most of them live right in East Texas. Alan and Joanna went to the same schools and both were active in drama. After college, they drifted apart. Kemp's syndicated radio show has a substantial audience."

"Were you able to find out how recently he left Brussels?"

"We're still digging. I'll have more information later today."

Belle sipped her coffee, magically preserving her lipstick. Dixie was always amazed at women who could eat, drink, and smoke without so much as a smudge.

"So where do we go from here?" Dixie asked.

Belle looked thoughtful. Instead of answering, she said, "What did Sarina mean about an apprenticeship?"

Dixie explained their visit to Stoned Toad Productions. She tried to tell it objectively.

"You sound like you approve of what she did," Belle said.

"Of course I don't *approve*. But I'll admit I admire the kid's spunk. If she hadn't pulled the valentine stunt, the deal with Alroy Duncan might've gone without a hitch."

"But she *did* pull the valentine stunt, and she must have known how upset Joanna's been these last two months. Somewhere deep inside, that girl wanted to hurt her mother."

"Maybe Joanna should be spending her money on a shrink instead of a bodyguard."

"Ouch! I'll let you tell her that." Belle set aside her coffee and rose decisively. "I want you to stay on the case, Flannigan. It can't do any harm. We're not a hundred percent certain the stalker's not in Houston."

Dixie couldn't argue, since Belle's philosophy mirrored her own.

"You're calling the shots, Ric." Only the job would feel a lot like training camp now, where there's no real danger, but you act as if there were.

"Speaking of caution, get the battery checked in that mobile phone and keep the damn thing with you. I want to be able to locate Sarina in a heartbeat—at all times."

"Done." Dixie showed her the phone attached to her belt. With Belle Richards, you could screw up once and get off with a warning. If you screwed up twice, you might as well fold your tent and move to South America.

"By the way—" Belle plucked a sheet of paper from her in-box. "You were right about the publisher of those first cards. Only a handful of stores carry the label, all in the San Diego and Los Angeles area, including a store in North Hollywood."

"Convenient. I hope somebody's talking to that store owner."

Belle nodded. "Discreetly."

"Right. So, what do we tell Joanna?"

"Nothing, for now. Trust me, Sarina was right about the way she'd take it. I've seen Joanna go ballistic with much less provocation than this."

"Weird out, Sarina would say."

"That's a fairly apt description." Belle opened a narrow closet and slipped her suit jacket off a hanger.

The image of a woman weirding out reminded Dixie of something that had haunted her since the evening news.

"Ric, did you hear about the Carrera case?"

"What about it?"

"Brenda worked on that for a while. I'm wondering how she's taking it."

"It was never much of a case, Flannigan. The DA's staff couldn't put together enough hard evidence against the mother. They had to drop it. And the civil case wasn't Brenda's concern."

"Have you ever known Brenda *not* to be concerned when a case she cares about goes south?"

"What are you getting at?"

"I don't know . . ." The hell of it was, she *didn't* know what she was getting at, only that she had a hunch Brenda was stressed to the max lately. Dixie had learned long ago to heed her hunches.

"Keep your nose glued to the right case, Flannigan. The Carrera woman's disappearance—"

"*Disappearance?*"

"What have we been talking about?"

"You tell me. I was talking about Patricia Carrera winning custody of her son, and worrying how another failure might affect Brenda."

"Then you missed the latest." Belle shrugged into her designer jacket. "Carrera was scheduled to pick up the boy from his grandparents last night, but she never showed. No one has seen her since she drove away from her house a winner."

Dixie flashed on another winner, Lawrence Riley Coombs, found raped and beaten in Memorial Park hours after he threatened Brenda Benson. Memories of her final weeks as ADA, and her own frequent bouts with rage and confusion, blipped through Dixie's mind like strobe lights. Every time a smug felon walked away free, Dixie saw the blind lady of justice corroding a bit.

She prayed she was wrong about ADA Brenda Benson, but her hunch indicator was shooting off the scale.

Chapter Twenty-five

Lawrence Coombs adjusted the seat in his Jaguar so he could watch the red Porsche Targa sitting across the parking garage from him. He sipped a cup of hot coffee. His mouth was no longer tender but ugly and misshapen from the stitches. Every time he looked in a mirror, he thought about the bitch who ruined his face and what he was going to do once the trial was behind him. The bounty hunter must have been pissing scared to bring her ADA friend and come after him. He appreciated their nerve, but Dixie Flannigan and friend were going to wish they'd never been born.

The anticipation filled him with energy, made his whole body hum like locusts in a balmy twilight. When the humming reached its extreme ecstasy, he would know what to do. Didn't want to rush it.

Now look at the bonus he'd won with his patience. Pretty Sarina Page, daughter of the hot-shit actress.

Traffic sounds filtered through his closed window. The morning had turned crisp. He'd wanted to linger in bed, but the bounty hunter's day started before sunup, so now his did, too. This time, he'd orchestrate the moment perfectly. Plan his moves. Take Dixie and her sweet sidekick to some quiet location, where there'd be no interruptions from nosey, loud-mouthed reporters. No cops. Just the three of them and all the time in the world to enjoy one another's company.

Lawrence watched the two women now, exiting the sky-walk from the Transco office building, talking as they walked. He envisioned their smiling faces tight with pain.

As they climbed into the Porsche, Lawrence started the Jaguar's engine, his body humming exquisitely.

Chapter Twenty-six

"I missed breakfast," Sarina grumbled, leaning against the red brick beside Brenda's front door as Dixie rang the bell.

"So did I. We'll only be here a few minutes. Then we'll eat."

She'd decided to ask Brenda outright if she knew anything about Carrera's disappearance. Lots of parents who battered their children were getting help one way or another, trying to work out their problems. Maybe Carrera, in a sudden flash of conscience, had decided her son was better off with his grandparents, and decided to simply get in her car and keep driving. No reason to think Carrera's disappearance was in any way connected with the attack on Coombs. But Dixie knew she'd never shake that haunting feeling until she heard Brenda's take on it.

It was Gail—a younger, taller, darker version of her sister—who answered the door. The separation of nearly a decade showed most in the sisters' personalities. Brenda was work-driven, determined to make a difference. Gail's interests were more political, fast-lane, high-rolling. She dated a young Texas senator who had aspirations for the governorship.

"Well, hey, Dixie!" Gail had her sister's whiskey voice. "Brenda's already gone. Was she expecting you?" Her gaze flitted from Dixie to Sarina.

"Actually, it was you I wanted to talk to." Not true, but not a bad idea. "You have a minute?"

"Sure, a minute, if you don't mind talking while I dress. We're putting together mailers today for the primaries."

She opened the door wide, and Dixie introduced Sarina as they entered the modest but attractive home.

"Smells like banana bread in here," Sarina commented, a hopeful note in her voice.

"Fresh from the bakery. Would you like some? I made hot chocolate to go with it."

Sarina glanced at Dixie, then at the portable television above the breakfast bar. "If it's no trouble."

With Sarina happily engaged in her two favorite activities, eating and channel surfing, Gail led Dixie through the family room, filled with enough potted plants to start a nursery, to her bedroom, all chintz, ruffles, and girlie gizmos. The only unplanned clutter was a tray of makeup on the dresser and the closet door hanging open. After pulling out a green slacks suit and a white blouse, Gail shut the closet door.

"What's up? I've lived with Brenda two years and you've been here maybe ten times, never at eight-thirty in the morning."

"I'm worried about her. She's lost some important cases lately, and I think she's taking it hard."

"Brenda doesn't like losing any better than I do." Gail slid the green pants on under her robe.

"Has she said anything to you about quitting?"

"Leaving the DA's staff? No way."

Maybe Brenda didn't confide in her little sister. "Has she seemed distracted lately? Upset about anything?"

Gail turned her back, tossed off her robe, and slipped into a bra, snapping it in front. "Brenda's always distracted. Always buried in a case."

Was Gail being evasive, or had she really not noticed anything unusual? "Did she talk to you about the Lawrence Coombs case?"

"That sicko was all she talked about for weeks." Gail eased the white silk blouse over her shoulders and turned around to button it, smiling. "After what the Avenging Angels did to him later, Bren didn't seem as upset about losing. Maybe the court should take a lesson — let the victim decide the punishment, put a real quick stop to crime."

Victim? "What makes you think it was Regan Salles?"

"Regan wasn't the only woman he messed up." She scooped the makeup tray off the dresser and headed for the bathroom.

Dixie followed, pausing to inch open the door to Brenda's bedroom as they passed it. Clothes littered the chairs, but the bed was made.

She watched from the hallway as Gail applied black mascara to her blond lashes.

"Actually, I'm surprised Brenda's gone already." The prosecutor was usually a late sleeper.

Gail leaned close to the mirror, separating the thickly coated lashes with a straight pin. "I didn't even see her this morning. She was gone before I got up."

Interesting.

"Did she mention the Carrera case? You remember the boy, Paulie, his mother liked to lock him up, punish him?"

"I remember. Brenda had to drop that case." She blinked at the mirror, then added another layer of mascara. "Why do you ask?"

Dixie wondered if her lashes felt heavy with all that goop on them. "The grandparents filed a civil suit. Looks like Carrera beat that one, too. Only she never picked her son up from his grandparents, and now Carrera's disappeared."

Driving over, Dixie had bought a newspaper and had read

the brief article at stoplights. As ordered by the judge, Paulie Carrera's grandparents had readied the boy and his belongings to be transported home. When Patricia didn't show by nine o'clock, and didn't phone with an explanation, they called their lawyer, who alerted the police. Checking Carrera's home, the police found nothing out of the ordinary. She hadn't been missing long enough to start a full-scale investigation.

Gail glanced at Dixie in the mirror. "Well, hey. Good damn riddance. As long as the kid's okay, Carrera can drop dead." She carefully outlined her lips with a bright red pencil, painting just outside the lip line, making them look full and sexy. Dixie watched, fascinated, as she filled in the pencil line with red lipstick, blotted it, powdered over it, then reapplied everything, adding a spot of lighter color in the center of the lower lip.

Deciding to come clean with what worried her, Dixie said, "Think Brenda might have anything to do with Carrera disappearing?"

"You mean like wrapping her in chains and throwing her off the Galveston bridge?" Gail picked up a wide-toothed comb and fluffed her hair, pulling a few casual wisps over her ears.

"When I was sixteen, I talked Mom into letting me have a cat. One weekend Brenda came home from college, and Mom had gone on one of her weekend getaways. I'd gone home with a friend from school, and we'd forgotten to leave the cat any food or fresh water. Brenda embarrassed me in front of my friend's parents, *dragged* me to the store, where she bought a whole case of cat food, then home, where she made me clean the bowl and fill it with that smelly fish paste. I had to pay Brenda back for the cat food by doing her laundry and washing her car every weekend she came home—at twenty-five cents an hour. The cat ran away a week later, but I was still paying Brenda back for months."

She dabbed a scented cream on her wrists. "If Brenda thought Carrera would hurt that kid . . . well . . . she might do whatever she thought necessary to stop it." She pushed the makeup into a drawer, tossed a towel into a hamper, and snapped off the bathroom light. "Hate to hurry you along, but I gotta get downtown."

On their way out the door, Dixie said, "After college, I lost track of Brenda, until four years ago, when she applied for a position as ADA. I know she was living out of state, and wasn't working in any legal capacity, but—"

"You didn't know she was married?" Gail frowned. "I'm not surprised—she won't even talk to me about it."

"How long was she married?"

"A few years, I suppose. Ask her."

Chapter Twenty-seven

Patricia Carrera stood alone in the dark, her bladder so full she feared it might burst, and listened to the scrabbles and squeaks draw closer. How long did her jailers plan to leave her here?

Suppose they decided not to return at all?

Trying to escape had gotten her nowhere, although she had finally freed her hands, wrenching and pulling until the tape stretched, thinned, and developed a tiny tear. She worked the tear until it separated. Then she struggled furiously with the chain holding her to the slimy wall, bracing her feet and yanking with all her strength. To no avail. Following the chain to its connection, she found a metal eyelet in the plaster and tried to pry the chain loose with her fingers. When that didn't work, she tried to break the lock that fastened the leather collar around her neck, digging her fingernails under the leather surrounding the lock.

Now her hands were torn and bloody, and she was exhausted. Yet nothing had changed. The chain still imprisoned her to the wall. She could not sit or lie down unless she was willing to have the collar choke the life out of her. Anyway, she'd rather die standing than sit on that filthy floor.

At first she'd heard the rustling and squeaking only around the walls, but after a while the mice—or rats?—had ventured nearer, until she felt one of them nip at her shoe. Darting away without thinking, she nearly snapped her neck. Now she remained as far from the walls as she could get, in this one spot for what seemed like forever, so tired she could barely stand up. Twice she'd nodded off, only to be jerked awake by the collar as she sagged against it.

She had to concentrate on keeping her muscles contracted so as not to lose the water from her bladder. No matter what else happened, she would *not* lose her water, would not squat like an animal, her own urine splashing up at her from the filthy concrete floor. That was too disgusting to think about.

Her jailers would have to return soon, demanding she sign their stupid papers. She would agree—but only if they let her out of this room first, gave her water to drink and the use of a bathroom to . . . wash up. Then she'd tell them to stuff it!

They couldn't force her to sign. What could they do, other than kill her? She'd never been afraid of dying, and she refused to believe she was going to die now.

They wouldn't leave her here indefinitely, would they?

She'd always gone back for Paulie.

Chapter Twenty-eight

"Belle said you were a lawyer," Sarina said quietly when they were back in the Porsche. She sat fiddling with a mechanical device of some sort.

"Yep." Dixie entered rush-hour traffic on Interstate 59, squeezing between a Ford van and a big-assed 1968 Cadillac that rattled like it was about to fall apart. If she remembered right, Brenda had a case on the docket later this morning. A midmorning break would be just right to pull her aside for a firm-but-friendly chat.

"All those years in law school," Sarina said, "and you just quit?" The gadget in her lap made a pounding sound, like a judge's gavel.

Dixie glanced at the kid. Sarina wasn't the first to ask that question. It wasn't easy to answer.

"I spent a lot of time learning a lot of other things, and I'm not putting those to good use, either. The law is still there. I still know how to use it. Right now I'm . . . a bit burned out." To put it mildly.

"Like Dad." She punched a button and the gadget elicited a groan. "He can't get the juicy parts anymore, so he grunges out, fishing, golfing."

Dixie cut in front of a truck, reminding herself smugly that she hadn't quit at the bottom of her career, but at the top. "A few years of grunging out can be useful in rearranging priorities."

"But you *could* still practice law, you said, right? Remember that boy who sued his parents for divorce—?"

"A kid can't divorce his parents."

"Okay, maybe it was a boy in a film, but suppose a kid wanted to make her parents send her to a certain college, instead of someplace lame, like Harvard?"

"Is this kid anyone we know?" Dixie slid the Targa over a lane, to pass a Greyhound bus. She hated riding behind diesel fumes. "Like you, perhaps?"

"Could I do that? You're a lawyer—"

"Criminal, not civil law, but never mind that. In Texas, Sarina, you'll be just as much an adult at seventeen as your parents. You can live on your own. You can go to any school that will have you, as long as you can pay the tuition. You can get a job, pay taxes, get married, drive a car, do anything any other adult can do."

"*Me* pay tuition? Aren't parents responsible for that?"

"Your parents' responsibility ends when you become an adult."

The thing in Sarina's lap boomed to life: "Objection, your honor!" The male voice, with exactly the right amount of sarcasm, sounded familiar.

Dixie slid a glance at Sarina. "What was that?"

"Sam Waterston. *Law and Order.*"

"You just happen to have a recording of *Law and Order*?"

"Only the best parts. I record sounds, then copy to my hard drive for manipulation, and save them to my Datman." She shoved the sound player into the deep pocket of her poncho and scooped up Dixie's morning newspaper.

Dixie took the Houston Avenue exit into town, glad to drop

the conversation. Her adoptive parents had spent plenty
sending her to law school, even with scholarships. The day
she brought home her license, framed in mahogany and
gold leaf, Barney's face had glowed with pride.

"This is incredible." Sarina's voice came from behind the
Amusements section. "*Star Voyager* starts tomorrow." She
folded the paper in quarters, the movie ads prominent.
"There's a special sneak preview today at six."

"I didn't notice movies on your mother's list of approved
sightseeing attractions."

Sarina poked her head up long enough to pull a face.
"Same director and effects team that worked on *Star Exile*.
Which, in case you don't remember, had only the best new
effects since *Close Encounters of the Third Kind*."

"I saw *Close Encounters*." Dixie had loved it, sitting on the
edge of her seat, shoveling popcorn, practically alone in the
theater, having caught a midday showing. She couldn't convince any of her friends to join her. But that was years ago.
"Never heard of *Star Exile*. Was it recent?"

"Last year."

"Must've been obscure. I catch all the SF movies."

"Not a movie, Dixie, a spectacular film experience.
There's a difference."

"Okay, but *Star Voyager* starts officially tomorrow, right?
That might be a better time to see it. At a matinee." Although
Dixie didn't believe Joanna's stalker had traveled to Houston, she didn't like the idea of taking the kid to a movie theater during peak attendance.

"*Tonight* is when it's happening. Tonight is like opening
your presents on Christmas morning, putting on your new
skates, and beating the other kids out to the street. Tonight is
when we see the film fresh, before critics spoil it." A hangdog
expression overtook the girl's features, then her excitement
burst through again. "They're using some of the primitive
slow-mo effects Ray Harryhausen designed for *Jason and the
Argonauts*, but with a new twist on the lighting."

Dixie secretly enjoyed all those old films, when she could catch the cable reruns.

As Sarina talked, her puppet materialized from her over-sized bag, and she began adding odd bits of metal and plastic to it with a small pliers and screwdriver.

"Effects aside, this is going to be the biggest independent film to hit the theaters until summer." Sarina looked anxiously at the dash clock.

"It's still morning," Dixie said. "Six o'clock is nearly nine hours away. Besides, we'll have a much better chance of getting good seats at a matinee."

"*Matinee?*" She made it sound like something to scrape off your shoe. "Dixie, we *have* to see it *tonight.*"

Since Belle was paying her to keep the kid entertained, while also keeping her safe, and since the kid wanted to see a movie, Dixie supposed she'd have to take her.

"*Maybe* we can make the preview. But no promises. First, I have to link up with a few people."

Sarina grinned as she fitted a tubular piece along the puppet's side. She swiveled the piece upright and pointed it like a rifle, miniature bayonet attached.

Several blocks from the courthouse, Dixie parked at a meter in front of a cinder-block building with one wall that had been covered with graffiti and painted over black so many times the concrete looked smooth as glass. The wall's location was much too tempting for the local tag artists. It faced a dead-end alleyway partially blocked by a Dumpster, a perfect canvas with just enough privacy.

Dixie dropped two quarters in the parking meter and ushered Sarina to a narrow stairway. No banister. Dixie eyed the steps and her snazzy new cane. If she pulled this off, she'd need a handful of painkillers afterward.

"Come on, crip." Sarina wrapped an arm around Dixie's waist, and before she could protest, she was being half tugged, half carried up the stairs.

On the building's second floor, an energetic decorator

had brightened a previously dark hallway by installing sky-lights and painting the walls a cheery daffodil yellow. The office doors all boasted shiny brass hardware. Dixie opened the one with a nameplate announcing RAMÓN ALVAREZ, GRAPHOLOGIST.

Ramón was possibly the best handwriting analyst Dixie had ever worked with on forgery and fraud cases, but he was an arrogant little prick. As an expert witness, he was useless. Since the information she needed now would never be used in court, Ramón was perfect. As the door swung inward, she heard his rapid treble voice raised in irritation.

"Charlie, Charlie, Charlie, Charlie, Charlie, what are you doing to me, man? I do the work, I get paid, blap! No waiting for you to collect squat. Your customer is your business. *You*, Charlie, are *my* customer. You get the bill, you pay the bill. Otherwise, I might have to ask my big, beefy cousin Palómo to come stand on your face." The receiver slammed into its cradle.

Dixie rapped the door as she pushed it wide.

Ramón's round brown head, much too big for his skinny neck, needed shaving again. A gold, diamond-chipped loop sparkled in his left ear. He wore a buttery leather jacket, with no shirt under it, tattered denim jeans sporting a western belt with an enormous silver buckle, brown socks, and no shoes. His Cordovan loafers were parked neatly beside the door. "Can't think with shoes on," he'd told her once.

"Ramón, who is this beefy cousin I've never met? Like the Wizard of Oz, all smoke and noise?"

"You do not want to meet Palómo, Dixie Flannigan. And for you, I can think of many ways to pay, so you never worry about Palómo." Ramón's double entendres were as full of smoke as his threats, but Dixie always paid up immediately to avoid misunderstandings. Ramón bounced to his feet from behind a stained and battered desk, salvaged no doubt from a yard sale. He didn't believe in incurring overhead costs. His office was the smallest in the building, with no window and scarcely room enough for himself and one client to sit down. Dixie waved Sarina to the only guest chair and placed the envelope of stalker notes on Ramón's desk.

"I need everything you can tell me about the person who wrote these."

He emptied the envelope. "Faxes? You expect me to work from faxes?" Then he spotted the valentines. Dixie had included them to keep him alert. "Have these been dusted?"

"They're okay. Don't worry about prints."

He opened the top card. "Red ink. Were they all in red ink? Says something if they were. Felt tip. That's not good."

"They were all written in red, but maybe not with the same pen." She glanced meaningfully at Sarina, who was all eyes and interest.

Ramón plucked a fax from the stack and turned it upside down, comparing it with an upside-down valentine.

"What're you pulling here, Dixie Flannigan? Two different people wrote these. See the downstrokes on this one?" He waved the faxed copy. "Hard. Angry. But this—" He dropped the fax and thumped the card with a flick of his stubby index finger. "Steady ink flow. Artistic. Probably traced. Forgery case?"

"Not exactly. When can you have something for me?"

"Not today. I have too much work today. Maybe tomorrow. But call first, *always* call first. Drop in like you did today, maybe I'm here, maybe not. Maybe I'm working in my jockey shorts. Call. We'll talk tomorrow." His phone rang. He shoved everything back in the envelope and shooed Dixie and Sarina out the door.

Back in the hallway, as soon as Dixie had closed the door behind them, Sarina skipped ahead and turned to walk backward.

"Ramón-the-bald looked at those notes two seconds— maybe three, max—and he knew they weren't the same. How did he do that so fast? Is that creepy?"

"Ramón can be creepy, all right. Plenty of practice." But the graphologist's abilities had amazed Dixie often enough.

She'd used him once on a drug case, to compare the handwriting of a boy who died a crack user. Before his death, the boy's handwriting had deteriorated, just as his brain and body had. Ramón pinpointed the week the kid started using. By questioning the boy's friends, Dixie had learned of a recent acquaintance, which resulted in the arrest of a new pusher in town. Too bad Ramón made such a bad impression on judges and juries.

At the courthouse, she found another rare parking place at a meter. A new cold front had blown in. Wind whipped around the buildings, tumbling leaves and candy wrappers along the sidewalks. As Dixie stepped out of the Porsche, the wind spit road dirt in her eyes.

They located the court where Brenda's case was being presented and found a pair of aisle seats. The defendant was a thirteen-year-old who'd brought his father's handgun to school to scare the bullies who beat him up every day for his lunch money. The gun scared them, all right, especially after it blew a hole in one boy's shoulder.

A young girl sat sloe-eyed and solemn in the witness box; Brenda spoke to her softly, using simple, direct questions and soothing hand motions. Brenda's hands, slender, with long coral nails, spoke as expressively as her words. Some of her opponents claimed she mesmerized juries with those hands, and Dixie didn't doubt it. Today, however, Brenda's manicure appeared ragged.

For twenty minutes, Dixie watched her friend skillfully question the reluctant witness. Then the judge granted defense counsel's request for a recess. Dixie caught up with Brenda at the prosecutor's table.

"How about coffee and a donut, Counselor? My treat."

"Donut?" Brenda flashed a smile. "Trying to fatten me up before self-defense class tomorrow?"

"Okay, a bran muffin. How about it?"

"Sorry. No time right now. How's that cushy job?" She glanced at Sarina, who had perched on the other end of the table and was digging in her bag. "Is Joanna Francis as beautiful in person as on the screen?"

"Beauty is as beauty does, as my sainted Irish adoptive mother used to say."

"Ah. Does that mean you managed to piss off the boss your very first day?"

"I've been my usual charming self." But Dixie couldn't keep the grin off her face. Her reputation for being difficult was founded on fact. "I'm afraid Ms. Francis doesn't appreciate my charm."

"Should I find that surprising?" Brenda tucked her papers into a tan leather briefcase. As she headed toward the door, Dixie fell in stride beside her.

"Not much I do would surprise you, Benson. We know each other too well, which brings me back to lunch, since you can't do coffee now. How about it?"

"Sorry, I have an important errand to run that will eat into my lunch hour. Maybe tomorrow."

Dixie wanted to talk now. She crooked a finger at Sarina to follow as she walked with Brenda out of the courtroom. The teenager fell in step a few paces behind them, but Dixie motioned her into protective range.

"Hear about Patricia Carrera disappearing?" Dixie murmured to Brenda.

"From nearly everybody I talked to today. Frankly, I hope the woman fell into a deep dark ravine where she can't hurt that child anymore."

"You and everybody who worked on the case, from what I understand." Down the hall ahead of them, Dixie saw Julie Colby and Grace Foxworth, the woman whose daughter was in a coma, thanks to Lawrence Coombs. As Dixie watched, Grace Foxworth opened a pack of cigarettes. Part of Julie's job was woodshedding the victims and witnesses—keeping them calm, preparing them for court. The process often created a bond that lingered even after the case was finished. Dixie wondered if smoke breaks had become a bonding time for people who still indulged. She didn't miss the worried look Julie tossed Brenda as they passed each other in the hall.

"What you said about Carrera falling into a ravine," Dixie said, "is that only wishful thinking? Or do you know something about it?"

Brenda rummaged through her shoulder bag, not looking at Dixie. When she finally plucked a wad of keys from the purse, her eyes remained averted. She snapped the latch shut and sorted out her car key.

"What are you getting at?" she asked.

The elevator stopped. People poured out.

Dixie lowered her voice. "I'm worried about you, Bren. Two nights ago, you were upset enough about Coombs' acquittal to consider trashing your career. I've known you a long time, and I think I can tell whether you're really riled or mildly pissed off. You were fuming."

They stepped into the elevator car. Sarina slouched into a corner, but Dixie could see her eyes following the conversation.

"The jury should have put that reptile away so long he wouldn't remember what a woman looked like, much less have enough lead in his pencil to rape one," Brenda whispered. Her hands tightened on her shoulder strap, stretching the skin over her knuckles.

"Hearing Coombs got a dose of what he likes to dish out, the Brenda I know would have called her friends together for a suds party. Instead, I can't seem to get your ear for three minutes. I find myself wondering why."

"I haven't been avoiding you. I've been busy." Brenda's expression was inscrutable, but her fist stayed clenched around the purse strap.

They exited the elevator, and then the building. Dixie kept a wary eye on Sarina as they strode along the breezy sidewalk toward a parking garage. The wind had turned colder. Dixie zipped her jacket.

"What errand is so important you schedule it during lunch? You hate rushing around the city at lunchtime."

"Since when did I start reporting to you, Dixie? If I remember right, you left the kitchen when you could no longer stand the heat. Some of us have to hang in there the best way we can."

They'd arrived at Brenda's Mazda. Oily black mud had splashed and dried on the rear fenders. The car was scarcely a year old, usually spotless. Dixie had driven Brenda to every auto dealer in town to find the perfect car, a car that "spoke to her." The white Miata, which Brenda affectionately christened Miles, must have whispered sweet nothings, because Brenda fell in love at first purr of the engine, and treated the auto better than some people treat their pets. Changed the oil every three thousand miles, hand-washed it twice a week, with bumper-to-bumper detailing monthly, and gave it a quick pass-over with a damp chamois anytime it got so much as a flyspeck.

"You must *really* be busy to neglect Miles," Dixie commented.

Brenda's knuckles were white as she turned the key in the door lock. One nail had broken off at the quick.

"Dixie, what if you *knew* who was involved in the Coombs assault? With your high-minded ideals, what would *you* do with that knowledge?"

Dixie wasn't sure how to answer. Coombs was the sort of monster who should be locked away, yet a jury had acquitted him. Legally, he was free to resume life as before, which for him meant preying on unsuspecting women. The only legal mechanism for dealing with that was to wait until he assaulted another woman, and pray the victim filed charges.

Everyone involved in the case knew Coombs was guilty, and Dixie couldn't deny the moment of jubilation she'd felt on hearing he'd been the victim instead of the victimizer for a change. But whoever assaulted Coombs was technically guilty of the same sort of crime Coombs himself had committed, assault and rape. Only God and State were allowed to mete out punishment. Did that mean monsters who could flummox the system should be exempt from punishment?

Not in Dixie's eyes. Such dilemmas had driven her from practicing law. If she knew for certain who Coombs' attackers were, would she turn them in?

"How about the Carrera disappearance?" she countered quietly. "Is the same someone involved in that?"

Brenda jerked the car door open.

Dixie studied the emotions playing over her friend's face as she tossed her briefcase and handbag to the passenger seat. Was that emotion guilt or fear? Maybe both.

"Bren, I'm not hypocritical enough to feel sorry about Coombs. But we both know that rough justice is not the answer to plugging all the holes in the legal system. There's good reason a jury is always made up of twelve individuals— and never the same twelve. Otherwise, personalities, one-upmanship, or the herd instinct to follow the strongest leader would begin to color their decisions. If you know the people responsible for the assault on Coombs—"

"I don't need a second conscience, Dixie. One is plenty." Brenda slid onto the contour seat and tried to yank the door shut. But Dixie grabbed it.

"Once a stone starts rolling downhill, it gathers speed. It gets harder and harder to stop. You can stop this one. Now."

"Dixie, butt out!" Brenda stabbed a key in the ignition.

Still holding the door against Brenda's effort to close it, Dixie leaned in. "If you were me, Bren, would you butt out?"

The attorney's face crumpled briefly, then she put the car in gear and began to pull away.

"When you're ready to talk, call me." Dixie stepped back so the car door could swing shut. "Otherwise, three o'clock tomorrow for defense class, right? We'll teach this one together."

Brenda nodded stiffly. The car screamed out of the parking garage. Dixie considered butting out, as Brenda had requested. She didn't like confronting her own attitudes about justice; so why should she pressure Brenda? If the prosecutor knew, or suspected, who the Avenging Angels were, and if she was handling the situation in as professional a manner as she could, Dixie's meddling wouldn't help any.

And what if Brenda herself was involved—could Dixie turn her in?

Years earlier, in a seedier part of the city, Brenda had saved Dixie from a crucial moment of bad judgment. The punk brother of a drug dealer Dixie was prosecuting beat a twelve-year-old witness to death. Dixie arrived to talk to the boy she planned to call as a witness and found him bleeding in a pile of dirt and broken crockery. He'd stumbled into a potted plant before falling from the balcony outside his family's apartment four flights up. From the beginning, he'd been frightened, but willing to testify because he wanted the drug dealers out of his neighborhood before his younger brothers were old enough to be enticed.

The boy hadn't lived long enough to name his assailant, but Dixie knew who'd killed him. Brenda had been surprised when Dixie didn't tell the responding officers who she suspected.

"No evidence," she'd told Brenda. "They'd never hold him on it." The truth was, Dixie wanted the satisfaction of personally pushing the punk's face in. So what if she lost her job and landed in jail for assault and battery?

Brenda kept reasoning with Dixie, rolling out every homily in the book: "You can't save the world. Stick to your job, let the cops do theirs. You have to trust the system." One old saw finally hit home: "If you wallow in their dirt, Dixie, you'll never feel clean again."

Was Brenda wallowing in dirt now? Or was she protecting someone else? Maybe Clarissa Thomas and her husband had decided to go after Coombs rather than be terrorized by him. Or maybe Regan had rounded up a few friends and decided to mete out the justice Coombs escaped in court. Either way, Dixie could've left it alone if it stopped with Coombs. But what if one taste of vengeance wasn't enough?

When did the dirt get too deep, too messy, to merely brush off? Dixie couldn't ignore her instinct that Brenda was in trouble.

And back at the courthouse, there was at least one other person who seemed worried about her: Julie Colby.

Chapter Twenty-nine

"Since your meeting was a washout, we have time to go to Alroy's studio. I think he did some of the effects on *Star Voyager*." Sarina's words came in a rush, as if heading off whatever Dixie planned to do next.

Dixie herded the girl back toward the courthouse.

"There's someone else I need to talk to."

A Metro bus wheezed to a stop at the corner, chuffing the air with diesel fumes.

"Okay, you've got things to do." Sarina stubbornly slowed her pace, allowing the WALK light to change. "Only let's not lose sight of who the paying customer is here."

"Belle Richards is the paying customer."

"And my mother pays Richards. Doesn't that give me some say in where we go?"

"Sarina, your mother doesn't even know yet that you visited Duncan's studio the first time. I notice you didn't volunteer that information—invented a trip to NASA, instead.

Did you have your cover story picked out before realizing you wouldn't be carting around town on your own?"

Sarina's expression turned sulky. "In L.A. I go wherever I want."

"I doubt it." Otherwise, she wouldn't need to visit an effects studio in Houston. "Did you have a bodyguard in L.A.?"

"At home I have school, and tennis instruction, and debate club, and foreign language tea parties, and every other distraction my mother can throw at me. Her agent either drives me or sends someone. I'm lucky I get ten minutes free time to brush my teeth."

Dixie's pager signaled a call from Ryan. Glad to end the argument with Sarina, she punched in her nephew's number on her cell phone. She was accustomed to handling Ryan's brand of persistence.

"Aunt Dix, you didn't get the cast off yet, did you? Everyone wants to see it."

"You mean laugh at it, don't you? Self-defense instructor breaks foot in skirmish?"

"I thought you broke it at that hotel downtown. That's what I told everybody. Where's Skirmish?"

"A skirmish is an insignificant battle."

"Mom said it was pretty significant. Said you gave the guy a new face."

Amy bragging about her sister's escapades? *Un*credible, as Sarina would say. "You know I'll only be assisting tomorrow. Ms. Benson is your instructor for another week or two."

"Sure, that's okay. She taught us some cool moves."

By the time Dixie assured him her cast would be available for inspection the next day, she and Sarina had reached the courthouse entrance. Julie Colby and Grace Foxworth stood outside, surrounded by puffs of pale smoke. As support staff, Julie was responsible for making sure witnesses showed up at court as scheduled, so a prosecutor's case could proceed smoothly. It was entirely possible that Julie had access to

Brenda's calendar and would know where the prosecutor was headed right now.

"I won't be long," Dixie told Sarina, stepping between the girl and a trio of briefcase-toting men who pushed past. "Then maybe we'll check out one of the cultural attractions on your mother's punch list."

"Yawn." Sarina hung back a pace as Dixie approached the two women.

Grace Foxworth blew smoke skyward as she flicked the ash off her cigarette and a regal appraisal over Sarina. Today she appeared almost radiant compared to the anxious woman Dixie had seen at the Coombs trial. Had her daughter's health taken an upward turn? She carried the same alligator bag, but with a striking spice-red pantsuit, silk animal-print scarf knotted around the collar, perfectly coordinated. Caterpillar turned butterfly.

Julie Colby had bundled her long, athletic body into a navy wool coat and a red and green silk muffler. Everything about the paralegal was long, from her chestnut hair to the thin cigarette between her slender fingers. Like Brenda, she'd been trying to quit smoking, but dealing with the victims of rape and abuse didn't make it easy. She looked down the street, in the direction Dixie and Sarina had appeared, before widening her gray eyes and making introductions. When her gaze locked on Sarina, she smiled. A dimple appeared above her square jaw.

"You must be Joanna Francis' daughter." She gently extinguished her partially smoked cigarette against a brick. "You're as beautiful as your famous mother."

"Thanks," Sarina muttered, staring down at her shoes. Not the kid's favorite compliment, Dixie figured. And not the first time she'd heard it, either.

Grace Foxworth checked her watch, then snuffed her own cigarette and handed the box of ultralight Capri to Julie.

"Sorry to interrupt," Dixie told her.

"No, no, I was leaving." She looked at her jewel-encrusted

watch again, a gold filigree band with an old-fashioned dial surrounded by tiny diamonds—or what looked like diamonds to Dixie's untrained eye. Gold earrings and a matching brooch were similarly encrusted. The simple gold cross encircling her throat seemed oddly out of place.

"I heard about your daughter's . . . incident," Dixie said. "I hope she's better."

The woman smiled, radiantly. "I believe she *is* better today. I do! The doctor says there's no change, but a mother *knows*." She opened the alligator handbag to take out her keys. "I have to run! Julie, thank you for . . . everything. Dixie, Sarina, lovely to meet you." She strode briskly away, toward a row of cars parked at meters.

"I'm afraid I need to move along, too," Julie said. "Was there something you needed from the office? I saw you walk out with Brenda."

"She drove away before I could find out where she's going for lunch."

Julie frowned. "Brenda told me this morning she needed to take a personal day if the trial finished early—we expected the recess, you know."

"She didn't mention where to reach her in case of an emergency?" Dixie took Sarina's arm and followed Julie into the building.

The witness coordinator shook her head. "I suggested Brenda take *several* days. She pushes herself too hard."

They reached the elevators. Julie punched the UP button as Dixie regarded Grace Foxworth beyond the glass entrance, climbing into a beige Ford sedan. According to Dixie's contact, Coombs had reported that at least two people assaulted him, and the only one who'd spoken was a woman. The Foxworths had been witnesses in Coombs' trial. Their daughter was in a coma, therefore unable to name her attacker, and only the fact that she'd been dating Coombs gave any reason to suspect him. Yet the couple had attended every day of his trial. Dixie made a mental note to talk to the Foxworths.

But her basic philosophy when seeking information was to "look for the loudest mouth." The loudest mouth in the Coombs case was Clarissa Thomas, the witness who'd found Regan Salles tied to a park bench. Clarissa's husband had been concerned enough about Coombs to buy a gun.

When the elevator doors opened, Julie looked anxiously at the stream of people pouring out. "I need to get upstairs, but . . . if there's anything else—?"

Dixie thought about riding up and wheedling a look at Brenda's calendar, but Sarina had positioned herself against a wall, busy with her puppet and too far away to corral easily.

"Can you get me some addresses?" Dixie asked Julie as she stepped into the elevator. "Clarissa Thomas, Regan Salles?"

Holding the doors open, Julie shook her head vaguely. "Clarissa's listed under her husband's name, Donald, but Regan had to move, and we got her an unpublished number to be safe from Lawrence Coombs. I know you used to work with Brenda, but . . . I really can't give out personal information."

Dixie expected as much. Brenda wouldn't value Julie's help the way she did if the woman were indiscreet. All right, then, she'd start with the loudest mouth.

Chapter Thirty

Patricia Carrera was thirsty. Her tongue was so dry it felt swollen, and her mouth tasted of vomit. She stood with her eyes closed, half asleep, not daring to fall fully asleep. Even if her short chain would allow it, she couldn't bear the thought of finding herself on the floor with the dirt and the slime and the crawly things.

A rat nipped at her shoe. She kicked it, connecting with a satisfying thud and hearing a squeal of pain. That should keep the filthy creatures away for a while.

She was cold. In the absolute dark, she had no idea whether it was day or night, but the temperature had dropped. Now she heard the wind whisk past the building, faintly, as if at a distance. Breathing the cold air made her chest want to close up, although her asthma had not been active in years. She could smell mold, the floor was probably thick with it. That would irritate her asthma as much as the cold air. No inhaler. She hadn't needed one in a very long time. Not like Paulie, who used one daily. But he'd outgrow it, just as she had.

It was the dust and heat that bothered Paulie. Sometimes that old cabinet could get plenty hot, and she would hear him wheezing, shut up in there without his inhaler. But he had to learn to deal with it, just as she had.

"Asthma, my foot," her mother would say when Patricia began to wheeze. "You're a whiner. Take yourself a deep breath, child. Stop all that coughing, and get that kitchen floor mopped before your daddy gets home, or I'll give you something to whine about." Meaning Patricia would get a strapping when Daddy wasn't around to stop it.

A deep breath was exactly what Patricia couldn't do. The fumes from the bucket and the exertion of pushing the mop made the wheezing and coughing worse. At night she would lie absolutely still and think about floating on a cloud. Sometimes the wheezing would stop. Other times, she coughed into her pillow until she thought her lungs would come right up through her throat, and she prayed for God to take her during the night.

But she outgrew the asthma, and so would Paulie. He just needed to toughen up.

Patricia shivered and tried not to think about the heaviness in her bladder. She held herself absolutely still. A cough now would surely release her urine.

She hated the mold, hated the *smell*, aware that minuscule spores were invading her nostrils with every breath. She imagined the blackish green fungus coating the insides of her nose, then creeping over the membranes of her sinuses, flourishing in the moist warmth of her lungs until mold filled them and grew back out of her nose and mouth, mottled her face and spread like a blackish green blanket over her body. By then, of course, she'd be long dead.

One of the rats crept closer. Hearing the soft *clickety-click* of toenails, she tensed. She wanted to kick it, but what if the effort caused her to cough? She'd wet herself. But she couldn't let the damn thing chew on her shoes.

Or maybe she could.

Maybe she could bait it, holding still until she felt the rat's teeth on the leather, then quickly lift her foot, bring it down SPLAT on the thing's head. Grind the flea-bitten monster into the dirt and hope the others got the message.

What if the rat bit right through to her skin? Or she succeeded in killing one of them and others crowded round to devour their dead brother? Patricia's stomach heaved at the thought.

She heard another click, louder this time, and not at her feet, but at the door. The turn of a key in the lock.

The real monsters had returned.

Sudden tears stung Patricia's nose, and a stream of warmth trickled down her inner thigh.

Chapter Thirty-one

"Your friend with the cool ride sounded like she didn't want any help. Does that mean we can do something fun now?" Sarina slouched sullenly alongside Dixie as they approached the Porsche.

"Movie at six. Anything else has to come from that list of cultural activities your mother provided. And I have one or two more people I need to talk to."

Dixie slid behind the wheel as Sarina slammed the passenger door. When they had eased away from the curb into downtown traffic, Dixie powered on her cell phone. Information listed two Donald Thomases. The first lived in a part of town where Clarissa's designer outfits would surely invite mugging. Dixie memorized the address for the other.

As soon as she snapped the cell phone off, Sarina said casually, "If you're off to see another friend now, you could drop me at the cineplex to catch an early show. I won't tell if you don't."

"Not a chance, kid."

"Since Mother's stalker is still in L.A., what could happen? You can earn your pay without me yammering in your ear, while I catch some new films. Is that not a terrific plan?"

"The plan is to find one or two cultural activities in this town that will interest even you."

Scowling, the girl brought the Datman out of her pocket, thumbed the controls, and produced a groan that sounded like something out of a grave in *Tales From the Crypt*. She replayed the hideous groan over and over until Dixie was ready to snatch the recorder and pitch it out the window. Instead, she clicked on the radio, tuned it to a country station, and defied the girl to touch it.

The Thomases resided in Hunter's Way, a middle-class neighborhood in Southwest Houston. The two-story house had a circular brick driveway, a broad porch with white columns, and double oak doors flanked by leaded glass and brass lanterns. Classy, even for the classy neighborhood.

The garage doors were closed. No car in the driveway. As the streets were quiet, with an open view, and the front door was only a few paces from the curb, Dixie allowed Sarina to stay in the car while she checked to see if anyone was home. When she knocked, a tinny voice, heavily accented, answered through a speaker.

"Yes, please. May I help you?"

"Is Clarissa Thomas in?"

"No, thank you."

"I'm not selling anything. How about Donald Thomas, is he in?"

"No. Thank you, please. Good-bye."

"Wait! Any idea when one of the Thomases will be home?"

"Mr. Thomas comes maybe at six."

"And Mrs. Thomas?"

"Shop until drop. You come this afternoon, please."

The speaker went firmly silent.

Irritated at the persistent dead ends, Dixie stepped away

from the porch and flipped open the cell phone to make a call she didn't want Sarina to hear. A familiar male voice answered.

"G.F., Incorporated."

"Cute, Brew. When did the Gypsy Filchers incorporate?" A small group of young people, most homeless for one reason or another, and formerly in trouble for one reason or another, had banded together to act like Robin Hood and his Merry Men, robbing from wealthy Houston merchants and giving to charities that rarely made the list of United Way recipients. Whenever a loaded grocery truck disappeared during a driver's coffee break, the groceries might end up on the shelves of a halfway house. The truck would be found later, parked at a supermarket, a string of Gypsy beads dangling from the rearview mirror.

Dixie carefully remained ignorant of any details, but believed the kids might otherwise be selling sex or drugs on street corners and committing far worse crimes. The DA's office was aware the gang existed, would probably round them up if there were ever enough evidence, but the Gypsy Filchers were not a priority.

The kids also raised money in more legitimate ways—roadside car washes, puppet shows in malls, vending sales at the festivals that popped up every spring and fall. Dixie tossed a few bucks their way when she needed information from the street or from a computer. Brew, one of the management trio, had lost the use of his legs as a kid, in a playground accident. He lived much of his life through computers, and had access to enough data about the daily crimes that went down to put plenty of small-time crooks behind bars. Right now, what Dixie needed was fairly simple.

"Can you find out which hospital has a Foxworth listed in long-term care?"

"Foxworth, Foxworth—that's the chick was assaulted in a local art gallery a few months back."

Dixie hadn't heard where the assault took place, but Brew read every major on-line newspaper in the country.

"Including her room number, if you can get it. I also need the Foxworths' home address."

Brew said give him two minutes on the hospital, then, scarcely missing a beat, rattled off the address. It was only a few miles from the Thomas residence.

Sliding into the driver's seat again, Dixie noticed Fire Dweller now sported an extra pair of arms, complete with viselike pincers.

"Are you starving yet?" she asked Sarina.

"Boredom does not affect my appetite."

"Did you check out your mother's list?"

She grimaced. "There's a metal sculpture show at the Museum of Modern Art. I could handle that."

"Sounds good. We'll get lunch somewhere near the museum. First I have another stop or two to make."

Dixie had just parked in front of the Foxworth house when the call came from Brew. The hospital was Memorial Southwest. Not far at all.

"One more thing," Dixie said as he was about to ring off. "Find out if anyone saw or heard anything in Memorial Park around the time Lawrence Coombs was attacked."

"Memorial Park? You're talking about one big stretch of pine trees."

"He was found about fifty yards from the Crestwood entrance."

"Right, like that helps." He disconnected.

The Foxworths' neighborhood was older than the Thomases', and the house smaller, hidden behind a tangle of shrubbery, but far from shabby. Dixie insisted Sarina go along this time.

The doorbell was answered by the sad shrunken man Dixie had last seen in the courtroom. He blinked at her from behind silver-rimmed eyeglasses. Pouches of loose skin beneath his eyes gave him the gentle, melancholy expression of a basset hound. A clock chimed inside the house.

"Didn't expect guests," he said. "Expected my wife for lunch, but not guests. Did she tell me you were coming?"

"We only met briefly." Dixie introduced herself and Sarina. "I had a few questions—"

"Well, then, Lowell Foxworth here. Come in, come in." He waved them inside. "Always glad to have luncheon guests. Always plenty. Like to cook, you see. Leftovers from last night. Didn't know we were having guests, or I'd have made fresh."

"We didn't come for lunch—"

"Nonsense, come in, have a seat. No, no, no—" He'd started to lead them toward a living room, or maybe the dining room Dixie could see just beyond it. "Let's eat in the den. Cozier there. You'll be more comfortable—especially you, young lady. What was your name again?"

"Sarina."

"Beautiful name. Sarina."

He led them into a room that would've been spacious if a baby grand piano weren't occupying half of it. A vase of deep red roses, beads of baby's breath woven among them, sat on a crocheted scarf draped over the gleaming lacquered finish. The tantalizing aroma of roasted meat drifted from the kitchen.

"Here we are. Sit yourself right here while I bring in the tea. You do like iced tea, don't you, child? Or would you prefer Pepsi? I like Pepsi-Cola myself from time to time. My daughter and I drink it. Grace prefers tea, but I don't mind a Pepsi-Cola now and again."

"Pepsi's great."

"I thought as much. Sit down now, sit down." He rolled one of the chairs out for Dixie. "You have a beautiful daughter. Take care of her. She's precious."

Mumbling, repeating the word "precious," Foxworth shuffled into the kitchen. He wasn't an old man, probably not yet sixty, but he had doddering mannerisms that Dixie hadn't seen in his wife at all.

Near the table, a wall of custom-built bookshelves held more volumes than it was ever intended to hold, books stacked in front of books, laced with religious ornaments and a gallery of framed photographs. In one picture, Lowell and

Grace Foxworth, a decade younger, perched together on the
sofa Dixie had glimpsed in the living room. A girl of about
fifteen with a halo of light brown curls sat between them.
Dozens of other photographs showed the young woman
growing up. Beverly Foxworth didn't favor her dark, regal
mother at all, or her sad-eyed father. But there were no baby
pictures. Adopted? In the most recent photo, Beverly wore
the gold cross Dixie had seen earlier today around Grace
Foxworth's neck. Or a damn good replica.

The mantel clock, carved distinctively in an art deco leaf
design, chimed again. This time the Westminster melody
lasted twice as long, signaling the half hour.

"Are you here about Beverly, then?" the man called from
the kitchen.

Not exactly. She was here to find out if Grace or Lowell
Foxworth had taken their grief to Memorial Park, along with
a big club, and beat hell out of the man who stole their
daughter's youth . . . health . . . innocence. "Your wife said
Beverly is improving."

He returned, carrying tall glasses of dark amber liquid. He
placed the nonbubbly in front of Dixie. A slice of lemon was
hooked over the tea glass.

"There's sugar," he said, "right behind you on the bookshelf. Fructose, only thing Beverly lets us use, not the blue
stuff, or the pink, says it's all bad anyway so just go easy and
enjoy. Fructose. You'll like it okay." He rested his melancholy gaze on Sarina. "Beverly is not improving, no matter
what Grace told you. The doctors tell us maybe she will im-
prove when she wakes up, perhaps not. Perhaps she will not
wake up at all. Grace hears what she wants to hear."

Sarina's eyes widened over the top of her glass.

"Your daughter's in a coma?" she blurted.

He nodded and picked up the recent photograph.

"This is my Beverly. Precious girl. You'd like her. Everybody
likes Beverly. You must hear her play the piano sometime.
Better than Grace, even." He handed the picture to Sarina,
then shuffled back to the kitchen.

Dixie felt like an imposter, sitting here at the man's table, trying to gather information that might incriminate him or his wife. She didn't have to *use* the information, she told herself. And maybe there was no connection between the violent assault on Coombs and the disappearance of Patricia Carrera. Maybe this time her niggling suspicions were all wrong.

Anyway, Dixie couldn't imagine this man as part of a reprisal party. He was too gentle to have done what was reportedly done to Lawrence Coombs, no matter how much rage and frustration festered inside him. She wasn't nearly as certain about his wife. Grace Foxworth was a formidable woman, intense even in her photographs.

"Beverly looks so . . . *healthy*," Sarina whispered.

"Very healthy," Lowell called from the kitchen.

Sarina looked stricken. The man had better hearing than she'd expected.

"A healthy girl, my Beverly. Going to be a physician, maybe, not like those doctors with needles and pills—a natural doctor, herbs, minerals, always good fresh vegetables, good meat. Except sometimes we drink Pepsi-Cola together."

He returned with a tray bearing three steaming dishes. Dixie stood to help, but he waved her back.

"Sit. You are guests. We don't have guests so often anymore."

The food smelled wonderful. Beef tips stir-fried with a colorful array of peppers, squash, and beans. The clock chimed, extending the Westminster melody by another few bars.

"Aren't we going to wait for your wife?" Dixie asked.

"Grace?" He waved the idea away. "She knows, lunch at eleven forty-five. If she wants to eat, she's here. If not—" He shrugged. "Grace lives at the hospital. And the churches. I will take supper to her later. I go mornings, nights. Between, I have to work. Hospitals are not free."

"What kind of work do you do?" Dixie sampled the beef. Excellent. The vegetables were al dente, the way Parker cooked them.

"Jeweler. Thirty-seven years."

Dixie noticed he wore a gold filigree wedding band on his left hand and a broad, flat initial ring on his right, a single sapphire embedded in one corner. She recalled Grace Foxworth's diamond-encrusted pin and earrings. Not a symbol of ostentatious wealth, then, but of craftsmanship.

He'd paused at his own meal to watch Sarina. "You have a boyfriend?" he asked quietly.

"Me?" Sarina chewed and swallowed. "No. Too busy."

"Good. Take your time. Date a boy your own age. I tell Beverly the same, but—" He waved a hand, dismissing his daughter's response.

Lawrence Coombs would be ten years older than the Beverly shown in the latest photograph. Dixie's conscience twitched at the thought of asking questions that would only bring this man more grief, but dammit, they had to be asked.

"I noticed you and your wife at Coombs' trial. It must have been a blow, seeing him acquitted."

Lowell put down his fork.

"That man! He was in this house, sat at this very table. Such a gentleman, bringing flowers, candy, wine. I tell Grace, this man is not right for our Beverly, but Grace, I think Grace was a little bit in love with him herself. She said, let the girl enjoy." Lowell's voice cracked. He picked up his Pepsi glass and sipped—with a shaking hand, Dixie noticed. "Now, this thing he did. Took my daughter first, then my wife. Grace is not the kindly woman she was before. And me . . ." He sipped again, set the glass down, and stared into his plate. "I never knew I could hate so much."

The mantel clock chimed, this time a full minute, playing the Westminster carillon followed by twelve bongs.

Chapter Thirty-two

Patricia shielded her eyes from a blinding light.

"*Surprise*, Trisha. Surprise, surprise." Betty Boop's screechy voice.

Two shapes moved into the room. Patricia's relief was like waking from a nightmare to discover it's not a dream. They pushed close, until their warm breath brushed her cheek.

"Did you think we weren't coming back for you?" Betty Boop demanded.

"No —" Patricia's throat was so dry she could barely speak. She swallowed. "No, I knew you'd come back. You said you would." As she'd always—always—gone back for Paulie.

"Are you ready to sign those papers?" The brunette's coarse whisper.

"I . . . I want some water," Patricia said firmly. "And I want to go to the ladies' room." She had to hold strong with her plan, no matter how much they frightened her. She would get what she wanted, then she'd refuse to sign their silly papers. Where was the redhead? she wondered.

"From the smell of you, sweetie," screeched the blonde, "you made your own ladies' room right here on the spot. Whew, what a stench you've made, spewing at both ends. A stench!"

Patricia flushed with embarrassment, but she kept silent, wanting them to hurry and let her go.

The light that blinded her moved to illuminate something. She blinked. A clipboard and a pen.

"Sign the papers," the brunette said.

Betty Boop poked Patricia's ribs. "Or maybe you're beginning to like it here?"

No! She couldn't stand it if they left her alone again! But she'd fought Steve's parents to keep Paulie, and she'd won. The court said Paulie was hers. She wasn't going to sign those papers no matter what they threatened.

"I want some water," she said. "And a ladies' room."

In the doorway a match snapped and flared. By its light, Patricia saw Raggedy Ann's bright mop. Raggedy Ann was the one who frightened her most.

She held the match to the tip of a cigarette. A stream of smoke wafted into Patricia's face. Patricia coughed, and her bladder leaked a few drops.

"Sign the papers, Trisha," the redhead crooned, the yarn wig tangled around the vacant plastic face.

"Weatherman predicts a hard freeze tonight." Betty Boop giggled. "This room will get awfully uncomfortable. Awfully, awfully. Especially with you in those wet panties."

"I won't sign anything until you give me some water," Patricia insisted stubbornly. "And let me go to the bathroom." But she worried they might actually leave—

Then her face was full of smoke and she coughed, and couldn't seem to stop coughing. Urine gushed down her legs. Her coughing ended in a wheeze, and she felt the familiar, dangerous tightness in her chest that she had not felt since her last attack as a child.

"Jeez, she's a wheezer," said the blonde. "Guess we know where little Paulie inherited his asthma."

"It's the smoke . . . and the cold. I just need to warm up. Please—" Another spasm of coughing choked off her plea.

"Sign the papers." Raggedy Ann said it calmly. "Then we'll put you on a nice warm airplane."

"After you take a shower, dearie. Wouldn't want you grossing out the other passengers."

"Paulie's mine," Patricia gasped. "I won't sign him over to Steve's prissy parents."

Sudden pain—hair twisted brutally in a fist—brought tears to Patricia's eyes. She gasped, sucking in rancid air that started a fresh round of coughing. Pain lanced her scalp, and then she realized they'd bound her hands again.

"Does it hurt?" The redhead's mouth pressed close, her breath moist on Patricia's cheek as the hair twisted tighter. "Paulie said it hurt him a lot when you pulled his hair."

"I never—"

"Yes, Trisha. Yes, you did. But you were always careful not to leave a mark anyone would notice. Who would notice a little missing hair?"

She yanked. Patricia screamed as the strand tore free, sending a rip of agony all the way to her teeth.

"Hey. That's enough." The brunette's gruff voice. "She'll sign our papers now, won't you, Patricia?"

"*I won't let her* sign them," said the redhead. "Not until she feels the misery Paulie felt. How about the hot poker trick, Trisha? That's a good one."

She yanked Patricia's head back by the hair, but this time the pain was nothing compared to the threat of the cigarette near her face. A hand clamped under her chin, forcing her toward the heat.

"Let her go," the brunette whispered roughly. "Let her sign the papers."

The cigarette held steady. Patricia could feel it through her eyelid.

"Pull her eye open and tape it," said the redhead.

"No—"

Hands pried at her eyelid, but she shut it tight, tears sliding down her cheeks.

"Open it!" said the redhead.

Fingers pried the eyelid open. Tape plastered her lashes to her forehead.

The cigarette glowed hotly, a quarter inch from her eyeball. Smoke bit at her nostrils, choking her—but if she coughed, her own movement could bring the glowing tip against her eye.

Her tear ducts spilled over, blurring her vision. Mucus streamed down her lip. Her lungs ached from the effort of not coughing.

"Don't worry, Trisha," Raggedy Ann crooned. "I won't let the cigarette actually touch you. That would leave a mark, wouldn't it? But the heat alone will raise a blister on that eyeball, swell up big as an egg. And hurt! Remember what Paulie said? Said he thought he'd die, it hurt so bad."

The heat was a burning auger boring slowly through her brain. The struggle to breathe was like a hot poker turning in her chest.

Patricia tried to remember why she didn't want to sign their papers. Why shouldn't she give them Paulie? Why would she want to spend the rest of her life saddled with such a sniveling, whining brat? He'd never been anything but a burden, never learning the lessons she taught him. Why not sign their papers?

She never knew there could be such pain. "Aw—" She choked, trying to steady her wheezing lungs to push out the words. "Awright."

"*All right?*" Raggedy Ann demanded. "All right, *what*? Does 'all right' mean you want to sign the papers, Trisha?"

"She wants to sign. Let her go."

"I want to hear her say it. Trisha, the good Lord wants you to *beg* to sign those papers."

"I—" She tried to spit the words out, but another spasm of coughing racked her body, her lungs stretched to bursting, raw, as if they'd been sandpapered. She *could not* breathe. Blackness edged her vision.

"Back off!" snapped the brunette. "Let her sign the damn papers."

"Beg me, Trisha," the redhead crooned. "Tell me how much you want to sign. Tell me you'll be a good girl and get on that plane. *Beg*, Trisha. The way little Paulie begged you to stop hurting him."

Please Mommy please. Please. She'd only done what would make him strong! She tried to form words, but her wheezing lungs weren't drawing any air.

"P—please."

"She said *please*," Betty Boop cheered.

"Now, back off," said the brunette.

Then the cigarette was gone but not the pain. The cruel hands released her bonds and Patricia fell. And signed.

Afterward, the hands lifted her, washed, dressed, and transported her, pressed a plane ticket and boarding pass into her grasp. Patricia's eye swelled shut, but she could breathe again. For an instant she considered turning around and going home. But Raggedy Ann's breathy whisper propelled her forward, into the airport, onto a plane headed somewhere safe.

Chapter Thirty-three

Spotting the crowd queuing up for movie tickets, Dixie knew she'd made a mistake bringing Sarina here. Nearly half the people at the cineplex were dressed as space creatures.

"Outstanding! These costumes are all from the first movie, *Star Exile*."

"Outstanding" was not the word Dixie would've chosen, but the ones that came to mind were not meant for gentle ears. Joanna's stalker may or may not be in Houston, but this bizarre crowd would make a bodyguard's job nearly impossible.

"Look!" Sarina pointed to a white Cadillac limousine parked at the curb. "Only the director or producer would arrive in a stretch. Or maybe one of the stars."

Judging by the girl's tone, movie stars weren't nearly as important as production people. Dixie guided her into the ticket line. When she tried to pull away to talk to someone, Dixie held her wrist until they moved inside the lobby, where more bedlam awaited.

"That's the director." Sarina pointed to a man wearing a white tuxedo with rhinestone trim and white hand-tooled boots. Two women alongside him wore identical white cocktail dresses, white fur draping their shoulders, rhinestones sparkling at their ears and necks. "The twins were *killed* in *Star Exile*. In this film they come back as cyborgs."

Dixie raised a skeptical eyebrow.

"Half human, half robot." Sarina skipped forward to join the cluster of groupies eager to speak to the director, but Dixie grabbed her arm.

"A cyborg, is that what you've been building with your bits of plastic and metal?"

"Not quite. Different technologies."

Dixie tugged her toward the concession stand. "Let's buy some popcorn and find a seat before they're all taken."

The number of people milling around made her edgy. It was impossible to tell who they were. Or, in some cases, whether they were male or female.

At the counter, they squeezed between a six-armed serpent and a two-headed gorilla. Dixie ordered popcorn and drinks.

"Anything else?" she asked Sarina.

"Milk Duds. Look, there's Alroy!"

Sarina shot off across the room before Dixie could collar her. The boy behind the snack counter slapped a candy box beside the other items, and Dixie dropped some bills on the counter, keeping one eye on Sarina. Alroy Duncan had trimmed his light hair and beard for the occasion. Even from the distance, the effects guru's emerald eyes glowed with intensity. He waved one of the twins over to try on a metallic helmet and torso.

Balancing the cardboard snack tray, Dixie threaded her way among Duncan's growing audience as he explained how the cyborg costume was created.

"First we make a head mold, right? Then construct the helmet out of polyurethane, and vacuform the body and arms. The suit's only used in close-ups, so we stop it here at mid-thigh."

Fascinated, Dixie watched half the girl's face disappear behind mechanical eyepieces and knobby protuberances. Like a transformer toy, her right arm and hand converted to a laser blaster.

"How does she operate the laser?" Sarina asked. Puppy-dog enthusiasm gushed through every word.

"She doesn't. We take care of it off-camera." Duncan snapped on the cyborg's left arm, then picked up a remote control module, too small for his broad hand. He turned toward a piranha-faced space creature, a superbly realistic model about the size of a large dog. "Watch this. Ready?"

The twin raised her blaster. Duncan fingered the remote. *Zzzing!* A red beam shot out, striking the creature in the chest. The creature howled; flesh and blood burst from his wound.

A collective gasp issued from the crowd. *Zzzing!* More flesh tore loose. *Zzzing!* The creature screeched and groaned and writhed, and stopped dead.

For a moment, the crowd was silent. Then someone applauded, someone else chuckled, and the whole room broke into applause and cheers.

The first blast had sent Dixie's adrenaline into overload. It took only a second for her to realize there was no danger, but in that second she also recognized the position she'd be caught in had the gun been real and pointed at Sarina. With her hands full of sodas and popcorn, the only way to stop a bullet was to launch herself in front of the girl. She stashed the tray on empty counter space to free up her hands.

"That one was a puppet, see?" Duncan was saying. "But we do the same thing with body padding."

Dixie's heart pounded furiously. She scanned the crowd. If the stalker was here, he'd have been surprised and startled by the shooting, possibly even frightened, before he realized it was staged. Everywhere she looked, though, people were laughing, talking, immensely entertained. *No reason to think the stalker flew to Houston*, she reminded herself.

But your job is to assume he did.

"Hey, Hap! Tori! You missed it," Sarina called, darting off again.

Hap Eggert, the red-haired techie from Joanna's film crew who'd carried the shivering star a wrap, had entered the cineplex with the young woman from wardrobe, Tori Pond. Sarina met the pair mid-lobby and pointed toward the wounded space creature.

Watching the crowd, Dixie strolled toward them. No one seemed to pay undue attention to Sarina as she reenacted the scene for her friends, complete with shooting motions and sound effects.

Eggert's gangly, freckle-faced friendliness made Dixie think of county fairs, apple pie, and Opie on the old Andy Griffith TV show. Pond was almond-eyed, darkly pretty, and a few years older than Sarina. Before Dixie could reach them, the trio rejoined the cluster around Alroy Duncan.

"Actually, it's old technology," Duncan was saying as Dixie walked up. He grinned at his circle of fans. "Seen it a zillion times, right? But it still works."

"Smooth, though, the way you handled it." Sarina's eyes shone.

"Will you present that same outdated technique at Illusions?" Pond asked.

Apparently, the young wardrobe tech wasn't as taken with Duncan as Sarina was. Perhaps she viewed him as competition.

Duncan twinkled at her. "Along with some nifty computer imaging."

"Like the fight scene you simulated for *Devil's Walk?*" Pond challenged. She tossed a guarded look at Sarina. "By the time you finished 'simulating,' most of Joanna's clothes were ripped away—"

"The devil had sharp claws. Or maybe those clothes you

made weren't constructed for action scenes." Frowning, Duncan turned away to answer another question.

"What was that all about?" Dixie whispered to Sarina, urging her toward the theater doors.

"Duncan got his big break on *Devil's Walk* 'cause all the big effects houses were booked up. One of the effects went screwy, but it was no big deal."

Something tickled Dixie's cheek; she whipped around to find a graceful cat-woman sweeping down the aisle, fluffy striped tail swinging haughtily in her wake. Where did the people come up with these outfits?

Sarina grinned. "Dixie, this crowd is nothing, compared with what we'll see Friday."

"What do you mean? What's happening Friday?"

"Didn't you see the newspaper ad? This preview is the beginning of the Illusions Film Festival. Three whole days!"

"And you expect to go?"

"Every serious effects artist in the *country* will be there. Festivals are where you find out who's got the edge-cutting ideas and who's only working for the buck, afraid to take chances."

"Why do I get the feeling you've been planning this all along?" Dixie maneuvered her into the theater, to a back row. Taking the aisle seat for herself, the next one for Sarina, she tossed the kid's denim bag on the third seat, as if saving it for someone.

"I wanted you to see how terrific this is before you start weirding out. I bought my ticket as soon as Mom insisted I come with her to Houston. The festival is the greatest thing that could have happened."

"I thought your apprenticeship was the greatest."

"Okay, second greatest."

"We can't go. It's too dangerous."

"Dixie! Illusions is the *ultimate* film festival. It's the Lamborghini, the Taj Mahal, the Da Vinci of festivals. I can't *not* go."

"You're not hearing me, Sarina. It's too dangerous."

"You'll be with me," Sarina pleaded. "And we can get another bodyguard. We can get *two* more bodyguards, *three*."

"The entire Secret Service couldn't keep you from getting killed in a room packed with space creatures and laser blasters—not to mention your habit of dashing off to talk to everyone who grabs your interest."

"I swear I won't leave your side the whole three days."

"Sarina—"

"You can handcuff me to your arm."

A dull ache pulsed behind Dixie's eyes. She hated disappointing the kid, but there was no way she could take Sarina to a film festival. Having registered in advance, the kid had left a trail the stalker could easily follow. He might be biding his time for an optimum moment when hundreds of costume-clad festival attendants gave him perfect cover.

During a particularly loud and bloody battle on whatever-the-hell planet, Dixie's pager signaled a call from Belle Richards. She scanned the theater, saw nobody whose gaze wasn't riveted to the screen, and whispered to Sarina that she'd be right outside the door. Propping it partially open with her shoulder to catch the hallway light on her cell phone keypad, she punched in Belle's number.

"What's up, boss?" She leaned against the door, facing so she could keep one eye on Sarina and still pitch her voice away from the folks trying to view the movie.

"Dug up some ancient history about Alan Kemp. Don't know if it's worth anything, but you may have noticed he uses a cane."

"Cane, umbrella, Burberry, and perfect vowels. I figure it's part of his European affectation. He doesn't limp."

"Maybe the limp's not obvious, but he has a genuine injury, one that's given him trouble over the years." Papers rattled. "Small-town newspapers print the handiest stories. Seems Kemp and a cousin were climbing a sycamore tree, daring each other to jump from progressively higher limbs. On Alan's final jump, he broke both ankles. Complications caused the bones to heal slowly, ending his dream of a sports career. Later, Kemp became interested in drama, and was evidently quite good. Would've landed some leading roles, except for those trick ankles. They give out after he's been on them a few hours."

"So he took up journalism?" Dixie moved aside to let a man laden with popcorn and drinks enter the theater.

"Kemp has actually done quite well, especially in foreign markets." When Belle paused, Dixie could hear her pencil tapping on the desk, could picture the point making tiny gray dots on Belle's blotter. "Now here's your chance to win the sixty-four-dollar question, Flannigan." *Tap, tap, tap.* "Name the cousin who dared Alan to take that last jump."

"Joanna Francis."

"Dead on."

"You think he's harbored a grudge all these years, and the notes are meant to drive his cousin nuts?"

"Seems a long shot, but I wanted you to know about it. I'd feel better if Kemp caught the next flight out of town."

"You do expect me to perform miracles. Anything else I should know? Anything on John Page, or the two techs I asked about, or—" Dixie almost said "Bubble Butt Barton," but realized Belle probably hadn't seen the obese director. "Or Barton?"

After more paper rustling, Belle replied, "John Page is shooting a TV pilot in the Florida Keys. He's been there for the past three weeks."

"Where was he when Joanna received those first cards?"

"Los Angeles. Handy, huh? Here's the stuff on Eggert. He works freelance. He's worked on some of Joanna's other films. Unmarried, lives with his mother, who's something of a lush. He's in high demand, considered a top-notch lighting designer—look at the ending credits next time you and Parker watch a video, you could easily see Eggert's name on the list. But the other tech—"

Three people moved up the aisle, blocking Dixie's view of Sarina. Swinging the door wide to let them exit, Dixie craned to get the kid in view again.

"Tori Pond," Belle continued, "is a whole different story from Eggert. She's been knocking around Hollywood for ten or twelve years. Never seemed to get a break, until Joanna put in a word with her own production company. Her parents are dead, she lives alone in East L.A. Wait—"

Belle mumbled, "Thanks," to someone, then came back again. "Okay, just got this in—David Barton directed two other movies Joanna starred in last year. At least three actresses on his films have been stalked, but Barton was never a suspect."

"Maybe he is now. Here's something new to work on—" Dixie asked her to find out about the effects incident on *Devil's Walk*, then disconnected. Ready to head back into the theater, she thought about Alan Kemp and the snapshots Casey James had taken on the movie set. She scanned the rows of spectators, all mesmerized by yet another space battle, and dug around in her memory until she found the reporter's cell phone number. Casey answered on the second ring.

"When you worked with Alan Kemp," Dixie asked, "did he seem content being a reporter?"

"Honey, you ask the damnedest questions."

"Did he ever mention wanting to be a film star himself?"

"Oh, don't we all? Me, now, I only wanted to sleep with them. Used to make snake bets on the pretty ones—Mel Gibson, Harrison Ford, any of the Baldwins."

"Snake bets?"

"Who had the longest, thickest, hardest, droopiest. Who wasn't circumcised. Paid bathroom attendants to find out. Vicarious sex, honey. The best kind. Imagination is *so* much better than the real thing."

"I thought you were working legitimate stories back then."

"This was for *fun*. Now, what's got you so worked up about Alan Kemp?"

"What you said about his visit here during Joanna's shoot not being a coincidence. Did he ever suggest there was bad blood between him and Joanna?"

"I can't recall his ever mentioning her at all. But what you said before, about his wanting to act . . . he did do some live theater work. Talked about going to New York, where the 'real' actors hang out. I don't know if he ever did."

"What do you know about John Barton?"

"Asshole extraordinaire," Casey said without hesitation. "Now, when is it my turn to ask questions?"

"Don't I always come through for you, Casey?"

"I'm not sure that's intentional. But okay, you're on a tab. Barton is good enough at what he does that he can get by with being a horse's patoot. He makes cable movies that a tremendous number of couch potatoes like to watch."

"How's his sex life? Who does he—"

"Barton's snake is buried so deep in fat even he hasn't seen it in years. But if your question is who does he play with, Barton has a different dewy-eyed starlet on his arm every week, and none of them go home with him. He's either gay or too proud to beg. Now, as much as I'd like to keep running up your phone bill—"

"One more question—"

"With you, Counselor, it's always one more question."

"What do you know about an agent named Marty Ahrens?"

"Joanna's agent?" For the first time, Casey hesitated. "Not much to know. He doesn't make a lot of noise, but he does right by his clients. Takes care of them, if you know what I mean."

"Spell it out for me."

Another hesitation. "Marty has been around Hollywood since the days when publicity was generally a good thing. He never handled any really big names, but he's never backed a complete loser, either. He knows how to move a client's career forward."

"That's the biggest whitewash I've ever heard from you, Casey. What're you not telling me?"

"Listen, Marty's a nice guy. If I was an out-of-work actor, he'd top my list of agents to hire. But as a reporter, honey, I know Marty only lets go of information when he has money riding on it."

Dixie couldn't decide what to make of Casey's last remarks. Apparently, Marty was the person Joanna should thank for keeping her "accidents" this past year out of the tabloids. Was he also counseling her not to go to the police with the threats from her number-one fan?

Noting that Sarina had attracted no attention, and was still flanked by two empty seats, Dixie decided to make one last call. Les Crews, the profiler at Quantico, should've received the stalker's messages from her by now.

She dialed his office number. Crews often worked late, but tonight he wasn't there. After listening to his abrupt recording, "You know what to do. Do it," she left a brief message.

Chapter Thirty-four

Later, having delivered Sarina safely back to the hotel, Dixie halted the Porsche outside her gate and watched a thin, comforting trail of gray chimney smoke ascend into the sky. The porch light was on, and the kitchen light. The television glowed faintly through the living-room window. The house looked warm and inviting.

Shivering in the night air, she reached for a shopping bag on the floorboard. Inside was a bottle of Parker's favorite wine and a valentine card. The holiday was still two days away, but she and Parker had gone to bed the night before without settling their problems—her job, the yacht party—and they'd both rushed off this morning, scarcely exchanging a word. She sensed a rift opening between them. Dixie wanted to close it, wanted to make things right, only she didn't have a clue how to do it. She hoped the valentine would say it for her.

She flicked on the interior light and took the valentine

out of the bag. The message wasn't terribly mushy: *Every day in so many ways, you brighten my life.*

Quickly, before she could think about it too much, Dixie wrote, "Love you," signed the card, and shoved it into the envelope.

The third item in the bag was a housewarming gift for Parker's new place. The carpenters had finally departed, the painters were painting their last few strokes, the floor coverings and appliances had been installed. The house was due to be completed at the end of the week. She hadn't asked, but she suspected he'd move his stuff out over the weekend, and she hated it. With Parker physically so far away, the rift could only open wider. The gift was a brass door knocker—not even a little mushy.

Mud met her at the back porch, sniffing his worried whine around her cast and demanding more affection than usual. With the strained atmosphere in the house, he probably felt as disconcerted as she did.

The kitchen smelled like fresh-baked cookies. A plate of brownies sat beneath a huge vase of red roses, a pink, heart-shaped balloon bobbing above them. The inscription on the balloon read *You're the sweetest!*

The first night Parker had stayed in her house, a prisoner, he'd scrounged ingredients from her near-empty cabinets to make brownies, the best she'd ever tasted. A rush of tenderness misted Dixie's eyes. Evidently, he wanted to make up, too.

Hearing Parker's footsteps behind her, she blinked away the silly moisture.

"It's not quite Valentine's Day," he said. "But—"

When he didn't finish the sentence, Dixie's anxious mind leaped ahead to finish it for him . . . *but I won't be here to celebrate Valentine's Day. . . .*

When he reached to embrace her, she turned into it, facing him. "I brought some wine. For dinner."

" 'Quick, bring me a beaker of wine that I may wet

my mind and say something clever.' " He grinned. "Aristophanes. Neat guy." Wiggling his eyebrows, he did his truly awful Humphrey Bogart imitation. "But if we're not careful, sweetheart, we'll turn into a pair of old winos."

"A glass a day keeps the heart at play."

"Then a bottle a day ought to keep us hale halfway into the next century."

His playful blue eyes locked with hers, and he closed the distance between them, his lips soft and inviting. She'd never loved a man the way she loved this man. Never needed anyone, yet she needed him, needed his essence to recharge her being, his humor to recharge her spirit. She couldn't imagine living without him—her and Mud whining at each other over frozen dinners.

"How's the kid?" Parker murmured when he finally let her lips go, arms still tight, lifting her. Her breasts flattened against his chest, their hips touching where it mattered, her toes and the heavy cast barely brushing the floor.

"The kid is still a pain in the butt, but a likable pain."

One hand slid down to her buttocks, drawing her into him, to feel the hard length of him against her belly. His mouth parted against hers, tongue flicking across her lips. A familiar warmth rose on her skin everywhere he touched, and where he hadn't touched—yet. The shopping bag slid from her fingers as he lifted her higher and carried her to the bedroom. In moments they were naked beneath the covers, the intensity of their need stunning them both. Later, they slept, curled together. Dixie awoke with the comforting scent of his skin deep in her nostrils, his chest hairs tickling her nose. She never wanted to move.

"Are you awake?" she murmured.

"Mmmmhmm."

She could feel the rumble of his breathing against her cheek. She was thirsty, and she had to pee.

"Want some wine now?"

"Mmmmhmm."

"Coffee and a brownie?"

"Mmmmhmm."

"Which of us is going to get it?"

"Which of us is on top?"

"I don't know. Me, I think."

"Mmmmhmm."

She nosed around on his chest until she found the hard nub of a nipple and slipped it into her mouth. For a moment, she enjoyed the tiny intimacy, then she caught the nipple between her teeth.

"Ow!"

"If I get the wine, you don't get to sleep."

She scrambled off the bed and into the bathroom.

"Woman, you are cruel!" he shouted after her.

Ten minutes later, they were propped against pillows, wineglasses, coffee, and brownies on a tray between them. On the muted television, the closing credits of a medical drama rolled across the screen.

Dixie lifted the shopping bag onto the bed and pulled out the remaining contents. His smile broadened at the wrapped package, a blaze of multicolored designer hearts against a pink background, tied with a wiggly red bow.

"For the grand opening of your new home," Dixie told him.

He shook the heavy box, listening. No sound, the knocker was shrink-wrapped.

"What is it?" His face held the eagerness of a kid at Christmas.

"See that string holding it together? Pull it, open it. Find out."

He tore open the package. The round brass knocker, shaped like a hinged hatchway on a ship's hull, was inscribed with his last name, Dann, in bold letters. He grinned.

"It's perfect! Where did you find this?"

"In the museum shop." After viewing the metal sculpture at the Contemporary Arts Museum that afternoon, she'd coaxed Sarina across the street to the Museum of Fine Arts. They'd spent the whole time in the tourist trap, Sarina helping her make the decision between the knocker and a brass pelican umbrella stand. Maybe she'd buy the umbrella stand later, for his birthday—or whenever.

"I love it. Thank you." He kissed her. "What else is in the bag?"

"A card." But suddenly it seemed woefully inadequate, expressing the wrong sentiment. "To be saved until Valentine's Day."

"Oh." He slid open a drawer on the nightstand. "I guess that means we have to save this one, too." He held up a square pink envelope.

"No, it doesn't." She wanted that envelope.

She reached for it. He held it out of her grasp.

"Fair's fair. Give me mine, I'll give you yours."

Dixie considered it, but she wanted time to buy him a better one, a card that really expressed how she felt—humorously, of course, without too much goo.

"We'll wait," she said. "Otherwise, Valentine's Day will seem anticlimactic."

"It's only two days away. Friday."

"Yep."

"Maybe we could spread the holiday into the weekend, spend the whole three days together . . . at my place. Invite Amy and Carl and Ryan down on Sunday."

She squirmed inwardly. If Joanna's film schedule had been extended by the rain, Dixie's job wouldn't be finished by the weekend. Of course, Belle could get someone else for those two days. But what if Dixie convinced Belle to let her out of the deal, and something happened to the kid? Dixie would never be able to live with that. And wouldn't Sarina be disappointed having a new bodyguard? Not to mention that Dixie would miss the mule-headed twerp.

In a way, she was shielding Sarina from Joanna's overprotectiveness as much as from the stalker. At sixteen—seventeen, a girl should have freedom to choose her own interests, as long as they didn't include drugs or selling her body on street corners. If Dixie quit the job now, Belle would be forced to hire someone who might not like Sarina as much as Dixie had come to.

"You don't even have a bed at your new house yet," she reminded Parker.

"You can help me buy one."

A newscast saved her from having to answer. She turned up the volume.

"*Police are stymied over the latest development in the Carrera case. Today the boy's grandparents received a notarized letter from Patricia Carrera relinquishing custody of her son, Paulie.*"

"The woman's nuts," Parker said. "Went to all that trouble to win, then gave the kid back?"

"Damned unlikely," Dixie mused.

"What do you mean?"

She hesitated. Her hunches weren't always easy to put into words.

"You know about the Avenging Angels' assault on Lawrence Coombs."

"Yeah. Wish I'd been right there with them."

Dixie shook her head. "I agree, but it can't work like that. A lynch mob, no matter how just it may seem in the moment, is still a lynch mob. It doesn't think, it doesn't reason, it rides on a surge of hatred."

"What's that got to do with the Carrera boy?"

Dixie sighed. "Nothing, I hope. But Brenda gathered evidence against Carrera, trying to make a state case against her for child abuse. It fell apart when Paulie couldn't testify, and the school nurse who turned it in hadn't observed enough consistency or frequency in the boy's injuries to build a case. Nevertheless, Brenda was convinced the mother was guilty. She steered the young attorney hired by the grandparents through the Open Records Act and copied him with everything in her files, certain the grandparents would win custody in a civil trial."

"But they lost."

"Right, and everybody knew Paulie would be showing up with bruises and burns as soon as Carrera had him in her hands again."

"Then you think she didn't send that letter and disappear willingly?"

Dixie shrugged. "It's possible the trial woke the woman up. Abuse is complicated. It usually goes back generations in a family. Kids get caught in a love-fear relationship, protecting the parent—they'd rather endure more abuse than jeopardize the family. In some cases, abuse is the only attention a kid gets."

"Maybe I can buy that in some backwoods burg, Dixie. But newspapers, magazines, television—hell, even the movies are filled with stories of abuse situations—usually followed by a hotline number to call for help."

"The most abusive people rarely see themselves as abusers. They express frustration the way their parents did—with punishment that to us seems extreme, but to them is merely necessary discipline. They truly believe that terrible old adage, 'Spare the rod and spoil the child.'"

"Then what the friggin hell do we have psychiatrists and psychologists for?"

"Hey! Yelling at me won't change anything."

"Sorry. It's just damned frustrating. We live in a civilized world, with systems to help people in trouble. Yet this eight-year-old boy is terrified to admit his mother beats him up every night? Makes me want to find the woman, knock *her* around some, let her see how it feels."

"I know." Dixie was quiet, thinking about that for a moment. "Carrera refused to see a psychologist, except for the court-prescribed evaluation, and she continued to claim she never hurt Paulie."

"If she believes she hasn't done anything wrong, why would she suddenly decide to give the kid to his grandparents?"

"What if she didn't? What if that wasn't her signature on the letter?"

"They'll check it out, won't they?"

"Maybe not too carefully."

"You have to admit, Dixie, the boy's better off."

"I'm sure he is. But what about whoever's responsible for Carrera's sudden change of heart?"

"They deserve a friggin medal."

Part of Dixie had to agree. "But where does it stop?" *And how much does a certain ADA know about Carrera's whereabouts?*

The newscaster had segued to yet another story that triggered an alarm in Dixie's mind.

"Two suspects in the Ramirez liquor store robbery-assault case were released today when a witness failed to pick them out of a lineup. Fifty-year-old Raymond Ramirez died from blows to the head. His sixteen-year-old niece remains in critical condition. Charges against Gary Ingles and Sid Carlson have been dropped for insufficient evidence."

The Ramirez case had raised the hackles of everyone who knew about it. The prosecution hadn't fallen on Brenda's desk, but Dixie recalled Brenda's bitterness the morning Ramirez and his niece, Celeste, were found. Carlson and Ingles had been implicated in five other robbery-assault cases. No one died in those incidents, but a seventy-one-year-old man had been paralyzed. The fact that the two suspects had now been released in no way exonerated them; it only meant that fear of retribution had silenced the witnesses.

When Parker rose to clear away their tray, Dixie leaned across the pillows to the bedside phone and dialed Brenda's number.

Gail answered, sounding rushed.

"Sorry, Dixie, Bren came in and then left. Said she'd be real late again."

"Again?"

"She's hardly been around the last couple nights—but aren't you seeing her later?"

"Did she say she was seeing me tonight?"

"No, but . . . when she said she was going out with the guys for drinks, I naturally thought she meant 'gals.' Brenda never goes out with guys."

"She didn't say where?"

"No. Listen, my ride's outside. We're off to shop for hot dogs and baked beans for the weekend. Got to rally the forces, get them knocking on doors. Want to help?"

"Not my thing. But leave a note for Brenda to call me— no matter how late she gets in."

When Dixie cradled the phone, she found Parker studying her again.

"You have a look about you, Dixie. A look I've come to associate with those times you leave here hell-bent on a quest and come home injured."

"I'm not going anywhere tonight. I'm staying right here."

He continued eyeing her. "You aren't planning to get mixed up with these Avenging Angels, are you?"

"Join up with them? You think I'm nuts?"

"Or go after them. Let the police handle it."

"Brenda's a friend. You don't turn away from friends when you're needed."

"And you can't help a friend if she doesn't want to be helped. What if you learn something that makes you an accessory? Something you're better off not knowing?"

"I'm not in any danger here, Parker. I only want Brenda to know she has a friend when she needs one." It wouldn't be the first time Dixie had turned suddenly deaf and dumb when confronted with information she didn't want to pass along.

He smiled thinly. "Dixie, your absolute loyalty is one of the qualities that makes you special. I admire that." Taking her hand, he coaxed her to her feet. "I've been holding out on you. Come on."

"Where?"

"Never mind, just come in the kitchen with me."

"If it's something to eat—"

"Nope." He led her to the table, to the roses, gorgeous and

fragrant. The pink balloon had worked itself free and bobbed near the ceiling. "Take a look at this."

He handed her a snapshot that had been propped against the vase.

"It's beautiful." She didn't really know much about boats, but this sailboat was midget-size, compared to the Berinsons' yacht.

"A real sweetheart. Thirty-six feet on deck, twenty-nine-foot waterline, eleven-and-a-half-foot beam. Suitable for both bluewater sailing and sailing around the bay."

"Are you planning to buy this?" Dixie pictured them sailing to Belle's Caribbean condo — what a terrific time that could be, just her, Parker, Mud, and a remote Caribbean island.

"Maybe. The owner only took it out twice before getting transferred to Denver. Now he's into skiing. He's willing to drop the price to turn a quick sale. Thought we could try it out tomorrow night—after you drop your teenage anchor back at the hotel. Moonlight sail, just the two of us."

Sounded romantic. "I'd love that. But wouldn't Friday night be even better —when we can sleep late the next day?" Sarina would be okay with another bodyguard for a couple of hours.

"I'm already holding off two buyers who want to see this honey. And I don't want it unless you like it."

"Really?"

"Of course, *really*. Who else would I want sailing beside me?"

Dixie tried not to envision the blonde aboard the Berinsons' yacht. Tried, unsuccessfully. "I'm not much of a sailor. . . ."

"We'll have fun teaching you."

Chapter Thirty-five

Lawrence Coombs watched the lights wink out in Dixie Flannigan's house and sneered to himself in the darkness.

So the sexy little cunt had a boyfriend, did she? So hot for each other they hadn't even noticed the bedroom shade was up. Not expecting anyone would be watching, out here in the boondocking country.

But Lawrence had followed the red Porsche, thinking he might have some fun tonight. He touched his lip where her teeth had bitten through, leaving two ugly red scars. The monster dog that came sniffing around her on the porch, big as half a horse, squelched that idea fast.

He started the Jaguar's engine and, without turning on the lights, backed quietly out to the road. He'd looked forward to sharing tonight's adventures with Marianne when he visited the nursing home tomorrow. Never mind. Plenty of time, no need to rush. He knew other women who'd do for tonight. Couldn't disappoint his dear mother.

Without warning, the nauseating scent of her overwhelmed

him. Imaginary, of course, she was eighty miles east, tucked up in her high-railed bed. Paralyzed fully on one side, partially on the other, she still managed to scoot around and fall to the tile floor when the aides failed to put the rails up. After his visits, though, she always quieted right down.

Lawrence reached a particularly dark patch of highway and realized he'd forgotten to turn his lights on. Rather interesting, riding along in the darkness. Spying a sedan twenty yards ahead of him, he speeded up until he was on its bumper, then flicked his headlights on bright, just before passing. As the sedan swerved toward the shoulder, Lawrence chuckled. One major cleaning job would be needed on that car seat tomorrow.

The thought of a urine-saturated seat reminded him again of the nursing home. On his last visit, they'd talked about Regan Salles—or rather, he'd talked. Marianne had only rolled her eyes frantically when he described the many ways he'd penetrated Regan.

"It's not as if the cunt was a virgin, Marianne," he'd explained. "Like you, she's had more dicks sticking in her than a porcupine has quills."

Marianne hadn't smiled at his jab of humor. But then she never smiled anymore. He wasn't sure she could.

Once, that smile had been all he could think about. Growing up, he'd liked nothing better than to crawl on his mother's lap, snuggle between her big soft breasts, and smell the warm skin of her neck. He watched her smile when his father kissed her there, just beneath her ear, and Lawrence began doing the same, when he was too big to sit on her lap.

But the smile that emblazoned itself on his brain was the one he'd seen through a crack in his closet wall. His parents' clothes closet had once backed up to his own, then had been replaced with shelves to hold books, television, stereo. Marianne had sent him to clean his room after school that day, when baseball practice was canceled, told him not to show his face until every corner was spotless—which meant cramming as much stuff as he could into his closet. Standing on a chair, he pushed some sweaters aside on a high shelf and noticed a sliver of an opening that angled right into his parents' bedroom. He hadn't meant to spy. He just leaned without thinking, looked through the hole, and saw his mother's radiant smile. She was naked. Lying on the bed, head thrown back against a pile of pillows, eyes closed, a look on her face that Lawrence had never seen. And the man with his hand between her legs, causing that smile, that *look*, was not his father.

Between his own legs, Lawrence had felt a throbbing heat . . . not the first time his penis had grown hard—he was almost fourteen—but this was different. His face felt hot, his mouth had filled with saliva, like at the dinner table when his favorite dishes were served. His penis wanted to pop right through his jeans. Unable to pull himself away from the intoxicating scene, he watched his mother arch against the pillows, her mouth falling open, her big soft breasts flattened slightly, each with a stiff brown nipple pointing outward. When the man leaned forward and slipped his mouth over one of those nipples, Lawrence's balance had teetered on the chair. Bracing himself with one hand on the closet shelf, he quietly unzipped his jeans and slid his other hand around the throbbing flesh, where every nerve in his body suddenly seemed to have gathered. There was no thought, no reality, except the delicious sensations raging through him. And then it was over.

He stood with a handful of slime, stretched precariously on a wobbly chair, spying on his mother. He felt so disgusted that at first the awfulness of what he'd seen didn't register. His eyes had been only on her. But realization settled in his mind like a canker sore. His mother was having sex with a strange man—in the very bed his father would sleep in that night.

Wiping his hand down the side of his jeans, he wanted to run, to get as far as possible from the embarrassment beyond his closet—

No! The man would have to come out of that room, into the hall. . . . A weapon!

Lawrence searched hurriedly for something, anything! He yanked open bureau drawers and rifled his desk, before finally reopening the closet door and snatching his baseball bat, leaning in a corner behind his shirts. He swung it, remembering the *thup!* of a ball hitting the wood, and aching to feel that *thup!* as it hit the man's head. He swung the bat again, then stormed into the hall to wait.

As he crouched in the hallway's afternoon shadows, he saw the whole episode again, dark lashes fluttering against her flushed cheeks, nostrils flaring with each breath, red lips parting as she arched. Sweat beaded Lawrence's lip, and he wiped it with a hand that still smelled of his own semen.

His parents' bedroom door opened. The man came out and turned silently down the hall, his mother watching him go, a filmy robe failing to conceal the patch of dark hair that drew Lawrence's gaze. His fingers flinched around the bat's neck, but he couldn't move. Then the man was gone. His mother shut the bedroom door, never noticing her son watching from the shadows.

After a long while, he put the bat away in the closet, not even glancing at the evil sliver of light above the top shelf. In the bathroom, he washed his hands and scrubbed his face with cold water. He spent the rest of the afternoon waiting on the front steps for his father's car to drive up, practicing the words in his head to tell what he'd seen. But when the long gray Lincoln turned into the drive, the words stuck in his throat. They never became unstuck, not that night nor the next time the man—and all the other men—visited his parents' bedroom.

He stopped going to baseball practice, circling around and silently entering the house instead, heading straight for the closet, for the exotic sights and smells and sounds that poured through the crack above the shelf. He hated himself for it, but staying away was not an option he even considered. He lived for those moments, imagining *he* was the one causing the smile, the soft moans, the moisture that glistened on his mother's skin.

The day his father walked into the room, Lawrence had his eye to the crack and his meat in his hand. His father's stricken face was like a winter gale, freezing him where he stood. Freezing the pair on the bed. In those frozen seconds, his father aged and died. Then, slowly, he turned and retraced his steps, shutting the door behind him with extreme care.

It was almost five years and many men later that he killed himself, carbon monoxide from another long gray Lincoln, the day after his son left for college. When the phone call came, Lawrence drank himself sick, knowing the complicity he shared in his father's death. Marianne had killed him, all those years ago. But Lawrence had kept quiet—a coward crouched uselessly in a corner with his baseball bat.

A truck's headlights glared in the rearview mirror. Adjusting it, Lawrence noticed his freeway exit approaching. College had taken him away from Marianne—he'd stopped thinking of her as Mother, and certainly couldn't call her Mom or Mommy—but college hadn't erased those days in the closet, nor the sight of his father's face. At first, he spent holidays and spring break anywhere but home. But after the first year, he returned to his old room each summer, and after college, he'd returned for good.

At forty-three, Marianne could still turn heads, and the men she brought to the house were often closer to her son's age than her own. Lawrence had long ago sealed up the crack in the closet wall, but he didn't need to watch. He could see the entire show in his mind—flushed cheeks, fluttering lashes, and that smile.

Taking the exit, he opened the Jaguar's glove box, removed the mobile phone and a fold of pink notepaper, and dialed a number. Lying now in her reeking room— Lawrence paid plenty to keep Marianne in the best, but the stench of sick old people still permeated the air—she could not smile or even respond to the stories he told of his own sexual pleasures, beyond rolling her phlegmy eyes or waving that one clawlike hand. But he loved watching her die a little every time he visited.

"Hello?"

"Dottie, darlin'." Lawrence sniffed the pink, honeysuckle-scented paper. "I am four blocks from your house and starving for a glimpse of your sweet face."

This would be a good night to give the randy Dottie a thrill while he waited for the time and place to do Dixie Flannigan. One thing he prided himself on was patience.

"Hope you won't mind, pretty lady, if I pop in for a nightcap."

Chapter Thirty-six

Sid Carlson peeled a twenty from a wad of bills as big as his fist and dropped it on the bar.

"Another round here," he told the bartender.

Sid was wearing his "IF YOU CAN'T TAKE A JOKE . . ." T-shirt, red with white letters, and hoping the bartender would give him a hard time, give him a reason to lift the edge of the shirt and show the final two words. What Sid would do next, depending on the bartender's attitude, was to either laugh at the cocksucker's surprised expression or put a fist through his stupid face. Whichever happened didn't matter much to Sid. He was having a great time celebrating. No one was going to spoil it.

The bartender set two cold mugs of Budweiser on the bar, precisely, so as not to spill foam down the sides of the mugs.

"You're getting better," Sid told him. "That's a nice head. Ain't that a nice head, Gary? Not a perfect head, a perfect head would be three-quarters of an inch above the top of the mug, without a drop spilled. This one's maybe half an inch, beer right up to the rim, then the head above that, and no beer wasted. Nice."

"Nice," Gary echoed. He slurped Budweiser through the foam, leaving a thin bead on his upper lip, which he raked off with a swipe of his thumb.

Gary rarely spoke much more than a mouthful of words in one gulp, which was all right with Sid. One thing Sid hated was some rattle-mouth bastard all the time yapping in his ear. When Gary had something to say, he said it. Otherwise, he kept his yap shut.

"Give our friend down there another round, too," Sid said. There were only three people in the place, so there was no way the bartender could get confused about who was meant. "Then drop another handful of quarters in the juke-box and play our favorite song."

Sid's favorite song was "I've Got A Tiger By The Tail," by Buck Owens. He'd never heard it until a couple months ago, right here on this jukebox. Somebody told him it was an old song, from sometime back in the sixties, but that didn't matter to Sid, who was born in '65 and wasn't old enough to remember much that happened in that decade. Who the fuck cared what happened back then, anyway? Who the fuck cared what happened last fuckin week, for that matter? Sid only cared about right now, this minute, and what happened from here on out. Right now, he was celebrating. And give Gary Ingles his due for not being a yapper, truth was, Gary wasn't much of a hell-raiser, either.

Fellow in the shadows at the end of the bar lifted his glass in a silent salute, meaning "Thanks."

Earlier, the joint had been rocking pretty good. Sid had won a few games of pool, had even lost a couple games without pushing anybody's face in for cheating. He and Gary had bought a couple of rounds for the house, not telling anybody exactly *why* they were celebrating. Of course, their mug shots had been on TV, so a few guys recognized them, knew they were celebrating being out of the slammer and squeaking by that robbery charge, but nobody knew what they were *really* celebrating. Nobody knew how many tills him and Gary had raked clean before they got nabbed. Twelve in all, not counting the citizens they held up in parking lots. Twelve, and tonight was his and Gary's anniversary, one year exactly from the first job they pulled together. It was just too goddamned perfect, being released from jail on the very day of their anniversary. So they had to fuckin celebrate.

One by one, everybody in the bar had gone home, except him and Gary. And that quiet bastard shuffling cards at the end of the bar. Not playing solitaire or anything, just shuffling, over and over.

Sid could go for a few hands of poker; hell, *that'd* be the way to finish celebrating. Case of cold Bud, bag of greasy Whataburgers, and a deck of hot cards.

His mom would say it was poker that got him and Gary in trouble with the law, got them knocking over convenience and package stores to pay their debts, but Mom had it all wrong. They robbed stores 'cause it was *fun*. Nice that it gave them pocket money and poker money and general fartin-around money, but the truth was, they got more money sometimes off the people they robbed in parking lots than from stores, the way everybody stuck their big bills in these fuckin safes, idiot clerks not knowing how to open the goddamn things, just poke the money through the fuckin slot.

But him and Gary had wised up and started casing a place before they hit it, looking to see if it had a safe. Your Stop & Go, Circle K, Spec's Liquor pretty much all had safes, but the mom-and-pop stores tried to get by staggering their bank deposits. What him and Gary did was wait till the first and fifteenth, nights people got paid, especially if it fell close to a weekend, then hit the store just before closing, after the whole neighborhood had come in to buy their beer and ice cream.

Anyhow, the mom-and-pop places were the most fun. Catch an old couple late at night like that, they *begged* you to take the money and not hurt anyone. Take an old guy alone, he might get feisty, pull a gun out from under the counter. But not when there was a woman in the place. One whack at the woman, the old guy practically pisses his pants begging you to rob him and "*not hurt anybody.*" That last job, they'd got a bonus, the geezer having a young sweet-thang in there, helping out.

The more Sid thought of it, a poker game would be a damn fine way to celebrate. He picked up his beer mug and ambled down the bar.

"You shuffle them cards anymore, won't have any marks left. That your special deck, or what?"

"New deck." The guy nudged a cellophane wrapper wadded up in the ashtray.

"Don't s'pose you know where a fellow could get into a good game tonight?"

The guy looked him over for a minute from the shadows, not straight on but out the side of his eye, like. Sure was a wiry little fucker, not much meat on him.

"Might," he said.

Kind of a croaky voice, like he smoked too much, only Sid hadn't seen him smoking since he'd been in the bar. Knit cap pulled low, blond hair poking out near the ears, big, heavy coat for such a mild night. Face and hands smooth as a woman's. Probably queer, but what the hell, everybody had to follow his own call, Sid always figured. Sure was tight with his words, tight as Gary, maybe, only Sid didn't think anybody could be as tight with words as Gary.

"Me and my friend over there are celebrating," Sid said. "A good game'd be the ticket, seeing as how the bar will soon shut down for the night. Just a friendly game, mind, no high rolling."

The long look again, like he's thinking whether Sid is okay to bring round to his buddies, then a glance down the bar at Gary. "You got money?"

"Hell yeah, I got money. Always got poker money."

Little fucker glanced at the clock. Bartender hadn't called last round yet, but he would in the next five minutes.

"Friends down the street are starting a game at two, goes till five. Win or lose, stops at five o'clock sharp."

"Fuck, if I can't take my share of a pot in three hours, something's seriously wrong."

"You up for it?"

"Hell yeah, Gary and me. And we'll bring along a case of brew, just so there'll be no hard feelings when we walk away with all your dough." Sid grinned, thinking about it. "Your friends'll say, 'Motherfuckers cleaned us out, but at least they brought the beer.' "

"You got a car?"

"Hell yeah, we got a car. Need a ride or something?"

"I'll call ahead, make sure there's room for two more at the table, then you follow me. Got to be there by two, sharp."

While the little fucker made his call, Sid talked the bartender into selling him a case of Bud at discount. He settled up, shorting the tab by seventy-five cents, and waited for the bartender to open his mouth, tell Sid to fork over. Then he laughed and flipped up the bottom of his T-shirt, showing the last two words: FUCK YOU. The bartender's face turned red, and his eyes got mean, but he didn't say anything. Smart fucker.

Gary lifted the case of beer off the counter. One of your strong silent types, that was Gary.

Sid heard the telephone receiver clunk down.

"Hey, what's your name, anyway?" Couldn't call their new poker friend Little Fucker out loud, man might take offense.

"John." Little fucker opened the door, dark clothes instantly blending into the dark night.

Sid took out his keys and headed toward the only two cars left in the parking lot, parked side by side. Bartender's ride was probably round back. He opened the trunk so Gary could set the case of beer inside. Saw the little fucker open his own trunk, wondered if he kept his poker money in there. Not a bad place, guy breaks into your car never thinks to look in the trunk for money. Except, of course, if they steal the whole car, you lose money and all—

Whop!

Sid turned at the sound, like a watermelon bustin' open, falling off the back of a truck, hitting the hot asphalt and *whop!* That same wet sound.

Only it wasn't a watermelon, it was Gary's head that got busted, and now something was swinging at Sid—

Whop!

Sonofabitch, that hurt! He fell against the car, fingering the side of his skull, which felt half-crushed, and thinking he was going to vomit. In the meager light, he saw shapes, movement, someone setting the case of beer on the ground and someone else shoving Gary into the trunk.

Then Sid felt a fist grab his collar, pushing him toward the other car. He bucked, swung an elbow and heard a satisfying grunt, then felt a *whack!* against his shin—*must've broke the goddamn bone, it hurt so*—and him falling, being shoved inside the fucker's car. Then the trunk lid closed over him.

"Hey!" he yelled. "What the fuck's going on? Let me out of here!" He banged on the lid with his fist.

A moment later he heard an engine start, then another, and they were moving, his body crushed into confinement, feeling every stone in the gravel parking lot. Blood seeped from his hair onto his neck. He reached up to wipe away the blood just as the car bounced over a curb, turning onto the paved road, and his head slammed against the trunk lid.

"Fuck!" Pain darted down his neck into his shoulders, and he gasped, sucked in a gulp of dusty, oily air, and sneezed, his head banging the lid again.

This time it hurt too bad to curse. Tears stung his eyes, and his anger was suddenly huge and rampant. He wanted to hit something, HURT SOMEBODY, but he couldn't even turn over, he was so cramped. He lay still for a few minutes, one arm shielding his head from further injury, his face mashed against the gritty mat.

He thought about it, wondered why anyone would bother to kidnap him and Gary. Neither of them had any family to pay ransom. They weren't worth anything, except for the wad of bills Sid was carrying, say a thousand bucks, give or take a few, maybe a couple thousand more stashed away.

He didn't know what the fuck was happening, but sooner or later they'd have to let him out, and he wasn't coming out bare-handed. Feeling around for something to use as a club—wrench, jack handle, anything—his fingers touched something hard and cold. He stretched, trying to hook a finger around it, but the goddamn spare tire was in the way, him twisted around it like a fuckin pretzel. He squeezed his head between the spare and the trunk lid, gaining a couple inches, and he could tell the thing was metal, could feel a smooth indentation like a handle grip. He dug his finger into the groove and tried to slide it toward him.

It wouldn't slide.

Stretching harder, his ear being ripped off by the rubber tread, the other one losing skin on the rough metal, he gritted his teeth and pincered the handle between his first and second fingers, dragging it toward him.

His goddamn fingers were slimy with sweat, sliding off the metal like snot on a doorknob, and the fuckin tool—whatever the goddamn thing was—didn't budge.

Sid lay still for a count of ten, forcing his muscles to relax, his anger to simmer down. A cool head, a strong arm, a stiff dick, and a steady heart, that's what winning was all about, and he had it, aces full, all he had to do was concentrate. He concentrated on having long, thin muscles, muscles that could stretch forever, fluid like a snake. He wiped his hand on the tire tread, chafed his fingers against the rubber until they felt rough and tacky, then took a breath and blew it out slow through his mouth. Flexing his fingers, he eeled his arm toward the tool, stretching, stretching, pincered the handle again between his fingers, and slid the tool toward him an eighth of an inch, a quarter. Sweat seeped from his brow into his eyes, but he closed them, ignoring the salty sting, and concentrated on pulling the tool another quarter inch closer. A little more and he could reach it with his thumb, get a real grip on it, but not yet, not yet, keep edging it closer. And then his thumb moved up to take the place of one finger, more strength now, but don't go too fast. The handle maybe an inch and a half wide and flat, except for the groove that ran around the inside, and now it was in his hand and it felt like maybe twelve, fourteen inches long, like maybe a monkey wrench. Heavy.

When that little fucker—John, was that the name he said?—when the little fucker opened the goddamn trunk he was going to goddamn lose some teeth.

Chapter Thirty-seven

Dixie awoke abruptly to the hushed ring of a telephone. Expecting an update from Brew, she'd turned the ringer down on the cordless and placed it close to her side of the bed. She scooped it up and padded down the hall to the kitchen to avoid waking Parker.

"Found a homeless," Brew told her, "says he was in Memorial Park Monday night. Might've seen Lawrence Coombs being chaperoned down one of the trails."

"When can I talk to him?"

"That might be a problem. This dude's as hard to find as a midnight shadow, and just about as talkative."

"I'll find him. What does he look like? Where does he hang out?" Something tickled Dixie's nose. Brushing at it, she felt a string dangling over her face, and it took a moment to realize it was the pink helium-filled balloon.

"Dixie, even if you find the dude, he'll spook and run." Brew hesitated. "There's one person who might be able to put you close to him."

"All right, whatever."

"You won't like it."

Uh-oh. Dixie knew instantly who he meant. She got along fine with two of the trio who managed the Gypsy Filchers. The other distrusted and disliked her. Although Dixie no longer represented the law, she'd found it impossible to soften the girl's attitude. "Ski?" she asked.

"Bingo. She's one of the few people Loser talks to."

Dixie groped for the balloon string, wrapped it around a finger. She was thoroughly awake now, and eager to find out whatever she could, even if it meant dealing with Ski. "Loser? I hope that wasn't the name his parents christened him."

"Louis, I think, Louis Boggs. But Loser's what he answers to. When he answers at all."

Louis Boggs. She'd heard the name somewhere. Dixie nudged a gingham curtain aside to look out at the night sky. The world looked beautiful at this early hour, especially through the tapestry of pine and pecan trees that encircled her home. Wishing life could be as peaceful as it felt, she fastened the balloon string to the curtain tieback. "When can we do this?"

"Just a minute." Brew's voice became muffled, as if he'd placed his hand over the phone. Then he came back. "Ski says she'll take you to where Loser bunks down, but no promise he'll be around tonight. Meet her at the Diamond Shamrock on Memorial, just east of the park."

"It'll take me twenty minutes."

"She'll be there."

Dixie grabbed some clothes from the bedroom closet and clumped back into the kitchen, pulling them on and cursing the bulky cast that refused to slide through any but the widest jeans. She had split the seams on a pair of her older ones, but they must be in the laundry. She grabbed some scissors and cut her way into these.

Fifteen minutes later, she turned off the 610 Loop onto Memorial Drive. Worrying about Brenda had kept her awake late into the night. If the Avenging Angels had stopped with one victim, Coombs, Dixie would simply forget it, bury her concerns, and move on. And maybe they *had* stopped there. She wished she believed they had. She hoped it was only her own fertile imagination inventing the connection between the Coombs reprisal and the disappearance of Patricia Carrera.

If Brenda would just talk to her, tell her the venting of anger had taken its course, Dixie would stop worrying. Brenda Benson had a soft heart but a strong survival attitude. She'd realize the chances of getting caught for the Coombs assault were low, with the Houston police as angry as anyone else about the jury's decision. But a continuing crusade was certain disaster. HPD didn't like civilians trying to do their job. If a pattern of vigilantism became apparent, they'd step up the investigation—and even if Brenda were only guilty by association, it would cost the prosecutor her job and reputation.

Dixie stopped for a signal light and spied the green glow of the Diamond Shamrock sign several blocks ahead. Glancing at her watch, she decided right now might be the one time she'd catch Brenda at home. The prosecutor would be pissed, being awakened at this hour, but Dixie could handle pissed. She punched the number on her cell phone.

After the third ring, the answering machine picked up. Her friend was either a heavy sleeper or keeping strange hours. Dixie left a message. Turning into the Diamond Shamrock station, she powered the phone off and began searching the darkness for a willowy young woman with platinum hair, delicate features, and deadly hands. In a sheath at the small of her back, Ski carried a set of stilettos. Dixie had seen the target she used for practice, the bull's-eye mushy from being punctured with a consistently tight grouping. Ski wasn't her real name, of course. All the Gypsy Filchers used street names.

Ski emerged from a narrow shadow flanking the old building, dressed in her usual black turtleneck and black jeans. She moved like a cat, swift and graceful, sliding into the passenger seat of the Targa, carrying a small grocery sack, folded over at the top.

"Dumb choice of wheels, Flannigan. You think Loser's going to talk when you climb out of a rolling red money pit smelling like law?"

Good point. Dixie had grown so comfortable tooling around in the Targa, not having to worry about the clutch, she hadn't considered how it would look to a homeless. "How far are we going? Maybe we can park it somewhere and walk." Dixie had brought her cane.

The girl nodded. "Drive around the corner to the Skylane Apartments. Park at the curb."

Dixie eased back onto Memorial Drive, glad to hear a note of cooperation in Ski's voice. Chronologically, the girl was roughly Sarina's age, but in street years at least a decade older. College had never been an option, high school probably just a nuisance. Dixie wondered if introducing the two girls might awaken Sarina's awareness of how good she had it.

The Skylane Apartments were vintage 1980s, new for the neighborhood, actually. This end of Memorial Drive had been gentrified many times over. The building provided covered parking, by extending the second floor out farther than the first, but no guard or gate. Dixie found a spot where she could pull the Targa well off the street. She followed Ski, with her grocery sack, into the parking area. It smelled of motor oil and trapped exhaust fumes.

Ski switched on a penlight and focused it into the backseat of the first car they came to.

"What are you doing?"

"Looking for Loser." Ski swept the slender beam into a car on the other side of them.

Homeless. Naturally, he wouldn't be in one of the apartments. An abandoned car would be a good home, if your only other option was a concrete doorway. But none of these cars, Fords, Chevys, Toyotas mostly, looked abandoned.

Ski moved on, shining the penlight into each vehicle.

"Why here?" Dixie asked. "Does he know someone who lets him sleep in their backseat?"

"Shhh. If he hears us, he'll run."

It took ten minutes to finish combing the parking lot, with no sign of Loser Boggs. When Ski headed back toward the Porsche, Dixie asked, "So what do we do now?"

"Go to the next set of apartments. This is his neighborhood."

Dixie didn't have to ask why this neighborhood. Street people typically found an area that suited them and stayed close. Maybe he'd grown up here, either on the lower income side, which would indicate homelessness due to poverty or drugs or general laziness, or the high income side, which would suggest mental illness. Not that poor people didn't sometimes have loose screws, but schizophrenia was one thing money couldn't cure, and it produced a tidal wave of homeless after the government cutbacks on mental health facilities.

The next apartment complex was definitely upscale — Mercurys, Accords, the occasional Cadillac.

"What does he do," Dixie asked, "break into a different car every night?"

"He doesn't break in, just tries all the doors until he finds one unlocked."

Moving with her feline grace, Ski went through the same drill, sliding between the cars and focusing the penlight into one backseat, then another. They'd searched two-thirds of the lot when the narrow beam fell on a mound of curly brown hair. Ski waved Dixie back, then opened the Buick's rear door.

"Loser?" She spoke softly, like a mother waking a child. "It's Ski. Can we talk?"

The mound of hair sat up. The car's interior light came on, and Dixie caught a glimpse of curly beard beneath a long, downturned nose.

"Ski?" the single word sounded both surprised and agreeable.

"I brought a friend, Loser. Can we all talk?"

"Friend? Where?"

"She's right here." Ski opened the door wider. "I brought some milk and Strawberry Newtons."

"Newtons." He scooted to make room. "Come in, Ski. Bring the Newtons."

"I want my friend to come, too, Loser. Is that all right with you?" Ski had made no move to get into the car. She waved Dixie closer.

"*Your* friend?" He sounded skeptical as his gaze swept toward Dixie, the moisture of his eyes reflecting the orange light of a nearby sodium vapor lamp.

"She can be your friend, too. I brought lots of Newtons."

"Okay."

He scooted to the far side of the velour-covered seat. Ski got in and handed Loser the paper sack. Dixie leaned her cane against the car and slid in beside her. Loser Boggs wore three tattered sweaters, only the bottom one fully buttoned, and a pair of corduroy pants that looked as if another pair might be hiding beneath them. His collar-length brown hair appeared clean, and his beard soft. He opened the bag eagerly.

Dixie had questioned skittish witnesses before. She knew not to move fast, though she wanted to start shooting questions at him. Ski had done such a good job so far, Dixie decided to let her continue.

As he popped an entire Strawberry Newton into his mouth, then turned his attention to opening the milk, Dixie glanced at her watch, wondering how soon the Buick's owner would be needing the car. The sun wouldn't be up for several hours.

Ski looked at Dixie, and when she nodded, turned back to Loser. "You told me you saw something scary in the park on Monday."

He fished another cookie out of the package, started to pop it in his mouth, then seemed to realize he wasn't the only one in the car, and offered it to Ski.

"Thank you. Loser, what was it you saw in the park?"

He studied the mouth of the milk carton. "Nothing."

"But you said—"

"*Heard* something scary." He gulped the milk. "Saw some people, then heard them."

His words were hesitant, but clear and well formed.

"What exactly did you hear?" Dixie asked carefully.

He darted a suspicious look from Dixie to Ski.

"It's okay," Ski murmured. "She's a friend."

He finished chewing another cookie, eyeing Dixie the whole time.

"Heard someone getting hit."

"How could you tell? Screams, shouts . . . blows—?"

"Grunts. The kind when someone's face is in a pillow, Dad going after him with a strap, sayin', 'Don't cry or you'll get ten more whacks just as hard.' "

He popped another cookie in his mouth. Dixie noticed he no longer looked anxious, just suspicious.

"You said you saw them . . . ?"

"Between the trees. Walking in the park."

"Men? Women?"

"One of them was small, a woman, I think. All dressed in dark clothes—except this one guy."

"Guy? You could tell?"

"White shirt, suit pants. Like he'd taken off his jacket after work, loosened his tie. Like that. The others all wore jeans, dark jackets, and those knitted caps that fit down over your ears." He looked at Ski and smiled. "I don't like hats."

"You have nice hair," she said, smiling back.

"You have nice hair." He offered her another cookie, but she hadn't even tasted the first one.

Something about Loser Boggs' smile triggered a memory, and Dixie figured she'd probably had him on a docket at one time or another. Trespassing, maybe.

"How many people were there?"

"Four."

"And only one was a woman?"

"Didn't say that. Dark. Hair covered with those knitted

caps?" He shrugged. "One might've been a woman, or a short man. Maybe all men. Maybe all women."

"Except the one in suit pants."

He nodded and scarfed up another cookie.

"Did you see his face?"

"Nope. Had a bag over his head."

Shit! It had to've been Coombs. Dixie wanted to ask Loser if he saw someone being taken into the woods with a bag over his head, why he hadn't *done* anything. But she knew. Street survival meant keeping your eyes and your mouth shut.

They talked while Loser finished the cookies and milk, but she learned nothing else of value. Brenda was taller than Dixie's five-foot-two, but not a lot taller. She might be the one Loser guessed to be a female. But Regan was fairly small, too. Clarissa was tall—not as tall as her husband, who had suggested his wife carry a gun. Clarissa wouldn't be a victims' rights volunteer if she didn't believe victims needed protection, and her husband obviously shared her beliefs. Dixie recalled Clarissa's loud accusations at the Suds Club, claiming Brenda's protection methods hadn't worked. Had she and her gun-toting husband decided to follow their protective instincts a step further?

Dixie also recalled Lowell Foxworth's statement that his wife had hardened after their daughter's hospitalization. Grace Foxworth had to be nearly six feet tall. Dressed in jeans and a dark jacket, and viewed from a distance, she'd pass for a man. And as much as Dixie had liked Lowell, he obviously carried an enormous hatred for the man who destroyed his family.

Having started poking around for her friend's sake, Dixie realized she was now just as concerned about the Foxworths, the Thomases, and Regan Salles. What worried her almost as much as the police catching up with them was their own potential for self-destruction. Decent people couldn't live easy with lawlessness and brutality, especially the vicious sort of assault issued on Coombs. Anger and guilt would surely start to eat at one or another of the Avenging Angels, until they turned on each other. She truly hoped their vengeance had run its course.

By the time she arrived home, the sky had lightened. In an hour Dixie's clock radio would signal time to get dressed and pick up Sarina. She entered the house silently. In the dim glow of a nightlight, Parker's sailboat snapshot caught her attention. She picked it up. She liked the idea of a romantic moonlight sail. She liked even more that he had arranged it to not interfere with her job.

At times Parker's caring made her feel so damn good. So why at other times did it made her feel smothered, manipulated, forced to choose between doing what made her feel good and what she knew was right?

Stripping her clothes off as she walked, Dixie gimped softly into the bedroom and drew back the curtains to glance out. The first ribbons of melon-colored sunlight wouldn't show for another half hour or so. And today was only Thursday. She could wait until after their moonlight sail to decide what to do about the weekend. She slipped under the covers and snuggled against Parker's broad, warm back.

Chapter Thirty-eight

Sid Carlson flexed his fingers around the monkey wrench and concentrated on the noises outside the trunk. Since the car stopped rolling, five, ten minutes ago, he'd heard low voices, doors banging, scuffling sounds like something being dragged. Now somebody was fartin around with the trunk lock. Sid hoped it was John, 'cause he was going to take the little fucker's head off.

Hearing a key slide into the lock, Sid gripped the wrench tighter, bracing his feet against the floor of the trunk. He'd hunkered himself into a ball, legs folded under him, ready to spring as soon as the lid opened. His knees hurt like hell from being bent double; he just hoped they wouldn't freeze up when he needed them.

In the darkness, he'd felt around with his fingers until he located the seam where the trunk lid joined the body, and now he stared at that spot, braced for the thinnest sliver of light to show. Wouldn't actually be light, of course, unless the sonofabitch parked under a street lamp, but Sid was watching for the slightest change from absolute blackness.

The lock clicked. A slip of gray showed through the crack. Sid unfolded, pushing up the lid with his back and swinging the monkey wrench in one swift motion.

He missed—*FUCK!*—and swung again, connecting this time and hearing a muffled curse as he fell headfirst to the ground, cracking his chin, getting a whiff of exhaust fumes. The wrench flew from his hand, clinked across the pavement, landing somewhere to his right. He tried to scramble after it, but one of the cocksuckers grabbed him by the collar and yanked him back, trying to pull him to his feet.

Sid wrapped an arm around the fucker's knees and heaved, pulling the sonofabitch down, hearing his tailbone strike the ground with a *whump* and him shrieking like a goddamn woman. The fucker would scream a hell of a lot harder before Sid got through. He snaked up on top, pinned the fucker to the ground, and sat on his stomach. Then Sid shot out a fist, a hammer blow to the fucker's nose. Blood spurted in Sid's face.

Hot damn! Nothing he liked better'n a good fight.

He reared back again, ready to loosen a few teeth with the next punch, but somebody grabbed his arm, somebody else kicked him in the head. He felt the boot heel flatten his ear, snapping his neck hard and making a popping sound inside his head. Then someone grabbed his other arm, lifting him up, dragging him across the concrete, ankles bumping over a threshold.

He blinked in the sudden dim light. Saw a clutter of boxes marked Bacardi, Budweiser, Chardonnay, Chivas, a storeroom, maybe, smelling of dust and rat turds, the boxes alphabetical. Stupid way to warehouse liquor, in Sid's mind. Smarter to shove all the hooch in one corner, all the beer in another, get rid of the fuckin wine. Sour damn crap nobody but women and queers drank, anyway.

And then he saw Gary, and Sid's stomach curled in on itself like a clam drying in its shell.

The fuckers had tied Gary to a wooden pallet loaded with boxes in the center of the room, Gary naked except for the rope looped around his neck, lashing his wrists and connecting him to the pallet. Gary was on his knees, slumped over a case of Miller Lite, a single shop light hanging overhead, the big guy's eyes wide open but not seeing, cheeks streaked with dirt, mouth working with no words coming out. Sid knew Gary was reliving The Nightmare.

"Cut him loose," Sid said quietly. Not yelling or anything, but real reasonable, 'cause he wanted it done now, RIGHT NOW, without any flak, and then they could do what the hell they wanted with him as long as Gary was out of it. "Cut him loose and I won't give you no more trouble."

"Trouble?" A squeaky voice, hell, it was a woman, sounding like she had a cold. Or a nose bleed. "We're the ones dishing out trouble, little man."

They had peeled off Sid's leather jacket and shirt, tied his hands behind him, and now the one Sid'd hit, the woman, was pulling off Sid's clothes. Her face was bloody. Sid wished it'd been that little cocksucker John he'd hit, but he wasn't sorry about the woman. Seeing the blank terror in Gary's eyes, Sid wished he'd shoved the cunt's fuckin nose bone straight into her brain.

His muscles twitched with rage that had bunched up inside him. He looked at Gary, laying there like a bitch dog ready to be mounted, and felt sick and helpless.

"Gary can't take being tied up," he said. "Cut him loose."

"You seem more worried about your good-looking friend than about yourself." A low voice in his ear, sexy. Another goddamn woman? "Are you and Gary asshole buddies, Sid? Is that why you're so worried about him?"

Shit! It wasn't like that, never had been like that. He loved Gary, that's all. In school, Sid'd been a snot-nosed runt, and Gary had taken care of him, saved his puny ass from being beaten to a pulp more times than Sid could count.

He jerked his wrists apart, twisted them, but the tape held tight, no give. He had to do *something*, though, to cut Gary free.

He lunged forward, breaking John's grip and shoving aside the tall bitch with the sexy voice. Then he turned and kicked her halfway across the room, liking the rush it gave him, wishing he was Chuck Norris or Bruce-fuckin-Lee. Stumbling, though, with his hands tied, throwing him off balance. He aimed for John-the-little-fucker's nuts, and missed, kicked his thigh instead.

The tall bitch darted out of the way. She was dressed like the others, dark pants, sweatshirt, knit cap. Couldn't see her face good. She grabbed a push broom out of the shadows, holding it by the bristle end, and jabbed it at him. Without his hands to fend off the blows, Sid could only dodge: the broom handle caught him under the ribs, again in the gut, and then a hard stiff jab in the soft spot right above his stomach knocked the wind out of him.

He managed to stay on his feet, but she swung the next blows overhand, the crazy bitch strong as a wild hog, coming down hard on his back and his neck and his head. He stumbled toward Gary, fell to one knee trying to think of something, *anything*, he could do to get Gary loose.

"Hang on, guy," he muttered. "We'll get out of this." Saying it but not believing.

The next blow caught Sid above the ear, knocking him sideways, his head going dull inside like wet cotton.

"Bring him over here," someone said. "Give him a front-row seat for the show starring his asshole buddy."

Then they were tying him seated against a crate, arms stretched backward, the rope looped once around his neck. Sid shook his head, trying to clear it. Blood from a gash on his face spattered the floor. The pain in his head was like a firecracker exploding.

Someone grabbed his hair, jerked his head back.

"You remember little Celeste, don't you, Sid?" The sexy

voice, purring close at his ear. "Celeste's uncle must have felt about as angry and helpless as you do right about now."

Who the fuck was she talking about, *Celeste*?

"Remember tying her up, making her uncle watch while you beat and raped her?"

Celeste. The sweet-thang they'd took as a bonus. Well, it was no more than what the shithead old store owner deserved, taking his deposit to the bank early. Here they'd been watching the place all fuckin week, ready to rake in a big load, and barely got sixty fuckin dollars outta the fuckin till.

"We're going to give your friend the same treatment you gave Celeste. You get to watch all the fun until your own turn comes."

"No!" He lowered his head to butt her, but the rope yanked him back, choking him. "C'mon now, listen," he gasped. "You got to let Gary go. He didn't do anything, I was the one did the girl and beat the old man."

"Celeste said it was *both* of you."

"Well, she's wrong, that's all."

She smoothed his hair back out of his face. Sid could see the other one across the room, wrapping black tape around the handle end of a sawed-off broomstick for better grip, the wood beaded with nail heads like the ones him and Gary kept under the car seat. Like the ones they'd used on the girl and the old storekeeper. Sid felt his bowels go weak.

He knew what was coming, and so would Gary. Gary would know better than anybody.

Even as a kid, Gary had been a looker, the girls twitching around him, old ladies patting him, saying what a fine big boy he was. When his ma died, Gary was nine, maybe ten. People around said the old man went home drunk one too many times and finally beat her to death, which was his right, her being his property and all. Then instead of looking for another wife, the old man started using Gary for a woman. Gary got real moody after that, and real quiet.

A few years later—Gary would have been twelve—his pop got in trouble and had to come up with a bunch of

money to pay a debt. Gary said the old man'd acted weird all
week, even when he was drunk, treating Gary nice and
inviting guys from all over the county to a party that
weekend. The old man's friends, sure, but also guys he didn't
even know.

Turned out Gary was the entertainment, chained to a big
staple his pop drove in the floor by the bed. Every man who
came paid at the door, then used Gary any way he wanted.

Besides the sex part, they beat him. Beat him with everything within reach in that old house. Every few hours, the
old man would shove Gary into the bathroom, tell him to
clean himself up, and Gary would swallow a handful of
water. But nobody bothered to feed him. Gary said he
probably couldn't have kept food down anyway.

It took two weeks for Gary to heal enough to go back to
school and nearly a year for him to get up enough nerve to
kill the old man. Then him and Sid lit out on their own.
They'd been hanging out together ever since. Most of the
time Gary was like anybody else, except maybe a bit more
quiet. And sometimes he'd get real moody until he got a
chance to use his big fists on some geezer, give out a little of
what he'd taken on that nightmare weekend. One thing
Gary still couldn't stand, though, even for a minute, was
being tied up.

The mousy woman with the screechy voice struck the first
blow, a full roundhouse with the nail-studded broomstick
across Gary's ass as he lay slumped over the Miller Lite box.
Gary's head snapped up, back arched, his mouth and eyes
opened wide with astonishment. Sid felt the pain as if it were
his own, even as he saw the woman lower the broomstick to
deliver a different sort of pain to Gary's backside.

Sid's rage exploded. He kicked the tall bitch in the knee,
thinking maybe he heard a crack as his shoe connected
with bone.

She cursed and stumbled, but recovered fast, whirling
toward him, her own foot drawn back, and Sid suddenly remembered how they'd silenced the old man in the store.

Through his fear, he saw John coming in from the side, the cocksucker not even as big as the woman but reaching out to stop her, and then the woman's heavy black boot slammed into his mouth. His first feeling was sheer disbelief that anything could hurt so fuckin bad, then through a red haze of pain he felt teeth crumble on his tongue like peanuts.

Chapter Thirty-nine

"That's enough."

Sissy shook away the hand that had jerked her off balance. "It's not half enough." She looked down at Carlson's bloody mouth and itched to land another blow. "It's only a taste of what they did to Celeste and her uncle."

"Nevertheless, it's enough." The woman's voice was calm. *Back off*, the bright, hard eyes commanded, *I'm taking charge here*.

Sissy met the eyes with her own, her jaw muscles tensed with resolve. She would not be deterred from the Lord's work.

Silence thrummed the air like torque on an E string.

"Hey!" From across the room. "This one here's passed out. Passed right out."

"He's been out of it since we tied him up." Sissy spat the words. Ignoring the ache of her own knee where Carlson had kicked her, she booted a carton out of her way. "This is no time to turn squeamish. We have a job to do here."

"The job's finished." The bright hard eyes had not wavered. "We've done enough. Keep this up and we're as bad as they are."

"That's not true." Sissy fought the rage that made her want to lash out at her friends. They mustn't turn on one another. Together, they were God's Fist. "We administer justice, we don't attack innocent people."

"We've gone beyond justice."

The worm with the bloody mouth moaned. Sissy's foot twitched with the need to knock out the rest of his miserable teeth. "God's justice is an eye for an eye. These two have only begun to pay."

"They've paid and we're finished. Let's get out of here."

"Hey, listen to me over here! This guy's not breathing, I tell you. I think he's dead. DEAD!"

"Don't be silly." Sissy was out of patience. "Of course he's breathing."

"He's not. *He's not breathing!*"

"You're getting hysterical." Sissy strode to Gary Ingles' side, her injured knee smarting, and laid a hand on his wrist. No pulse. On his throat. Nothing. "How long has he been like this?"

"I don't know . . . I just . . . Oh, jeez, we've got to call an ambulance!"

The other one shoved Sissy aside and pressed a hand at Ingles' throat. "Cut him loose." Catching Ingles' jaw, she leaned down and breathed into his mouth.

"Stop that," Sissy said. "If he's dead, so be it. Raymond Ramirez is dead, too. And how many others?"

"I said *cut him loose!*"

Sissy watched her bleeding-heart friend turn Ingles on his back and continue breathing for him.

"One of you take over," the woman said between breaths, "while I try to start his heart."

"Oh, jeez, I couldn't. I can't!" The whine rose another octave. "Let's dial 911. Get someone here who knows what they're doing."

Sissy stepped back, disgusted. "Nobody's calling 911. The man's a killer and a rapist. He deserves to die."

"Eh?" Sid Carlson roused from his own stupor and sputtered through his ruined mouth. "Wha's goan on?"

"Shut up!" Sissy took three swift strides and kicked him between the eyes. It'd be fine with her if they were both dead.

Chapter Forty

Thursday, February 13

A rapid treble voice rang down the hallway as Dixie and Sarina approached the office of Ramón Alvarez, Graphologist.

"What are you telling me now?" he demanded. "First, you say you're depressed, so small, and descending, almost weeping off the page. Now, you bounce all over, up and down, up and down."

This time the graphologist was not yelling into his phone, but down at his desk, apparently at a page of handwriting. His door was propped open by a plastic basset hound that barked mechanically as Sarina's steps vibrated the floor. When Dixie rapped on the door with her cane, Ramón waved them over to the desk.

"Look at this. This handwriting wants me to think a patient has been cured. Does this look cured to you?"

Though Dixie hadn't a clue what he was talking about, she peered intently at the page of writing. Sarina had brought her rod puppet to work on, but appeared to find

Ramón's conundrum more interesting. She squeezed in behind Dixie.

The handwriting on the page bent left, then right, then left again. *My time here has been very productive . . .* read the first line. The irregular form had extra-large descending strokes on the *y* and *p*.

"This patient is *not* cured. Could I forgive myself if his mother took him from the hospital and then he tried to off himself again? I could not forgive that."

"You can detect suicide tendencies in this writing?" Dixie was impressed. She hadn't realized graphology was that precise.

"You don't see it?" Ramón thumped the paper, exasperated. He pushed the first page aside to reveal another, this one with small, tightly formed letters that descended to almost nothing at the end of a sentence. The two styles didn't seem as if they could be written by the same individual. "There!" He tapped the longest line with his stumpy finger.

"I don't have your keen eye, Ramón. Did you get a chance to look at the samples I brought yesterday?"

"Oh!" He waggled his head side to side. "Another imposter!"

Shuffling his folders, he produced one with FLANNIGAN printed boldly on the front. He spread the folder open. The top fax was of the first card Joanna received from the stalker, with the note: GOD BLESS YOU, JOANNA. THE MESSAGE IN YOUR NEW MOVIE HAS GIVEN ME REASON TO LIVE.

"Such sweet words, 'God bless you.' But such angry strokes. Look!"

Dixie looked. Couldn't see what he meant. He turned the page upside down, as he had the day before.

"Angry! You see these downstrokes? Heavy, made with great, angry pressure." He fanned the remaining faxes. "And this one."

The fax he indicated was the one that threatened Sarina: NO MORE MEN, JOANNA! IF YOU HAVEN'T THE STRENGTH TO

PRESERVE YOUR PURITY, I MUST HELP YOU. YOUR DAUGHTER WILL SACRIFICE FOR YOUR SINS.

"Angry! But these—" He flipped through the remaining faxed greeting cards. "Do you see anger here?"

Dixie had to admit the writing on these pages was much more consistent, though the downstrokes still appeared heavier, slightly wider, than the cross strokes. She could understand the stalker being furious when writing the Sarina note, but not that first message. And if he was angry when writing the first one, what calmed him down for the next two?

"Could the writer be unstable? Mentally ill?"

Ramón waved the notion aside. "Who can say? Insecure? Yes. Hot-tempered? Definitely. But from this I would not say someone is nuts."

"So what else *can* you tell me?"

Ramón lifted all five faxes from the file and fanned them like a deck of cards.

"He has—" The graphologist stopped and looked at Dixie. "You do realize I don't mean 'he' precisely? We cannot determine sex or age from handwriting."

"Yeah." Dixie knew that from past cases, but Ramón always reminded her.

"He has no connections, which would fool some analysts, thinking he purposely printed the notes to disguise the writing. But this does not fool Ramón. I believe he always prints with no connections. To disguise the writing, he used his off hand."

"*Off* hand?"

"Left, if he's right-handed." Dixie nodded, and Ramón continued. "No connections says he is a fussbudget. You know that word?"

"Yeah. He's into details, wants everything perfect."

"Good! Yes, he wants perfection, maybe is even a bit artistic. And look here, the capital letters in the middle of sentences. Do the words 'message' and 'given' have more importance to him than 'reason' or 'live'? I think not. This one is under extreme emotional pressure. Or he is lying."

Dixie examined the words. She had not actually thought of the letters as capitals, because they were only minutely larger than the others, but she could see now what Ramón meant.

"And this hook on the T-bar? Determined! This one will not be easily diverted from a cause."

Dixie probed for ten more minutes, but only a few points Ramón made seemed useful. The words "movie" and "daughter" and "sacrifice" were written more carefully than others, and these words all appeared in the "angry" notes. Also in these two notes, the words were widely spaced, but the letters were crammed closely together, which Ramón considered a sign of the writer's stress or tension.

When Dixie explained the difference between the faxed notes and the two cards Sarina had provided, Ramón's interest instantly escalated.

"How did you trace the letters, young lady? There's no seeing through this heavy card."

"Simple. I scanned one of the messages. The last one was still around when I heard Mother tell Marty I'd be going with her to Houston. Like I don't have a life! Then I extrapolated the letters I didn't have and printed out the messages on a two-part form Marty's secretary uses. The top page of the form has this transfer stuff on the back."

"So then you positioned this transfer just right and traced over the letters with a—what, a ballpoint?" He ran his finger lightly over the red lettering.

"Pencil. Very lightly, otherwise it made indentions and the blue carbon, or whatever, showed through the red felt tip." Sarina shrugged. "I had to practice a few times."

"Then this pastose, this flowing ink, is your work?"

"Yeah, I guess."

"I will tell you something about yourself." Ramón's chin lifted with his usual conceit. He knew damn well he was good. "Without seeing your own handwriting, not even a signature, I say you are sensual. I say you are very imaginative, warm, and pleasure-loving. You enjoy intense experiences. An artist, and perhaps a bit self-indulgent?"

Sarina's mouth dropped only a little. "Can you tell me if I'm going to make my first big movie before I'm eighteen? Spielberg did it before eighteen."

Scowling at her mother's list, Sarina sullenly chose the Houston Arboretum and Nature Center for her one concession to culture. Dixie mentally applauded the choice. They'd likely be the only two people on the trails on a brisk February morning. Luckily, the gates opened early.

Sarina breezed past the native specimens in the indoor botanical hall with scarcely a glance, spotting some stationery in the gift-shop window she wanted to pick up later for Joanna—probably to prove they'd been doing the things laid out for them. Most of the outdoor plants were winter skeletons. They walked three of the five miles of trails before the kid found something that actually interested her. A green froth of ancient ferns, live oak trees dipping their low-hanging, moss-laden branches near the water, a cool mist enveloping everything, the scene conveyed prehistoric earth like nothing Dixie had ever seen.

While Sarina sketched, Dixie found a rock to perch on. A pale sun promised to break through the overcast later, but at present the mild breeze over the water held an uncommonly sharp bite, even for February. Wriggling her butt to a more comfortable position on the rock, she powered her cell phone on. She'd resisted carrying the damn thing for months, but it'd proven so useful in the past few days, killing time in movie theaters and winter gardens, that she might actually kiss Belle Richards for insisting she anchor it to her belt. She dialed Brenda's home phone number: no answer. Dixie had pretty much given up on buttonholing her friend about the Avenging Angels, but she did need to confirm their self-defense class at Ryan's school later that morning. Glanc-

ing at her watch, she punched in the office number. Julie
Colby answered, sounding rushed.

"Brenda phoned in a message earlier," Julie said. "She
has some personal errands to take care of before lunch—
guess that includes your class. She really likes teaching those
kids. I know she'll miss it, now that you're—well, you *are* getting that cast off soon, I hope. Can't be comfortable."

Dixie assured her the cast would be off before the week
was out, ended the call, and immediately dialed Les Crews
at Quantico, hoping he wasn't out of town. He often lectured
in criminal justice programs across the country. Or out sick—

"Les! Dixie Flannigan. Hope you have a minute to talk."

"Fuck you, Flannigan."

Whoa! The man was often abrupt, even rude, but . . .
"Hey, Les, if this is not a good time—"

"What the hell's that piece of shit package you sent here?"

"My note—"

"Said you have a stalker. You want me to tell you who,
where, what color his eyes are, what the sonofabitch eats for
breakfast. I *read* your goddamn note. I don't like smartass
pranks taking up my time."

Pranks? "Les, what's going on? I sent a few stalker notes.
Thought you might see something in the wording that
would help us. That's it. If you don't have time—"

"You're telling me you didn't know they came right out of
one of my papers?"

"What?"

"*Loving Pursuit: The Faith Burrows Stalker.* I sent you the
goddamn paper five years ago."

No wonder the words had rung false when she'd read
them. Dixie had been working a sex offense case, and Les
Crews sent the stalking paper in a stack of similar but more
specific material on sex offenders.

She pulled out her pocket notebook and started scribbling.

"Sorry, Les. One of the messages seemed familiar, but I
didn't place it."

"Hell, when the Burrows case broke, and the stalking laws were getting a boost, that paper was published everywhere — including photographs of the goddamn letters Eckers wrote."

Crews sounded placated, more or less. And the case was coming back now. Eckers had been one of the stalkers convicted and sentenced in Arizona, right after voters made stalking a felony.

Hearing the *whir* of a camera's motor drive, Dixie looked around for Casey James. Dixie had phoned the reporter before leaving home that morning and asked if she'd bring copies of the shots she'd taken on Joanna's set Tuesday afternoon. Casey sat on a tree branch near ground level, elbow on a KEEP OFF sign. She was photographing Sarina.

"Les, a copycat *stalker*? Is that possible?"

" '*You must overcome your weakness, Faith. Your weakness is men.*' Does that sound close enough to you?"

Almost identical. Only, Joanna's stalker had said "illness." This was one of the notes Ramón had indicated was not written in anger. "How about the others?"

Dixie could hear the profiler's labored breathing and remembered he'd stopped smoking years ago, doctor's orders. She wondered if he'd started again. After a few seconds, evidently reading the copies she'd sent, he muffled the phone and cleared his throat.

"Here's one: '*If you haven't the strength to preserve your purity, I must help you. Your daughter will sacrifice for your sins.*' The Burrows letter read: '*If you haven't the strength to protect our unity, your children will sacrifice for your sins.*' Eckers maintained that he and Burrows were 'two halves of the same soul,' star-crossed lovers or some shit. Should've seen the crap we pulled out of his spare bedroom — animal skulls filled with black candle wax, acupuncture needles he'd been using to pierce his own skin. Sonofabitch even took pictures, him standing nude with three hundred needles sticking out of him. Sick goober bastard."

Dixie shivered, and knew it wasn't from the chilly wind.

"Anything you can tell us about *our* guy? The fact that he copied another stalker's letters, does that indicate anything?"

"Shit if I know. Copycats get a hard-on for the 'famed felon,' see themselves improving on their hero's techniques, certain they won't get caught. Burrows was a hometown nurse, not a TV actress. Husband, three toddlers. Eckers had a ten-year-old picture of his older sister, who looked amazingly like Burrows, taped to his mirror—where he took the snapshot of himself with the needles."

Dixie filled her notebook with information as fast as Crews spit it out. She'd sort out the relevant parts later, along with the stuff Ramón had given her. Right now nothing was making any sense.

"Les, I've dealt with plenty of stalker situations, but none where I was the one in charge of keeping the principal safe. Anything you can tell me?"

"Yeah. Think of the most sensible thing to do and do the opposite. You already know that responding to a stalker—returning unopened letters, changing the phone number, getting a judge to issue a restraining order—all of that only makes the goober more obsessed. So does having a bodyguard. They obsess on waiting for that instant when the principal is unguarded. Then they strike."

Dixie whipped her gaze to Sarina, still sketching her scene.

"The good news," Les continued, "is that most stalking cases extinguish with time."

True. Dixie had told many an anxious woman to be patiently wary, and eventually the jerk annoying her would give up. But Burrows had been kidnapped and raped while Crews and the local officials were trying to get enough evidence against Eckers to arrest him.

"One more question, Les, if you have another minute. You heard about our Avenging Angels, I take it?"

" 'Citizen participation in crime prevention' is the official term, Flannigan. Posse comatatus committees. *Vigilantes.*

Effective. Visit Montana, Idaho, South Carolina, see how they claim to have cleaned up their states through 'citizen participation.' "

"And what kind of behavior would I look for in a . . . vigilante suspect?"

"Hmmmm. Number-one thing to remember, vigilantes justify their actions on the grounds that *not* acting would've made them victims rather than victors. Every vigilante perceives some kind of danger. Just because the rest of us don't see it, doesn't mean the danger isn't real to them."

"And after the perceived danger is past?"

"If it's one individual? Might end right there. Your 'Angel' goes on with everyday life, probably with increased enthusiasm. If it's a posse, then you're dealing with different dynamics. The leader sometimes becomes addicted to the power. Won't let go. Shared responsibility makes their actions appear just and reasonable. Klansmen actually pass a weapon from hand to hand, demanding everyone handle it. The rush, the sense of self-importance, puts more and more 'evildoers' on their hit list, until the smallest infringement demands punishment. Remember the Salem witch-hunts?"

Crews sounded as if he was into one of his lectures. Dixie knew all this, but couldn't help being fascinated by Crews' passion.

"I love this quote," Crews chuckled, "from an American sergeant who joined in the interrogation of Vietcong prisoners. 'First you strike to get mad, then you strike because you *are* mad, then you strike for the sheer pleasure of it.' "

Mob rage. Dixie felt another chill. "I doubt the Angels were into pleasure when they assaulted Coombs." But she wasn't sure she believed it. "And the man was a rapist—"

"Of course! Deserved every swinging blow. When Francine Hughes took her last beating, poured gasoline around her husband's bed, set it afire, and walked away from a murder charge, women started believing their only escape from being a victim is to be the victor. Don't walk away, kill the bastard."

"Coombs wasn't killed."

"No, Flannigan, but are you dealing with an individual or a posse? If it's a posse, you might not've seen the end of it."

That's what Dixie hadn't wanted to hear. Loser Boggs had seen four figures in Memorial Park. One would be Coombs. Did three constitute a mob? "What do I look for in questioning suspects?"

Crews seemed to think about that for a few seconds. "I know you want a checklist, like with serial killers, but the truth is, vigilantes are ordinary people. What you look for is the suspect who appears more self-assured than usual. Satisfied. Unafraid. That is, if it's an individual. In a posse, group dynamics will either create such a feeling of self-righteousness that someone eventually brags to a friend. Or guilt causes someone to want out. When that happens, you get to scrape up the pieces."

Chapter Forty-one

"Intriguing conversation you had there." Casey's camera clicked off shots at Dixie. "Pardon my eavesdropping, but that's what I do best. Somebody wound you up and aimed you toward the Avenging Angels?"

Dixie hated being photographed, never knowing what to do with her face. She was tempted to stick out her tongue, but figured that'd be precisely the shot to end up on the front page of the *Houston Chronicle*.

"I can see your headline, Casey: 'Cousins Visit Arboretum.' Must be a slow day for news."

"You'll lead me to a juicy piece, Dixie. I have faith." She snapped off a few more shots of Sarina. "These just might surface in my gallery collection. The kid has the same body lines as her famous mother did in the early days, like a young gazelle, gangly and bursting with energy. This is the first time I've caught her totally still."

True, the kid could make you tired just walking along a path, the way she darted ahead and skipped from side to side.

Casey let the camera dangle from her stumpy neck. "Joanna did her best work in those early days. Goldie on *Guerilla Gold*? Always was a talented bitch. But then, you'd know that, being her *cousin*." An evil grin stretched the reporter's lips, somehow displaying pink gums without showing any teeth.

"Bitch?"

"Isn't that what we label every woman who claws her way to the top, Counselor?"

Dixie didn't miss the jab. In her own career, she'd been frequently referred to as the State's Courtroom Bitch. "Joanna has talent, beauty—"

"So do thousands of dewy-eyed dreamers in Hollywood. Three actresses starred in the pilot. Like the Three Little Pigs, they dropped one by one, each time replaced with lesser talent. Except for Joanna."

"You're saying she sabotaged her co-stars?"

"Joanna was smart enough to have a tough agent." Casey's piggy eyes narrowed at Dixie. "What did you think about our Angels striking again, big time?"

The fine hairs on Dixie's arms bristled. "Big time? What does that mean?"

Casey's camera flashed. Dixie cursed herself, falling for the reporter's bait.

"One down, one dead. Sid Carlson, Gary Ingles, respectively, as they say. I don't know any more than that. What about you, honey? Know anything I can use?"

"How would I know anything about the Angels? I'm curious, like everybody else."

"Everybody else is hoping these guys do a Batman and Robin number on the city. Interesting, isn't it, how our biggest heroes are vigilantes, cleaning up crime the cops can't deal with? Superman? The Lone Ranger? Wouldn't surprise me to find Dixie Flannigan on that list."

"You can't believe I had anything to do with what happened to Coombs or Carrera, much less Carlson and Ingles. My God, Casey, *murder*?"

"Heart failure is the early diagnosis on Ingles. While enduring the sort of beating the Ramirez girl suffered. And, honey, if you're not an Avenging Angel in fact, you are in spirit. Isn't that why you left the legitimate world of crime fighters, because you couldn't punish the offenders enough?"

A rush of heat filled Dixie's face. Casey had struck too close to the bone.

"I'm not part of any self-appointed justice committee. And if you print one word that suggests I am, Casey, you'll regret it."

"You know a lot more than you tell. No one else has figured Patricia Carrera as one of the Angels' targets."

Damn! "It's only a hunch."

"I've known you awhile, Counselor. You don't shoot in the dark without infrared. Like these photographs." She drew a packet from her coat pocket. "What's in these that has your hackles up?"

Dixie glanced at Sarina, still engrossed in her prehistoric sketch.

"Like I said, Joanna wants them. Something about a scrapbook."

Casey rolled her eyes, smiling toothlessly, and handed over the photographs. Dixie flipped through them, careful not to seem particularly interested.

"If you spot anything prime in there," Casey grumbled, "you're better than I am. Wasted day, except for the spats between director and crew—too clichéd to get excited about."

But Dixie had already found the photo she wanted. She flipped on past, then slipped the glossy prints back into their envelope. "Thanks. I owe you one."

"Don't think I won't collect, honey."

Dixie's thoughts flipped back to Casey's news.

Gary Ingles, dead. "How do they know it's the Angels this time?"

"Who else? Think we got two gangs of hotheads running around Houston?" She cocked her head, as if listening to an inner thought. "Come to that, maybe it's an angle—anything's possible in this town. Police aren't saying, only that they found the pair in a liquor warehouse, both beaten, the dead one sexually used and abused, as they say." She handed Dixie a folded page torn from a small notebook. "That other thing you wanted—and for this you owe me big time. The story that Joanna Francis was a doper came from an anonymous tip. I sweet-talked the reporter into giving me a description of Mr. Anonymous—not the name, but with this hairball I could probably have gotten the name, too, if he knew it. He didn't."

Dixie opened the notepaper. She wasn't surprised to learn that the anonymous tipster who nearly ruined Joanna's career a year earlier fit the description of a person in one of Casey's snapshots taken on the set two days ago. She tucked the note away with the photos.

Meanwhile, her mind raced with the news that the Angels had gone as far as murder. A liquor warehouse—to symbolize the Ramirez liquor store Sid and Gary robbed? One dead, as they'd left the old man dead. One raped, as they'd raped the old man's niece?

"What kind of shape is Carlson in? Can he talk?"

Casey shrugged. "Alive. That's all I know."

Maybe he'd be able to identify his assailants. Dixie waited for Casey to leave, then called Sergeant Benjamin Rashly at the HPD's Homicide Division. She and Rashly had worked together when Dixie was with the DA's office.

"Rashly."

Dixie heard the clink of Ben's pipe against his teeth.

"Thought you'd quit smoking."

"Who's this? Flannigan?"

"Quitters Anonymous. Remember the old *Twilight Zone* episode?"

"Never watched that show."

"Fellow signs up to quit smoking. He lights one cigarette, and his wife is abducted and tortured—given an electric hot-foot. Second time he's caught, she loses her little finger. Third time . . . Well, you get the picture."

"Jesus! That's nuts! What kind of idiot would sign a contract like that?" His smoker's voice was rough as a file.

"It was just a TV show, Rash."

"Now I remember why I never watched it. Flannigan, you didn't call to needle me about smoking."

"What's the story on Carlson and Ingles?"

He took his time answering. "Did I miss something? Mayor appoint you Chief of Police while I wasn't looking?"

Rashly never parted with information easily. Searching her mind for a scrap of street info to use as a bargaining chip, Dixie recalled a tidbit Brew had passed along about a connection between a DOA at the Port of Houston and recent burglaries in North Houston. It wasn't much.

But Rashly hesitated a second too long. He was interested.

"If you know something, Flannigan, don't do-si-do with me."

"Maybe it's nothing. Who can believe street talk?"

Dixie counted the seconds while Rashly gnawed the stem of his pipe—unlit, of course. Always grumpy, he'd become downright irascible after the city vetoed smoking in public buildings. But during Dixie's years as ADA, Rashly earned her respect with his dogged investigation techniques.

"What've you got?" he said, finally.

Dixie kept the report short and factual. The scratch of a ballpoint pen told her Rashly was taking notes. He didn't have to ask her source. One reason the local police never came down hard on the Gypsy Filchers was the useful information they occasionally provided.

Then she asked about the Ingles murder.

"You're a civilian now, kid. Got no business messing around in murder cases. What's your interest?"

Dixie wondered how much she could say without implicating Brenda.

"You noticed similarities, I take it, between the Carlson-Ingles beatings and the Coombs assault in Memorial Park."

"Homicide is on speaking terms with Sex Crimes, if that's what you're asking." Hearing the faint thumps and scrapes as he cleaned and refilled his pipe, Dixie could almost smell the fragrant Middleton's Cherry Blend he preferred over more exotic tobaccos.

"What about the disappearance of Patricia Carrera? Anything turn up on that?"

"Carrera? That's a civil case, Flannigan. Protective Services stepped out of it months ago. You going to ring in a divorce or two next? Try to tie it all up with organized crime, maybe some kind of government conspiracy?"

"Just a hunch, Rash."

"And I'm supposed to poke around in a civil lawsuit on one of your hunches?" But Rashly believed in the intuitive processes people in law enforcement often developed. "I'll kick it around. Doubt there's anything we can use there. Now, why are you telling me?"

"Thought you might reciprocate."

"Ask, Flannigan, or get off my phone."

"Coombs claimed one of his assailants was a woman. Did Sid Carlson get a look at his assailants? Male, female, how many?"

"Said there were three, all dressed in black clothes and wearing knit caps pulled low, covering their hair. He thinks two were women. The third he wasn't sure about."

She heard his pipe clink against an ashtray just before he cradled the phone.

Two women. Even dropping Carrera out of the equation, one of those women had to be Brenda. She was the only one connected to both cases. Unless . . .

Clarissa Thomas was one of the more unbridled, more headstrong of the Victims Advocates, and the Ramirez case had been all over the news right after it happened—two victims, an elderly man and a pretty young woman. Anyone following the story knew the beating and rape were particularly brutal. Clarissa would've followed the case. When Ingles and Carlson were released, she'd have been outraged.

And Clarissa was always the fire behind Regan. The person who'd convinced Regan to testify. Had she also convinced Regan to get even?

As Sarina finished her sketch and started walking back along the path, Dixie dialed the number she'd jotted down for Donald Thomas listed in Southwest Houston. No answer.

"That munchkin who was here." Sarina tucked her pad and markers into a leather portfolio she'd brought along. "Is it you or me she's following?"

"I'm not sure Casey cares, as long as one of us leads her to a sensational story."

"Will we?

"I hope not."

While Sarina purchased the stationery she'd spotted for Joanna, Dixie stopped at a pay phone that miraculously still had its Yellow Pages tucked into a niche. She opened to hair salons, and started calling all the numbers in the Post Oak/ Memorial area, where Brenda had mentioned Regan worked. On the fifth call, she hit a home run.

The receptionist said Regan could probably work Dixie in if she wanted to stop by the salon after two o'clock. That would allow time for her and Sarina to grab lunch after the self-defense class at Ryan's school. Dixie had told Parker she might get a sexy new hairstyle. Now was her big chance.

Chapter Forty-two

Dixie couldn't help feeling apprehensive every time she saw the seventh-, eighth-, and ninth-graders bunched together, boys feigning karate kicks, girls stealing glances and giggling. The skills they learned in this class, which the private school had agreed to try on an experimental basis, could be used as easily for violence as for self-defense.

Krav Maga, the Israeli technique, was brutal but effective. It took months to learn instead of years. But as in any martial art, mental discipline mattered most. And despite Dixie's insistence that gender didn't count, the raging hormones of puberty proved otherwise. Young males slapped and punched, young females posed and flirted.

They were old enough that she'd laid out the grim statistics in the first class: Every fifteen seconds, a woman is assaulted and beaten. Every 1.3 minutes, a woman is raped. Sixty-one percent of all rapes involve females under seventeen. The part she didn't tell them was that twenty-nine percent are females yet to reach their eleventh birthday. And sixteen percent of all *males* are sexually molested as children. She did talk about muggings, kidnappings, and assaults that might happen outside the family. She talked about drug pushers and peer pressure. And about weapons. She had issued every kid in the room a police whistle for emergencies and a leather thong for carrying it.

Twenty-three kids in the room, all from upper-middle-class homes. How many were already statistics? Dixie hoped what she taught them would someday change the dismal figures.

She looked at her twelve-year-old nephew and was glad she was only an aunt. How could any parent be sure of doing the right thing at the right time?

After the kids all signed her cast, and while they waited for Brenda Benson to arrive, Dixie wrote on the white board, as she did every session:

> *"Power of mind is infinite, while brawn is limited."*
> —Kochi Tohei

> *"Instead of trying to do everything well, do those things perfectly of which you are capable."*
> —Bruce Lee

Her intention was to show kids of both genders they had all the strength and ability needed to escape an attacker. They had only to practice using those abilities.

At five minutes past the time for class to start, Brenda had not arrived. Dixie introduced Sarina, who drew instant approving looks from the boys and awe from the girls.

"Who's the fox?" Ryan whispered, cutting his eyes at Sarina.

"My new assistant. Now get back there with your classmates." She turned to Sarina. "Do you mind? Nothing you can't handle, I promise."

Sarina grinned. "No sweat."

"Let's review briefly," Dixie told the class. "What's the best form of self-defense?"

"Escape!" they shouted in unison.

"Good. What else have you learned?"

"Use your whole body as a unit!" Ryan yelled.

"Right. Let's look at something new." Setting her cane aside, she positioned Sarina and told her to take her best punch. Dixie demonstrated how to deflect the blow and use the attackers' own force against her. "The next step is to keep moving and get to safety."

She paired the kids up and let them practice.

"You did pretty good there," she told Sarina. "I take it this is not all new to you."

"I got out of ballet by agreeing to take tai chi."

"Good choice. Although ballet is a terrific workout for defensive arts."

When the kids had practiced the exercise long enough to get restless, she held up her hand for quiet.

"What are the three skills to practice daily?"

"Run!"

"Dodge, deflect, and turn fast!"

"Thrust and twist!"

Brenda entered the gym just as Dixie and Sarina had demonstrated body-twisting to dislodge a hold. The prosecutor nodded brusquely at Dixie and stepped in to handle the next move. Dark circles under her amber eyes suggested she hadn't slept much the night before. Her makeup had been applied hastily. Her usual easy banter with the kids was replaced with a sharp command to take the moves seriously.

"Concentrate on watching your opponent," Brenda insisted. "When you move, your whole body, including the eyes, must move as a unit." She made the kids practice a hold-breaking thrust over and over.

"Your friend sure knows how to bum out a room," Sarina whispered to Dixie. "Totally uncheery in here all of a sudden."

The kids were feeling it, too. They'd stiffened up and gone quiet. Ryan shot a puzzled look at Dixie. She looked at her watch, waited a second, and stepped in, ignoring Brenda's sharp glance.

"Nice job!" Dixie put enough enthusiasm in her words, she hoped, to offset the gloomy atmosphere that had descended. "Now what are we going to practice this week?"

"Running," someone mumbled.

"Whoa, what was that wimpy answer?" Dixie grinned at them. "*What* are we going to practice this week?"

"Running."

"Dodge, deflect, and turn fast!"

"Thrust and twist!"

They were smiling again, at least. "And what's the best form of self-defense?"

"*Escape!*"

Dixie dismissed the class. But when she looked around for Brenda, the prosecutor had disappeared.

Chapter Forty-three

When Regan Salles smiled, she did it with her whole being, and suddenly the pouty sexpot became girl-next-door gorgeous. Discovering Sarina was the daughter of actress Joanna Francis elicited a wide-eyed, elated smile.

"*Joanna Francis?* Jeez! She's my favorite actress of all time. All time! I can't believe I'm actually talking to her daughter. Let me touch you!" She touched Sarina's arm with a glossy red fingernail that matched the red skirt peeking from beneath her black smock. "Sarina, you are going to walk out of here with the best hair ever—*best ever!* And you'll tell all your friends in Hollywood that you have 'Hair by Regan.' You will, won't you?"

Sarina slid a look at Dixie, who nodded her encouragement. When making the appointment, Dixie had impulsively given Sarina's name, recalling what the girl herself had said about having righteous connections and using them. Now it seemed to be paying off.

"I don't want my hair changed," Sarina clarified. "Just trimmed."

"Oh, I agree totally. Totally." But the eagerness in Regan's face suggested she would do more than a mere trim.

Dixie followed the pair to a shampoo room, twenty red basins lining two walls, a red reclining plastic chair snugged up to each basin. In three of the stations, hairdressers worked over customers of both genders. The other chairs were empty. Once Sarina was positioned for sudsing, Dixie sat on a vacant chair to watch.

"When Sarina's mother suggested she get her hair styled while they're in town," Dixie said, "I knew you'd be perfect for it. I saw what a change you made in Clarissa Thomas." This last was a guess, but a safe one, Dixie felt, considering how close the two women had become during the Coombs trial.

"Oh." Regan caught her full, glossy lower lip between her teeth. "You know Clarissa?"

"She's a member of Victims Advocates," Dixie hedged. "I've been trying to catch up with her for two days, but her maid keeps telling me she's 'shopping.' Got any idea where I might find her?"

Regan had soaped Sarina's hair and was now rinsing it.

"Why did you want to talk to Clarissa? Are you a reporter?"

The spin on that last word suggested being a reporter was right up there with being a movie star. Dixie decided to go with it.

"No, but I have a friend who wants to do a follow-up piece on the Coombs trial." Not entirely untrue. Casey James would love to do a follow-up, if it was juicy enough.

"Why *Clarissa*? I was the one—I—" Regan's voice suddenly went screechy. She shut the water off and poured conditioner on Sarina's hair. More than enough, Dixie thought. "I'm the one he—he attacked and—and—"

Regan rubbed hard at Sarina's hair. The girl grimaced, but didn't complain.

"Where would the follow-up piece be published?" Regan asked.

Dixie shrugged. "My reporter friend's a stringer. She works for several publications."

"Business was really good all during the trial," Regan said. "I was, like, almost a celebrity."

Dixie searched for the right bait to put on her hook. Apparently, Regan thrived on attention. Dixie pointedly glanced at the few occupied stations, then lowered her voice conspiratorially.

"How do you feel about what happened to Coombs after the trial?"

Regan's lips thinned. She finished rinsing the conditioner from Sarina's hair and wrapped a towel around it.

"Lawrence made me believe he really cared about me. Sent me flowers, candy—Lady Godiva, my favorite—even bought me this pin." She touched a gold heart pinned to her smock. "Real gold."

Dixie wondered how she could bear to wear it. But then, the hairdresser had paid dearly for that pin—why not wear it?

Regan released the lever that raised Sarina's chair from the reclining position.

"You have beautiful eyes," she told the girl. "Let me put a few highlights in your hair, and those eyes will brighten up till there's not a man alive could resist them."

"Red highlights?" Sarina seemed to like the idea.

Dixie wondered what Joanna would say, then decided to hell with it, Joanna *had* criticized the girl's hair, and Sarina would look terrific with red highlights. Anyway, didn't Hollywood types change their hair color every week?

"Or we could do platinum . . ."

"Red." Sarina was emphatic.

"All right!" Regan squeaked. "Have to dry you a bit first."

While she positioned the kid under the dryer, Dixie flipped open the cell phone and dialed Clarissa's number again. Just as the maid started to say, "No, Mrs. Thomas shopping," Dixie held the phone for Regan to hear.

"I suppose Clarissa will have to miss out on the interview," Dixie said, snapping the phone shut. "But I'm sure my friend would like to talk to you—find out how *you* feel about vigilante justice."

Regan's lips thinned again, but her eyes were bright and defiant. "The jury didn't do their job. They'd have acted differently if Lawrence had raped one of *them* . . . or one of *their* daughters."

"So you believe Lawrence Coombs got what he deserved—later?"

"What he deserves is to be locked up, locked up until his puny little thing withers with old age. But that wasn't going to happen, was it?" Her face flushed with anger and indignation.

Dixie couldn't decide whether she'd been involved in the brutal assault on Coombs or only wished she'd been.

"What about the recent vengeance killing of Gary Ingles? Do you think he got what he deserved?"

Regan stiffened. "I . . . I don't know anything about that. I don't!"

But the fact that she did, indeed, know something about it was written in every rigid muscle of her face.

Chapter Forty-four

Regan skipped up the steps of the tiny garage apartment Clarissa had rented for her, thinking about the wonderful job she'd done on Sarina Page's hair. When her mother saw what a change Regan had made, taming that girl's shaggy mess and putting some zing in it, why, Joanna would want the same person to work on her own hair, wouldn't she? And wouldn't she want that person to move right out to Hollywood, do her hair every single day?

Regan had always known deep in her heart that a truly wonderful moment would come along one day, and she'd have to be quick enough to grab that moment before it passed. Today she'd reached out and grabbed!

A siren whooped, and Regan froze, listening, until it faded into the distance. Whew! She sure was jumpy.

Maybe she should go right in and pack her things. *Hollywood*. Regan had never been there, but she'd seen the giant letters on television and always knew she could be cutting hair for Meryl Streep or Demi Moore. Ever since

Lawrence . . . beat her up so bad . . . why, she still didn't understand what had gotten him so mean, she'd *told* him he could park his shoes under her bed any night he wanted . . . anyhow, ever since then, Regan had come to hate Houston.

Now was the moment she'd waited for all her life. Sarina had said to come by the movie set and she'd introduce Regan to her mother. Regan's whole body had quivered with anticipation. She just hoped she wouldn't make a fool of herself.

Reaching the landing, she turned her key in the lock—

Someone stepped from the shadows.

Regan gasped, dropping her keys. "Oh! Jeez, I thought you were the cops."

"Why would you expect the police?" Her visitor picked up Regan's keys, inserted one deftly into the lock, then pushed the door wide so Regan could enter. "Was it you who called them?"

"I just—I didn't want that man to *die!*"

"It was God's will for Gary Ingles to die. And for Sid Carlson to spend a long, painful time reflecting on his sins. Why can't you see the divine symmetry of what occurred last night?" She closed the door behind her and loosened her coat buttons.

Regan took off her fake fur jacket and tossed it on the sofa. She didn't want to think about Gary Ingles or God's Fist right now. She wanted to pack. She didn't want to be in Houston anymore, even if Joanna Francis wasn't—

No, she wouldn't jinx her good luck.

"Why didn't the paramedics save him?" she asked earnestly. "You told me—"

"I *told you*, the Lord works miracles according to His own agenda." Her gloved fingers tightened around the silk encircling her neck.

"I didn't hit him hard enough to kill him. I *didn't*. I don't want to go to jail."

"Nobody's going to jail, Regan. Unless you told the police something you shouldn't, there's really nothing to worry about."

"Nothing to worry about? We *killed* a man. That's not going to go away." Regan gnawed at the lipstick on her bottom lip.

"You can't honestly believe the police are going to waste their time worrying about Ingles' death." The woman crossed the cluttered living room to the kitchen, took two of Regan's teacups off their hooks, and began filling them with water.

Well, she could have tea if she wanted, but Regan wasn't wasting any more time. She went into the bedroom, just an alcove, really, the whole apartment being one big space, and pulled her suitcases out of the closet.

"You didn't mention going on a trip."

"Just . . . for a while." Regan was afraid if she said her new dream out loud it might go *poof!* Like a big pink bubble bursting. "It makes me crazy waiting around, expecting the cops to knock on my door."

"There'll be no cops knocking on your door. You're worrying about nothing."

"*Nothing?* You keep saying that, but we *killed* a man. That's not *nothing*. We should have stopped after Lawrence."

"Weren't you furious about Carrera and her son?"

"Of course I was. We all were."

"Little Paulie is safe now. We accomplished what the court failed to do."

"That doesn't change the fact that we killed a man." Regan felt another flood of tears pressing behind her eyes. She didn't want to cry and ruin her makeup, but . . . jeez! "It . . . it *was* an accident. We didn't plan for that man to die. That should count for something."

"God's will is done. If He intended Gary Ingles to live, the man would have lived."

Regan watched her set the cups in the microwave and remove two tea bags from a canister.

"I hate it when you talk like that." Opening her dainties drawer, Regan began scooping up handfuls, throwing them into the suitcase. "What makes you think God has any interest in what happens to us? Where the hell was God when Lawrence hurt me? Or Beverly? Where was God when Patricia Carrera hurt her son? Where—"

The woman—suddenly right in Regan's face—slapped her. Regan cringed. "Ow!"

"This will all quiet down before you know it. Ingles' death will land in the unsolved pile. There's nothing to lead the police to us." She glanced at the open suitcases. "That is, unless one of us does something crazy, like running away."

"Crazy? You think I'm crazy for wanting to get out? You're the one who's crazy, talking about being God's Fist, part of some divine scheme to punish the unholy. Thinking you're God's avenger."

"I told you, this is not about vengeance. It's about stamping out cruelty and waking people up to the weakness of man's law. Now, calm down, and nothing will happen to any of us. God watches over His chosen."

Outside, a siren whooped. Regan pushed past and flung an armful of sweaters into the suitcase.

"*You* can wait around, expecting God to take care of you, but *I'm* leaving." Regan jerked open the closet door and grabbed a handful of hangers—

"What—?" Something was around her neck! "Stop!"

Dropping the clothing, she clawed at the scarf squeezing off her breath. She tried to scream, but only a dry wheezing sound came from her mouth.

Arching backward, Regan struggled to shake the woman off—

She felt herself pushed, through the clothes, to the back of the closet. Her face slammed into the wall. The silk twisted tighter around her throat, yanked her back—

Slammed her into the wall again.

The pulse of blood roared inside Regan's brain. Brilliant pinpoints of light darted like fireflies . . . in the deepening fog.

Chapter Forty-five

Memorial Hospital Southwest advertised as a "not-for-profit health care system." Dixie wasn't sure what that meant, but she could see the hospital planners had gone to some trouble creating an atmosphere of wellness rather than illness. Nevertheless, the overwhelming sensation she felt within the long-term care unit was of walking through the twilight of death.

Beverly Foxworth lay motionless and alone, waxy skin as white as the sheets. A single window, thin drapes drawn wide, let in a stream of cool winter sunlight that fell precisely across Beverly's still hand lying atop a pale blue blanket. The comatose woman looked far younger than her twenty-five years.

A yellow rose in a slender green vase adorned the bedside table. A copy of *Pride and Prejudice* lay beside the vase, a silver clip holding the reader's place. Did Grace Foxworth read aloud to her daughter, Dixie wondered, and where had Grace gotten off to? She "lived at the hospital," according to her husband. When she wasn't at church. Dixie glanced at her watch. Dinnertime.

Sarina's new hairstyle fell in a sleek cap around her face, threads of red-gold glistening among the straw-blond strands. A concerned frown creased the teenager's brow as she repositioned the only guest chair, drawing it close to the bed. She watched Beverly's face as if expecting her to awaken.

"How long has she been like this?" Sarina whispered.

"A few months."

"Are you trying to find the man who did this? Is that what's with all the questions to Mr. Foxworth and the hairdresser?"

"Not exactly." How did she explain the sardonic whims of justice? "The man was already tried and found not guilty."

Sarina's young face turned to meet Dixie's, frown lines deepening in perplexed intensity.

"Then who did it?"

Dixie sighed inwardly. "That's where it gets complicated. The man acquitted was the only suspect, and Beverly was comatose when she was found. She never described her attacker."

"So he's free—to do this again?" Sarina looked horrified.

"I'm afraid so." Actually, Coombs had never been tried for assaulting Beverly Foxworth. If the young woman ever regained consciousness, the DA would have another crack at him—providing they thought the case against Coombs was stronger than their last one.

Sarina's young features hardened. She turned back to Beverly, picked up one fragile hand, and held it in her own. A nurse came by, checked the monitors, jotted a note on Beverly's chart, and moved on.

When Dixie's pager shuddered against her waist, she reached to turn it off and knocked it out of its clip. Picking it up, she recognized the number as Parker's. She stepped to a telephone on the nightstand to return his call, stretching the cord to its full length to have some privacy. A photograph of the Foxworths sat near the phone, a gold cross and chain, like the one Beverly wore in the photograph, draped over it.

"Everything's set for tonight," Parker told her.

The boat ride. Dixie's innards went all soft. "What does a woman wear on a moonlight sail?"

"Warm, comfortable clothes. The weather is supposed to be fair, but you'll need a heavy coat. Gets nippy on the water."

No problem. She had tossed an all-weather coat in the Porsche's trunk that morning, along with her new deck shoes. "This time it's just the two of us?"

"You, me, the boat, the sea, and the laughing old man in the moon."

"Which of us is sailing the boat?"

"You get to read the instructions, while I man the sails."

"*Instructions?* Don't you know how to sail it?"

"Never had it out before."

"But you've sailed other boats, haven't you?" Parker was from Montana. Not much chance to practice sailing in the frozen mountains.

"Don't worry, I'll keep us afloat. And I've stocked the galley with sandwiches and hot chocolate. Come prepared to relax and enjoy."

Sounded irresistible. He rattled off directions to the slip where the boat was docked.

"See you at ten o'clock, latest," Dixie promised. She disconnected, and almost instantly got another page.

"Where are you?" Belle's voice held a note of urgency.

"Near the Southwest Freeway and Beechnut." Visiting one of Coombs' victims probably wouldn't meet with Belle's approval, so why mention it? "What's up?"

"Joanna got another card from the stalker."

Dixie straightened and looked at Sarina. She had picked up the book and was reading aloud, too softly for Dixie to make out the words.

"What's the message?"

" 'To my special friend: Just want you to know how special you are to me.' The stalker's added, 'I'm disappointed, Joanna. This was to be *our* special time. Now there's only one day left.' The word 'our' is underlined."

" 'One day left'? What does that—?"

"The filming's back on schedule. Joanna says they'll finish tomorrow."

"Who would know that?"

"Everyone in the cast and crew, I suppose, and anybody they happened to tell."

"That narrows it to most of Houston." Dixie wondered if the downstrokes on the stalker's words would reveal surging anger. "Whether Joanna likes the idea or not, we need someone watching her until she gets on that airplane."

Dixie would be dropping Sarina off early that evening to attend a dinner party the production company was throwing for the cast and crew. Dixie wasn't invited. Anyway, she planned to do some snooping around the set while no one was there. She couldn't be in two places at once.

"Trust me, Flannigan, she won't go for it. This message doesn't threaten her, and she gets this sort of mail often enough that it doesn't upset her. Except for Sarina. I've already flapped my gums on the subject until they're bloody." When Belle paused and Dixie didn't fill in the silence, the attorney said, "You think 'only one day left' indicates the stalker's about to make a move?"

"Who knows what to think? But why risk it?"

Belle heaved a sigh with a hint of defeat in it. "I think you're right that we need another operative, just to be safe, but it has to be somebody invisible."

"Operative. I like that word. I suppose the hottest female defense attorney in Texas wouldn't have ordinary gumshoes working for her. She'd hire *operatives*."

"I've been reading detective novels lately, picking up all sorts of interesting tidbits. You ought to try it."

"If this jerk really means business, Ric, only the best is good enough. It has to be somebody who can do the job."

"You can't mean Hooch."

"He's the best."

"I said *invisible*. Somebody to blend with the crowd. Flannigan, that's not Hooch."

"If ever there were the perfect place for Hooch to blend in, it's on a movie set."

"The set of *Frankenstein*, maybe."

"That's a low remark, and not a bit worthy of you."

Before Belle could launch a full-blown argument, Dixie disconnected and dialed a pager number for the Gypsy Filchers.

Chapter Forty-six

It was approaching darkness when Hooch and Ski slipped out of the shadows and joined Dixie across from the Four Seasons Hotel. She wanted Sarina to meet them. Her mother might be obstinate, but the kid deserved to know who to approach for help if she needed it.

"Holy humbug," Sarina murmured as the pair neared them. "What role is he made up for?"

The gray scar that marred Hooch's face started at the corner of his right eye, bisected the bridge of his nose, and permanently sealed the left corner of his mouth, where an ax blade had split his jaw. Standing six-foot-four, 285 pounds, Hooch made grown men want to crawl into a hidey-hole.

His unfortunate appearance resulted from a wound suffered as a child, a blow that had nearly split his skull in half. In a Halloween fright show, Hooch could be the major frightmonger without a speck of makeup. When he walked down a street, people crossed to the other side. Yet he could shadow a person for days, never lose them, and never be spotted. He was one of the trio who had organized the Gypsy Filchers—a team with more skills, talents, and accomplishments among them than many a well-trained army. Hooch was responsible for most of their training. With him on the job, Dixie could enjoy her moonlight sail.

"This guy's going to stay nearby tonight in case you need him." Dixie explained briefly about the latest greeting card, then opened the car door and stepped out.

"What's horrible?" Hooch said, grinning from the good side of his mouth. He'd coined the greeting from one of his favorite fiction detectives and used it the way other people said, "What's happening?" Hooch claimed it made people smile a little before they ran away screaming.

Ski cast a long, curious gaze at Sarina. She and Hooch were both dressed in black jeans, dark crew neck sweaters, and dark jackets. Dixie made introductions.

"Hooch is going to follow you and your mother to the restaurant," Dixie explained to Sarina. "He'll hang around outside until the dinner is over, then follow you back here."

"Cool! With another bodyguard, we can go to the festival tomorrow."

The kid was persistent, Dixie had to give her that. "Right now let's concentrate on tonight."

"Dixie, Mother's weird fans are *not* interested in me."

"Maybe not. But humor me tonight. If anything strange happens, find Hooch. He'll be close."

"Like gum on your shoe," he agreed.

"Mother doesn't know about this, does she?"

Dixie shook her head, and Sarina grinned. Putting one over on Joanna seemed to brighten her outlook on the evening.

Ski stayed behind with the Porsche while Dixie ushered Sarina inside the hotel and alerted security that Hooch was on the job. As Dixie retraced her steps through the hotel lobby, her pager signaled a message—surprisingly from Brenda Benson. Back in the Porsche, she returned the call.

"Dixie, thank God—" Brenda's tired voice was barely audible over a bad connection.

"What's wrong, Bren?"

"I need to talk. Not on the phone"—static—"meet at my house . . . an hour?"

Dixie glanced at the dash clock. She needed at least forty-five minutes for the task Ski was helping her with, and it was a twenty-minute drive to Clear Lake, where the boat was located. Brenda's house was a short distance in the opposite direction. A tight squeeze, but if Brenda finally wanted to talk—

"Sure. What's up?" She turned the key to start the Porsche's engine.

"I—I thought it would stop with Coombs"—more static—"out of control. I need—I have to trust—"

"I'll be there." She disconnected and called Parker to say she might be a few minutes late. No answer on his cell phone. She left a message at his office, praying he'd bother to check the machine.

Chapter Forty-seven

Dixie wished the three production trailers weren't parked on such a well-lighted street. She'd seen the small signs that first day on the set, WARDROBE, CAST/CREW, BURTON.

Sidling up to the one she wanted, she scanned the distance across the shooting area, where Ski was distracting the guard. Two jobs with the girl in two days—phenomenal. Even Brew had been hesitant when Dixie requested Ski's help. Ski's hatred of Dixie was based on the girl's own problems with a juvenile law enforcement officer, and her temper was apt to flare unexpectedly. But she was perfect for tonight's task. There wasn't a man alive who wouldn't be distracted by champagne curls above delicate features and a slip of body that moved like liquid mercury. Only if the guard was female would Ski be facing a challenge.

Dixie slid her hands into a pair of thin plastic gloves, then gripped the Lock-Aid tool she'd brought from home, a handy gadget shaped like a pistol. Stick the key end into any lock, except possibly high security, pull the trigger, and after a few brisk clicks, the lock fell open like magic. She'd confiscated the tool from a young pro vowing to go straight—never expecting to use it herself. But occasionally, it proved handier than shirt pockets. Carefully, she inserted the tool into the trailer lock.

Made sense, she figured, the director having a trailer all his own— obesity plus ego. Was it Burton's call for Joanna to share space with everyone else on the set? Perhaps he was equally nasty to all his stars, but one thing was certain, Burton had ample opportunity to make Joanna's life miserable. He didn't need to send threatening notes.

Dixie still hadn't discovered why Alan Kemp showed up in Houston at the same time as Joanna. But if he carried a grudge for the fall that broke his ankles and put an end to his acting, why choose now to get even? According to Casey, his syndicated radio show aired all over the world. His career as a journalist was about as good as it gets.

The trailer's lock clicked open. Dixie cast another glance at Ski and the guard, then eased the door wide enough to slip inside the trailer. As she stuffed the Lock-Aid back in her pocket, the photographs Casey James had given her fell out. The one that had interested Dixie showed Tori Pond waiting for Joanna outside the wardrobe trailer. Tori had applied for a job the same month the stalker's notes started appearing.

But Tori Pond seemed totally smitten with the lighting tech, Hap Eggert. Then again, maybe Dixie's hunch was dead wrong this time. She'd know in a few more minutes.

She gathered up the photos and snapped the trailer door shut. Her penlight picked out racks of clothing, a dressing table with jars of makeup and brushes, a blow-dryer hanging from a hook beside the mirror. On shelves above the clothing were stacked shoe boxes and hatboxes, all neatly labeled. Dixie saw the box Alroy Duncan had sent over with Joanna's headpiece.

The effects wizard had been high on her suspect list for a while, primarily because she questioned his motives for apprenticing Sarina. But when the success of *Devil's*

Walk escalated Duncan's career, he had relocated to Houston. Why would a stalker move away from the object of his obsession?

Beneath the headpiece box hung the slicker Hap Eggert had taken to Joanna as she shivered in the rain that first day.

Dixie limbered her hands in the plastic gloves and began the search.

"How long is this going to take?" Ski had asked as they drove downtown.

"If what I'm looking for is where I expect to find it, we'll be finished in less than an hour."

"And if you aren't?"

"Then we might have a long night." Dixie wasn't about to waste this opportunity. Tomorrow the shoot would wrap up. Saturday morning Joanna and Sarina would be on a plane back to L.A. If Dixie couldn't identify the stalker before then, she'd worry about the kid indefinitely.

"Didn't I hear you promise to meet someone?" Ski had argued. "Guess promises don't mean much to you, Flannigan."

"It won't take that long."

Now, Dixie prayed she could find the evidence she needed with the first pass. She wanted to keep that appointment with Brenda. After evading her for three days, the prosecutor was finally willing to talk: Dixie wanted to be there for her.

Nor did she plan to miss her moonlight cruise with Parker.

But the worry that something might happen to Sarina after she flew back to L.A., something Dixie could've prevented by doing the job right, filled her with an unexpectedly stinging disquiet.

According to Ramón, the cryptic messages were written by someone who showed anger at the wrong times. That fact spelled "emotionally unstable" to Dixie in flashing neon letters.

No. She was ending this stalker business. Right here. Tonight. If necessary, she'd search every inch of the set to find what she knew had to be there.

And, finally, behind the last rack of beaded evening dresses and fur coats brushing the floor sat a black leather travel bag. Dixie trained her penlight over the brass lock—no sweat opening that one—to a matching leather luggage tag. Dixie unsnapped the tag to a business card behind a clear plastic window: HAP EGGERT, LIGHTING DESIGN.

Bingo!

That first day on the set, she'd seen the techie emerge from the *wardrobe* trailer. Eggert's friendship with Tori Pond might be real or merely convenient, but this trailer would provide more privacy than the one used by the entire cast and crew, more privacy than the equipment trailer, where other techs would be constantly in and out.

Dixie inserted the Lock-Aid tool into the brass keyway, squeezed the trigger, and listened to the metallic *clicks*.

Eggert's mother had been one of the original stars on *Guerilla Gold*, facing the same bright future as Joanna Francis. Joanna became a star; Eggert's mother became a penniless drunk.

As a techie, Eggert had "been in the business forever," according to Sarina. "Works lighting, sometimes camera crew, whatever," she'd said. He could've easily gained entry to all the sets where Joanna experienced "accidents."

The lock snapped open. Dixie swung the lid back to reveal technical lighting schematics and a jumble of files. Gingerly, she rifled the files. Near the bottom, stuck between two technical manuals, she found the Les Crews article on the Burrows case—the stalker's name Eckert. Had the name similarity stimulated Eggert's latest assault on Joanna's career? From the beginning, Dixie had felt the stalker's messages were too tame to take seriously. If Eggert's original intent was merely to distract Joanna into making stupid mistakes, without drawing police attention, the notes made more sense. Only when the actress failed to respond with sufficient fear had Eggert's anger exploded, showing in his handwriting.

In a file folder marked simply STOCK, Dixie found a packet of note cards bearing the same simplistic art style as on the stalker's cards. The logo on the back of the packet, SUNSHINE GRAPHICS. *Double bingo.*

Dixie snatched her cell phone out of its clip and punched in a number. Eggert's travel case contained enough evidence to prove he'd sent the threatening greeting cards and to start an investigation into Joanna's "accidents" during the past year. Set the right wheels in motion and Eggert would be picked up for questioning tonight before he finished his fancy steak dinner. Considering the "extreme emotional pressure" Ramón had noted in Eggert's handwriting, and the urgency in his most recent message, the sooner he was in custody the better.

"Houston Police Department. Sergeant—"

Dixie disconnected. Never mind the fact that evidence gained by illegal entry would be thrown out—Texas law being tougher than most states'. Never mind that none of Eggert's notes had specifically threatened harm. Belle had entrusted Dixie to keep Joanna's troubles confidential.

Pushing the phone back on its clip, she scanned the suitcase contents, a frustrated sigh slipping softly from her tense mouth. Then she arranged the stalker cards, the Crews article, and all Eggert's files, with exacting care, as she'd found them, snapped the lock shut, resnapped the luggage tag, and placed the travel bag back behind the coats and evening dresses. She'd let Belle Richards decide how to handle discovering the evidence.

After relocking the trailer, she stepped into the shadows and dialed Ski's pager number to signal they were finished here. The Gypsy Filcher would slide into the night.

Pointing the Porsche toward the restaurant where the film

crew was having dinner, she called Belle at home and explained what she'd found.

"We need to finish this tonight," Dixie added. Her meeting with Brenda and her romantic sail with Parker would be delayed, but what she had in mind wouldn't take long. She told the attorney what was needed and where to meet her.

When Belle arrived at Ruth's Chris Steak House, Dixie had already briefed Hooch. Then, while Dixie phoned the restaurant, feigning an urgent message from Eggert's mother, Belle and Hooch waited for him by the hostess station, a duo of quiet authority and grotesque muscle. The toughest street hood would've come along nicely, and Eggert was far from street tough. When they emerged, his freckled face betrayed his guilty amazement at being caught.

"You can't prove anything," he stated bitterly after Dixie told what she'd pieced together.

"Yes, we can, if it comes to that." Lies were useful at times. "Instead, we have a proposal. You're going to leave the country. Right now, tonight. Work on foreign films a few years. Meanwhile, Marty Ahrens has agreed to get your mother into a clinic, and when she's sufficiently dried out, to get her some decent parts."

"Hah! She begged that old fart to take her on. He turned her down cold."

"He won't turn her down this time, provided she gets sober."

A spark of hope flitted across his face. Then he looked away, tension and defeat hardening his boyish features.

"She won't do it. I've tried before."

Maybe she wouldn't. Maybe she'd continue to wallow in self-pity rather than put forth an effort.

"But this time she'll have Joanna Francis encouraging her." Marty Ahrens had agreed that Joanna owed the woman that much, and he would see that she owned up to it.

In the end, Eggert agreed, convinced his only alternative

was jail. Belle and Hooch would drive him straight to the airport. On the way, he'd write a note mentioning an unexpected opportunity. Belle would see that his things were packed up and sent along later.

Getting Eggert's agreement took far longer, though, than Dixie had hoped. When she called Parker and Brenda to explain, she got only recordings.

Chapter Forty-eight

"Aunt Dix! Parker's buying a boat! Have you seen it yet?"

The call from Ryan came before Dixie reached Brenda's house.

"I'm going sailing on it later tonight." At least she hoped the date was still on.

"You could pick me up! I've already done my homework."

Amy's voice, in the background, said, "Tomorrow's a school day, Ryan. Anyway, you'll get to sail on the weekend. Now, let me talk to her." Into the phone, Amy said, "Dixie, what should I bring for dinner Sunday?"

Sunday? Parker had said he wanted her approval on the boat before buying it. "Bring where, Amy?"

"To Parker's housewarming. You don't mind, do you? I mean, he did say the boat was your valentine's gift, and we don't want to horn in if this is a special weekend for you two, or whatever, but Parker insisted we come for dinner and sailing. Carl's bringing a proposal from his people-finder friend, the one who wants a partner."

"My valentine gift?" Dixie turned into Brenda's neighborhood.

"Oh, dear! He said you'd see it tonight. I didn't spoil anything, did I? Dixie, I remembered how much you liked that cruise you took. On the schooner? I suppose I told Parker you'd liked sails better than motors, with all that noise. I didn't spoil anything, did I?"

"No." Dixie wasn't sure how she felt about Parker setting all this up without discussing it with her first. He'd made a big hit with her family from the first moment they'd met, and she liked that. But now she felt they were all ganging up on her about that partnership proposal. As for the boat—well, she *had* mentioned to Amy that she liked boating better than flying. Pulling to the curb in front of Brenda's red brick bungalow, Dixie cut the engine. "Guess I'll see you on Sunday, Sis. I have to go—"

"Wait! What should I bring? What does Parker need for his new house?"

"Everything. Tables, chairs, a television. Amy, I think he must be planning to take you guys out to eat."

"Oh. Then I'll bring . . . some flowers. A house always looks brighter with fresh flowers."

Brenda's house appeared dark, except for the single gaslight in the front yard and a floodlight illuminating the driveway. But the garage door was up, and Miles, Brenda's Miata, was parked inside.

Dixie wanted to be ticked off at Brenda for sounding so mysterious, but after her success with Hap Eggert, she felt too damn good to be angry at anybody. The fact that Brenda finally wanted to talk was all that mattered.

Leaving the Porsche at the curb, Dixie strolled up the driveway toward the back of the house, expecting to see a light in the kitchen window. Her heartbeat cranked up a notch when she found the rear of the house as dark as the front.

Behind her in the trees, Dixie heard a noise, like footsteps. "Brenda?"

No answer. Just trees rustling, maybe.

With her eyes trained on the space behind her, Dixie approached the back door and tapped with her cane. No sound stirred inside the house.

She opened the outer storm door and rapped hard on the wood door frame while peering through the glass insets. The door moved inward. Unlocked.

Instantly, Dixie stepped away from the house and strode back to her car. She lifted the trunk lid, removed the .45 from its case. Snapped the safety off. Placing her cell phone on silent, she crossed the lawn to check the front door. Locked.

A car started up somewhere in the darkness.

Circling again to the back, she ducked beneath windows that appeared secure, at least from a glance. She eased open the storm door, listening for sounds inside. Nothing.

Pushing the inner door flat against the wall, she stepped swiftly inside—she'd be a standing duck silhouetted against the moonlight. Listened. Silence, except for a cricket chirping in the depths of the darkened house.

A nagging part of Dixie's mind said forget caution, find Brenda, she may be hurt—*why would she ask you to meet and not be here? How long ago did you talk to her? Miles parked right there where he should be—Brenda's okay, just in a hurry to get to the goddamn bathroom or something—*

But an ache in Dixie's gut said it was too late. Something bad had already gone down.

In those few seconds her eyes adjusted to the darkness, and she saw the door frame—splintered. Someone had kicked the back door in.

A bar stool lay on its side in the kitchen walkway. Cabinet doors hung open. A yellow box of plastic leaf bags had spilled out on the floor.

From the direction of Brenda's bedroom, a single faint light seeped down the hallway. Total blackness in between.

Dixie didn't like that blackness. Wide-open room, potted plants thick as a forest—ficus, palm, something bushy, dozens of goddamn places to hide. Couldn't skim along the wall for all the goddamn plants. Go straight through the door and her back would be wide open.

Still no sound.

Brenda could be lying hurt inside that bedroom, or the bathroom, if she rushed to take a pee and maybe fell. Sixty percent of home accidents happen in the bath. That would explain not closing the garage . . . assailant already inside—

Wouldn't Brenda have noticed the busted door?

Someone *followed* her inside, then. Brenda rushes in, turns the thumb bolt to lock the door, habit, hurries to the bathroom—

Dixie crouched low and padded lightly, quickly past the kitchen bar, .45 following her line of vision—squeezed past the bar stool—*watch the goddamn clumsy cast*. Back against the door frame, she scanned right, willing her eyes to sense any tiny movement, any shadow that didn't look like a palm or a ficus . . . scanned left. . . .

Nothing.

Going in low and fast, she crossed the open room. Nothing to shield her until she reached the hallway.

Stopping, she searched for movement in the faint light. Nothing.

Smarter to search each room she passed, but no time if Brenda was in that bedroom, hurt. Back against the wall, past Gail's closed bedroom door, no light under it.

Scan. Then fast around the corner—

Now she could see the lighted room, Brenda's bedroom.

Crouched low, Dixie sidled to the doorway, bobbed a look, then back for cover. Bright inside. More signs of a struggle. Lamp overturned, slipper chair knocked against the bed, bureau drawers pulled out, clothing tossed—

Searching for something?

No sound, except the damn cricket. No movement.

Perfume in the air, strong. Shalimar, Brenda's scent.

The door was open to the master bath, light on inside. Dixie scanned as she moved. Nothing. Softly, swiftly on the carpet, she crossed to the open bathroom. Slid a glance around the door.

No one there.

Movement—

Her trigger finger tightened.

A cricket hopped on the tile floor.

Dixie took a steadying breath and studied the mess. Bathroom drawers tossed, cabinet doors open, cosmetics knocked into the sink, perfume bottle shattered on the floor. Shalimar leaked between the tiles, cloying in the still air.

Beside the toilet, as if flung there—during a struggle?— lay a glossy black wig and a plastic mask, the translucent face of a woman.

Dixie made a quick search of the remainder of the house, including Gail's bedroom, bath, and huge walk-in closet. Nothing appeared out of place. When she felt certain the house was empty, she began turning on lights, scouring each area, moving back toward the kitchen. No sign of Brenda or Gail. A few more indications of a struggle—plants knocked over, a vase broken beside the sofa.

Someone had been waiting, had forced the door after Brenda entered. They fought. Wherever she was now, Brenda hadn't wanted to go.

The footstep Dixie'd heard outside—the car starting—

Damn! Had she been that close behind them?

Returning to the master bedroom, she looked for anything that might indicate who'd been here. No clue. In the bathroom, she stooped to examine the mask and wig, not touching them. They lay beside a drawer that had been jerked from the cabinet. Spilling from the same drawer was a bundle of dark clothing, a black knitted cap, a blousy print dress with an apron attached. A set of keys lay partially buried under the black hair. Dixie nudged the hair aside with a fingertip and recognized the police whistle Brenda carried on her key ring, house and car keys fanned around it.

Flipping open her cell phone, Dixie dialed 911 as she retraced her steps through the house. She gave the location and reported what she'd found when arriving to meet her friend, not voicing any suspicions. She told the 911 operator she'd wait in her car. In this part of town, police would arrive quickly. To avoid answering questions about the .45, she stowed it back in the trunk.

Waiting in the driveway, she dialed Parker's pager again, again got no answer, and dialed his office to leave a message. Listening to the ring, she studied Brenda's Miata. Light rays from the overhead floodlight spread into the garage, falling on a slender splash of yellow hanging from the passenger door.

Parker's machine answered.

Slender splash of—

Dixie's chest tightened.

Splash of yellow—

A thin shiver walked down her spine.

Yellow-blond. Yellow-blond hair.

Slender splash of yellow hair.

Staring at the spill of blond locks, she heard the tone signaling to record a message.

She felt welded in place.

There was an explanation, some silly, simple explanation. Another wig, a blond wig—

"I'm at Brenda's," she told the machine.

She had to look.

"Something's happened . . . maybe you shouldn't count on me . . . tonight."

Oh, Jesus. She didn't trust her legs to walk the distance. Only fifteen, maybe twenty feet. But her legs felt like rubber, soft, limp, the leaden cast heavier than it had been all day.

She had to look.

Dixie closed her eyes. Swallowed the bile that climbed her esophagus.

As she raised her lids, flickering lights approached in the distance. Police. Let *them* look.

Yellow-blond hair. Mellow yellow.

Maybe Brenda was alive. Hurt but alive.

Dixie had stood there only seconds, but *too long. Move!*

She jogged to the passenger side, tinted windows obscuring what was inside, and jerked the door open. The interior light flicked on.

Dixie gulped a steadying breath.

Brenda lay on the seat, legs bent against the opposite door, one shoe off, gray skirt and white blouse twisted, shoulders and head trailing off the seat to the carpet, yellow hair hanging over the door frame, spilling to the concrete.

Then, as she saw Brenda's face, Dixie's breath seeped out with a thin moan. Dark, bloated with blood. The ugly bruise like an obscene necklace beneath a twisted silk scarf.

Dixie touched the impossibly still wrist. The skin was warm.

Moving her thumb, she pressed harder. The pulse had to be there. *It had to be there.*

A police car rumbled into the driveway, red and blue lights flickering across Dixie's vision, bouncing off Miles' shiny white paint and Brenda's yellow hair.

There was no pulse.

Chapter Forty-nine

Parker Dann toweled his hair, then wrapped the blue-striped terry cloth around his waist before venturing into the bedroom. No curtains yet. The way he figured it, the only windows that needed covering were in rooms where he was likely to be naked. Otherwise, why spend all that money for an ocean view?

Why spend another chunk on a sailboat? He'd been wrestling with that question for days. Wanted something he and Dixie could enjoy together besides the ten o'clock news. Maybe distract her from the work she did that he hated.

He pulled on a T-shirt still warm from the clothes dryer. Smelled fresh. The new shower worked fine, too. Steaming hot, with an adjustable spray that had massaged his stiff muscles back to life. Stiff from taking a nap on the carpet. After making sandwiches to eat aboard the boat later, he'd stretched out with Mud for a nap. Killing time. Wasn't due to meet Dixie until ten. And he'd been up since before dawn, the drive from Richmond to Clear Lake taking nearly two hours, once traffic got heavy. By leaving early, he'd cut that in half.

Mud padded in and stood watching him dress.

"Patience, fellow. We're almost there."

He patted the dog's ugly head before turning on the hair dryer. Mud had surprised him, liking to sail. Truth was, Mud liked just about anything these days except staying at the Richmond house alone. Dixie refused to notice.

The dog trotted alongside as Parker loaded the picnic basket, a cooler of drinks, and a thermos of coffee into the Cadillac. When Mud clamped the yellow Frisbee between his big jaws and carried it to the car, Parker loaded that, too. But he wondered if it was better to disappoint the dog now or later. Couldn't play Frisbee on a sailboat.

Pausing to take a mental inventory of what else they might need, he threw in two extra blankets. It'd be cold on the water. Dixie probably wouldn't think to dress warm enough. Then he remembered the heart-shaped box of chocolates he'd bought weeks ago, hidden on the top kitchen shelf, too high for Dixie to see without a stool. He retrieved it and buried it under the blankets.

As he scooped up his wallet and pocket change, he noticed the message from Dixie on his pager. Probably phoned while he was in the shower. He dialed her cellular number and got a busy signal. Then her pager.

"Three to one she's calling to say she'll be late," he told Mud. "So what's new, right?"

He phoned the weather bureau for an update: cold and clear.

Mud nudged his hand, wanting to be scratched. Parker obliged.

"Perfect night, with that big full moon out there. All those stars. Be a shame to waste it."

He tried her number again, got another busy signal.

"Okay, fellow, let's move it out." Locking the door, he admired the new brass knocker in the yellow glow of the porch light, then bounded down the steps behind Mud. Galveston beach houses, he'd learned, were built twelve feet off the ground to allow for storm floods.

"What about wind damage?" he'd asked the architects. "What do we do to keep the house from blowing away in a hurricane?"

"Build it in Arizona." They'd laughed hard before showing him the structural enhancements they'd made for storm protection.

Twenty minutes later, he and Mud reached the Clear Lake sales office and stopped to pick up the keys to the boat. His message light was blinking. He punched the speaker button. The first message was from Dixie.

"Hey, guys, I may be a few minutes late, but don't give up on me. Say, what are we eating out there? I'm starved!"

"What'd I tell you?" he asked Mud. The dog yawned and sat down as another message queued up.

"I'm at Brenda's . . . something's happened . . . maybe you shouldn't count on me . . . tonight."

"Dammit, Dixie!" Parker threw the keys across the desk.

Mud whined and sniffed at the answering machine.

"Sorry, boy. Looks like we've been stood up."

Mud looked at Parker and barked, then whined at the machine again. Parker rewound the tape.

"What's up? You've heard Dixie on the speaker before."

Mud continued to nose nervously around the answering machine, a high thin note issuing from his muzzle.

"Want to hear it again? Is that it?" Parker punched the RE-PLAY button.

Mud watched the speaker intently while Dixie told them again not to count on her. When Parker reached to rewind, Mud barked.

"What the hell, Mud—" Then he heard it, a thin moan.

He rewound the tape and turned up the volume. After

Dixie finished talking, he heard a long pause followed by a gasp, a metallic creak, and that awful moan.

Mud barked and turned to stand beside Parker.

Muffled noises . . . nothing recognizable . . . then a loud clatter, as if the phone had dropped. The buzz of a dead line.

Parker stroked Mud's side, needing the comfort himself.

"It's not what you think, boy. She's fine."

Mud barked.

"She's at Brenda's," Parker muttered. "She's fine."

Mud nudged his hand. Parker started to pat, but the dog shrugged him off and moved toward the door.

"Wait, fellow. I don't know where Brenda lives. We'll call her." He located the telephone directory and flipped it open. Lots of Bensons with the first or second initial B, but no Brenda. He looked under attorneys, found none that came close, then dialed information.

"This is an emergency. I need a home number for State Prosecutor Brenda Benson."

The operator spelled the last name, then said, "That's an unpublished number, sir."

"Okay, *you* call it. This is an *emergency*. There could be someone in trouble at that number." He explained the message he'd received, not mentioning it was from a cellular phone. Cell phones were notorious for going dead when you needed them.

The operator hesitated, then asked for his name, and apparently dialed the number. He could hear it ringing.

"I'm sorry, there's no answer."

"Are you sure the line's okay?"

"Yes, it's fine. I'm sorry—"

"Wait. Give me the address."

"I can't do that on an unpublished number. I'm sorry. Would you like me to connect you with the police or fire department?"

If Dixie was into something she wanted kept quiet,

sending in the cavalry wouldn't help her any. *What was the name of that homicide detective . . . ?*

"Sir?"

"Never mind, Operator." He disconnected and flipped through the directory to City Government, Police Department.

Mud paced between the desk and the door, nudging Parker's leg every time he passed.

"Wait a minute, will you? We can't charge out of here without knowing where to go."

Finding nothing that looked helpful, he dialed Belle Richards' home, got her machine, and left his cell phone number. The only other person he thought might know where Brenda lived was Amy. He hated to worry her if it was nothing, but—

"Ryan? Parker. Is your mom there?"

"Yeah. How's the boat?"

"You'll find out for yourself on Sunday. Listen, I'm in kind of a hurry. Can you put your mother on?"

"Sure . . . *MOM!*"

"Parker?" Amy's voice. "What's wrong?"

Why would she think something was wrong? "Nothing. It's just . . . Dixie called and left a message she was at Brenda Benson's and forgot to leave me the phone number. Would you have it? Or even her address."

"Oh, my, no-o-o-o. Let me look, but I don't believe I've ever had that . . . She lives in Bellaire, though, doesn't she? Seems like Dixie said she lived just a mile or two from us."

Bellaire. Couldn't be more than a few square miles. He'd drive every street, if necessary.

The directory had fallen open to C. Hadn't that detective's name started with C? Parker ran his finger down the page, hoping to jog his memory. . . . Cash, Cashly, Chase . . . He stopped at Coombs, Lawrence Riley.

Coombs had threatened Brenda. What if . . . ?

Without consciously deciding to do it, Parker dialed Coombs' number.

"Hello?"

"Lawrence Coombs?"

"Yes. Who is this?"

Parker dropped the receiver back in its cradle. At least that sick sonofabitch wasn't the problem.

"Come on, Mud. Let's go find her."

Chapter Fifty

Ben Rashly ducked under the crime-scene tape and joined Dixie against the garage wall.

"You okay, kid?"

"Yeah." Dixie was numb.

Behind them, someone from the Medical Examiner's office was bent over Brenda, on a stretcher, where they'd moved her after photographing the scene.

"Come on out where you can get some air. You look like you're going to throw up."

Dixie rubbed her forehead. "She was a good friend, Rash." Her voice had gone shrill. She took a breath to slow the fluttering in her chest.

Rashly placed a hand on her arm to lead her away from the garage, but Dixie resisted, feeling the need to be right here, where it had happened, until she'd figured it out. Her toe touched her cell phone. When had she dropped it? The plastic cover had broken open, the battery spilled out.

"I talked to her a little more than an hour before I got here. She was . . . worried. Scared, I think."

"Scared of what?"

"I don't know, but maybe that's what she was planning to tell me. I think she called from the car—the connection was terrible—on her way home. Somebody must've been waiting—but dammit, her keys were inside the house. Why would she go in, then come back out without her keys? Miles would've been locked—unless she intended to leave again. Except she knew I was coming."

Dixie studied the Miata, willing it to reveal what had taken place. Except for smudges where Brenda's heel had kicked the driver's inside door, the car appeared clean. Maybe the fingerprint technician would find something.

"You know more than you're saying, Flannigan." Ben's voice was gentle but firm.

"Honest, Rash, I don't *know* anything." But she took a stab at relaying her hunch that Brenda was involved somehow in the attack on Lawrence Coombs, the disappearance of Patricia Carrera, and the death of Gary Ingles.

The detective bit the stem of his pipe, talking around it.

"An hour, you said. Plenty of time to search a house, find what you want, strangle somebody, and get away."

"But she wasn't at home yet when I talked to her."

"The mess in that bathroom looks like she surprised a burglar."

"A burglar stealing her bath gel?"

"The bedroom was tossed, too. Women usually keep their jewelry in the bedroom."

"Rash, why would a burglar bring her back out to the car to kill her?"

"Somebody she knew, then. Maybe one of her vigilante buddies. You saw that mask and wig?"

Dixie shrugged. "Maybe she went to a costume party."

"Maybe. But the bunch who jumped Carlson and Ingles were wearing dark clothes and knitted caps, like the cap hanging out of that bathroom drawer." He studied Dixie for several seconds. "Coombs threatened her. But why would she go after Carrera and Ingles?"

"Because monsters shouldn't be loose in society. Rash, we don't know that stuff was hers. Maybe she'd taken the mask and clothing as evidence, and threatened to expose . . . someone." *Someone eventually brags to a friend*, Les Crews had said. *Or guilt causes someone to want out.*

A hungry pack turning on the weak member? Only, Bren wasn't weak. Stubborn, maybe. Dixie crossed her arms against the memory of her friend's stubborn lungs, refusing to respond as the paramedics labored over her. *Dead.* Dixie couldn't get her mind around that. She'd *talked* to Brenda, alive and well . . . and frightened. . . .

"Her skin was still warm. Why the hell didn't I come when she called me?"

"Don't think like that, kid." Rashly took the pipe out of his mouth and used it to point toward the darkness beyond the garage. "You know the killer may've been hiding out here when you went inside."

The noise in the trees. She told him about the footstep, or whatever it was.

"Maybe Brenda got away from the killer and ran—but dropped her keys in the scuffle—and the killer caught up with her out here. Then I arrived before he had a chance to go back after the evidence."

"Possible." Rashly drew a hiss of air through the cold pipe. "Benson didn't go down without a fight. We may get a skin sample from under her nails." He took her arm again. "Come on out of here. I gotta have a smoke."

This time, Dixie grudgingly allowed him to guide her. But she noticed one of the officers lift some trace evidence from the shadow of the car's right front wheel, a cigarette, only partially smoked.

Brenda didn't allow anyone to smoke inside her car.

Dixie stopped the officer before she bagged the butt.

It was thin, with a narrow gold band around the deep filter.

"Capri," Dixie said, remembering Grace Foxworth. Striking in her spice-red pants suit and radiantly optimistic about her comatose daughter, Grace had shared her pack of Capri with Julie outside the courthouse.

Chapter Fifty-one

Parker slid the Cadillac to the curb near a driveway crowded with police vehicles. He'd spotted Dixie right away, standing near the garage, inside a roped-off area. Talking to her friend, the Homicide cop. Parker's runaway pulse slowed. She was okay. Whatever the hell had happened here, Dixie wasn't the one on the stretcher being lifted into a coroner's van.

Mud stood on the passenger seat, pressing his nose to the window.

"No dice, boy. The last thing she needs is us mucking around over there." But Parker sympathized with the dog's eagerness to jump out and give her a good licking.

The full moon they'd intended to enjoy on the lake tonight hung high above oak and pine trees. High above the police department's halogen flood lamps. The effect was like a low-budget film. Grainy. Unreal.

Watching her, Parker felt clammy and disoriented. The frantic energy of the past hour was draining out of him. Whatever had occurred here, Dixie appeared in complete control. Her keen mind would already be speculating, calculating. He admired her ability to focus on a problem, excluding all other considerations. But it frightened him, too. Had their ruined evening infringed on her thoughts at all?

Dixie Flannigan brought a quality of contentment to his life he'd never before experienced. She drew from him the desire to look further into the future than next week or next month. But was there a next week or next month in their relationship?

She stood less than fifty feet away, but in a world removed from everything he knew or cared about. A vile world of savagery and pain. A world she moved in daily.

He watched her cross her arms against the cold and wished he were beside her, wrapping a blanket of comfort around her. Far away from tragedy and death. He could feel the curve of her warm body molding against his own. Smell the fragrance of her hair. Hear her peaceful breathing as she slept.

Mud whined and nosed his arm.

"This is no place for us, boy. Let's go home."

Chapter Fifty-two

Dixie arrived home shortly before midnight, having spent hours going over her story with Rashly. He would investigate the whereabouts of Lawrence Coombs, Julie Colby, Regan Salles, the Foxworths, and the Thomases. Parker's Cadillac was parked near the back door, its trunk open, a couple of cartons loaded inside.

As Dixie gimped toward the house, her foot aching miserably, he came out the back door, carrying another box. Mud alongside. The dog padded over and licked her fingers, a worried whine barely audible on his warm breath.

"Your pager was off tonight," Dixie said.

He didn't look at her. "I was in the shower. What about yours?"

Dixie felt at her waist. Gone. She must've dropped it searching Brenda's house. "Sorry about the boat. Did you get my messages?"

He set the box in the trunk, and began rearranging things to fit.

"Dixie, I don't care a damn about the boat." He sounded tired, defeated.

"Brenda's dead."

"I know. I . . . caught a newscast." He looked at her then, and the expression in his eyes made her want to weep. "I'm sorry about your friend. I know you two went way back."

"But you're mad at me for not showing up tonight."

"No. Mad doesn't even come into it." The cartons were cocked up, and he shoved one back to make more room. "All right, I was mad at first. Then . . . your cell phone was still on when you . . ." He sighed, and in that one long breath Dixie heard all the fear and frustration he'd suffered. "What the hell happened?"

She explained, leaving out the parts that would worry him most, like searching the house. But he knew how to fill in the blanks.

"You could've been killed, too."

"I didn't see anyone . . . and there was no time. I was worried about Brenda."

"Yeah." Another long sigh. "That's what scares me. You never worry about yourself. I kept calling your cell phone, your pager. I knew you wouldn't blow off the trip without an explanation. Unless something was wrong." He tried to shut the trunk, but one box was still too high. "I drove Bellaire, one street after another, knowing *whatever* had happened, I was too late. Do you understand how helpless that feels?" He wrenched the box aside and slammed the trunk lid with more force than necessary. "You were in trouble, Dixie, *and I couldn't do a goddamn thing about it.*"

"She was a friend."

"Yeah, that's what I've been telling myself, how could I fault you for helping a friend?" He raked a hand through his hair.

"Parker, I didn't realize—I never intended to worry you."

"I know." He shook his head wearily.

Dixie ached for him. But what could she say? Words couldn't erase the past few hours. She'd had no idea what he was going through—which was exactly the point he was making—she never considered how her actions affected him. She was used to getting along fine without anybody worrying about her. Guilt curled like a worm in her gut. Guilt over Brenda. And Parker.

She didn't want to ask the next question, wasn't sure she wanted to hear the answer. . . .

"Where does this leave us?"

Parker's gaze roamed over her face as if memorizing it. His usually expressive features held no clue to what he was thinking.

"I don't know," he said.

Then he reached out one of his big arms to draw her close. As he tightened the embrace, a shudder went through him, and he wrapped his other arm around her, pulling her tight, enveloping her completely, as if renewing his own strength from her closeness.

"Dixie . . ." His voice was thick, and a knot rose in her own throat. "It's hard to imagine you not being part of my life." He spoke so softly she felt rather than heard his words. "These last two months, the best part of every day has been the time I spent with you. I love you so damn much it tears me up inside to think of losing you."

They stood that way, holding each other. Mud tried to nose between them. *It'll be okay*, Dixie told herself. *We'll talk and we'll be together and it will be okay.*

"I think, maybe, we need some distance for a while to sort things out," Parker said. "I've always thought of myself as a man who could take care of the people he loved. But with you . . . I guess you don't want that protection, and . . . I'm not cut out for the passive role."

She pulled back to look at him. "You're not passive—"

"Dixie, I don't expect an ordinary relationship for us. It didn't start that way, and there's not an ordinary bone in your body. But I can't continue with you. Not until I come to grips with the danger you draw constantly into your life."

"I guess I don't think of it as danger."

"No, you never do." He kissed her forehead, pressed his lips there for several seconds. Then gruffly, "I don't have to leave tonight. I know you just lost a friend."

She didn't want him to leave. But she wouldn't want him to leave tomorrow, either, or the next day.

"It's okay. But . . . when will I see you?"

"I'll call."

Dixie sat on the porch with Mud and watched Parker's taillights disappear beyond the gate. Tears she'd been fighting to suppress spilled over and flooded her cheeks.

Mud licked them away.

Chapter Fifty-three

Friday, February 14

Technically, with Joanna's stalker gone, Dixie was relieved of Sarina duty. But she didn't relish spending the day alone. She called Belle just after dawn.

"Any reason I shouldn't pick up the kid, spend today kicking around town as usual?"

"At your rates? Eggert's on a plane headed for Australia. The job's finished."

"But Joanna's film won't finish shooting until tonight. And Sarina's bright enough to get in trouble on her own." Dixie had already decided to stay on the job, with or without pay. But if Richards, Blackmon & Drake could be pressed into paying the freight, why not let them?

Belle's pen tapped a steady rhythm as she considered it.

"Okay. I haven't had a chance yet to tell Joanna about Eggert. But keep Sarina away from Duncan's studio until Marty Ahrens has a chance to soften Joanna up on the subject of her apprenticeship."

"Would I do otherwise?" Not with the Illusions festival starting today.

Dixie carried the phone to the bathroom. Her eyes looked like two burn holes in a mattress, and her body felt as if she'd been holding up the house all night. A few good SF films might just take her mind off her miseries. Besides, Rashly had ordered her to stay out of his way while he followed up on the Avenging Angels suspect list.

There was no answer at the Four Seasons Hotel suite. Sarina had probably slipped out early, determined to attend the festival and expecting Dixie to argue. Pointing the Porsche toward Rice University campus, where Illusions was being held, Dixie placed a call to Rashly.

"Any news on the names I gave you? The Foxworths? The Thomases? Regan Salles?"

"If you'd turned over that information earlier, Flannigan, we'd already have checked them out."

And maybe Brenda wouldn't be dead. "I didn't have any information. I was just poking around."

"You knew Coombs threatened Benson."

"Defendants threaten prosecutors, Rash. And Brenda wasn't sexually violated. Did he have an alibi for last night?"

"He was settled in with a tall whiskey and an X-rated video when we picked him up for questioning."

"Did he say anything?"

"Yeah. 'Talk to my lawyer.' "

"Nobody ever said Coombs was stupid, just mean as a cold snake."

"Doesn't mean he murdered your friend."

"No." But she'd rather suspect Lawrence Coombs than anyone else on her list. That cigarette could've been dropped anytime.

"What about the scarf she was strangled with? It had a distinctive pattern." Red apples on pale green silk. "And Brenda doesn't wear scarves." But the scarf *had* seemed familiar.

"Maybe it was the sister's. Haven't located her yet." Dixie

heard the clunk of Rashly's pipe on an ashtray. "But your friend Benson was in this vigilante business up to her eyebrows, Flannigan."

"Okay. I can picture Brenda going after Coombs. Even Carrera—*if* that's what happened with Carrera—but the Ingles murder, no way."

"The ME said the blows didn't kill Ingles. Had a weak heart."

"Not weak enough to keep him from beating Ramirez to death and raping his niece." Dixie had reached the campus. "Gotta go, Rash."

She disconnected and scanned a sea of cars. Not a chance of parking close to the Media Center.

Chapter Fifty-four

Sarina stood at the open door of the Media Center Theater, frowning at the crush of students inside. Codswallop! Not even standing room. She'd expected the early showing of *Night Freaks* to be prime-seat, center-center, enveloped in sounds and effects, alone at last with the best. Uncredible that so many people jumped bed at dawn to see an obscure flick. This festival had drawn more film students than any L.A. seminar she'd attended.

Now what? Most of the booths weren't set up yet. After the check-in and opening speeches, the movie was *it*, the only game going until the ten o'clock panels started.

"Looks like we'll have to hike over to Hamman Hall, pretty lady," drawled a sexy male voice behind her. "Hear they're setting up to show some outtakes from the *X-Files*."

An old guy, maybe thirty-five, forty, but with eyes like the deep Pacific on a clear day. Actor, probably.

Sarina examined the list of presentations. "*X-Files* is not listed on the schedule until tonight."

"The folks producing this shindig must've scrambled around after realizing what a turnout they had. Usually, Hamman Hall is reserved for live theater and chamber music, but it handles film all right in a pinch. Don't know about you, but I'm not standing around twiddling my thumbs for two hours."

He strolled toward the door.

"Wait! I'll walk with you." The map showed Hamman Hall as a tiny block all the way across the campus. This guy seemed to know where he was going.

He wasn't dressed like an actor, at least not an out-of-work actor. More GQ—cashmere pants, blue turtleneck sweater, tweed blazer, and the shiniest black shoes Sarina had ever seen. Producer? Agent? Too important to wear a name tag. Talent scout, maybe. Whatever, introducing him to Alroy Duncan might make her some points.

"You're Southern," she guessed. "Does that make you from around here?" South Carolina had its own film culture taking shape. He could be South Carolina gentry, the way he carried himself, slow-talking, easy-walking.

"Born and bred, as they say, right here in Houston."

"Is there as much filmmaking going on in Texas as we hear about on the coast?"

"At least."

He took her arm to lead her around the curb. His touch sent a shiver of expectation through her. She'd never been heavy into dating, too busy carving a niche. Boys usually fell into two categories, super-stud melonheads and gifted gay-cats. Neither was date-mate status. An older man might be interesting.

They came to a student cafeteria, and she suggested they grab a muffin. She'd missed breakfast again.

"No time, if we want to catch the opening credits."

"On X-Files? Show me five minutes, any episode, I'll quote the credits. Verbatim."

He smiled and veered toward the cafeteria, his hand on her elbow. The tingle stayed when he dropped his hand.

She scooped up a muffin and bottled water.

"Never watched it, myself," he said.

"*Un*possible. You're missing the *Twilight Zone* of the nineties. Low on effects, but high on story."

He insisted on paying, even though he hadn't picked up anything for himself. Guy her age would *not* have paid. Dating an older man could be interesting, all right.

They'd crossed half the campus, according to her map. Not many students wandering around. Classes already in progress.

"What's your take on crash-and-burn? I'm past that, myself, but pyrotechnics is its own trip. Set the string just right, perfect combo of pop and sizzle. Stand back, flick the Bic, and glory in the fireworks. Can anything be more intense?"

"You, pretty lady, are intense. Ten minutes we've been talking, and I've felt more heat than from my fireplace on a cold night."

"Isn't fire what it's all about? You start out, you don't know quite what to do or how to do it, but you *must* perform. And that's when the sweetest work is done. When the fire goes out, that's when you start mimicking what's gone before. That's when I hope I have guts enough to quit."

They'd reached a quiet brick building. Sarina didn't see any students, unless they were all inside taking up the good seats.

He opened the glass door for her. Old guys did things like that. The lobby was empty.

"Where is everyone? Are you sure this is the right building?"

"Absolutely. They're probably still sorting out the equipment downstairs. Come on."

He led the way down a stairwell to a door marked RE-HEARSAL ROOM A. Sarina could hear the hum of a furnace but little else.

He opened the rehearsal-room door. When she looked in—nobody there, a sofa, some chairs—his hand clamped the back of her neck like a vise.

Chapter Fifty-five

A canopy of ancient live oaks shuddered in a brisk, cold wind blowing from the north. A fine February day ahead, the weatherman promised. Yet already a fresh bank of rain clouds the color of mold were rolling in from the north, looking as ill-natured as Dixie felt after the previous night's tragedy.

Pushing through the Media Center door with her cane, she instantly entered an alien world: colorful, noisy, smelling of urethane and crackling with activity. Every square inch was crawling with life, workshop organizers attending to last-minute details, vendors setting up displays. Dixie was glad not to have the stalker to worry about.

From the look of the crowd, every movie enthusiast within a hundred miles had attended the festival, many of them cloaked in anonymity provided by elaborate costumes. A nine-foot silver-skinned humanoid, hairless head skimming the ceiling, picked his way through the crowd. If Sarina were inside such a garb, Dixie would never find her.

Mesmerized, she bumped into a tentacled green blob with six eyes.

Belle had once talked Dixie into dressing for a Halloween party. At a rental agency, she'd found racks of Scarlett O'Hara, Raggedy Ann, and Wicked Witch of the West trappings, but nothing to compare with what she saw here.

Muscling through the line, she bought a day pass and received a six-page listing of vendors, films, workshops, locations of off-campus screenings, events planned for the three-day weekend, and a map of the campus.

She noticed a sign announcing a showing of *Night Freaks*. The auditorium door was shut, the feature already in progress. Sarina would likely be inside.

Stepping into the darkened theater, Dixie blinked, disoriented, then waited by the entrance for her eyes to adjust. On the screen, opening credits rolled across grainy black-and-white images. Splashes of green suggested someone had filmed the action through an infrared lens. Disco music established the period as the seventies.

Dixie searched the throng of furred, feathered, scaly creatures for a thatch of strawberry-frosted blond hair, but the lighting was inadequate to distinguish color even a few seats away. She fished out her penlight and played its meager beam down the aisle and across the rows. Receiving only minor curses, she muttered "Sorry" after each, and knew five minutes later that Sarina wasn't in the audience.

Gimping outside again, her leg already aching, she eyed the maze of vendor tables and pushed on. With a start, she recognized ahead of her the silver hair and hesitant gait of Alan Kemp. As she watched, Kemp stopped at a vendor table and addressed a woman sitting behind it. Plump, sprightly, about fifty years old, she was reading a document. At Kemp's approach, the woman removed her reading glasses, laid aside the document, and stood up to shake hands.

Dixie sauntered up to Kemp's side. "You're the last person I'd expect to find at this conference."

Kemp frowned, obviously as surprised as she was.

"Ms. Flannigan?" His eyes flickered to the manuscript lying on the table.

Dixie strained to make out the words printed on the cover.

"Mr. Kemp's screenplay," the woman said, gesturing at the manuscript. "A good one, as far as I've read."

"Actually, I came to Houston to attend this conference," Kemp said, invoking his phony European accent. "Professor Pendercall has been kind enough to entertain the possibility of helping me obtain the interest of a Hollywood producer. Joanna would play the lead."

The plump woman's eyebrows shot up. "With your cousin in the title role, you'd stand a better chance of finding backers."

"So far I haven't found the right moment to ask her," Kemp admitted.

Meaning he hadn't found the guts, Dixie thought. But that cleared up the nagging question of why he was in town.

"Have you seen Sarina here this morning? We were supposed to meet at the hotel. I guess she got impatient."

"No," Kemp said. "If I run into her, I'll tell her you stopped by."

Dixie excused herself and hobbled back into the main aisle. According to the map, the Stoned Toad Productions booth was on the far side of the lobby. Sarina would certainly hook up with Alroy Duncan. Dixie melted into a crowd heading in that direction.

She found the effects tech seated in front of a computer, surrounded by costumed spectators. As he tapped a keyboard, images on a giant, wall-mounted monitor mutated, multiplied, and shattered into molten chrome.

"Every creature we've ever created," Duncan was saying, "is stored on disk in interchangeable parts."

Dixie wedged between two spectators and positioned herself at his elbow.

"Seen Sarina yet?" she asked, just loud enough for Duncan to hear.

He glanced up. "Sarina? No—" Then he amended, "Yes! I was carrying in boxes, and she was going out the other door."

"Out? Where?"

Duncan scratched his beard and shrugged, his attention back on his work. "Can't say. Had a guy with her."

"What guy? What did he look like?"

"Tall, good-looking. Too old to be a student." He tapped the keyboard, working magic on the screen for his spectators.

Dixie stepped away from the booth and studied the schedule. Everything seemed to be happening right here in the Media Center or in off-campus theaters. Nothing else looked promising, except a student cafeteria. Eating was one of Sarina's favorite pastimes.

But after dragging her heavy cast halfway across the campus, she found Sarina was not at the cafeteria. The cashier recalled seeing a girl with reddish-blond hair, though.

"Came in with a guy—" He looked at his watch. "About thirty-five, forty minutes ago. Bought a cranberry muffin."

Chapter Fifty-six

Scuffling, whimpering noises came from behind a sofa. An animal?

Sarina didn't know, but it was part of whatever bad was going to happen, not in any shocker film, but real-life bad, feel it, touch it, *smell* it bad.

Mouth, wrists, and ankles taped, she couldn't stop shaking.

*Un*cool. Totally uncool. Even tied up in the dark, didn't the heroine always figure a way out? She should *do* something.

The door opened. He came in again, with another silk tree. What was the deal with all the fake plants? He'd lugged in five—from the theater prop room, Sarina figured. Trees, shrubs, flowers. Grouped around a bench in a corner.

He caught her staring and smiled. When he smiled, it was hard to believe this was all for real. Except for tying her up, he'd been nice, really, really nice. Apologized for taping her mouth. "Can't risk any noise," he'd said, "when the other guest arrives." *What other guest?*

Think! Why was she here? Was this a joke? College kids harassing the out-of-town dweeb?

"Hey, pretty lady." He knelt beside her. Stroked her cheek.

He had a good voice, a good, *kind* voice, and a soft touch. Whatever he was up to, it couldn't be anything really bad. A gag to get a producer's attention, maybe. Actors pulled all kinds of crazy stunts to get producers to notice them. Screenwriters, too. If he'd just *asked*, she could've told him she had connections. Producers, directors—her mother was *Joanna Francis*, her father *John Page*—

"How do you like the decor?"

He meant the bench and trees. A baseball bat leaned against a potted shrub. Looked like a day in the park.

Sarina tried to answer, tried to tell him about her righteous connections.

"Amazing what can be thrown together in a pinch. But it's . . . not quite right . . . yet." He stood, pondering the scene he'd created. "Lighting. Yes, we need the proper mood, before your friend arrives."

Friend?

Did he mean Dixie? She was her only friend in Houston. Except Duncan, but who would know about Duncan, unless they'd been followed—

Oh! Oh, no. This guy couldn't be the stalker. Mother's stalkers were never really dangerous. Never.

Was that the deal? Was he using her as bait to trick her mother into coming?

He went out, but this time he left the door open a crack. If she could crawl to the door, hide before he returned—

She scooted her hips and feet, hip-walking, inching like a worm as fast as she could across the floor—and made it. Turning sideways to the door, she elbowed it open and scooted through, squirming backward now, and down the hall—which way, dammit? Right! Opposite the way they came in. Inching, inching, inching—*yards* to go and she could only get there in pissy little inches—

"Darlin', is this how you repay my hospitality?"

He caught a handful of her collar.

Sarina screamed behind the tape. She wriggled and kicked the wall with both feet.

Yanking her away from the wall, he set down the lamp he was carrying, then dragged her back into the room. She yelped and shrieked, straining to pull free.

"You disappoint me, Sarina." He shoved her against the wall. She fell on her side, and he grabbed her hair to jerk her erect. Slapped her.

She cried out with the pain. Her eyes filled with tears. She shrank away from him, whimpering behind the tape.

"Sorry, pretty lady. Can't have you wandering off before the show starts."

He kissed her face where he'd struck her.

"Don't make me hurt you." With a thumb, he stroked a tear off her cheek. "Rest up, darlin'. You're the star player today."

Sarina shivered.

Star player? What did that mean?

He brought the lamp in, an old-fashioned street lamp, white globes on a wrought-iron base, like in that old Gene Kelly movie. He positioned it near the bench, turned it on, then turned off the overhead light. Only his "stage" was lit now, the rest of the room dark.

Someone would come. The building had been wide open. They'd walked right in. Drama classes, rehearsals, something had to be going on today, or why leave the doors unlocked?

She had to stop this silly crying. It clogged her nose so she couldn't breathe.

Dixie would come.

Dixie would know exactly where she'd gone this morning,

probably was already on campus, headed to Hamman Hall right now.

Sarina wished her shoe had a James Bond razor built into it. Or a *Star Voyager* laser blaster. The real thing, not f/x.

She wished she could stop shaking.

She wished she knew what was making that scuffling noise.

Chapter Fifty-seven

"I saw her, sure. Noticed her hair. Wouldn't mind having mine done simple like that, with those cute highlights. That's why I noticed."

The young woman seemed familiar with the campus, willowy body, asymmetrical sandy hair, a complexion nearly the same hue. She carried a red book bag stuffed with software manuals and was the twentieth person Dixie had shown the photograph to.

"Could you tell where she was headed?"

"Toward Hamman. That direction, anyway. I have an audition there later today, for a part in *Tiny Alice*. That's why I noticed. Wondered if auditions had already started. But I'm sure they're later, way later, like four o'clock. Thought I'd check the schedule, just to be sure. But I'd remember. I'm perfect for this role, wouldn't want to miss out—being late, you know, for tryouts—and somebody else get the part, *my part*, just because I was late. Huh-uh. I know they're at four."

Dixie prayed for patience. "Anything happening at Hamman Hall to do with the film festival?"

"No, you want the Media Center. Nothing's at Hamman today except, like I said, tryouts at four o'clock."

"But you saw this girl—headed toward Hamman Hall?"

"Yeah. Nice-looking man with her."

Maybe Sarina had met another "soul mate" like Alroy Duncan, and they'd gone for a walk. Or had she developed an interest in special effects for live theater? "What else is around that area that might be part of the festival?"

"Nothing. Natural Science. Geology Lab." She hefted her load in preparation for moving on. "Bet that cast itches. Say, how do you think I'd look with red highlights?"

Jaundiced. But Dixie's cast hadn't itched, until now. "Go for it."

Nice-looking man with her. As Dixie walked, the cast itching like crazy, a single raindrop fell on her cheek. She frowned at the threatening cloud bank, quickened her pace, and dialed Belle's number. What the devil would've taken Sarina so far from the Illusions hubbub? Something felt wrong about it.

"Are you certain Hap Eggert got on that plane last night?" The cell phone worked fine after she'd replaced the battery and twisted a rubber band around the plastic piece that held it in.

"Yes. Why?"

"Probably nothing. Sarina was already gone when I arrived at the hotel, so I assumed she went to this festival she's been yammering about. So far I haven't located her. Maybe I just haven't walked enough yet." Dixie disconnected, wishing now that she'd brought the car. Hamman Hall hadn't looked nearly as far on the map.

To take her mind off her aching foot, she dialed Ben Rashly. "Anything new?"

"The Thomases and Foxworths are coming in for interviews. But our killer beat us to Regan Salles."

Dixie stopped walking. "Regan's dead?" She pictured the woman's eager face as she'd realized Sarina might be her ticket to a Hollywood hair salon. "How?"

"Strangled with a scarf, same as your friend."

"Rash, I saw Regan yesterday afternoon. How long—?"

"Dead twelve to eighteen hours. We know she left the salon about three."

Right after she'd finished Sarina's hair.

"Looked like she was packing for a trip," Rashly continued. "We found another mask in her apartment, like the one at Benson's. This one with a blond wig."

"Neither Coombs nor Carlson described their assailants as masked, did they?"

"No . . ."

He hesitated, and Dixie knew he was debating whether to disclose a piece of information. Pushing him wouldn't help. She could hear the draw of air through his pipe.

"We found another body," he said, finally. "Sexual assault. This one looks a whole lot like the work of Lawrence Coombs, except this time he used a knife. Went all the way."

Oh, God, not Gail Benson.

"White woman," Rashly continued. "Thirty-five. ID'd as Dottie Anderson."

Not Gail. Not Julie or Clarissa Thomas or Grace Foxworth. Didn't make the death any less terrible, but less personal.

"How?" Dixie asked.

"Bled to death. Sometime Wednesday night. Another interesting item—Marianne Coombs died early this morning. Stroke. Her son, who makes up his own come-and-go privileges at the nursing home, had been sitting with his mother for an hour when it happened."

"Is that supposed to make me feel sorry for him? Why the fuck didn't we lock the bastard away when we had the chance?"

"We, Flannigan? *We* at Homicide slam the bastards in jail. It's you lawyers who let 'em out." He banged the phone down.

Dixie didn't blame him for being mad. The body count was mounting, and his clues led nowhere. She wondered if Dottie Anderson was the vivacious brunette Coombs had danced with at the Parrot Lounge the night he'd broken her foot. Seemed like an eternity ago. Virtually every woman in the club that night was envious. How would they feel now? And how the hell could a man be so charming one moment and so malevolently savage the next?

By the time she reached Hamman Hall, leaning heavily on the cane, storm clouds had turned the sky that mottled purple that warned of heavy rain. The air felt fresh with ozone. Dixie's clothes and hair were damp. She hobbled up the steps as the first cloud opened.

Wide brick steps swept from the sidewalk, through glass panels, into the lobby. Dixie saw no one around. The place was lighted and the doors were unlocked. But the building felt deserted, the way an office building feels in the dead of night, with only the mechanical hum of a heating unit, fluorescent lighting, and computer equipment to fill the silence.

Outside, the rain had dropped a curtain around the building, blurring the landscape into a watery mosaic. At least ducking in here had kept her from getting drenched.

A flyer tacked beside the ticket window announced tryouts for *Tiny Alice* at four o'clock. Double doors led to the auditorium. Two more doors appeared to be office entrances. To the right of the auditorium, a tiled ramp angled downward, another angled upward. The lobby's architecture was designed for longevity, efficiency, and handicap access. Dixie definitely could use the latter.

In the auditorium a steep semicircular bank of red chairs led down to the empty stage. Heavy brown curtains flanked the walls, absorbing sound and softening the light. Not a soul visible, not a sound to indicate anyone backstage. Perhaps there were discussion rooms downstairs, handling overflow from the Media Center. The acoustics probably dampened any sound from below.

Dixie spied an exit door to the right of the stage. The

ramp from the lobby likely led to the same area, but she decided to cut through the auditorium, in case something was happening directly behind the curtain—a tour, perhaps, that she couldn't hear from fifty feet away.

Halfway down the stairs, the silence became oppressive. Dixie could no longer hear the rain pelting the brick walkway outside. The building felt as if it were wrapped in dense blankets. Obviously, the acoustics were well designed to amplify from the stage upward and dampen any noise coming from outside or elsewhere in the building. Beyond the exit door, there might be dozens of people.

But when she opened the door, more silence greeted her. Only the hum from the furnace seemed louder.

The area had been roughly sectioned off into smaller rooms, all painted white. This was the work area, behind the scenes, the guts of the building. Most of the lights were off, probably to conserve energy until the building was in use, which meant it was not in use now. Nothing going on, so why would Sarina and her friend have come here? Perhaps the young woman Dixie stopped had been mistaken.

While she was here, though, might as well check the remaining rooms. The first door she opened was a closet. Mops, brooms, and a rolling cart with cleaning fluids blocked the passage to a row of cluttered shelves on the back wall. The next door opened to an empty room.

Around a corner, Dixie saw a faint light under a door marked REHEARSAL ROOM A.

Chapter Fifty-eight

Sissy lay cramped in the dark.

Trapped.

The stench of her own sweat and blood and urine invaded her nostrils. Her head throbbed. Pain seared her lungs with each breath.

Where was she?

Panic gripped her as she tried to move. Hands tied. Aching from constriction. Darkness wrapped her completely.

Sweat dampened her skin. Her clothes felt soaked with it.

Ankles tied, knees drawn painfully against her chest. She lay on her side, hardness beneath her.

Where was she?

She remembered going to Brenda's. Pleading with her to complete the task God had given them. To walk the path God had lighted. *Regan was a mistake,* Sissy told her. *Regan was weak, and God had called her home, but Brenda—*

Brenda was strong.

The death of Gary Ingles had been an omen. God had

reached out and touched Ingles' heart, stopping it. A sign that He was with them.

Man's law, mankind's *justice?* A joke! Strength was in the people, rising up together to demand their own justice.

Sissy coughed. Pain knifed her ribs.

Where was she?

She lifted her bound hands to explore the darkness.

Plastic.

Dear Lord, this could not be happening.

Oh, dear God. Plastic! Her stomach knotted in dry heaves.

A whimper escaped her lips. Her mind raced . . . and words spilled in a hoarse whisper—

The Lord is my shepherd . . . I shall not want. . . .

A thudding blow halted her prayer.

Chapter Fifty-nine

Sarina worked her arms behind her back, trying to loosen the tape that bound them together. She'd been sitting here in the dark forever. The silence was crazy-making. What was he waiting for?

He stood near the door, in the shadows. Just standing there! Not moving, not talking.

"Shhh!" he'd said when Sarina tried to tell him, grunting behind the tape, that her nose was running and she couldn't breathe. He'd noticed, and jerked her head back, wiped her nose ungently with his handkerchief. Then he told her in a low, hard voice to keep quiet.

The noises started again behind the sofa. He'd kicked something, and the noises stopped.

After that, Sarina kept absolutely still, trying hard not to provoke him. But her nose continued running, and she couldn't stop sniffling.

The doorknob turned.

Sarina froze. Had he seen the knob turn?

She wanted to scream a warning, but with the tape, and her nose clogged, she could only make this small, sick little squeal. She scuffled her feet on the floor, bumping, bumping, banging as hard as she could.

"Shhhhh!"

The door swung open.

Seeing Dixie in the doorway Sarina squealed and scuffled louder than ever. Dixie wouldn't see him standing beside the door, wouldn't be able to see anything but his stupid "stage."

Dixie raised her hand and felt along the wall beside the door, probably for a light switch.

"Sarina?"

Chapter Sixty

A hand clamped over Dixie's wrist and jerked her into the room.

"Seems like we've had this dance before, pretty lady. Now it's my turn to lead."

She choked down on the cane and swung the brass knob at Coombs' ribs.

He dodged.

She kicked her heavy cast at his shin, connecting, but not hard enough. His broad palm slammed the side of her head, sending a volley of pain through her jaw and cheekbone. Before she could recover, he grabbed her arms, yanked them behind her. She heard the rip of tape coming off a roll.

Move! While he's busy with the tape—

Gulping a breath to clear her head, she wrenched sideways, stomped with the cast where she hoped his foot would be—

But he was too quick. He whipped the tape around her

wrists, thrust a hand in her hair, and jerked her head up, forcing her to look at him.

His minted breath caressed her cheek.

"I *do* like the way you fight, darlin'." He tossed her cane in a dark corner. "But here we are in this fine theater, and this is my show. You're only a player."

Probing her pockets, he found the Kubaton, then ripped the cell phone off her belt and tossed them both. His hands cupped her breasts. Giving one cruel squeeze, he shoved her against the wall.

Hands bound, the cast throwing her off balance, Dixie slumped to the floor in a heap. Her good leg twisted painfully beneath her. Trying to right herself, she heard a choking whimper—

And with sparkling clarity Dixie realized how fast her mildly annoying morning had turned to stone disaster. *Sarina!*

Squirming around, she spotted the girl, mouth taped, eyes wide, legs thrust out straight and duct-taped together at the ankles. A bruise stained her temple. Otherwise she appeared to be okay, just scared.

Just scared? She was a kid, she was terrified.

Along with the fear in Sarina's eyes, Dixie recognized something that turned her heart to jelly . . . hope and *expectation*. She expected Dixie to make the horror go away.

Of course she did.

Dixie's body felt rigid—with contrition and her own measure of fear. Her one purpose had been to keep this child safe. Yet, Sarina was in severe danger because Dixie attracted a monster into their wake.

Wriggling upright, she scooted toward the girl, willing her face to butch up. Show some resolve.

"It's okay, kid," she lied.

Coombs jerked Dixie's feet out straight, thumping her against the wall. A jolt ricocheted down her spine.

"Relax, pretty lady. You talk when I say to talk." He taped her cast, binding it to her other ankle. "We have hours to play, and no one to bother us. I've already tested the sound."

He crossed to the door and twisted the lock. "You can scream until your lungs burst."

Dixie scanned the room desperately, cataloging details, searching for opportunities. Four plain white walls. Concrete floor. Boxes. Sofa. Two chairs. And a carefully assembled scene in one lighted corner.

When she glanced back, Coombs was watching her.

"Nice, yes? Remind you of anything?" He tenderly repositioned a silk ficus nearer the lamp. "It's not a real park bench, but close enough."

Dixie's heart drummed into double time. *Regan Salles— beaten, raped, and found tied to a park bench. And then Coombs. Beaten, sodomized. Tied to a bench.*

She strained her wrists to loosen the bonds. Scrubbed the tape on her cast against the floor. Ignored Coombs' confident chuckle.

A sound came from behind the sofa. Coombs' head snapped toward it. He smiled.

"Ahhh." He reached behind to drag out a bulging leaf bag. Something inside the bag moved. Something alive.

Dixie recalled the open box of green plastic garden bags strewn across Brenda's kitchen. Someone had kicked Brenda's back door open. Someone strong.

But Brenda was *killed* in the *garage*, in the front seat of her Miata.

And her sister Gail was still missing. On a handshaking tour, she'd said.

A moan came from the bag as Coombs muscled it upright against the wall.

Had he killed Brenda? Or had he merely been there when she was murdered? Watching. Plotting his revenge— *the foreplay's over, darlin'*—when the killer left the garage, Brenda already dead, and entered the house, using Brenda's keys.

A woman's habit, to lock a door behind her, any door. A cautious woman in a dangerous city always locked doors. *One of the Angels?*

Coombs, following the killer, kicks in the locked door. Catches the killer searching Brenda's bedroom.

It's the two of them who scatter the wig, the clothes, the mask—break the bottle of Shalimar.

Once Brenda's killer is knocked out, convenient to use a leaf bag for camouflage. Carry it through the trees to his car. Toss it in the trunk—*the noise outside Brenda's house.* . . .

On the bathroom floor, beside the black wig, Dixie could see Brenda's key chain—dropped there by the killer. . . .

Gail wouldn't need Brenda's keys to enter her own house.

And Dixie remembered now why the green and red scarf around Brenda's neck had looked familiar. She'd seen it first outside the courthouse.

Coombs tossed away the plastic tie securing the leaf bag, and skinned the plastic down over a semiconscious body. Hair snarled, mouth taped. Face and arms bruised. Eyes dazed, unfocused.

Brenda's killer.

"Pretty maids all in a row," Coombs drawled.

Rashley could stop looking for Julie Colby. *Had she been in that damn bag all night?*

Dropping to one knee, Coombs tore the tape from Julie's mouth. When she cried out, he stroked her tangled hair, almost lovingly, then pulled her roughly forward and pressed his mouth to hers. She tried to twist away, but he gripped her chin, fingers digging into her bruised cheek. She whimpered.

"Heard your mother died this morning, Coombs. Guess she never realized what a monster she raised."

Coombs lifted his face from Julie's.

"You, darlin', don't know *shit.*" His fist shot out, busting Dixie across the mouth.

Behind her, Dixie heard Sarina gasp.

Quiet, kid. Don't draw his attention.

He wiped a fingertip across Dixie's lip. The finger came away smeared with blood.

"Blood kin, now, aren't we, darlin'?" His eyes held a malicious glow as he touched the ruddy scar on his mouth. "You taste mine, I taste yours . . . ? And this lady—" His tone went hard, his words aimed like darts at Julie's face as he separated a strand of her hair. "Did you think I'd *ever* forget your voice—cunt?"

He twirled the hair around his finger.

"Remember what I told you that night in the park?" Slowly, he wound the strand tighter.

Julie's mouth opened as if to protest, but only a gasp escaped. When Coombs yanked the strand of hair, Julie's neck arched.

"Noooooooooo—"

"No, what?"

But she pressed her lips together and glared at him.

"Give it up, Coombs." Dixie tasted blood from her split lip. "You won't beat the court this time. This time there are three of us."

His contented eyes rested on hers. "And how many do you think will be talking when I leave here?"

Dixie flashed on Rashly's account of another rape victim. *This time he used a knife. Went all the way.*

Julie screamed. Coombs spread the ripped-out hair on the floor.

"One." Smiling, he reached for another strand.

Steeling herself to Julie's screams and Sarina's soft sobs, Dixie worked her wrists to loosen the tape. *Tryouts at four o'clock.* Hours away. But Alroy Duncan had seen Coombs with Sarina.

Why would anyone ask? With the stalker no longer a threat, no one would be worried about them until they didn't return from the festival.

Five clumps of hair lay on the floor, arrayed in a tidy line, before Coombs seemed to grow bored with Julie's pain. Her screams had quieted to heart-wrenching whimpers. Whatever horror the woman had endured before he brought her here must have blunted the pain and focused her rage. Her furious gaze stayed riveted on Coombs. She seemed unaware of Dixie or Sarina. And if what Coombs wanted was to frighten his other two captives, Julie Colby had served his purpose. When his gaze flicked to Sarina, Dixie's scalp crawled with sweat.

Sarina's face turned bone white.

Do something!

"Coom—, um, Lawrence . . ." Dixie drawled. She licked her dry lips. "Why don't we have a go at it? You and me. Finish what you started back at the Parrot Lounge."

He smiled. "If I recall rightly, pretty lady, you didn't want it back then."

"We didn't know each other then. It's different—"

"Turn it off, darlin'. Why should I settle for used goods when I have sweet Sarina?"

Snick!

Dixie flinched toward the sound. A box cutter lay in Coombs' palm, thin, flat, not much bigger than a pack of chewing gum. Buck apiece in any hardware store. Single-edged razor, ready in a flash.

With one swipe, he sliced the tape binding Sarina's ankles. He hauled the slender girl to her feet, startled and terrified, like a field rabbit Dixie had frightened once when she turned on her porch light.

"There's a lot to be said for experience," Dixie persisted, working her wrists ruthlessly against the chafing duct tape.

Sarina keened softly as Coombs dragged her toward the bench. Her bewildered gaze swung toward Dixie, pleading.

"Lawrence!" Dixie foraged her memory. What did she know about him? What triggered him? Turned him on? Off? What would make him abandon the girl to deal with either of the two older women in the room? She regarded Julie, bleeding, bruised, limp as a rag doll. *Do something.* "Is that really your style, Lawrence? Go for the weak ones? Too young and scared to fight back?"

"You'll get your turn, darlin'." He snapped the tape from Sarina's mouth. "You can scream now, pretty lady."

No! Dixie shook her head at Sarina. She remembered

now—what Coombs enjoyed most was a woman's terror. He fed on it.

Sarina tightened her lips, but her eyes widened with fright.

Coombs yanked the girl's shirt open. Buttons popped to the floor.

Sarina opened her mouth as if to scream. Then she darted a terrified glance at Dixie, and clamped her lips together again, sobbing without sound.

Hooking a finger behind her bra, he sliced the fabric, releasing her small breasts.

"Sweet. Not much in size, but real." Coombs stroked one breast with the knife blade. Sarina shrank away from it. "Make a nice trophy, pretty lady."

Her face turned waxen. A nervous cry escaped her tightly closed mouth. She tried to back away, but stumbled into the bench.

"Scared of the knife, darlin'?" Coombs circled Sarina's nipple with the blade. The razor left a thin pink trail.

Frantically, Dixie cast about for a weapon. *Anything!* Sarina's poncho and tote lay in a heap. With a swift glance at Coombs, she inched sideways until her fingers locked on the tote's strap. She eased it behind her.

Panic palsied her fingers as they searched the bag. She dropped it, had to grab it up again and start over. Sweat slid down her neck—

Calm down. She'd be useless if she let herself get psyched. Pushing the panic deep, where it couldn't get at her, she worked her fingers through the bag's contents—

There! How had she missed it? The damn thing was huge, too huge to pull out past the other crap in there. Dixie swallowed, willed her trembling fingers to slow down, and counted, one . . . two . . . carefully extracting the rod puppet from the folds and papers and gizmos, she turned the mass of points and edges to find the sharpest—the puppet's bayonet blade. She rubbed it against the tape binding her wrists. Not as sharp as she'd hoped.

Her fingers cramped.

Biting down on the pain, she kept rubbing. And kept working her cast against the floor.

Coombs teased Sarina with his knife, tasting her fear like a kid with the first lick of an ice cream cone. The more terrified Sarina became, the greater his arousal.

And the less sense of his audience, maybe. Dixie counted on that. With enough time, she knew she could get free. Duct tape was strong, yet all she needed was a nick to start ripping it.

But how much time did she have until Coombs let the knife cut deep enough to do real damage? And how could she lessen Sarina's fear without attracting Coombs' attention to her own busy hands and feet?

"Lawrence, you're like a little boy at a slasher film," she taunted, the words for Sarina more than Coombs. "Getting pumped by the special effects. The bench, the goofy plants." *This is not real, Sarina. It's part of his script, manufactured for our benefit.* "Who's your hero, Lawrence? Freddy Krueger? Jason? Pinhead?"

Sarina swiveled her gaze to Dixie.

"This girl's had *lessons* in screaming," Dixie said. "Real bloodcurdling shrieks, learned first day in acting class. Used in every nickel-a-frame horror film. Right, kid?"

Sarina's eyes lost a fraction of their terror. She screamed, aiming the sound directly at Coombs.

"Not bad," he murmured. "Nice, seeing a little fight in those pretty gray eyes." He trailed the knife blade down her cheek.

Sarina cringed.

"It's only make-believe, Lawrence," Dixie said firmly. "The ingenue never fights back. Screams, faints, swoons, flails her arms, but she never *really* fights back. Sarina knows exactly how to *play* the fragile victim. It's all just make-believe."

Coombs pivoted toward Dixie. "Shut up, or I'll tape your mouth." He shoved Sarina behind the bench and pulled the tape roll from his pocket. "We'll see how *good* an actress she is."

Dixie could feel her own bonds beginning to stretch, but not enough to wrench her hands free.

Sarina was trying to wriggle out of Coombs' grasp. But the man's strength was too much for her. He used his body weight to bend her over the bench while he taped her wrists, one to each bench arm.

Sarina's terrified gaze locked on Dixie. She was smart *and* tough, Dixie reminded herself. She'd be okay once they got through this. *She'd be okay.*

If they got through this alive.

The girl stiffened and went suddenly still as Dixie heard fabric tear. Sarina's jeans fell around her knees.

Another rip of fabric, and Coombs held Sarina's panties. She kicked and squirmed furiously. The box knife hit the tile floor and skidded across the room.

Coombs ignored it. "I like a woman with fire, darlin'."

Dixie heard the clink of his buckle and a zip as he opened his fly. A fresh wave of fear tightened Sarina's face.

"Bet you never had a man between those sweet thighs."

Fury fueled Dixie's actions as she sawed at the tape binding her wrists. The damn stuff would not give! Too many layers.

Coombs' attention was totally on Sarina now, face flushed with arousal.

Damn the tape! She rose clumsily to her knees, heels against the wall. Launching herself like a projectile, she lunged at the bench, falling into it, shoving it backward, smashing Coombs against the wall, Sarina screaming—

The thinner tape on Dixie's ankles snapped. She scrambled to her feet and swung the heavy cast at Coombs' shins. But her hands were still bound, and when he slugged her, blackness swirled like smoke inside her head.

She heard a screech behind her—not Sarina—

Coombs' fist swung again, hitting Dixie solid on the

jaw, knocking her backward and splattering the wall with blood.

As Coombs grabbed for his pants, Dixie came back, head lowered, butting upward—but hitting only his muscled shoulder as he dodged. He backhanded her to the floor.

Another earsplitting screech.

Julie Colby flew at them, the box knife in her hand, her face deformed with rage. Still screeching, she hacked at Coombs' face.

He sidestepped, but he was against the wall. His hand flew up to block the ferocious blows.

Julie sliced at his face, his chest, his stomach, and when he lowered his hands to protect his manhood, she went for his face again. Enraged, Coombs struck out with both arms, knocking her aside, and tried to move past, but she flew back at him, the knife arcing—

Dixie shoved the bench away, and Sarina with it. Let them fight, she just wanted to get the girl to safety. "Are you okay?"

Sarina nodded. "Get me loose."

"I will." But not yet.

A nauseating crack of bone snapping—a scream—Coombs had broken Julie's knife arm. She fell against the wall, the weapon again in Coombs' bloody grip.

The look in his eyes said Julie was about to die. He raked the blade across her throat.

Her eyes widened in surprise.

"God's Fi—" she murmured. Then her body fell sideways, into Coombs. The knife tumbled to the floor.

With one final twist, Dixie ripped the tape from her hands. She dropped to the floor, scrambling madly. *She couldn't reach—the goddamn knife—*

Coombs grunted, threw himself at her.

Dixie's fingers closed on a weapon. She turned and slammed it into Coombs' ear. Screaming, he raised both hands to his bleeding head.

She slammed it into his face, punched it into his unprotected stomach, then tossed the broken puppet aside and finally scooped up the knife.

With one hand on his collar and the knife at his throat, she threw him face first against the wall and kicked the back of his knees.

"Down. Down to the floor."

He resisted, but pressure from the blade convinced him. He sank to his knees.

"All the way. Facedown."

Eyes straining toward the knife, he stretched out flat. With a knee in his back, Dixie released his collar to grope for the tape.

"Give me your hands."

He complied.

She sliced off a tape strip and fastened his wrists.

Then she freed Sarina. As she helped gather her clothes together, Dixie had the compelling urge to count the kid's fingers and toes.

Sarina snatched up the bloody puppet. "Wait'll we tell Mother it was Fire Dweller who saved us. *Un*credible!"

Chapter Sixty-one

February 14 — that night

Dixie lay curled in a chair, Mud's muzzle resting on her lap, as they waited for the ten o'clock news. The heart-shaped balloon, partially deflated, bobbed overhead. She'd found one of Parker's lumberjack shirts in the laundry room, plaid cotton flannel, soft from uncounted washings. Wearing it against her bare skin, she wondered what he was doing in his big new house.

Wondered if he was alone.

Wondered if he missed her as much as she missed him.

Mud's ears pricked forward. A second later, the phone rang.

"Happy Valentine's Day." Parker's deep voice rumbled over the phone line.

"Happy Valentine's to you, too." Why couldn't she ever think of anything brilliant to say when she needed to?

"I caught a newscast, heard your name mentioned."

"Hang around with celebrities, it's bound to rub off."

"How many bruises?" He said it lightly, but she could hear the worry in his tone.

"One." The others were too small to count.

"How's the kid?"

"A few bruises, but that kid's tougher than she looks—about as timid as Tabasco." Being a minor, Sarina had been spared all but a short interview with the cops—with Belle present for moral and legal support. What mattered to Dixie was that the girl had come through without any physical injuries or, apparently, any debilitating psychological ones. "She'll be okay."

Dixie herself had suffered a sustained ass-chewing from Belle, before reminding the attorney that twenty-four-hour protection might've prevented Sarina from leaving the hotel alone. That ended Belle's diatribe, but not the worms of guilt that crawled through Dixie's gut every time she closed her eyes and saw Sarina's terror. Those minutes at Hamman Hall, when she'd felt unable to help the girl, had given her a good dose of what Parker must feel at times.

"Guess you've had a long day."

"Yeah." She'd spent too much of it telling various police officers what had happened, and the rest of it with a doctor examining her jaw where Coombs had popped her. But at least she'd talked the doc into finally removing the cast. "Got my clutch foot back. How's the boat?"

After a stretch of silence, Parker said, "Had to let it go."

Well, hell. "Sorry. I know you wanted it."

"There's always another good deal around." He hesitated. "I have a confession to make."

Oh, God. Dixie thought about the blonde and didn't know if she wanted to hear this.

"I stole your pillow," he said.

"My pillow?"

"It smells like you. . . ."

Dixie buried her nose in the collar of his plaid flannel shirt. "That's okay. I can get another pillow."

"I miss you."

Dixie dropped a hand on Mud's warm, furry neck.

"We miss you, too. Why don't you drive in and watch the news with us?"

Parker's sigh came long and low and heartsick. "I wish it were that easy, Dixie."

The good stuff never comes easy. "Do you think it's impossible?"

Another unbearable silence.

"I think when people are thrown together under stressful conditions, emotions can get tangled."

Tangled? What does that mean? "Is this a new way of saying 'Let's just be friends'?"

"Dixie, this was the emptiest day of my life, until I heard your voice. I sure don't want to be strangers."

A huge gray lump wedged itself under Dixie's heart. *Friends or strangers.*

"Are those our only two choices?"

"Maybe down the road we'll see some others. Why don't we just say good night now and talk again tomorrow?"

Dixie looped the dangling balloon string around her finger as she stalled for something—*anything*—to say that would make a difference. Words were so damned useless.

"Good night, Parker."

Epilogue

FALLEN ANGEL MURDERED

by Casey James

The grave marker bears a shocking epitaph: *Julie Ann Colby, Beloved Daughter, Murder Victim.* But since her death, police have uncovered a chilling tale of a young woman's double life: one that garnered respect in the legal community, the other tormented by failed justice, rage, and retribution.

Investigators instrumental in obtaining a murder conviction against Colby's killer said that Colby, a witness coordinator for the Harris County District Attorney, led the vigilante group called "Avenging Angels." The

group consisted of three women who allegedly beat and tortured at least three men
and possibly one woman during a four-day
vengeance spree.

"Two of these women worked in the
justice system. They chose their victims
carefully, and carried out their crimes carefully," said Homicide Detective Ben Rashly.
"All of their victims had been prosecuted and
found innocent or had been suspected and released for insufficient evidence."

In a bizarre twist, Colby, the alleged leader
of the group, is the primary suspect in the
strangulation deaths of the other two so-called
Avenging Angels: hairdresser Regan Salles and
prosecutor Brenda Benson.

According to sources close to the investigation, the verdict in the Lawrence Riley
Coombs trial last February triggered the
formation of the Avenging Angels. Coombs
had been tried and found innocent of raping
Salles.

A friend of Colby, Victims Rights Volunteer
Clarissa Thomas, said Colby acted "spooky"
following the rape trial.

"We were all upset when the jury let
Coombs go," Thomas said. "But Julie was so
calm it was almost spooky. She told us,
'Lawrence Coombs escaped man's law, but he
won't escape God's Fist.'"

According to Thomas, Colby recruited
Benson and Salles to exact vengeance on
Coombs. "They wanted me to go along, but I
was too scared," Thomas said.

In the trial that ended today, a jury of
seven women and five men deliberated only

twenty minutes before convicting Coombs of first-degree murder of Julie Colby. Prosecutors said they will seek the death penalty when the punishment phase begins tomorrow.

About Chris Rogers

Chris Rogers lives in Houston, Texas, where she is at work on her next Dixie Flannigan novel.

If you enjoyed Chris Rogers's RAGE FACTOR, you won't want to miss any of the exciting mysteries in the Dixie Flannigan series.

Look for BITCH FACTOR, the first Dixie Flannigan mystery, at your favorite bookseller.

And, coming in hardcover from Bantam Books in February 2000, look for CHILL FACTOR, the third book in this bestselling mystery series.